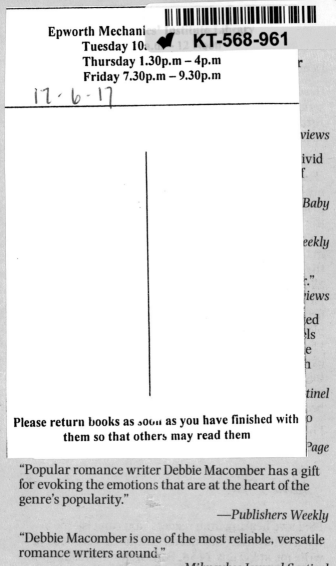
views

ivid

Baby

eekly

r."
views

ed
ls
e
h

tinel

o

Page

"Popular romance writer Debbie Macomber has a gift
for evoking the emotions that are at the heart of the
genre's popularity."

—*Publishers Weekly*

"Debbie Macomber is one of the most reliable, versatile
romance writers around."

—*Milwaukee Journal Sentinel*

Dear Friend,

Here you have it, volume two of the Midnight Sons series, which includes *Daddy's Little Helper* and *Because of the Baby*. I hope you've enjoyed the series so far. I know I enjoyed writing it.

Midnight Sons was my first venture into writing six closely connected books. I loved the way it expanded my horizons as an author. Because I felt I needed to know what Alaska was really like before starting the first book, my husband and I flew to Anchorage and then on to Fairbanks and eventually landed in the tiny town of Bettles, which is situated above the Arctic Circle. That trip, and the research it allowed me to do, added a great deal of personal pleasure to the writing of these stories. I'm grateful for everything I learned and saw in Alaska. We had plenty of adventures (some of them hilarious), and I feel the experience of spending time there brought extra texture and authenticity to the books. Keep in mind that the Hard Luck stories were written in the mid-1990s, before cell phones, DVDs and the internet became part of our everyday lives.

I hope you're eager to return to Hard Luck and the men—and few women!—who live there.

Debbie Macomber

PS: I love hearing from readers. You can visit me at www.debbiemacomber.com, find me on Facebook or write me at PO Box 1458, Port Orchard, Washington 98366.

DEBBIE MACOMBER

Alaska Nights

MIRA

MIRA®

ISBN-13: 978-0-7783-3018-9

Alaska Nights

For questions and comments about the quality of this book, please contact us at CustomerService@Harlequin.com.

www.MIRABooks.com

Printed in U.S.A.

Midnight Sons

Alaska Skies
  (*Brides for Brothers* and
  The Marriage Risk)
Alaska Nights
  (*Daddy's Little Helper* and
  Because of the Baby)
Alaska Home
  (*Falling for Him,*
  Ending in Marriage and
  Midnight Sons and Daughters)

This Matter of Marriage
Montana
Thursdays at Eight
Between Friends
Changing Habits
Married in Seattle
  (*First Comes Marriage* and
  Wanted: Perfect Partner)
Right Next Door
  (*Father's Day* and
  The Courtship of Carol Sommars)
Wyoming Brides
  (*Denim and Diamonds* and
  The Wyoming Kid)
Fairy Tale Weddings
  (*Cindy and the Prince* and
  Some Kind of Wonderful)
The Man You'll Marry
  (*The First Man You Meet* and
  The Man You'll Marry)
Orchard Valley Grooms
  (*Valerie* and *Stephanie*)
Orchard Valley Brides
  (*Norah* and *Lone Star Lovin'*)
The Sooner the Better
An Engagement in Seattle
  (*Groom Wanted* and
  Bride Wanted)
Out of the Rain
  (*Marriage Wanted* and
  Laughter in the Rain)
Learning to Love
  (*Sugar and Spice* and *Love by Degree*)

You...Again
  (*Baby Blessed* and
  Yesterday Once More)
The Unexpected Husband
  (*Jury of His Peers* and
  Any Sunday)
Three Brides, No Groom
Love in Plain Sight
  (*Love 'n' Marriage* and
  Almost an Angel)
I Left My Heart
  (*A Friend or Two* and
  No Competition)
Marriage Between Friends
  (*White Lace and Promises* and
  Friends—And Then Some)
A Man's Heart
  (*The Way to a Man's Heart*
  and *Hasty Wedding*)
North to Alaska
  (*That Wintry Feeling* and
  Borrowed Dreams)
On a Clear Day
  (*Starlight* and
  Promise Me Forever)
To Love and Protect
  (*Shadow Chasing* and
  For All My Tomorrows)
Home in Seattle
  (*The Playboy and the Widow*
  and *Fallen Angel*)
Together Again
  (*The Trouble with Caasi* and
  Reflections of Yesterday)
The Reluctant Groom
  (*All Things Considered*
  and *Almost Paradise*)
A Real Prince
  (*The Bachelor Prince*
  and *Yesterday's Hero*)
Private Paradise
  (in *That Summer Place*)

Debbie Macomber's
  Cedar Cove Cookbook
Debbie Macomber's
  Christmas Cookbook

CONTENTS

The History of Hard Luck, Alaska

Hard Luck, situated fifty miles north of the Arctic Circle near the Brooks Range, was founded by Adam O'Halloran and his wife, Anna, in 1931. Adam came to Alaska to make his fortune, but never found the gold strike he sought. Nevertheless, the O'Hallorans and their two young sons, Charles and David, stayed on—in part because of a tragedy that befell the family a few years later.

Other prospectors and adventurers began to move to Hard Luck, some of them bringing wives and children. The town became a stopping-off place for mail, equipment and supplies. The Harmon family arrived in 1938 to open a dry-goods store, and the Fletchers came soon after that.

When World War II began, Hard Luck's population was fifty or sixty people all told. Some of the young men, including the O'Halloran sons, joined the armed services; Charles left for Europe in 1942, David in 1944 at the age of eighteen. Charles died during the fighting. Only David came home—with a young English war bride, Ellen Sawyer, despite the fact that he'd become engaged to Catherine Harmon shortly before going overseas. Catherine married Willie Fletcher after David's return.

After the war, David qualified as a bush pilot. He then built some small cabins to attract the sport fishermen and hunters who were starting to come to Alaska; he also worked as a guide. Eventually he built a lodge to replace the cabins—a lodge that was later damaged by fire.

David and Ellen had three sons, born fairly late in their marriage—Charles, named after David's brother, was born in 1960, Sawyer in 1963 and Christian in 1965.

Hard Luck had been growing slowly all this time, and by 1970 it was home to just over a hundred people. These were the years of the oil boom, when the school and community center were built by the state. After Vietnam, ex-serviceman Ben Hamilton joined the community and opened the Hard Luck Café, which became the social center of the town.

In the late 1980s, the three O'Halloran brothers formed a partnership, creating Midnight Sons, a bush-pilot operation. They were awarded the mail contract, and they also deliver fuel and other necessities to the interior. In addition, they serve as a small commuter airline, flying passengers to and from Fairbanks and within the northern Arctic.

In 1995, at the time these stories start, there are approximately one hundred and fifty people living in Hard Luck—the majority of them male.

Now, more than twenty years later, join the people here in looking back at their history—particularly the changes that occurred when Midnight Sons invited women to town. Women who transformed Hard Luck, Alaska, forever!

For Janet and Claude Robinson.
Thank you for all the warmth in a cold climate.
We appreciated your generosity and hospitality.

DADDY'S LITTLE HELPER

One

September 1995

The new schoolteacher wouldn't last.

It didn't take Mitch Harris more than five seconds to make that assessment. Bethany Ross didn't belong in Alaska. She reminded him of a tropical bird with its brilliant plumage. Everything about her was *vivid,* from her animated expression to her sun-bleached hair, which fell to her shoulders in a frothy mass of blond. Even blonder curls framed her classic features. Her eyes were a deep, rich shade of chocolate.

She wore a bright turquoise jumpsuit with a wide yellow band that circled her trim waist. One of her skimpy multicolored sandals dangled from her foot as she sat on the arm of Abbey and Sawyer O'Halloran's sofa, her legs elegantly crossed.

This get-together was in her honor. Abbey and Sawyer had invited the members of the school board to their home to meet the new teacher.

To Mitch's surprise, she stood and approached him before he had a chance to introduce himself. "I don't believe we've met." Her smile was warm and natural. "I'm Bethany Ross."

"Mitch Harris." He didn't elaborate. Details wouldn't be necessary because Ms. Ross simply wouldn't last beyond the first snowfall. "Welcome to Hard Luck," he said almost as an afterthought.

"Thank you."

"When did you get here?" he asked, trying to make conversation. He twisted the stem of his wineglass and watched the chardonnay swirl against the sides.

"I flew in this afternoon."

He hadn't realized she'd only just arrived. "You must be exhausted."

"Not really," she was quick to tell him. "I suppose I should be, considering that I left San Francisco early this morning. The fact is, I've been keyed up for days."

Mitch suspected Hard Luck was a sorry disappointment to her. The town, population 150, was about as far from the easy California lifestyle as a person could get. Situated fifty miles north of the Arctic Circle, Hard Luck was a fascinating place with a strong and abiding sense of community. People here lived hard and worked harder. Besides Midnight Sons, the flight service owned and operated by the three O'Halloran brothers, there were a few small businesses, like Ben Hamilton's café. Mitch himself was one of a handful of state employees. He worked for the Department of the Interior, monitoring visitors to Gate of the Arctic National Park. This was in addition to his job as the town's public safety officer—PSO—which meant he was responsible for policing in Hard Luck. Trappers wandered into town now and then, as did the occasional pipeline worker. To those living on the edge of the world, Hard Luck was a thriving metropolis.

Lately the town had piqued the interest of the rest of the country, as well. But Bethany Ross had nothing to do with that. Thank heaven, although Mitch figured she'd stay about as long as some of the women the O'Halloran brothers had brought to town.

Until recently only a small number of women had lived here. Not many were willing to endure the hardship of being this far from civilization. So the O'Hallorans had spearheaded a campaign to bring women to Hard Luck. Abbey was one of their notable successes, but there'd been a few equally notable failures. Like—who was it?—Allison somebody. The one who'd lasted less than twenty-four hours. And just last week, two women had arrived, only to return home on the next flight out. Bethany Ross had actually applied for the teaching job last spring, before all this nonsense.

Unexpectedly she smiled—a ravishing smile that seemed to say she'd read his thoughts. "I plan to fulfill my contract, Mr. Harris. I knew what I was letting myself in for when I agreed to teach in Alaska."

Mitch felt the heat rise to his ears. "I didn't realize my...feelings were so transparent."

"I don't blame you for doubting me. I don't exactly blend in with the others, do I?"

He was tempted to smile himself. "Hard Luck isn't what you expected, is it?"

"I'll adjust."

She said this with such confidence he began to wonder if he'd misjudged her.

"Frankly, I didn't know *what* to expect. With Hard

Luck in the news so often, the idea of moving here was beginning to worry me."

Mitch didn't bother to conceal his amusement. He'd read what some of the tabloids had written about the town and the men's scheme to lure women north.

"My dad was against my coming," Bethany continued. "It was all I could do to keep him from flying up here with me. He seems to think Hard Luck's populated with nothing but love-starved bush pilots."

"He isn't far wrong," Mitch said wryly. If Bethany had only been in town a few hours, she probably hadn't met the pilots currently employed by Midnight Sons. He knew Sawyer had flown her in from Fairbanks.

It was after repeatedly losing their best pilots for lack of female companionship that the O'Hallorans had decided to take action.

"Midnight Sons is the flight service? Owned by the O'Hallorans?" she asked, looking flustered. "Sawyer and his brothers?"

"That's right." Mitch understood why she was confused. Immediately following her arrival, she'd been thrust into the middle of this party, with twenty or more names being thrown her way all at once. In an effort to help her, Mitch explained that Charles O'Halloran, the oldest of the three brothers, was a silent partner.

Charles hadn't been so silent, however, when he learned about the scheme Sawyer and Christian had concocted to lure women to Hard Luck. Still, he'd changed his tune since meeting Lanni Caldwell. Earlier in the week, they'd announced their engagement.

"Is it true that Abbey—Sawyer's wife—was the

first woman to come here?" Her eyes revealed her curiosity.

"Yes. They got married this summer."

"But...they look like they've been married for years. What about Scott and Susan?"

"They're Abbey's children from a previous marriage. I understand Sawyer's already started the adoption process." Mitch envied his friend's happiness. Marriage hadn't been nearly as happy an experience for him.

"Chrissie's your daughter?" Bethany asked, glancing over at the children gathered around a Monopoly game.

Mitch's gaze fell fondly on his seven-year-old daughter. "Yes. And she's been on pins and needles waiting for school to start."

Bethany's eyes softened. "I met her earlier with Scott and Susan. She's a delightful little girl."

"Thank you." Mitch tried hard to do his best for Chrissie, though sometimes he wondered whether his best would ever be enough. "You've met Pete Livengood?" he asked, gesturing toward a rugged-looking middle-aged man on the other side of the room.

"Yes. He owns the grocery?"

"That he does. Dotty, the woman on his left, is another one who answered the advertisement."

Bethany blinked as if trying to remember where Dotty fit into the small community. "She's the nurse?"

He nodded. "Pete and Dotty plan to be married shortly. The first week of October, I believe."

"So soon?" She didn't give him an opportunity to answer before directing her attention elsewhere.

"What about Mariah Douglas? Is she a recent addition to the town?"

"Yup. She's the secretary for Midnight Sons."

"Is she engaged?"

"Not yet," Mitch said, "but it's still pretty early. She just got here last month."

"You mean to say she's lived here an entire month without getting married?" Bethany teased. "That must be some sort of record. It seems to me the virile young men of Hard Luck are slacking in their duties."

Mitch grinned. "From what I've heard, it isn't for lack of trying. But Mariah says she didn't come to Hard Luck looking for a husband. She's after the cabin and the twenty acres the O'Hallorans promised her."

"Good for her. They've fulfilled their part of the bargain, haven't they? I read that news story about the cabins not being anywhere near the twenty acres. Sure sounds misleading to me." Fire flashed briefly in her eyes, as if she'd be willing to take on all three O'Hallorans herself.

"That's none of my business. It's between Mariah and the O'Hallorans."

Bethany flushed with embarrassment and bent her head to take a sip of her wine. "It isn't my business, either. It's just that Mariah seems so sweet. I hate the idea of anyone taking advantage of her."

They were interrupted by Sawyer and Abbey. "I see you've met Mitch," Sawyer said, moving next to Bethany.

"He's been helping me keep everyone straight," she told him with a quick smile.

"Then he's probably mentioned that in addition to

his job with the Department of the Interior, he's our public safety officer."

"Hard Luck's version of the law," Mitch translated for her.

"My father's a member of San Francisco's finest," she murmured.

"Well," Sawyer said, "Mitch was one of Chicago's finest before moving here."

"That's right," Mitch supplied absently.

"I imagine your head's swimming about now," Abbey said. "I know mine was when I first arrived. Oh—" she waved at a woman just coming in the door "—here's Margaret. Margaret Simpson, the high school teacher."

Margaret, a pleasant-looking brunette in her thirties, joined them. She greeted Bethany with friendly enthusiasm, explained that she lived on the same street as Sawyer and Abbey did and that her husband was a pipeline supervisor who worked three weeks on and three weeks off.

Mitch hardly heard the conversation between Margaret and Bethany; the words seemed to fade into the background as he found himself studying Bethany Ross.

He wanted to know her better, but he wouldn't allow himself that luxury. Although she claimed otherwise, he didn't expect her to last three months, not once the brutal winter settled in.

But she intrigued him. Tantalized him. The reasons could be as basic as the fact that he'd been too long without a woman—six years to be exact. He'd buried Lori when Chrissie was little more than an infant. Unable to face life in Chicago, he'd packed their bags and headed north. As far north as he could get. He'd known at the time that he was running away. But he'd felt he had no choice, not with guilt and his own self-doubts nipping at his heels. He was out of money and tired of life on the road by the time he reached Hard Luck.

And he'd been happy here. As happy as possible, under the circumstances. He and Chrissie had made a new life for themselves, made new friends. For Mitch, the world had become calm and orderly again, without pain or confusion. Without a woman in their lives.

He certainly hadn't expected to meet a woman like Bethany—a tropical bird—in Alaska.

She wasn't precisely beautiful, he decided. She was…striking. He struggled to put words to her attributes. Feminine. Warm. Generous. Somewhat outrageous. Fun. The kids would love her. He'd spent ten, possibly fifteen, minutes chatting with her and wanted more of her time, more of her attention.

But he refused to indulge himself. He'd learned all the lessons he ever wanted to learn from his dead wife. The new schoolteacher could tutor some other man.

Bethany yawned and tried to hide it behind the back of her hand.

"You must be exhausted," Abbey said sympathetically. "I can't believe we've kept you this long. I'm so sorry."

"No, please, it was wonderful of you to make me feel so welcome." To her obvious chagrin, Bethany yawned again. "But maybe I should leave now."

"She's dead on her feet," Sawyer said to no one in particular. "Mitch, would you be kind enough to escort her home?"

"Of course." He set down his wineglass, but truth be known, he'd rather have declined. He was about to suggest someone else do the honors when he realized Bethany might find that insulting.

She studied him, and again he had the impression she could read his mind. He looked away and searched the room until he found his daughter. Chrissie was sitting near the door to the kitchen with her best friend, Susan. The two were deep in conversation, their heads close together. He didn't know what they were discussing, but whatever it was seemed terribly important. Yet another scheme to outsmart the adults, no doubt. Heaven save him from little girls.

He turned to Bethany Ross. "If you'll excuse me a moment?" he asked politely.

"Of course. I'll need a few minutes myself."

While Mitch collected Chrissie, Bethany bade the members of the school board good-night.

They met just outside the front door. He didn't have to ask where she lived—the teacher's living quarters were supplied by the state and were some of the best accommodations in town. The small two-bedroom house was located on the far side of the school gymnasium.

Mitch held open the passenger door so Chrissie could climb into the truck first. He noticed how quiet his daughter had become, as if she was in awe of this woman who would be her teacher.

"I appreciate the ride," Bethany told him once he'd started the engine.

"It's no trouble." It was, but not because of the extra few minutes' driving. But then he decided he might as well let himself enjoy her company, since the opportunity was unlikely to be repeated. Once the eligible men in Hard Luck caught sight of her, he wouldn't stand a chance. Which was probably a good thing...

"Would you mind driving me around a bit?" Bethany asked. "I didn't get much of a chance to see the town earlier."

"There's not much to see." It occurred to him that he might enjoy her company too much, and that could be dangerous.

"We could show her the library," Chrissie said eagerly.

"Hard Luck has a library?"

"It's not very big, but we use it a lot," said the girl. "Abbey's the town librarian."

Sawyer's wife had worked for weeks setting up the lending library. The books were a gift from the O'Hallorans' mother and had sat in a disorganized heap for years—until Abbey's arrival. She'd even started ordering new books, everything from bestselling fiction to cookbooks; the first shipment had been delivered a week ago, occasioning great excitement. It seemed everyone in town had become addicted to books. Mitch had heard a number of lively discussions revolving around a novel. An avid reader himself, he was often a patron, and he encouraged Chrissie to take out books, too.

"Ms. Ross should see the store," Chrissie suggested next. "And the church and the school."

"What's that building there?" Bethany asked, pointing to the largest structure in town.

"That's the lodge," he said without elaborating.

"Matt Caldwell's fixing it up." Again it was Chrissie who provided the details. "He's Lanni's brother."

"You didn't meet Lanni Caldwell," Mitch explained. "I told you about her—she's engaged to Charles O'Halloran."

"I met Charles?"

"Briefly. He was in and out."

"The tall man wearing the Midnight Sons sweatshirt?"

"That's right."

Chrissie leaned closer to Bethany. "No one lives at the lodge now 'cause of the fire. Matt bought it, and he's fixing it up so people will come and stay there and pay him lots of money."

"The fire?"

"It happened years ago," Mitch told her. "Most of the damage was at the back, so you can't see it from here." He shook his head. "The place should've been repaired or torn down long before now, but I guess no one had the heart to do either. The O'Hallorans recently sold it to Matt Caldwell, which was definitely for the best."

"Matt's going to take the tourists mushing!" Chrissie said. "He's going to bring in dogs and trainers and everything!"

"That sounds like fun."

"Eagle Catcher's a husky," Chrissie added.

Mitch caught Bethany's questioning look. "That's Sawyer's dog."

"He belongs to *Scott*," his daughter corrected him.

"True," Mitch said with a smile at Chrissie. "I'd forgotten."

"Scott and Susan are brother and sister, right?" said Bethany. "Abbey's kids?"

"Right."

Mitch could tell Bethany was making a real effort to keep everyone straight in her mind, and he thought she'd done an impressive job so far. Maybe a memory for names and faces came with being a teacher.

"Are there any restaurants in town?" Bethany asked. "I'm not much of a cook."

Mitch glanced her way. Their eyes met briefly before he looked back at the road. "The Hard Luck Café."

Bethany nodded.

"Serves the best cup of coffee in town, but then Ben hasn't got much competition."

There was a pause. "Ben?"

"Hamilton. He's a bit of a grouch, but don't let that fool you. He's got a heart of gold, and he's a lot more than chief cook and bottle washer. Along with everything else, he dishes up a little psychology. You'll like him."

"I—I'm sure I will."

Mitch drove to the end of the road. A single light shone brightly in the distance. "That's where the cabins are," he said. "Mariah's place is the one on the far left." Mitch had lost count of the number of times the youngest O'Halloran brother, Christian, had tried to convince his secretary to move into town. But Mariah always refused. Mitch was just glad *he* wasn't the one dealing with her stubbornness.

He turned the truck around and headed back toward the school. When he pulled up in front of Bethany's little house, she smiled at him.

"Thanks for the tour and the ride home."

"My pleasure."

"Chrissie," Bethany said, her voice gentle, "since I'm new here, I was wondering if you'd be my classroom helper."

His daughter's eyes lit up like sparklers on the Fourth of July, and she nodded so hard her pigtails bounced wildly. "Can Susan be your helper, too?"

"Of course."

Chrissie beamed a proud smile at her father.

"Well, good night, Chrissie, Mitch," Bethany said, then opened her door and climbed out.

"Night," father and daughter echoed. Mitch waited until she was inside the house and the lights were on before he drove off.

So, he thought, *the new schoolteacher has arrived.*

Bethany was even more exhausted than she'd realized. But instead of falling into a sound sleep, she lay awake, staring at the ceiling, fighting fatigue and mulling over the time she'd spent with Mitch Harris.

The man was both intense and intelligent. That much had been immediately apparent. He stood apart from the others in more ways than one. Bethany suspected he wouldn't have bothered to introduce himself, which was why she'd taken the initiative. She'd noticed him right away, half-hidden in a corner, watching the events without joining in. When it looked as if the evening would pass without her meeting him, she'd made the first move.

There was something about him that appealed to her. Having lived with a policeman all her life, she must have intuitively sensed his occupation; she certainly hadn't been surprised when Sawyer told her.

He reminded her a little of her father. They seemed to have the same analytical mind. It drove her mother crazy, the way Dad carefully weighed each decision, considered every option, before taking action. She'd bet Mitch was like that, too.

It was one personality trait Bethany *didn't* share.

She would've liked to know Mitch Harris better, but she had the distinct impression he wasn't interested. Then again…maybe he was. A breathless moment before she'd introduced herself, she'd recognized some glint of admiration in his eye. She'd been sure of it. But now she wondered if that moment had existed only in her imagination.

All the same, she couldn't help wondering what it would be like to see his eyes darken with passion before he kissed her….

She was far too tired; she wasn't thinking clearly. Bethany closed her eyes and pounded the pillow, trying to force herself to relax.

But even with her eyes shut, all she saw was Mitch Harris's face.

She hadn't come to Hard Luck to fall in love, she told herself sternly.

Rolling onto her other side, she cradled the pillow in her arms. It didn't help. Drat. She could deny it till doomsday, but it wouldn't make any difference. There was just something about Chrissie's father….

"Ms. Ross?"

Bethany looked up from the back of her classroom. Chrissie and Susan stood by the doorway, their faces beaming with eagerness.

"Hello, girls."

"Um, we're here to be your helpers," Chrissie said. "Dad told us we'd better make sure we *are* helpers and not nuisances."

"I'm sure you'll be wonderful helpers," Bethany said.

The two girls instantly broke into huge grins and rushed inside the room. Bethany put them to work sorting textbooks. This was the first time she'd taught more than one grade, and the fact that she'd now be handling kindergarten through six intimidated her.

"Everyone's looking forward to school," Chrissie announced, "especially my dad."

Bethany chuckled. Mitch wasn't so different from other parents.

The girls had been working for perhaps twenty minutes when Chrissie suddenly asked, "You're not married or anything, are you, Ms. Ross?"

A smile trembled on her mouth. "No."

"Why not?"

Leave it to a seven-year-old to ask that kind of question. "I haven't met the right man," she explained as simply as she could.

"Have you ever been in love?" Susan probed.

Bethany noticed that both girls had stopped sorting through the textbooks and were giving her their full attention. "Yes," she told them with some hesitation.

"How old are you?"

"Chrissie." Susan jabbed her elbow into her friend's ribs. "You're not supposed to ask that," she said in a loud whisper. "It's against the human-rights law. We could get charged with snooping."

"I'm twenty-five," Bethany answered, pretending she hadn't heard Susan.

The girls exchanged looks, then started using their fingers to count.

"Seven," Chrissie breathed, as if it were a magic number.

"Seven?" Bethany asked curiously. What game were the girls playing?

"If a man's seven years older than you, is that too old?" Susan asked, her eyes wide and inquisitive.

"Too old," Bethany repeated thoughtfully. She perched on the edge of a desk and crossed her arms. "That depends."

"On what?" Chrissie moved closer.

"On age, I suppose. If I was fourteen and wanted to date a man who was twenty-one, my parents would never have allowed it. But if I was twenty-one and he was twenty-eight, it would probably be okay."

Both girls seemed pleased with her answer, grinning and nudging each other.

Bethany responded to their odd behavior with a joke. "You girls aren't thinking about dating fourteen-year-old boys, are you?" she asked, narrowing her eyes in pretend disapproval.

Chrissie covered her mouth and giggled.

Susan rolled her eyes. "Get real, Ms. Ross. I don't even know what the big attraction is with boys." Then, as if to explain her words, she said, "I have an older brother."

"Would you tell us about the man you were in love with?" This came from Chrissie. Her expression had grown so serious Bethany decided to answer, despite her initial impulse to change the subject.

"The man I was in love with," she began, "was a guy I dated while I was in college. We went out for about a year."

"What was his name?"

"Randy."

"Randy," Chrissie repeated with disgust, turning to look at her friend.

"Did he do you wrong?"

Bethany laughed at the country-and-western phrasing, although she was uncomfortable with these questions. "No, he didn't do me wrong." If anyone was to blame for their breakup, it had been Bethany herself. She wasn't sure she'd ever really loved him, which she supposed was an answer in itself. They'd been friends, and that had developed into something more—at least on Randy's part.

He'd started talking marriage and children, and at first she'd agreed. Then she'd realized she wasn't ready for that kind of commitment. Not when she had two full years of school left. Not when she'd barely begun to experience life.

They'd argued and broken off their unofficial engagement. The breakup had troubled Bethany for months afterward. But now she understood that what she'd really regretted was the loss of their friendship.

"Do you still see him?" Chrissie asked.

Bethany nodded.

"You *do?*" Susan sounded as if this was a tragedy.

"Sometimes."

"Is he married?"

"No." Bethany grew a little sad, thinking about her

longtime friend. She did miss Randy, even now, five years after their breakup.

Both Chrissie and Susan seemed deflated at the news of Bethany's lost love.

"Would it be all right if we left now?" Chrissie asked abruptly.

"That's fine," Bethany told them. "Thanks for your help."

The two disappeared so quickly all that was missing was the puff of smoke.

If nothing else, the girls certainly were entertaining, Bethany thought. She returned to the task of cutting large letters out of colored paper.

The sun blazed in through the classroom windows, and she tugged her shirt loose, unfastened the last few buttons and tied the ends at her midriff. Then she pulled her hair away from her face and used an elastic to secure it in a ponytail.

Half an hour later, most of the letters, all capitals, for the word *September* were pinned in an arch across the bulletin board at the back of the room. She stood on a chair and had just pinned the third *E* when she felt someone's presence behind her. Twisting around, she saw Mitch standing in the open door.

"Hi," she said cheerfully, undeniably pleased to see him. He was dressed in the khaki uniform worn by Department of the Interior staff. His face revealed none of his emotions, yet Bethany had the feeling he'd rather not be there.

"I'm looking for Chrissie."

Bethany pinned the *R* in place and then stepped down from the chair. "Sorry, but as you can see she isn't here."

Mitch frowned. "Louise Gold told me this was where she'd be."

Bethany remembered that Louise Gold was the woman who watched Chrissie while Mitch was at work. She'd briefly met her the day before. In addition to her other duties, Louise served on the school board.

"Chrissie was here earlier with Susan."

"I hope they behaved themselves."

Bethany recalled their probing questions and smiled to herself. Pushing back the chair, she said, "They were fine. I asked Chrissie for her help, remember?"

Mitch remained as far away from her as possible. Bethany suspected he'd rather track a cantankerous bear than stay in the same room with her. It was not a familiar feeling, or a pleasant one.

"She must be over at Susan's, then," he said.

"She didn't say where she was headed."

He lingered a moment. "I don't want Chrissie to become a nuisance."

"She isn't, and neither is Susan. They're both great kids, so don't worry, okay?"

Still he hesitated. "They didn't, by any chance, ask you a lot of personal questions, did they?"

"Uh…some."

He closed his eyes for a few seconds and an expression of weariness crossed his face. He sighed. "I'll look for Chrissie over at Susan's. Thanks for your trouble."

His gaze held hers. By the time he turned away, Bethany felt a little breathless. She was sure of one thing. If it was up to Mitch Harris, she would never have left San Francisco.

Well, that was unfortunate for Mitch. Because Bethany had come to Hard Luck with a plan, and she wasn't leaving until it was accomplished.

Two

"Daddy?"

Mitch looked up from the Fairbanks paper to smile at his freckle-faced daughter. Chrissie was fresh out of the bathtub, her face scrubbed clean, her cheeks rosy. She wore her favorite *Beauty and the Beast* pajamas.

His heart contracted with the depth of his love for her. No matter how miserable his marriage had been, he'd always be grateful to Lori for giving him Chrissie.

"It's almost bedtime," he told his daughter.

"I know." Following their nightly ritual, she crawled into his lap and nestled her head against his chest. Sometimes she pretended to read the paper with him, but not this evening. Her thoughts seemed to be unusually grave. "Daddy, do you like Ms. Ross?"

Mitch prayed for patience. He'd been afraid of this. Chrissie had been using every opportunity to bring Bethany into their conversations, and he knew she was hoping something romantic would develop between him and the teacher. "Ms. Ross is very nice," he answered cautiously.

"But do you *like* her?"

"I suppose."

"Do you think you'll marry her?"

It was all Mitch could do to keep from bolting out of the chair. "I have no intention of marrying anyone," he said emphatically. As far as he was concerned, the subject wasn't open for discussion. With anyone, even his daughter.

Chrissie batted her baby blues at him. "But I thought you liked her."

"Sweetheart, listen, I like Pearl, too, but that doesn't mean I'm going to marry her."

"But Pearl's old. Ms. Ross is only twenty-five. I know 'cause I asked her. Twenty-five isn't too old, is it?"

Mitch gritted his teeth. After they'd driven Bethany home that first night, Chrissie had been filled with questions about the new teacher. No doubt she'd subjected Bethany to a similar inquisition that morning.

Mitch supposed all this talk about marriage was inevitable. The summer had been full of romantic adventures. Certainly Sawyer had wasted no time in marrying Abbey; it didn't help that Abbey's daughter was Chrissie's best friend. Then Charles had become engaged to Lanni, followed by Pete and Dotty's recent announcement. To Chrissie, it must've seemed as if the whole town had caught marriage fever. Bethany, however, had been hired by the school board last spring and had nothing to do with the recent influx of women.

"I like Ms. Ross *so* much," Chrissie said with a delicate sigh.

"You hardly know her. You might change your mind once you see her in the classroom." Mitch felt he was grasping at straws, but he was growing more and more concerned. He could hardly forbid his daughter to mention Bethany's name!

He wasn't sure what the woman had done to sprout wings and a halo in his daughter's estimation. Nor did he understand why Chrissie had chosen to champion Bethany instead of, say, Mariah Douglas.

Perhaps she'd intuitively sensed his attraction to the young teacher. That idea sent chills racing down his spine. If Chrissie had figured it out, others wouldn't be far behind.

"I won't change my mind about Ms. Ross," Chrissie told him. "I think you should marry her."

"Chrissie. We've already been over this. I'm not going to marry Ms. Ross."

"Why not?"

There was something very wrong when a grown man couldn't out-argue a seven-year-old. "First, we don't know each other. Remember, sweetheart, she's only been in town two days."

"But Sawyer fell in love with Abbey right away."

"Yes…" he muttered warily.

"Then why can't you put dibs on Ms. Ross before any of the other men decide they like her, too?"

"Chrissie—"

"Someone else might marry her if you don't hurry up!"

Mitch calmed himself. It was clear that his daughter had a rejoinder for every answer. "This is different," he said reasonably. "I'm not Sawyer and Ms. Ross isn't Abbey. She came here to teach, remember? She isn't looking for a husband."

"Neither was Abbey. I *really* want you to marry Ms. Ross."

Mitch clenched his jaw. "I'm not marrying Ms. Ross, and I refuse to discuss it any further." He rarely used this tone with his daughter, but he wanted it understood that the conversation was over. He wasn't getting married. End of story. No amount of begging and pleading was going to make any difference.

Chrissie was quiet for several minutes. Then she said, "Tell me about my mommy."

Mitch felt like a drowning man. Everywhere he turned there was more water, more trouble, and not a life preserver in sight. "What do you want to know?"

"Was she pretty?"

"Very pretty," he answered soothingly. Normally he found the subject of Lori painful, but right now he was grateful to discuss something other than Bethany Ross.

"As pretty as Ms. Ross?"

He rolled his eyes; he'd been sucker-punched. "Yes."

"She died in an accident?"

Mitch didn't know why Chrissie repeatedly asked the same questions about her mother. Maybe the child could tell that he wasn't giving her the whole truth. "Yes, your mother died in an accident."

"And you were sad?"

"I loved her very much."

"And she loved me?"

"Oh, yes, sweetheart, she loved you."

His daughter seemed to soak in his words, as if she needed reassurance that she'd been wanted and loved by the mother she'd never known.

After that, Chrissie grew thoughtful again. Mitch returned to his paper. Then, when he least expected it, she resumed her campaign. "Can I have a brother or sister someday?" she asked him. The question came at him from nowhere and scored a direct hit.

"Probably not," he told her truthfully. "Like I said, I don't plan to remarry."

"Why not?" She wore that hurt-little-girl look guaranteed to weaken his resolve.

Mitch made a show of checking his watch. He was through with answering questions and finding suitable arguments for a child. Through with having Bethany Ross offered up to him on a silver platter—by his daughter, the would-be matchmaker.

"Time for bed," he said decisively.

"Already?" Chrissie whined.

"Past time." He slid her off his knee and led her into her bedroom. He removed the stuffed animals from the bed while Chrissie got down on her knees to say her prayers. She closed her eyes and folded her hands, her expression intent.

Mitch could see his daughter's lips move in some fervent request. He didn't have to be a mind reader to know what she was asking. If God joined forces against him, Mitch figured he'd find himself engaged to the tantalizing Ms. Ross before the week was out.

Christian O'Halloran, youngest of the three brothers, walked into the Hard Luck Café and collapsed in a chair. He propped his elbows on the table and buried his face in his hands.

Without asking, Ben picked up the coffeepot and poured him a cup. "You look like you could use something stronger," he commented.

"I can't believe it," Christian moaned.

"Believe what?" Ben assumed this had to do with Christian's secretary. He didn't understand what it was about Mariah that Christian found so objectionable. Personally he was rather fond of the young lady. Mariah Douglas had grit. She had the gumption to live in one of those run-down cabins. No power. No electric lights. And for damn sure, nothing that went flush in the night.

"You won't believe what just happened. I nearly got my head chewed off by some feminist attorney."

Now this was news. Ben slid into the chair opposite Christian's. "An attorney? Here in Hard Luck?"

Christian nodded, his face a smoldering shade of red. "I was accused of everything from false advertising to misrepresentation and fraud. *Me,*" he said incredulously.

"Who hired her?"

Christian's eyes narrowed. "My guess is Mariah."

"No." Ben shook his head. Mariah might've been the cause of some minor troubles with Christian, but there wasn't a vindictive bone in her body. From everything he'd seen of her, Mariah was a sweet-natured, gentle soul.

"It isn't clear who hired the woman," Christian admitted, "but odds are it's Mariah."

"I don't think so."

"I do!" Christian snapped. "I swear to you Mariah's been looking for a way to do me in from the moment she got here. First off, she tried to cripple me."

"She didn't mean to push that filing cabinet on your foot."

"Is that a fact? I don't suppose you noticed how

perfect her aim was, did you? She's been a thorn in my side from day one. Now *this*."

"Seems to me you're getting sidetracked," Ben said. He didn't want to hear another litany of Mariah's supposed sins, not when there was other, juicier information to extract. "We were discussing the attorney, remember?"

Christian plowed all ten fingers though his hair. "The lawyer's name is Tracy Santiago. She flew in from some highfalutin firm in Seattle. Let me tell you, I've seen sharks with duller teeth. This woman's after blood, and from the sound of it, she wants mine."

"And you think Mariah sent for her?" Ben asked doubtfully.

"I don't know what to think anymore. Santiago's here, and when she's through discussing the details of the lawsuit with Mariah, she wants to talk to the others. To Sally McDonald and Angie Hughes." He referred to the two most recent arrivals—Sally, who worked at the town's Power and Light company, and Angie, who'd been hired as an administrative and nursing assistant to Dottie. Both of them were living in the house owned by Catherine Fletcher—Matt and Lanni Caldwell's grandmother.

"Are you going to let her?"

Christian raised his eyes until they were level with Ben's. "I can't stop her, can I? But then, I don't think a freight train would slow this Santiago woman down."

"Where is she now? Your office?" Ben asked, craning his neck to look out the window. The mobile office of Midnight Sons was parked next to the airfield, within sight of the café. He couldn't see anything out of the ordinary.

"Yeah, I had to get out of there before I said something I'd regret," Christian confessed. "I feel bad about abandoning Duke, but he seemed to be holding his own."

"Duke?"

"Yeah. Apparently he flew her in without knowing her purpose for coming. He made the fatal mistake of thinking she might've been one of the women I hired. Santiago let him know in no uncertain terms who and what she was. By the time they landed, the two of them were at each other's throats."

That they'd been able to discuss anything during the flight was saying something, given how difficult it was to be heard above the roar of the engines.

"If I were this attorney," Christian said thoughtfully, "I'd think twice before messing with Duke."

Ben had to work hard to keep the smile off his face. When a feminist attorney tangled with the biggest chauvinist Ben had ever met, well...the fur was guaranteed to fly.

The door opened. Christian looked up and groaned, then covered his face with his hands again.

Ben turned around and saw that it was Mariah. He lumbered to his feet, reached for the coffeepot and returned to the counter.

"Mr. O'Halloran," the secretary said as she timidly approached him.

"How many times," Christian demanded, "have I asked you to call me by my first name? In case you haven't noticed, there are three Mr. O'Hallorans in this town, and two of us happen to spend a lot of time together in the same office."

"Christian," she began a second time, her voice

quavering slightly. "I want you to know I had nothing to do with Ms. Santiago's arrival."

"Yeah, right."

Mariah clenched her hands at her sides. "I didn't know anything about her," she insisted, "and I certainly had nothing to do with hiring her."

"Then who did?"

Ben watched as Mariah closed her eyes and swallowed hard. When she spoke again, her voice was a low whisper. "I suspect it was my dad. He must've talked to her about my being here."

"And why, pray tell, would he do that?" Christian asked coldly.

Mariah went pale. "Would you mind very much if I sat down?"

The look Christian threw her said he would. After an awkward moment, he gestured curtly toward the seat across from him.

"You want some coffee?" Ben felt obliged to offer.

"No," Christian answered for her. "She doesn't want anything."

"Do you have orange juice?" Mariah asked.

"He has orange juice," Christian told her, "at five bucks a glass."

"Fine."

Another moment of strained silence passed while Ben delivered the four-ounce glass of juice.

"You had something you wanted to tell me?" Christian asked impatiently.

"Yes," she said, her voice gaining strength. "I'm sure my family's responsible for Ms. Santiago's visit. You see… I didn't exactly tell them I'd accepted your job offer. They didn't know—"

"You mean you were hiding from your parents?"

"I wasn't *hiding*," she argued. "Not exactly." She brushed a long strand of hair away from her face, and Ben saw that her hands were shaking badly. "I wanted to prove something to them, and this seemed the only way I could do it."

"What were you trying to prove?" Christian shouted. "How easy it is to destroy a man and his business?"

"No," she replied, squaring her shoulders. "I wanted to demonstrate to my father that I'm perfectly capable of taking care of myself. That I can support myself, and furthermore, I'm old enough to make my own decisions without him continually interfering in my life."

"So you didn't tell him what you'd done."

"No," she admitted, chancing a quick look in Christian's direction. "Not at first. It's been a while since my family heard from me, so I wrote them a letter last week and told them about the job and how after a year's time I'll have the title to twenty acres and the cabin."

"And?"

"Well, with Hard Luck being in the news and everything, Dad had already heard about Midnight Sons advertising for women. He…" She paused and bit her lower lip. "He seems to think this isn't the place for me, and the best way to get me home is to prove you're running some kind of scam. That's why he hired Ms. Santiago. I… I think he may want to sue you." She closed her eyes again, as if she expected Christian to explode.

Instead, he stared sightlessly into space. "We're dead meat," he said tonelessly. "Sawyer and I can forget everything we've ever worked for because it'll be gone."

"I explained the situation as best I could to Ms. Santiago."

"Oh, great. By now she's probably decided I've kidnapped you and that I'm holding you for ransom."

"That's not true!"

"Think about it, Mariah. Tracy Santiago would give her eyeteeth to cut me off at the knees—and all because you wanted to *prove something* to your father!"

"I'll take care of everything," Mariah promised. Her huge eyes implored him. "You don't have to worry. I'll get everything straightened out. There won't be a lawsuit unless I'm willing to file one, and I'm not."

"*You'll* take care of it?" Christian repeated with a short bark of laughter. "*That's* supposed to reassure me? Ha!"

Lanni Caldwell glanced at her watch for the third time in a minute. Charles was late. He was supposed to pick her up in front of the *Anchorage News,* where she was working as an intern. She should wait outside for him, he'd said. It had been ten days since they'd seen each other, and she'd never missed anyone so much.

They'd agreed to postpone their wedding until the first week of April. At the time, that hadn't sounded so terrible, but she'd since revised her opinion. If these ten days were any indication of how miserable she was going to be without him, she'd never last the eight months. Her one consolation was that his travel schedule often brought him to Valdez, which was only a short airplane trip from Anchorage.

Just when she was beginning to really worry, Lanni

saw him. He was smiling broadly, a smile that spoke of his own joy at seeing her.

Unable to stand still, Lanni hurried toward him, threading her way through the late-afternoon shoppers crowding the sidewalk.

When she was only a few feet away, she started to run. "Charles! Oh, Charles!"

He caught her around the waist and lifted her off the ground. They were both talking at once, saying the same things. How lonely the past days had been. How eight months seemed impossible. How much they'd missed each other.

It felt so good to be in his arms again. She hadn't *intended* to kiss him right there on the sidewalk with half of Anchorage looking on, but she couldn't stop herself. Charles O'Halloran was solid and handsome and strong—and he was hers.

His mouth found Lanni's and her objections, her doubts, her misery, all melted away. She hardly heard the traffic, hardly noticed the smiling passersby.

Slowly Charles lowered her to the ground. He dragged in a giant breath; so did she. "When it comes to you, Lanni," he whispered, "I haven't got a bit of self-control."

They clasped hands and began walking. "Where are we going?" she asked.

"We have to go somewhere?" he teased.

Lanni leaned her head against his shoulder. "No, but dinner would be nice. I'm starved."

"Me, too, but I'm even more starved for you."

Lanni smiled softly. "I'm dying to hear what came of the lawyer's visit to Hard Luck. What's this about

Mariah being the one who's filing the lawsuit? I don't know her well, but I can't see her doing that."

"I'll explain everything later," he promised, sliding his arm around her, keeping her close to his side.

"All I can say is that Christian deserves whatever he gets. He's been so impatient with her."

Charles's eyes met Lanni's, then crinkled in silent amusement. "Whose side are you on in this fiasco?"

"Yours," she said promptly. "It's just that I find it all rather...entertaining."

"Is that a fact?" He brought her hand to his lips and kissed her knuckles. "Christian's convinced we're in a damned-if-we-do and damned-if-we-don't situation."

"Really?" Her eyes held his. This could well be more serious than it sounded. "Is Midnight Sons in legal trouble?"

Charles held open the door of her favorite Chinese restaurant. "I don't know. Frankly, it's not my problem. Sawyer and Christian are the ones who came up with this brilliant plan to bring women to Hard Luck. I'm sure that between them they'll come up with a solution."

They were promptly seated and the waiter took their order. "Don't look so worried," Charles said, reaching across the table to take her hand. "As far as I'm concerned, this is a tempest in a teacup. Mariah's parents are the ones who started this, so I suggested we let Mariah work this out with them. Her father doesn't want to ruin Midnight Sons—all he really cares about is making sure his daughter's safe."

"I'd say Mariah can look after herself very well indeed. She's bright and responsible and—"

"Christian might not agree with you, but I do."

A smile stole across Lanni's features. "You're going to be a very good husband, Charles O'Halloran."

For long moments they simply gazed at each other. To Lanni, there was no better man than Charles. Of all the women in the world, he'd chosen to marry *her*—but then, she was convinced their falling in love had been no accident.

"I talked to your mother," she said, suddenly remembering the lengthy conversation she'd had with Ellen Greenleaf. Ellen had remarried a couple of years ago and was now living in British Columbia.

"And?"

"And she's absolutely delighted that you came to your senses and proposed."

"I proposed?" he repeated, his eyebrows raised. "Seems to me it was the other way around."

"Does it really matter who asked whom?" she said in mock disgust. "The important thing is I love you and you love me."

Charles grew serious. "I do love you."

Lanni would never doubt him. Slowly he raised her hand to his lips and kissed her palm. The action was both sensual and endearing.

"Does your grandmother know about us?" Charles asked.

Lanni shook her head. "Her health has deteriorated in the last few weeks. Half the time, Grammy doesn't even recognize Mom. Apparently she slips in and out of consciousness. The doctors…don't expect her to live much longer."

Charles frowned and his eyes were sad. "I'm sorry, Lanni."

"I know you are."

"I spent a lot of years hating Catherine Fletcher for what she did to my family, but I can't anymore. It's because of her that I found the most precious gift of my life. You. Remember what you said a few weeks ago about the two of us being destined for each other? I believe it now, as strongly as I believe anything."

Bethany had purposely waited three days before visiting the Hard Luck Café. She'd needed the time to fortify herself for this first confrontation. The night of her arrival, Mitch had confirmed what she already knew: Ben Hamilton owned the café.

Her heart skipped, then thudded so hard it was almost painful. Her palms felt sweaty as she pulled open the door and stepped inside. If she reacted this way before she even met Ben, what would she be like afterward?

"Hello."

Ben stood behind the counter, a white apron around his middle, a welcoming smile on his lips. Bethany felt as if the wind had been knocked out of her.

"You must be Bethany Ross."

"Yes," she said, struggling to make her voice audible. "You're Ben Hamilton?"

"The one and only." He sketched a little bow, then leaned back against the counter, studying her.

With her breath trapped in her lungs, Bethany made a show of glancing around the empty room. It was eleven-thirty, still early for lunch. The café featured a counter and a number of booths with red vinyl upholstery. The rest of the furnishings consisted of tables and mismatched chairs.

"Help yourself to a seat."

"Thank you." Bethany chose to sit at the counter. She picked up a plastic-coated menu and pretended to study it.

"The special of the day is a roast-beef sandwich," Ben told her.

She looked up and nodded. "What about the soup?"

"Split pea."

Ben was nothing like she'd expected. The years hadn't been as generous to him as she'd hoped. His hair had thinned and his belly hung over the waistband of his apron. Lines creased his face.

If he hadn't introduced himself, hadn't said his name aloud, Bethany would never have guessed.

"Do you want any recommendations?" he asked.

"Please."

"Go with the special."

She closed the menu. "All right, I will."

As he walked back to the kitchen, he asked, "How are things going for you at the school?"

"Fine," she said, surprised she was able to carry on a normal conversation with him. "The kids I've met are great, and Margaret's been a lot of help." Today was Labor Day; tomorrow was her first day of teaching.

She wondered what Ben saw when he looked at her. Did he notice any resemblance? Did he see how much she looked like her mother, especially around the eyes? Or had he wiped the memory of her mother from his mind?

"Everyone in Hard Luck's real pleased to have you."

"I'm pleased to be here," she responded politely. She was struck by how friendly he was, how genuinely interested he seemed. Was that why her mother had fallen in love with him all those years ago?

The door opened and Ben looked up. "Howdy, Mitch. Said hello to the new schoolteacher yet?"

"We met earlier." Bethany thought she detected a note of reluctance in his voice, as if he regretted coming into the café while she was there.

Mitch claimed the stool at the opposite end of the counter.

"I don't think she's contagious," Ben chided from the kitchen, then chuckled. "And I'm pretty sure she doesn't bite."

Mitch cast Bethany an apologetic smile. Uncomfortable, she glanced away.

Ben brought her meal, and she managed to meet his eyes. "I... I meant to tell you I wanted to take the sandwich with me," she said, faltering over the words. "If that's not a problem."

"Not at all." He whipped the plate off the counter. "What can I get for you, Mitch?" he asked.

"How about a cheeseburger?"

"You got it." Ben returned to the kitchen, leaving Bethany and Mitch alone.

She looked at him. He looked at her. Neither seemed able to come up with anything to say. In other circumstances, Bethany would've found a hundred different subjects to discuss.

But not now. Not when she was so distracted by the battle being waged in her heart. She'd just walked up to her father and ordered lunch.

No, he *wasn't* her father, she amended. Her father was Peter Ross, the man who'd loved her and raised her as his own. The man who'd sat at her bedside and read her to sleep. The man who'd escorted her to the father-daughter dance when she was a high school sophomore.

The only link Bethany shared with Ben Hamilton was genetic. He was the man who'd given her life, and nothing else. Not one damn thing.

Three

On the first day of school, Mitch swore his daughter was up before dawn. By the time the alarm sounded and he struggled out of bed and into the kitchen, Chrissie was already dressed.

She sat in the living room with her lunch pail tightly clutched in her hand. She was dressed in her new jeans and Precious Moments sweatshirt.

"Morning, Daddy."

"Howdy, pumpkin." He yawned loudly. "Aren't you up a little early?" He padded barefoot into the kitchen, with Chrissie following him.

"It's the first day of school." She announced this as if it was news to him.

"I know."

"I'm Ms. Ross's helper," she said importantly.

Mitch had stopped counting the number of times a day Chrissie mentioned Ms. Ross. He'd given up telling her he wasn't interested in marrying the teacher. Chrissie didn't want to believe it, and arguing with her only irritated him. Eventually, she'd see for herself that there'd never be a relationship between him and Bethany.

He'd heard that Bethany had stirred up a lot of interest among the single men in town. Good. Great. Wonderful. In no time at all, she'd be involved with someone else, and his daughter would get the message.

Mitch hated to disappoint her. But, he reasoned, disappointment was part of life, and he wouldn't always be able to protect her. The sooner she accepted there'd only be the two of them, the better.

"I packed my own lunch," she told him, holding up her Barbie lunch pail.

"I'm proud of you."

She delighted in showing him what she'd chosen for her lunch. Ham-and-cheese sandwich carefully wrapped in napkins, an apple, juice, an oatmeal cookie. Mitch was pleased to see that she'd done a good job of packing a well-balanced meal and told her so.

He looked at his watch, gauging the time before they could leave. "What about breakfast?"

Although Chrissie claimed she was too excited to eat, Mitch insisted she try. "How about a bowl of cereal?" he suggested, pulling out several boxes from the cupboard. He wasn't much of a breakfast eater himself. Generally he didn't have anything until ten or so. More often than not, he picked up a doughnut or something equally sweet when he stopped in at Ben's for coffee.

"I'll *try* to eat something," Chrissie agreed with a decided lack of enthusiasm. He let her pour her own cereal and milk. His daughter was an independent little creature, which was fine with Mitch. In fact, he took pride in it.

By the time he'd finished dressing, she'd eaten her breakfast and washed and put away her bowl and spoon. She sat on the couch waiting for Mitch to escort her to school.

"Are you sure you need me, now that you're a second-grader?" Not that Mitch objected to walking his daughter to class. However, he had a sneaking suspicion that if her teacher had been anyone other than the lovely Ms. Ross, Chrissie would have insisted on walking without him.

"I *want* you to take me," she said with a smile bright enough to blind him. The kid knew exactly what she was doing. And being the good father he was, he had to go along with her. The way he figured it, he'd walk her to the school door and, if he was lucky, escape without seeing Bethany.

His plan backfired. Chrissie *had* to show him her desk.

"I'm over here," she said, taking him by the hand and leading him to the front row. "Ms. Ross let me pick my own seat." Wouldn't you know, his daughter had chosen to sit directly in front of the teacher's desk.

He tried to make a fast getaway, but Bethany herself waylaid him.

"Good morning, Mitch."

"Morning." The tropical bird was back in full plumage. She wore a black skirt with a colorful floral top; it reminded him of the shirt Sawyer had brought back from Hawaii. Her hair was woven into a thick braid that fell halfway down her back.

She did have beautiful hair, he'd say that much. It didn't take a lot of effort to imagine undoing her braid and running his fingers through the glossy strands.

He could see himself with his hands buried wrist-deep in her hair, drawing her mouth to his. Her lips would feel silky soft, and she'd taste like honey and passion and—

"Are you picking me up after school?" Chrissie asked, interrupting his thoughts.

Thank heaven she had. Apparently all Chrissie's chatter about Bethany was having more of an effect on him than he'd realized. His heart pounded like an overworked piston, his pulse thumping so hard he could feel it throb in his neck.

Bethany and Chrissie were both looking at him, awaiting his response. "Pick you up?" As a rule, Chrissie walked over to Louise Gold's house after school.

"Just for today," Chrissie said, her big eyes gazing up at him hopefully.

"All right," he agreed grudgingly. "Just for today."

Chrissie's face shone with her smile.

He would've told Bethany goodbye, but she was talking to other parents. Just as well. The sooner he got away from her, the sooner he could get a grip on his emotions.

Mitch wished he knew what was wrong with him. After vehemently opposing all talk about becoming romantically involved with Bethany Ross, he found it downright frightening to discover the effect she had on him.

Sawyer debated what exactly he should say to his brother. It wasn't often that he felt called upon to take Christian to task. But enough was enough. Christian had Mariah so unnerved the poor girl couldn't do anything right.

"She did it again," Christian muttered as he walked past Sawyer's desk to his own.

Sawyer looked up. "Who?" he asked in an innocent voice.

Seething, Christian jerked his head toward Mariah. "She can't seem to find accounts receivable on the computer."

"It's here," Mariah insisted, her fingers on the keyboard. Even from where Sawyer was sitting, it looked as though she was randomly pressing keys in a desperate effort to find the missing data. "I'm just not sure where it went."

"Don't you have it on a backup disk?" Sawyer asked.

"Yes…"

"Who knows?" Christian threw his hands in the air. "The backup disk's probably in the same place as the missing file. We could be in real trouble here." Panic edged his voice.

"She'll find it," Sawyer said confidently.

Mariah thanked him with a brief smile.

"Let me look," Christian demanded, flying out of his chair. "Before you crash the entire system."

"I lost it, I'll find it." Mariah didn't budge from her seat. The woman had long since won Sawyer's admiration, not least for the mettle she'd shown in dealing with his brother.

"Leave her be," Sawyer said.

"And risk everything?"

"We aren't risking anything. There's a backup disk."

Christian sat down at his desk, but his gaze remained on Mariah. Sawyer watched Christian. And Mariah did her level best to ignore them both.

"Fact is, I could use a break," Sawyer said. "Why don't we let Ben treat us to a cup of coffee?"

"Okay," Christian agreed reluctantly.

As Sawyer walked past Mariah's desk, she mouthed a thank-you. He nodded and steered his irritable brother out the door.

"I wish you wouldn't be so hard on her," he said the minute they were alone. It annoyed him to see Christian treat Mariah as if she didn't have a brain in her head.

"Hard on her?" Christian protested loudly. "The woman drives me insane. If it was up to me, she'd be out of here in a heartbeat. She's trouble with a capital *T*."

"She's a good secretary," Sawyer argued. "The office has never been in better shape. The files are organized and neat, and the equipment's been updated. Frankly I don't know how we managed without her as long as we did."

Christian opened his mouth, then closed it. He didn't have an argument.

"Okay, so there was the one fiasco with that attorney," Sawyer said, knowing that part of Christian's anger stemmed from the confrontation with Tracy Santiago.

Christian's mouth thinned and his eyes narrowed. "Mark my words, she'll be back."

"Who?"

His brother eyed him scornfully. "The attorney, of course. If for nothing more than pure spite. That woman's vicious, Sawyer. Vicious. And as if that's not bad enough, she took an instant dislike to all of us—especially Duke. She's out for revenge."

Sawyer didn't believe that. True, Christian had been the one who'd actually talked to her, but his brother's assessment of Tracy's plans for revenge sounded a little far-fetched.

"It's my understanding that everything was squared once Mariah talked to her. I don't think there's any real threat."

"For now," Christian said meaningfully. "But don't think we've heard the end of this. Yup, you mark my words, Santiago's gone for reinforcements."

"Don't be ridiculous. Why would she do that if no one's paying her fee? We've seen the last of her."

"I doubt it," Christian muttered.

Instead of going straight to Ben's, they strolled toward the open hangar. John Henderson, who served as a sometime mechanic and a full-time pilot, was servicing the six-passenger Lockheed, the largest plane in their small fleet.

When he saw them approach, John grabbed an oil rag from his hip pocket and wiped his hands. "Morning," he called out cheerfully.

Sawyer noticed that John had gotten his hair and beard trimmed. He wasn't a bad-looking guy when he put some effort into his appearance. Of course, there hadn't been much reason to do that until recently.

It occurred to him that Duke Porter might learn a thing or two from John. Duke might have fared better with the Santiago woman had he been a bit more gentlemanly. Sawyer had never seen any two people take such an instant dislike to each other.

"You're looking good," he commented, nodding at John, and to his surprise, the other man blushed.

"I was thinking of asking the new schoolteacher if

she'd have dinner with me Friday evening," he said. Sawyer noted that John was studying Christian as if he expected him to object.

"It's Thursday, John," Sawyer pointed out. "Just when do you plan to ask her?"

"That depends." Again John studied Christian.

"What are you looking at me for?" Christian snapped, his mood as surly with John as it had been earlier with Mariah.

"I just wanted to be sure you weren't planning on asking her yourself."

"Why would I do that?" The glance Christian gave Sawyer said he had more than enough problems with *one* woman.

John's face broke into a wide grin of unspoken relief.

Christian grumbled something under his breath as he headed out the other side of the hangar. Sawyer followed him to the Hard Luck Café.

As they sat down at the counter, Ben stuck his head out from the kitchen. "It's self-service this morning, fellows."

"No problem." Sawyer walked around the counter and reached for the pot. He filled two mugs. Meanwhile, Christian helped himself to a couple of powdered-sugar doughnuts from under the plastic dome.

"Getting back to Mariah," Sawyer said when he'd finished stirring his coffee. He felt obliged to clear this up; in his opinion, Christian's attitude needed adjustment.

"Do we have to?"

"Yes, we do. She's proved herself to be a capable secretary."

"The woman's nothing but a nuisance. She can't type worth a damn, she misfiles correspondence, and she habitually loses things. The accounts-receivable disaster this morning is a prime example."

"I've never had any trouble with her," Sawyer countered. "I've found Mariah hardworking and sincere."

"She makes too many mistakes."

"Frankly I don't see it. If you ask me, *you're* the problem. You make her nervous. She's constantly worried that she's going to mess up—it's a self-fulfilling prophecy, Christian. Besides," Sawyer added, "she's gone to a lot of trouble to work things out with her family and settle this lawsuit business. I admire her for that."

Christian obviously didn't share his admiration. "I wish they'd talked her into returning to Seattle. That's where she belongs."

Sawyer merely shrugged. "Face it—Mariah's going to stay the entire year. It's a matter of pride with her, and that's something we can both understand."

Christian looked away.

"She isn't so bad, you know." Sawyer slapped his brother affectionately on the back. "There's one thing you seem to have conveniently forgotten."

"What's that?"

Sawyer grabbed one of Christian's doughnuts. He grinned broadly. "You must've liked *something* about her. After all, you're the guy who hired her."

"In other words, I don't have anyone to blame but myself."

"You got it." With that Sawyer walked out of the café, leaving his brother to foot the bill.

* * *

In two weeks Bethany hadn't seen even a glimpse of Mitch Harris. The man made himself as scarce as sunlight in an Alaskan winter. He must be working overtime, and she had to wonder if it was—at least partly—in an effort to avoid her.

Bethany could accept that he wasn't attracted to her if that was indeed the case. But the night they'd met and each time afterward, she'd sensed a growing awareness between them. She knew he felt it, too, even though he doggedly resisted it. Whenever they were in a room together, no matter how many people were present, their eyes gravitated toward each other. The solid ground beneath Bethany would subtly shift, and she'd have to struggle to hide the fact that anything was wrong.

"Can I clean the blackboards for you, Ms. Ross?" Chrissie asked, interrupting her musings. The youngster stood next to Bethany's desk. It would be very easy to love this child, she thought.

Chrissie had been her student for two weeks, and it became increasingly difficult not to make her a teacher's pet. The seven-year-old was so willing to please and always looked for ways to brighten Bethany's day.

If Bethany had any complaints about Mitch's daughter, it was the number of times Chrissie introduced her father into the conversation. Clearly the girl adored him.

"Can I?" she asked again, holding up the erasers.

"Certainly, Chrissie. How thoughtful of you to ask. I'd be delighted if you cleaned the boards."

Chrissie flushed with pleasure. "I like to help my dad, too. He needs me sometimes."

"I'll bet you're good at helping him. You've been a wonderful assistant to me."

Once again the child glowed at Bethany's approval. "My dad promised to pick me up after school today," she said; she seemed to be watching for Bethany's reaction to that news. From other bits of information Chrissie had dropped, Bethany knew that Mitch occasionally collected his daughter after school. She herself hadn't seen him.

"With your dad coming, maybe you should skip cleaning the boards this afternoon," Bethany said. She didn't want Mitch to be kept waiting because Chrissie was busy, nor did she want to force him to enter the classroom.

"It'll be all right," Chrissie said quickly. "Don't worry, Dad'll wait."

Still, Bethany wasn't confident that she was doing the right thing, especially since Mitch seemed to be avoiding her so diligently.

The little girl was busy with the blackboards, standing on tiptoe to reach as far as she could, when Mitch walked briskly into the classroom. His movements were filled with impatience. His body language said he didn't appreciate having to come and look for his daughter.

As had happened before, his eyes flew to Bethany's, and hers to his. Slowly she rose from behind her desk. "Hello, Mitch."

"Bethany."

"Hi, Dad! I'm helping Ms. Ross. I'm almost done," Chrissie said lightheartedly. "All I have to do is go outside and get the chalk out of the erasers. I'll be back in a minute."

Mitch opened his mouth as though to protest, but before he could utter a word, Chrissie raced out the door.

Bethany and Mitch were alone.

They couldn't stop staring at each other. Bethany would've paid good money to know what he was thinking. Not that she was all that clear about her own feelings. Their attraction to each other *should* have been uncomplicated, since neither of them was involved with anyone else.

True, John Henderson, one of the bush pilots employed by Midnight Sons, had asked her to dinner. She'd accepted; there was no point in sitting around waiting for Mitch to ask her out, and John seemed pleasant.

The silence between them grew. Mitch's face was stern, his features set. Bethany sighed, uncertain how to break the ice.

"I hear you're going out to dinner with John Henderson this evening," Mitch surprised her by saying.

"Yes." She wasn't going to deny it.

"I think that's an excellent idea."

"My having dinner with John?"

"Yes."

Their eyes remained locked. Finally she swallowed and asked, "Why?"

"John's a good man."

It was on the tip of her tongue to ask the reason Mitch hadn't asked her out himself. Mitch was attracted to her, and she to him. The force of that attraction was no small thing. Surely it would be better to discuss it openly, even if they didn't act on their feelings. She longed to bring up the subject and see where it took them. But in the end she said nothing. Neither did Mitch.

Chrissie reentered the classroom, and Bethany slowly moved her gaze from Mitch to his daughter.

"The erasers are clean," Chrissie announced. Her eyes were huge with expectation.

"Thank you, sweetheart."

"You're welcome. Can I clean them again next Friday?"

"That would be very helpful."

"Have a nice evening," Mitch said as he walked out the door, his hand on his daughter's shoulder.

"I will, thank you," she called after them, but she didn't think he heard.

The encounter with Mitch left Bethany feeling melancholy. She accompanied Margaret Simpson to her house for a cup of coffee, hoping that a visit with the other teacher would cheer her up; however, she was distracted during their conversation. Once she arrived home, she turned on her CD player and lay down on the living room carpet, listening to Billy Joel—which said a great deal about her state of mind.

Instead of being excited about her dinner date, she was bemoaning the fact that it wasn't Mitch taking her out. It was time to face reality: he wasn't interested in seeing her. She told herself it didn't matter. There were plenty of other fish in the sea. But her little pep talk fell decidedly flat.

Because John was afraid he might get back late from a flight into Fairbanks, he'd asked if they could meet at the Hard Luck Café. Bethany didn't object. She showered and changed into a knee-length, chocolate-brown skirt, an extra-long, loose-knit beige sweater and calf-length brown leather boots. To dress up the outfit, she wove a silk scarf into her French braid. She looked good and she knew it. Her one regret was that Mitch wouldn't see her. She'd like him to know what he was missing!

To her astonishment, there were only two other people in the café when she arrived. The men, whom she didn't recognize, were deeply engrossed in conversation. They sat drinking beer at one of the tables.

"My, my, don't you look pretty," Ben hailed her when she took a seat in a booth near the window. Apparently he knew she was meeting John, because he filled two water glasses and tucked a couple of menus under his arm.

"Thank you."

"I heard John's got his eye on you."

Bethany didn't comment. Although she'd been in the café a number of times since her first visit, she was never completely comfortable with Ben. She'd moved to Hard Luck with an open mind about him. She had no plan other than getting to know this man who'd fathered her.

She'd learned about him only a year ago. Despite the initial shock, this new knowledge didn't change her feelings toward either her mother or Peter Ross. She just wanted to discover for herself what kind of man Ben Hamilton was. She certainly didn't intend to interfere in his life. Nor did she intend to embarrass him with the truth. The year might well come to a close without his ever finding out who she was.

In all honesty, Bethany couldn't think of a way to casually announce that she was his daughter. For a giddy moment, she was tempted to throw open her arms and call him Daddy. But no—he'd never been that.

Ben lingered at the table. "If you want the truth, I was surprised you were coming here with John."

"Really." Bethany picked up her water glass.

"I kinda thought you were sweet on Mitch."

The glass hit the table with an unexpected thunk, garnering the attention of the restaurant's two other occupants.

Ben rubbed the side of his face. "What I've seen, Mitch is taken with you, as well."

Bethany stared down at the table and swallowed nervously. "I'm sure that isn't true."

Low laughter rumbled in Ben's chest. "I've seen the way you two send looks at each other. I'm not blind, you know. Yes, sir, I see plenty—lots more than people think." He tapped his finger against his temple to emphasize the point. "I might be a crusty old bachelor, but I—"

"You never got married?" she interrupted him.

"No."

"Why not?" She turned the conversation away from herself, at the same time attempting to learn what she could about his life.

"I guess you could say I never found the right woman."

His answer irritated Bethany. Her mother was one of the finest women she'd ever known. The desire to defend her mother, tell this character about the heartache he'd caused, burned in the pit of her stomach.

"How...how long have you been in Alaska?" she asked instead.

Ben seemed to need time to calculate his answer. "It

must be twenty years now. The O'Halloran boys were still wet behind the ears when I made my way here."

"Why Hard Luck?" she asked.

"Why not? It was as good a place as any. Besides," he said, flashing her a grin, "there's something to be said for having the only restaurant within a four-hundred-mile radius."

Bethany laughed.

The door opened and John Henderson rushed in, a little breathless and a whole lot flustered. He hurried over to the table, and his eyes lit up at the sight of her. He seemed speechless.

"Hello again," Bethany said.

John remained standing there, his mouth open.

Ben slapped him on the back. "Aren't you going to thank me for keeping her company?"

John jerked his head around as if suddenly noticing Ben. "Uh, thanks, Ben."

"No problem." He turned to walk back to the kitchen, but before he did, Bethany's eye caught his and they shared a secret smile. For the first time Bethany felt she'd truly communicated with the man she'd come three thousand miles to meet.

Dinner turned out to be more of an ordeal than Bethany had expected. By the time he'd paid for their meal, Bethany actually felt sorry for John. During the course of their dinner, he'd dripped gravy down the front of his shirt, knocked over the sugar canister and spilled his coffee, most of which landed on her skirt. The man was clearly a nervous wreck.

"I'll walk you home," John said.

She waited until they were outside before she

thanked him. Although they were only halfway through September, there was a decided coolness, and the hint of snow hung in the air. Bethany was glad she'd worn her coat.

"Thank you, John, for a lovely evening."

The pilot buried his hands in his jacket pockets. "I'm sorry about the coffee."

"You didn't do it on purpose."

"What about your skirt?"

"Don't worry—I'm sure it'll wash out."

"You didn't get burned?"

She'd assured him she hadn't at least a dozen times. "I'm fine, John, really."

"I want you to know I'm not normally this clumsy."

"I'm sure that's true."

"It's just that it isn't often a woman as beautiful as you agrees to have dinner with me."

There was something touching about this pilot, something endearing. "What a sweet thing to say. Thank you."

"Women like to hear that kind of stuff, don't they?" John asked. "About being pretty and all."

Bethany hesitated, wondering where the conversation was heading. "I think it's safe to say we do."

It was difficult to keep from smiling. With someone else, she might have been irritated or worse. But not with John. Besides, the evening was so beautiful. The sky danced with a brilliant display of stars, and the northern lights seemed to sizzle just over the horizon. Bethany couldn't stop gazing up at the heavens.

"Is it always this beautiful here?"

"Yup," John said without hesitation. "But then they say that beauty's in the eye of the beholder."

"That's true." Bethany shrugged, a little puzzled.

"It won't be long now before the rivers freeze," he explained soberly.

"So soon?"

"Yup. We're likely to have snow anytime."

Bethany could hardly believe it. "Really?"

"This is the Arctic, Bethany."

"But it seems as if I just got here. It's still summer at home."

"Maybe in California, but not here." He looked worried. "You aren't going to leave, are you?"

"No. I signed a contract for this school year. Don't worry, I'm not going to break my commitment because of a little snow and ice."

They strolled past the school, and she glanced at the building with a sense of pride. She already loved her job and her students.

Soon her house was in sight. Bethany was deciding how to handle the awkwardness that might develop when they reached her front door. She didn't plan to invite John in.

"Thank you," Bethany said again when at last they stood on the stoop.

"The evening would've been better if I hadn't… you know."

"Stop worrying about a little coffee."

"Don't forget the sugar." He grinned as if he'd begun to find the entire episode amusing.

"Despite a few, uh, mishaps, I really did enjoy dinner," she told him.

John kicked at the dirt with the toe of his shoe. "I don't suppose you'd go out with me again."

Bethany wasn't sure how to respond. She liked

John, but just as a friend, and she didn't want to mislead him into thinking something more could develop between them. She'd made that mistake once before.

"You don't need to feel guilty if you don't want to," he said, his eyes avoiding hers. He cleared his throat. "I can understand why someone hand-delivered by the angels wouldn't want to be seen with someone like me." He glanced shyly at her.

Tempted to roll her eyes at that remark, Bethany managed a smile. "How about if we have dinner again next Friday night?" she asked.

John's head shot up. "You mean it?"

Bethany nodded. "This time it'll be my treat."

His smile faded and he folded his arms across his chest. "You want to buy *me* dinner?"

"Yes. Friends do that, you know." A car could be heard in the distance, driving slowly down the street.

"Friends?" The car was coming closer.

"Yes." She leaned forward and very gently pressed her lips to his cheek. As she backed away, she saw that the car had stopped.

Silhouetted against the moonlight sat Mitch Harris. He'd just witnessed her kissing John Henderson.

Four

October 1995

The first snowfall of the year came in the third week of September. Thick flurries drifted down throughout the day, covering the ground and obscuring familiar outlines. Mitch thought he should've been accustomed to winter's debut by now, but he wasn't. However beautiful, however serene, this soft-looking white blanket was only a foretaste of the bitter cold to follow.

He looked at his watch. In a few minutes he'd walk over to the school to meet Chrissie. He'd gotten into the habit of picking up his daughter on Friday afternoons.

Not because she needed him or had asked him to come. No, he wryly suspected that going to the school was rooted in some masochistic need to see Bethany.

He rationalized that he was giving Chrissie this extra attention because he worked longer hours on Friday evenings, when Diane Hestead, a high school student, stayed with her. That was the only night of the week Ben served alcohol. Before the women had arrived, a few of the pilots and maybe a trapper or two wandered into the Hard Luck Café. But with the news of women coming to town, Ben's place had begun to fill up, not only with pilots but pipeline workers and other men.

For the past three Friday nights, John Henderson and Bethany had dined at the café. They came and left before eight, when Ben opened the bar.

From the gossip circulating around town, Mitch learned they'd become something of an item, although both insisted they were "only friends."

Mitch knew otherwise. On Bethany's first date with John, he'd happened upon them kissing. Friends indeed! Even now, his gut tightened at the memory.

For the thousandth time he reminded himself that he'd been the one to encourage her to see John. He couldn't very well reveal his discontent with that situation when she'd done nothing more than follow his advice.

He'd tried to convince himself that discovering John and Bethany together—kissing—had been sheer coincidence. But it hadn't been.

As the public safety officer, Mitch routinely checked the streets on Friday nights. He'd seen them leave Ben's place on foot that first evening and had discreetly followed them. On subsequent Fridays he'd continued his spy tactics, always making sure he was out of sight. He wasn't particularly proud of himself, but he found it impossible to resist the compulsion.

Except for their first date, when he'd seen them kissing outside her house, she'd invited John in. The pilot never stayed more than a few minutes, but of course Mitch knew what the two of them were doing.

He kept telling himself he should be pleased she was dating John; Henderson was a decent sort. But Mitch *wasn't* pleased. At night he lay awake staring at the four shrinking walls of his bedroom. Still, he knew it wasn't the walls that locked him in, that kept him from building a relationship with Bethany.

It was his guilt, his own doubts and fears, that came between him and Bethany. This was Lori's legacy to him. She'd died and in that moment made certain he'd never be free of her memory.

Mitch checked his watch a second time and decided to head over to the school. The phone rang as he closed and locked the door, but he resisted the temptation to answer it. The machine would pick up the message, and he'd deal with the call when he returned to the office.

Mitch could hear excited laughter in the distance as the children frolicked in the snow. Chrissie loved playing outside, although there'd be precious little of that over the next few months.

By the time Christmas came, Hard Luck would be in total darkness. But with the holidays to occupy people's minds and lift their spirits, the dark days didn't seem nearly as depressing as they might have.

Mitch had just rounded the corner to the school when he saw Bethany. She was half trotting with her head bowed against the wind, her steps filled with frantic purpose. She glanced up and saw him and stopped abruptly.

"Mitch." Her hand pushed a stray lock of hair away from her face, and he noticed for the first time how pale she was. "It's Chrissie. She's been hurt."

The words hit Mitch like a fist. He ran toward her and gripped her by the elbows. *"What happened?"*

"She fell on the ice and cut herself. The school tried to call you, but you'd already left the office."

"Where is she?"

"At the clinic…" Bethany's voice quavered precariously. "I knew you were probably on your way to the school. Oh, Mitch, I'm so afraid."

It was bad. It had to be, otherwise Bethany wouldn't be this pale, this frightened. Panic galvanized him and he began running toward the clinic. He'd gone half a block before he realized that Bethany was behind him, her feet slipping and sliding on the snow. Fearing she might stumble and fall, he turned back and stretched out a hand to her. She grasped his fingers with surprising strength.

Together they hurried toward the clinic. It couldn't have taken them more than two or three minutes to reach the building, but it felt like a lifetime to Mitch. He couldn't bear the thought of something happening to Chrissie. His daughter, his joy. She'd given his life purpose after Lori's death. She'd given him a reason to live.

He jerked open the clinic door, and the first thing he saw was blood. Crimson droplets on the floor. Chrissie's blood. He stopped cold as icy fingers crept along his backbone.

Dotty Harlow, the nurse who'd replaced Pearl Inman, was nowhere in sight; neither was Angie Hughes.

"Dotty!" he called urgently.

"Daddy." Chrissie moaned his name, and the sound of her pain pierced his heart.

Dotty stepped out of a cubicle in the back. Her soothing voice calmed his panic as she explained that Chrissie had required a couple of stitches, which she was qualified to do.

Angie, who'd been talking to Chrissie, stepped aside when he came into the room. Chrissie sniffled loudly and her small arms circled his neck; when she spoke, her words came in a staccato hiccupping voice. "I…fell…and cut my leg real…bad."

"You're going to be fine, pumpkin." He pressed his hand to the side of her sweet face and laid his cheek on her hair.

"I want Ms. Ross."

"I'm here," Bethany whispered from behind Mitch.

Chrissie stretched out her arms and Bethany hugged her close. Watching the two of them together threatened his resolve, as nothing else could have, to guard his heart against this woman.

"You were very brave," Dotty told Chrissie, as she put away the medical supplies, and Bethany helped his daughter back into her torn jeans.

"I tried not to cry," Chrissie said, tears glistening in her eyes, "but it hurt too bad."

"She's going to need to take this medication," Dotty said, distracting Mitch. The nurse rattled off a list of complicated-sounding instructions. Possibly because he looked confused and uncertain, Dotty wrote everything down and reviewed it with him a second time.

"I can take her home?" he asked.

"Sure," Dotty said. "If you have any questions, feel free to call me or Angie."

"Thanks, I will."

"Can I go home now?" Chrissie asked.

"We're on our way, pumpkin."

"I want Ms. Ross to come with us. Please, Daddy, I want Ms. Ross."

Any argument he might have offered died at the pleading note in Chrissie's voice. There was very little he could have denied his daughter in that moment.

When they arrived at the house and went inside, Chrissie climbed on Bethany's lap, and soon her eyelids drifted shut.

"How'd it happen?" Mitch asked tersely, sitting across from Bethany. Even now, the thought of losing his child made him go cold with the worst fear he'd ever experienced. When he'd found Lori dead, he hadn't felt the panic that overcame him when a terrified Bethany had told him his daughter was hurt.

"I'm not sure," Bethany said. "As she always does on Fridays, Chrissie offered to clean the boards and erasers. My guess is that she took them outside and slipped. She must have cut her leg on the side of the Dumpster. One of the other children came running to get me."

"Thank God you were close at hand."

Bethany squeezed her eyes shut and nodded. When she opened them again, he noticed how warm and gentle they were as she looked down at Chrissie. "I don't mind telling you, it shook me, finding her like that," Bethany admitted. "You have a very special child, Mitch."

"I know." And he did. He felt a strange and unfamiliar blend of emotions as he gazed at the two of them together. One he loved beyond life itself. The other he *wanted* to love, and couldn't. He had nothing to offer her—not his heart, not marriage. And it was because he'd failed Lori, just as she'd failed herself. And failed him, failed her daughter. Day in and day out, his wife had grown more desperate, more unhappy. After Chrissie's birth, she'd fallen into depression. Nothing he said or did seemed to help, and he realized now that he hadn't paid enough attention, hadn't understood the reality of her despair. Mitch blamed himself; his lack of awareness had cost Lori her life.

"She's fast asleep," Bethany whispered, smoothing Chrissie's hair away from her temple. Her words freed him from his bitter memories and returned him to the present.

Mitch stood, lifting his daughter from Bethany's arms. He carried her into her room while Bethany went ahead to turn down the covers, then placed his daughter in her bed.

As soundlessly as possible they left the room, keeping the door half-open.

There was no excuse for Bethany to linger. She had a date with another man—but Mitch didn't want her to leave.

"I suppose you have to get ready for your dinner with John?" he said, tucking his hands in his back pockets.

"No." Her eyes held his and she slowly shook her head.

He was about to ask why, but he quickly decided he shouldn't question the unexpected gift that had been dropped in his lap.

"Chrissie and I rented a video to watch tomorrow," he said, hoping to hide his eagerness for her company. "We generally do that on weekends. This week's feature presentation is a three-year-old romantic comedy. Not my choice," he told her. "Pete Livengood's movie selection isn't the most up-to-date, but I think you'd enjoy it. Would you care to stay and watch it with me?" Heaven knew, Mitch wanted her to stay. About as much as he'd wanted anything in his life.

She gave a small, tentative smile and nodded. "But if it's supposed to be Chrissie's movie…"

"I'll get her another one tomorrow. Or—" he grimaced comically "—I'll watch this one again."

"Okay, then. How about some popcorn?" she asked.

He grinned almost boyishly. "You got it."

It wasn't until the kernels were sizzling in the hot oil that he realized they hadn't bothered with dinner. It didn't matter. He'd fix something later if they were hungry. He had several free hours before his patrol, and he didn't intend to waste them.

When the corn had finished popping, he drenched it with melted butter, then carried the two heaping bowls into the living room. Bethany followed with tall, ice-filled glasses of soda. He placed the bowls on the coffee table and reached for the remote control.

Normally he would've sat in the easy chair and propped his feet on the ottoman. He chose to sit next to Bethany, instead. For this one night, he was going to indulge himself. He needed her.

The movie began, and he eased closer to her on the comfortable sofa. He found himself laughing out loud at the actors' farcical antics and clever banter, which was something he didn't do often. Very rarely did he see the humor in things anymore. When he ran out of popcorn, Bethany offered him some of hers. Soon his arm was around her, and she was leaning her head against his shoulder. This was about as close to heaven as he expected to get anytime within the next fifty years.

Curiously time seemed to slow, not that Mitch objected. During one comical scene in the movie, Bethany glanced at him, laughing. Her eyes were a remarkably rich shade of brown. He wondered briefly if their color intensified in moments of passion.

He swallowed hard and jerked his head away. Such thoughts were dangerous and he knew it. He reverted his attention to the television screen. Another mistake. The scene, between the hero and heroine, played by two well-known actors, was the final one of the movie, and it was a love scene.

Mitch watched as the hero's lips moved over the heroine's, first in a slow, easy kiss, then with building passion. The actors were good at their craft. It didn't take much to convince Mitch that the characters they played were going to end up in the bedroom.

His breathing grew shallow as a painful longing sliced through him. The scene reminded Mitch of what he would never have with Bethany. In the same second, he realized with gut-wrenching clarity how much he wanted to kiss her.

As though neither of them could help it, their eyes met. In Bethany's he read an aching need. And he knew that what he saw might well be a reflection of his own.

There was a long silence as the credits rolled across the screen.

It was either throw caution to the winds and kiss her—or get out while he could still resist her. Almost without making a conscious decision, Mitch leapt from the sofa.

He buried his hands deep in his pockets, because he couldn't trust them not to reach for her. "Good movie, wasn't it?" he asked.

"Wonderful," she agreed, but she couldn't hide the disappointment in her voice.

"Mom, I'm so sorry." Lanni Caldwell stood in the doorway of the Anchorage hospital room. Her grandmother had died there only an hour before. "I came the minute I heard."

Kate looked up from her mother's bedside, her eyes brimming with tears, and smiled faintly. "Thank you for getting here so quickly." Lanni's father stood behind his wife, his hand on her shoulder.

Lanni gazed at Catherine Fletcher, the woman on the bed. *Grammy.* A term of affection for a woman Lanni barely knew, but one she would always love. Her heart ached at the sight of her dead grandmother. Over the past three months, Catherine's health had taken a slow but steady turn for the worse. Yet even in her failing physical condition, Catherine had insisted she'd return to Hard Luck. Dead or alive.

She would return.

Not because it was her home, but because Catherine wanted to go back to David O'Halloran, the man she'd loved for a lifetime. The man who'd left her standing at the altar more than fifty years earlier, when he'd brought home an English bride. The man she'd alternately loved and hated all these years.

"My mother's gone," Kate whispered brokenly. "She didn't even have the decency to wait for me.

Like everything else in her life, she had to do this on her own. Alone. Without family."

After spending the summer in Hard Luck, Lanni better understood her mother's pain. For reasons Lanni would never fully grasp, Catherine Fletcher had given up custody of Kate when she was only a toddler. At a time when such decisions were rare, Catherine had chosen to be separated from her daughter. Chosen, instead, to stand impatiently on the sidelines waiting for David's marriage to Ellen to disintegrate. When that didn't happen, Catherine had decided to help matters along. But Ellen and David had clung steadfastly to each other, and in the end, after David's untimely death, Catherine had let her bitterness and disillusionment take control.

All her life, Kate Caldwell had been deprived of her mother's love. She'd known that her mother had married her father on the rebound. The marriage had lasted less than two years, and Kate's birth had been unplanned, a mistake.

"Matt's on his way," Lanni told her parents. She'd spoken to her brother briefly when he phoned to give her his flight schedule. Sawyer O'Halloran was flying him into Fairbanks, and he'd catch the first available flight to Anchorage that evening. Lanni had arranged to pick him up at the airport.

After saying her own farewell to her grandmother, Lanni moved into the room reserved for family to wait for her parents. Her heart felt heavy, burdened with her mother's loss more than her own.

Footsteps alerted her to the fact that she was no longer alone. When she glanced up, she saw Charles O'Halloran.

"Oh, Charles," she whispered, jumping to her feet. She needed his comfort now, and before another moment had passed, she was securely wrapped in his embrace.

The sobs that shook her came as a shock. Charles held her close, his strength absorbing her pain, his love quieting her grief.

"How'd you know?" Although tempted, she hadn't phoned him, even though he was currently working out of Valdez.

"Sawyer."

She should've guessed his brother would tell him.

"Why didn't you call me?" he asked.

"I...didn't think I should."

Her answer appeared to surprise him. "Why not?"

"Because... I know how you still feel about Grammy. I don't blame you. She hurt you and your family."

They sat down together and Charles took both of Lanni's hands in his own. "I stopped hating her this summer. How could I despise the woman who was ultimately responsible for giving me you?"

Lanni swiped at the tears on her cheeks and offered a shaky smile to this man she loved.

"And after my mother told me the circumstances that led to her marrying my dad," Charles went on, "I have a better understanding of the heartache Catherine suffered. My father made a noble sacrifice when he married Ellen. I know he grew to love her. But in his own way, I believe he always loved Catherine."

"I'd like to think they're together now," Lanni said. Charles's father and her grandmother. "This time forever."

"I'd like to think they are, too," Charles said softly, and he dropped a gentle kiss on the top of her head.

Lanni pressed her face against his shoulder and closed her eyes.

"The memorial service will be in Hard Luck?" he asked.

"Yes. And Grammy asked that her ashes be scattered on the tundra next spring."

He nodded. "Do you know when the service is?"

"No." The details had yet to be decided. Lanni lifted her head and looked up at him. "I'm glad you came."

"So am I," he said. "I love you, Lanni. Don't ever hold anything back from me, understand?"

She nodded.

He stood, giving her his hand. "Now let's go see about meeting your brother's plane."

Mitch heard via the grapevine that Bethany had a date with Bill Landgrin. Bill's pipeline crew was working at the pump station south of Atigun Pass. The men responsible for the care and upkeep of the pipeline usually worked seven days on and seven days off. During his off-time, Bill occasionally made his way into the smaller towns that dotted the Alaskan interior.

What he came looking for was a little action. Gambling. Drinking. Every now and then, he went in search of a woman.

Mitch didn't know when or how Bill Landgrin had met Bethany. One thing was sure—Mitch didn't like the idea of his seeing Bethany. In fact, he didn't want the man anywhere near her.

Mitch understood Landgrin's attraction to Bethany all too well. It had been hard enough to sit idly by and watch her date John Henderson. The pilot was no real threat; Bill Landgrin, on the other hand, was smooth as silk and sharp as a tack. A real conniver, Mitch thought grimly.

There was no help for it. He was obligated to warn Bethany of Bill's reputation. *Someone* had to.

He bided his time, waiting until two days before she was said to be meeting Bill. As if it was a spur-of-the-moment decision, he'd stop by to see her after school. He'd make up some fiction about being concerned with Chrissie's grades—which were excellent.

He waited until he could be sure there was no chance of running into Chrissie. The last thing he needed was to have his daughter catch him seeking out Bethany's company. The kid might get the wrong idea.

Mitch had intentionally avoided Bethany since the night of Chrissie's accident. There was only so much temptation a man could take, and that evening had stretched his endurance to the breaking point.

He found Bethany sitting at her desk. Her eyes widened as he walked into the classroom. "Mitch, hello! It's good to see you."

He smiled slightly. "I hope you don't mind my dropping in like this."

"Of course not."

"It's about Chrissie," he said hurriedly, for fear Bethany would get the wrong impression. "I've been a little, uh, concerned about her grades."

"But she's excelled in all her subjects. She's getting top marks."

He was well aware that his excuse was weak. From the day school had started, he hadn't had to hound

Chrissie to do her homework. Not once. She would've gladly done assignments five hours a night if it meant pleasing Ms. Ross.

"I've been wondering about her grades since the accident," he said.

"They're fine." Bethany flipped through her grade book and reviewed the most recent entries. "I've kept a close eye on her, looking for any of the symptoms Dotty mentioned, but so far everything's been great. Is there a problem at home—I mean, has she been dizzy or anything like that?"

"No, no," he was quick to reassure her.

"Oh, good." She seemed relieved, and he felt even more of a fool.

Mitch stood abruptly and turned as if to leave. "By the way," he said, trying to make it sound like an after-thought, "I don't mean to pry, but rumor has it you're having dinner with Bill Landgrin this Friday night."

"Yes." She stared at him. "How'd you know that?"

"Oh," he said with a nonchalant shrug, "word gets around. I didn't know you two had met."

"Only briefly. He was on a flight with Duke and stopped in at the café the same time I was there," she explained.

"I see," he said thoughtfully. He started to leave, then turned back with a dramatic flourish. "What about John? Do you often date men you've just met?"

"What about him?"

"Why aren't you seeing him anymore?"

Bethany hesitated. "I don't think I like the tone of your question, Mitch. I have every right to date whomever I wish."

"Yes, of course. I didn't mean to imply anything

else. It's just that, well, if you must know, Bill has something of a…reputation."

She stiffened. "Thank you for your concern, but I can take care of myself."

He was making a mess of this. "I didn't mean to offend you, Bethany. It's just that I'm all this town's got in the way of law enforcement, and I thought it was my duty to warn you."

"I see." She snapped the grade book shut. "And I'm a policeman's daughter. As I told you earlier, I can take care of myself." She made a production of looking at her watch. "Now if you'll excuse me?"

"Yes, of course," he said miserably, turning to go. And this time he left.

Bethany wasn't sure why she was so angry with Mitch. Possibly because he was right. She had no business having dinner with a man she barely knew. Oh, she'd be safe enough. Not much was going to happen to her in the Hard Luck Café with half the town looking on.

It went without saying that she'd agreed to this dinner for all the wrong reasons. John Henderson had started seeing another woman recently. One of the newer recruits, a shy young woman named Sally Mc-Donald.

After nearly six weeks here, Bethany had to conclude that Mitch didn't want to become romantically involved. The night of Chrissie's accident, she'd felt certain they'd broken through whatever barrier was separating them. She remembered the way his eyes had held hers after the love scene in the movie. Bethany knew darn well what he was thinking, because she was thinking it, too. Then, when things looked really promising, Mitch had leapt away from her. Since that night, he'd had nothing to say—until now. Bethany was left feeling frustrated and confused.

When Bill Landgrin had asked her out, she'd found a dozen reasons to accept. She'd always been curious about the Alaska pipeline. It was said to stretch more than eight hundred miles across three mountain ranges and over thirteen bridges. Having dinner with a man who could answer her questions seemed innocent enough.

In addition, it sent a message to Mitch, one he'd apparently received loud and clear. He didn't like the idea of her dating Bill Landgrin, and frankly she was glad. Unfortunately, Mitch had to use his daughter's injury as an excuse to talk to her about Bill. That was what irritated Bethany most.

Mitch honestly tried to stay away from Bethany on Friday night. Chrissie was spending the night at Susan's, and the house had never seemed so empty. By seven o'clock, the walls were closing in on him. He'd had to grab his coat and flee.

He tried to look casual and unconcerned when he walked into Ben's café. A quick look around, and his mouth filled with the bitter taste of disappointment. Bethany was nowhere in sight.

"Looking for the new teacher, are you?" Ben asked as he dried a glass with a crisp linen cloth.

"What gives you that idea?" Mitch growled. He was in no mood for conversation. "I came here for a piece of pie."

"I thought you decided to cut back on sweets."

"I changed my mind," Mitch said. If he'd known Ben was going to be such a pain in the butt, he would've stayed home.

Ben brought him a slice of apple pie. "In case you're interested, she left not more than twenty minutes ago."

"Who?" he asked, pretending he didn't know.

"She wasn't alone, either. Bill insisted on seeing her home."

Agitated, Mitch slapped his fork down on the plate. "Who Bethany Ross dates is her own business."

"Maybe," Ben said, bracing both hands on the counter, "but I don't trust the man, and you don't either, otherwise you wouldn't be here. My feeling is that maybe one of us should check up on Bethany— see that everything's the way it should be."

Mitch was convinced there was more to this scenario than Ben was telling him. His blood started to heat.

"Since you're the law in this town, I think you ought to go make sure she got home all safe and sound."

Mitch wiped his mouth with the back of his hand. Ben was right. If anything happened to Bethany, Mitch would never forgive himself. In the meantime, if he did meet up with Bill, he'd impress upon the man that he was to keep away from Bethany Ross.

"So, are you going to see her?"

No use lying about it. "Yeah."

"Then the pie's on the house," Ben said, grinning.

Mitch drove to Bethany's, grateful to see that the lights were still on. He knocked loudly on the door and would have barged in if she hadn't opened it when she did.

"Mitch?"

"May I come in?"

"Of course." She stepped aside.

He walked in and looked around. If Bill was there, he saw no evidence of it.

She'd been combing her hair, and the brush was still in her hand. She didn't ask Mitch why he'd come.

He suspected she knew.

"Did Landgrin try anything?" Mitch demanded.

Her eyes narrowed as if she didn't understand the question.

"Landgrin. Did he try anything?" he repeated gruffly.

She blinked. "No. He was a perfect gentleman."

Mitch shoved his fingers though his hair as he paced the confines of her small living room. He didn't need anyone to tell him what a fool he was making of himself.

"Will you be seeing him again?"

"That's my business."

He closed his eyes and nodded. He had no argument. "Sorry," he said. "I shouldn't have come." He stalked toward the door, eager to escape.

"Mitch?"

His hand was on the doorknob. He stopped but didn't turn around.

"I won't be seeing Bill Landgrin again."

Relief coursed through him.

"Mitch?"

She was close, so very close. He could feel her breath against the back of his neck. All he had to do was turn and she'd be there. His arms ached to hold her. His hand tightened on the doorknob as though it were a lifeline.

"I won't see Bill again," she said in a voice so soft he had to strain to hear, "because I'd much rather be seeing you."

Five

A week after Catherine Fletcher's death, the town held a memorial service. Although she'd never met Catherine, Bethany felt obliged to attend. She slipped into the crowded church and took a place in the last row, one of the only seats left. It seemed everyone in Hard Luck wanted to say a formal goodbye to the woman who'd had such a strong impact on their community.

When news of Catherine's death had hit town, it was all anyone could talk about. Apparently the woman's parents had been the second family to settle in Hard Luck. Bethany knew that Catherine had grown up with David O'Halloran, although a lot of the history between the two families remained unclear to her. But it was obvious that Catherine had played a major role in shaping the town. Folks either loved her or hated her, but either way, they respected her feisty opinions and gutsy spirit.

The mood was somber, the sense of loss keen. Hard Luck was laying to rest a piece of its heart.

A number of people attending the service were

strangers to Bethany. The members of Catherine's family had flown in for the memorial, including an older couple she assumed was Catherine's daughter and son-in-law. Matt Caldwell, Catherine's grandson, lived in Hard Luck. Bethany had met him one Saturday afternoon at Ben's café. She remembered that Matt had bought the partially burned lodge from the O'Hallorans and was currently working on the repairs.

When they'd met, Matt had told her he planned to open the lodge in time for the tourist traffic next June. Bethany was tempted to ask *what* tourist traffic, but she hadn't.

Matt's younger sister, Lanni, sat in the front pew, as well, Charles O'Halloran close by. Bethany had heard that they were engaged, with their wedding planned for sometime in April. Even from this distance, she could see how much in love they were. It was evident from the tender looks they shared and the protective stance Charles took at his fiancée's side.

Abbey had told her about Charles and Lanni, and a little of the story about the O'Halloran brothers' father and Catherine Fletcher. Bethany gathered that for many years there'd been no love lost between Catherine and the O'Hallorans. Then again, she thought, perhaps that *was* the problem between the two families. *Love lost.* Maybe, just maybe, it had been found again through Charles and Lanni.

Silently Bethany applauded them for having the courage to seek out their happiness, despite the past.

Reverend Wilson, the circuit minister, had flown in for the service. He stepped forward, holding his Bible, and began the service with a short prayer. Bethany solemnly bowed her head. No sooner had the prayer ended than Mitch Harris slipped into the pew beside her.

He didn't acknowledge her in any way. She could have been a stranger for all the attention he gave her. His attitude stung. It hurt to realize that if there'd been anyplace else to sit, he would have taken it.

As the service progressed, Bethany noticed how restless Mitch became. He shifted position a number of times, almost as though he was in some discomfort. When she dared to look in his direction, she saw that his eyes were closed and his hands tightly clenched.

Then it hit her.

She knew little of his life, but she did know he was a widower.

Reverend Wilson opened his Bible and read from the Twenty-Third Psalm. "'Yea, though I walk through the valley of the shadow of death, I will fear no evil: for thou art with me; thy rod and thy staff they comfort me.'"

Mitch had traversed that dark valley himself, and Bethany guessed that he hadn't found the comfort the pastor spoke of. But it wasn't Catherine Fletcher Mitch mourned. It was his dead wife. The woman he'd loved. And married. The woman who'd carried his child. The woman he couldn't forget.

How foolish she'd been! Mitch didn't want to become involved with her. How could he when he remained emotionally tied to his dead wife? No wonder he'd been fighting her so hard. He was trapped somewhere in the past, shackled to a memory, a dead love.

Bethany closed her eyes, shocked that it had taken her so long to see what should have been obvious.

True, he was attracted to her. That much neither could deny. But he wasn't free to love her. Maybe he didn't *want* to be free. He probably hated himself for even thinking about someone else. His behavior at this memorial service explained everything.

Mitch leaned forward, supporting his elbows on his knees, and hid his face in his hands. He was in such unmistakable pain that Bethany couldn't sit idly by and do nothing. Not knowing whether her gesture would be welcome, she drew a deep breath and laid her hand on his forearm.

He jerked himself upright and swiveled in his seat to look at her. Surprise blossomed in his eyes. Apparently he'd forgotten he was sitting next to her. She gave him a quick smile, wanting him to know only that she was his friend. Nothing more.

Mitch blinked, and his face revealed a vulnerability that tore at her heart. She wanted to help, but she didn't know how.

As if reading her thoughts, Mitch reached out and grasped her hand. The touch had nothing to do with physical desire. He'd come to her in his pain.

He let go of her almost immediately, then rose abruptly and hurried out of the church. Bethany twisted around and watched him leave, the doors slamming behind him.

Mitch stalked into his office, his chest heaving as if the short walk had demanded intense physical effort. His heart hammered wildly and his breathing was labored.

He'd decided at the last minute to attend the memorial service. He hadn't known Catherine Fletcher well, but appreciated the contribution she and her family had made to the community.

Mitch had talked with her only a few times in the past five years. Nevertheless he'd seen his attendance at the service as a social obligation, a way of paying his respects.

But the minute he'd walked into the church, he'd been bombarded with memories of Lori. They'd come at him from all sides, closing in on him until he thought he'd suffocate.

He remembered the day he'd met her and how attracted he'd been to the delightful sound of her laughter. They'd been college sophomores, still young and inexperienced. Then they'd gotten married; they'd had the large, traditional wedding she'd wanted and he'd never seen a more beautiful bride. They were deeply in love, blissfully happy. At least he had been. In the beginning.

When they learned she was pregnant, a new joy, unlike anything he'd experienced before, had taken hold of him. But after Chrissie was born, their lives had quickly slid downhill. Mitch covered his head. He didn't want to remember any more.

He continued to pace in the silence of his office. Attending the memorial service had been a mistake. He'd suffered the backlash caused by years of refusing to deal with the pain, the guilt. Years of denial. Now he felt as if he was collapsing inward.

He'd never felt so desperate, so out of control.

"Mitch."

He whirled around. Bethany stood just inside the office, her eyes full of compassion.

"Are you all right?"

He nodded, soundlessly telling her nothing was wrong. Even as he did, he realized he couldn't sustain the lie. "No," he said in a choked whisper.

Slowly she advanced into the room. "What is it?"

He shook his head. His throat clogged. He stood defenseless as his control crumpled.

Bethany's hand fell gently on his arm. He might have been able to resist her comfort if she hadn't touched him. His body reacted instantly to the physical contact, and he lurched as if her hand had stung him. Only it wasn't pain he felt, but an incredible sense of release.

"Let me hold you…please," he said. "I need… I need you." He didn't wait for her permission before he brought her into his arms and buried his face in her shoulder. She was soft and warm. Alive. He drew in several lungfuls of air, hoping that would stabilize his erratic heart.

"Everything's all right," she whispered, her lips close to his ear. "Don't worry."

Her arms were his shelter, his protection. The first time he'd met Bethany, he'd promised himself he wouldn't become involved with her. Until now he'd steadfastly stuck to that vow.

But he hadn't counted on needing her—or anyone—this badly. She was his sanity.

He knew he was going to kiss her in the same moment he acknowledged how desperate he'd been for her. With a hoarse groan that came from deep in his throat he surrendered to a need so strong he couldn't possibly have refused it.

Their lips met, and it was like a burst of spontaneous combustion. He'd waited so long. He needed her so badly. One hand gathering the blond thickness of her unbound hair, he kissed her repeatedly, unable to get enough.

He was afraid his need had shocked her, and he sighed with heartfelt relief when she kissed him back as avidly as he was kissing her.

He moaned, wanting to tell her how sorry he was. But he was unwilling to break the contact, to leave her for even those short seconds.

Bethany coiled her arms tightly about his neck. Again and again he ran his hands down the length of her spine, savoring the feel of this woman in his arms. Their mouths met urgently, frantically. He felt insatiable, and she responded with an intensity that equaled his own.

Mitch broke off the kiss when it became more than he could physically handle. He felt that the passion between them might never burn itself out. At the rate things had progressed, the kiss would quickly have taken them toward something more intimate. Something neither of them was ready to deal with yet.

Bethany gasped in an effort to catch her breath, and she pressed her hand over her heart as though to still its frenzied beat. Her lips were swollen. Mitch raised his finger and stroked the slick smoothness of her mouth.

Slowly he raised his head and studied her.

She blinked, looking confused. Or dazed.

He felt a surge of guilt—and regret. "That should never have happened," he whispered.

She said nothing.

"I promise you it won't happen again."

Her eyes flickered with…anger? Before another second had passed, she'd turned and rushed out of his office.

Matt had found the day long and emotionally exhausting. He'd attended the services for his grandmother and the wake that followed.

His mother mourned deeply, and in his own way Matt did, too. His grief surprised him. Matt had barely known Catherine—Grammy, as Lanni called her. There hadn't been many visits over the years.

She'd always sent a card with a check for his birthday. Money again at Christmas. A Bible when he graduated from high school and later, she'd established a trust fund for him. This was the money he'd used to buy the lodge from the O'Halloran brothers.

His grandmother had never known how he'd used the money in the trust fund. By the time he was able to collect it this past summer, her health had disintegrated so much she no longer recognized him. Somehow Matt felt she would have condoned his choice. He liked to think she would have, anyway.

The memorial service and wake had gone well. Virtually all the townspeople had offered condolences, and many had inquired about his progress with the lodge.

The people of Hard Luck had been open and friendly since his arrival, but Matt tended to keep to himself. He was too busy getting the lodge ready to socialize much. He didn't dare stop and think about everything that needed to be done before he posted an Open sign on the front door. The multitude of tasks sometimes overwhelmed him.

Readying the lodge was a considerable chore, but his success depended on a whole lot more than making sure the rooms were habitable.

He'd have to convince people to make the journey this far north, and he'd have to provide them with activities. Wilderness treks, fishing, dogsledding. If his first order of business was getting the lodge prepared for paying customers, his second was attracting said customers.

He'd do it. Whatever it took, he'd do it. He had something to prove to—

His thoughts came to an abrupt halt.

Karen.

He worked fifteen-hour days for one reason, and that reason was Karen. Just saying her name produced an aching sensation in his heart, an ache that had started the day she'd filed for divorce.

What kind of wife filed for divorce without discussing the subject with her husband first? Okay, so maybe she'd mentioned once or twice that she was unhappy.

Well, dammit, he was unhappy, too!

He'd be the first to admit she had a valid complaint—but only to a point. True, he'd changed careers four times in about that many years. He was a man with an eye to the future, and opportunities abounded. But Karen had accused him of being self-indulgent and irresponsible, unable to settle down. That wasn't true. He'd always moved on to something new when the challenge was gone, when a job no longer held his interest.

He supposed he could understand her discontent, but he'd never thought she'd actually *leave* him. To be fair, she'd threatened it, but he hadn't believed her.

If she truly loved him, she would've stuck it out.

Matt shook his head. There was no point in reviewing the same issues again. He'd gone over what had led to the divorce a thousand times without solving anything.

The final blow had been when she left Alaska. Oh, he'd fully expected her to do well in her career. She was an executive secretary for some highfalutin engineering company. Great job. Great pay. When they'd offered her a raise and a promotion, she'd leapt at the chance. Without a word, she'd packed her bags and headed for California.

California? Even now he had trouble believing it.

He reached for a magazine and idly flipped through the pages, then slapped it shut. Thinking about Karen was unproductive.

California! He hoped she was happy.

No, he didn't. He wanted her to be miserable, as miserable as he was. The simple truth was…he loved her. And he missed her.

A year. You'd think he'd be over her by now. He should be seeing new women, going out, making friends. He might have, too, if he wasn't so busy working on the lodge. But if he had any free time and if there were single women available—like that new teacher, maybe—he'd start dating again.

No, he wouldn't.

Matt wasn't going to lie to himself. Not after today when he'd stood with his family and mourned the loss of his grandmother. His parents had been married for nearly thirty years now. Lanni and Charles had stood on his other side. Together.

Losing Grammy had been difficult for Lanni. Having spent part of the summer in Hard Luck cleaning out their grandmother's home, Lanni felt much closer to Catherine than he did. She grieved, and Charles was there to lend comfort.

The way his father comforted his mother.

But Matt stood alone.

It hurt to admit how much he'd yearned to have Karen beside him. His agony intensified when he was forced to recognize how deeply he still loved her.

He wondered if it would always be like this. Would he ever learn to let her go? Not that he had any real choice. The truth was, any day now he expected to hear she'd remarried.

There wasn't a damn thing to stop her. The men in California would have to be blind not to notice her. It wouldn't take long for her to meet some executive who'd give her the stability she craved. There wasn't a man alive who could resist her, he thought morosely. He should know.

His ex-wife was beautiful, talented, generous and spirited. Was she spirited!

A smile cracked his lips. Not many people knew that the cool, calm Karen Caldwell loved to throw things—mainly at Matt. She'd hurled the most ridiculous objects, too.

His shirt. A newspaper. Potato chips. Decorator pillows.

When her anger reached this point, there was only one sure method to cool her ire. One method that had never failed him.

He'd make love to her. The lovemaking was wild and wicked, and soon they'd both be so caught up in the sheer magic of it she'd forget whatever it was that had angered her.

Matt remembered the last time Karen had expressed her fury like a major-league pitcher. His smile widened as he leaned back in his chair and clasped his hands behind his head.

He'd quit his job. All right, he should've discussed it with her first. But he hadn't *planned* to go in and resign that day. It had just...happened.

Karen had been furious with him. He tried to explain that he was going to find something better. Accounting wasn't for him—he should've realized it before. He'd been thinking about a job more suited to his talents.

She wouldn't give him a chance to explain. Ranting and raving, she'd started flinging whatever she could lay hands on. Matt had ducked when she'd sent her shoes flying in his direction. The saltshaker had scored a direct hit, smacking him in the chest.

That had given her pause, he recalled, but not for long. Braving her anger, he'd advanced toward her. She'd refused to let him near her. When she ran out of easy-to-reach ammunition, she'd walked across the top of the sofa and leapt onto the chair, all the while shouting at the top of her lungs and threatening him with the pepper mill.

It hadn't taken much to capture her, and he'd let her yell and struggle in his arms for a few minutes. Then he did the only thing he could to silence Karen— kiss her.

Soon, the pepper mill had tumbled from her hands and onto the carpet, and they were helping each other undress, their hands as urgent as their need.

Afterward, he remembered, Karen had been quiet and still. While he lay there, appreciating the most incredible sex of his life, his wife had been planning their divorce. Less than a week later, she moved out and he was served with the papers.

The smile faded as the sadness crept back into his heart.

He modified his wish. He didn't want Karen to be miserable. If someone had to be blamed, then fine, he'd accept full responsibility for their failure. He deserved it.

He missed her so much! Never more than now. Whatever happened in the future with this lodge and the success of his business venture seemed of little consequence. Matt would go to his grave loving Karen.

Like his grandmother before him, he would only love once.

"You seem pensive," Sawyer said as he sat on the edge of the bed and peeled off his socks.

With her back propped against the headboard, Abbey glanced over the top of her mystery novel. "Of course I'm pensive," she muttered, smiling at her husband. "I'm reading."

"You're pretending to read," he corrected. "You've got that look again."

"What look?" she asked him with an expression of pure innocence.

"The one that says you're plotting."

Abbey made a face at him. How could Sawyer know her so well? They hadn't been married all that long. "And what exactly am I plotting?" She'd see if he could figure *that* one out.

"I don't know, but I'm sure you'll tell me sooner or later."

"For your information, Mr. Know-It-All, I was just thinking about Thanksgiving."

Sawyer cocked his head to one side, as if to say he wasn't sure he should believe her. "That's almost a month away. Tell me what could possibly be so important about Thanksgiving that it would occupy your mind now?"

"Well, for one thing, I was thinking we should ask Mitch and Chrissie to join us." She glanced at her husband in order to gauge his reaction.

Sawyer didn't hesitate. "Good idea."

"And Bethany Ross."

A full smile erupted on Sawyer's handsome face as he pointed his finger at her. "What did I say? You're plotting!"

"What?" Once more she feigned innocence.

"You want to invite Mitch *and* Bethany to Thanksgiving dinner?"

"Right," she concurred, opening her eyes wide in exaggerated wonder that he could find anything the *least* bit underhand in such a courtesy. "And what, pray tell, is so devious about that?"

His finger wagged again as he climbed into bed. "A little matchmaking, maybe? You've got something up your sleeve, Abbey O'Halloran."

"I most certainly do not," she said with a touch of righteous indignation.

"I notice you didn't suggest inviting John Henderson."

"No," she admitted.

"Isn't he the one Bethany's been having dinner with for the past few weeks?"

"They're friends, that's all."

"I see." Sawyer leaned over and deftly reached for one end of the satin ribbon tying the collar of her pajama top. He slowly tugged until it fell open.

"Besides, I heard from Mariah that John's interested in someone else now."

Sawyer idly unfastened the first button. "Is that right?"

Her husband's touch was warm, creating feathery sensations that scampered across her skin.

Sawyer's eyes dropped to her mouth, and his voice lowered to a soft purr. "Mitch has lived here for a few years."

"True." Her second button gave way as easily as the first.

"If he was interested in remarrying, he'd have done something about it before now, wouldn't you think?"

Abbey closed her book and set it blindly on the table next to the bed. "Not necessarily."

"Do you think Mitch is interested in Bethany?" Sawyer slipped his hand inside the opening he'd created.

Abbey closed her eyes at the feel of her husband's fingers. "Yes." The word sounded shockingly intimate.

"As it happens," Sawyer said in a husky whisper, "I agree with you."

"You do?" Her voice dwindled to a whisper. With her eyes still closed, she swayed toward him.

Sawyer's kiss was long and deep. The conversation about Mitch Harris and Bethany Ross stopped there.

Instead, Sawyer and Abbey continued their dialogue with husky sighs and soft murmurs.

Bethany walked into the Hard Luck Café shortly after ten on Saturday and sat at the counter. The place was empty. Ben wasn't in sight, either, which was fine; she wasn't in any hurry. Tired of her own company, she'd decided to take a walk and sort through what had happened between her and Mitch. Ha! she thought sourly. As if that was even possible.

There wasn't anyone she could ask about Mitch's past. And apparently *he* wasn't going to volunteer the information. He hadn't said one word about his life before Hard Luck, and no one else seemed to know much, either.

As for what had happened at the memorial service, Bethany had given up any attempt to make sense of it. For whatever reason, Mitch had turned to her. He'd kissed her with such intensity, such hunger.... Never before had she felt that kind of joy.

Then he'd apologized. And she'd realized he had simply needed someone. Anyone. Any woman would have sufficed. She just happened to be handy. The minute he saw what he'd done, he regretted having touched her.

"Bethany, hello! How are you this fine day?" As always, Ben greeted her with a wide smile as he bustled up to the counter. "We missed you at the wake after Catherine's memorial service. The women in town put on a mighty fine spread."

There was probably some psychological significance in the fact that she'd sought Ben out now, Bethany decided. If she wasn't so sick of analyzing the situation between her and Mitch, she might have delved into *that* question. As it was, she felt too miserable to care.

"I'm fine."

"Is that so?" Without her asking, Ben filled a mug with coffee. "Then why those little lines between your eyes?"

"What lines?"

"When I'm stewing about something, these lines always appear. Right there." He pointed to his own forehead. "Three of them. Seems to me you're cursed with the same thing. Can't fool a living soul, no matter how hard I try." He smiled, encouraging her to talk.

Bethany resisted the urge to tell him she'd come by those lines honestly. Inhaling a deep breath, she eyed him, wondering how much she dared confide in him about her feelings for Mitch. Darn little, she suspected. That she'd even wonder was a sign of how desperate she'd become. Still, maybe he could fill in a few details about Mitch's background. With no other customers present, this was the optimum time to ask.

"What can you tell me about Mitch?" she began.

"Mitch? Mitch Harris?" All at once, Ben found it necessary to wipe down the counter. He ran a rag over the top of the already spotless surface. "Well, for one thing, he's a damn good man. Decent, caring. Loves his daughter."

"He's lived in Hard Luck for how long?" She already knew the answer, but she wanted to ease Ben into the conversation.

"Must be around five years now."

She nodded. "I heard he worked for the police department in Chicago before that."

"That's what I heard, too."

"Do you know how his wife died?" Since Ben wasn't inclined to share any real information, she'd have to pry it out of him.

"Can't say I do." His mouth twisted to one side, as if he was judging what he should and shouldn't tell her. "I don't think Mitch has ever talked about her to anyone. Hasn't mentioned her to me."

Bethany heard the door open behind her. Their conversation was over, not that she'd gleaned any new facts.

"If you're curious about his wife," Ben whispered, "I suggest you ask him yourself. He just walked in."

For the briefest of seconds, she felt like a five-year-old caught with her hand in the cookie jar.

To her surprise, Mitch sat on the stool next to hers. He studied her for what seemed like minutes. "Hello, Bethany," he finally said in a low voice.

"Mitch." She refused to meet his eyes.

"I'm glad I ran into you."

Well, that was certainly a change.

Ben strolled over and Mitch asked for coffee.

"I'd like to talk to you, Bethany." He gestured toward one of the booths, the steaming mug in his hand.

She followed him to the farthest booth, and they sat across from each other. For a long moment, he didn't say anything, and when he lifted his head to look at her, his eyes were bleak.

"Bethany, I can't tell you how sorry I am. I don't know what else to say. I've lain awake nights worrying what you must think of me."

Confused and hurt, Bethany said nothing.

He gestured helplessly. "I'm sorry. What more can

I say? Talk to me, would you? Say something. Anything."

"What are you sorry for?" she asked, her voice almost a whisper. "Kissing me?"

"Yes."

Even now he didn't seem to realize she'd been a willing participant. "You needed me. Was that why?"

"Yes," he said, as if this was his greatest sin.

She hesitated, searching for the words. "Any other woman would have done just as well. Isn't that what you're really saying? It wasn't *me* you were kissing. It wasn't *me* you needed. I just happened to...be available."

He didn't disagree.

Six

"You're going to do it, aren't you?" Duke Porter asked John for the second time. An incredulous look contorted the pilot's features. "You're *actually* going to do it?"

"Yes," John said, irritated. He jerked the grease rag from his back pocket and brusquely wiped his hands.

Duke followed him to the far end of the hangar while John put away the tools he'd used. "You're *sure* this is what you want?"

John didn't hesitate. "I'm absolutely, positively sure."

"But you hardly know the woman."

"I know everything I need to know," he muttered. Duke was good at raising his hackles, but nothing was going to ruin this day. The engagement ring was waiting in his pocket. His eagerness to propose was nothing compared to the way he felt about Sally.

This time it was *his* turn. Earlier, he'd fallen all over himself in an attempt to court Abbey Sutherland. What he hadn't known was that Sawyer O'Halloran had stolen her heart without giving any of the others a chance.

Then there was Lanni Caldwell. John had never seriously considered her wife material, believing she'd only be in town for the summer. Duke might've been more interested in striking up a relationship with her, but once again they'd been beaten out by one of the O'Hallorans.

John liked Mariah Douglas well enough, but it was plain as the nose on your face that she had eyes only for Christian. Besides, the last thing he wanted to do was tangle with *her*. Daddy Douglas just might sic that attorney on him.

He'd had a shot with Bethany, the schoolteacher. In the beginning he was quite drawn to her. He knew she didn't share his enthusiasm, but he'd figured that, given time, their friendship might grow into something more.

Then Sally McDonald had arrived.

Sally, with her pretty blue eyes and her gentle smile. He'd taken one look at her and his heart had stopped beating. In that moment, he'd recognized beyond any doubt that she was the one for him. After John had met Sally, he didn't resent Sawyer for stealing Abbey away from him and the others. It seemed unimportant that Lanni was marrying Charles, or that Bethany Ross wasn't as keen on him as he'd been on her. Sally was the one for him.

"If you want my opinion…"

John glared at Duke. "I didn't ask for it, did I?"

"No," Duke said, "but I'm going to give it to you anyway."

John sighed loudly. "All right. If it's so important, tell me what you think."

"I can understand why you'd want to marry Sally—" Duke began.

"But you're thinking about her for yourself!" This explained why Duke was poking into something that was none of his concern.

"No way," Duke said, raising both hands. "I'm off women. Too many of 'em are like that lawyer, looking for any excuse to chew a man's butt."

"Tracy Santiago wasn't like that." John grinned broadly at the memory of their clashes. To be fair, he wasn't interested in her for himself, but he kinda liked the way she'd cut Duke down to size. "She was doing her job, that's all."

"Listen, if you don't mind, I'd rather not discuss that she-devil. She's gone, at least for now, and all I can say is good riddance. The woman was nothing but a nuisance."

John swallowed a laugh. He'd never seen Duke get this riled up over a woman. It seemed to his inexperienced eye that his friend protested too much. He figured that, this time, Duke had met his match. Too bad Tracy lived in Washington State and Duke in Alaska.

"About Sally…" The other pilot broached the topic again.

John could see there was no escaping his friend's unwanted counsel. "All right," he said, giving in. Duke was going to state his opinion whether John wanted to hear it or not. He might as well listen—or pretend to.

"Don't get me wrong here," Duke said, shoving his hands into his pockets as though he found this difficult. "I like Sally. Who wouldn't? She's a real sweetheart."

"Exactly."

"The thing that concerns me is…she's young."

"Not that much younger than Bethany. Or Lanni."

"True, only Sally's led a more sheltered life than either of them."

John couldn't argue with that. Sally had been raised in a British Columbia town with a population of less than a thousand. From what he understood, her family was a closeknit one. She'd attended a small, private high school and a church-affiliated college. When finances became too tight for her to continue her education, she'd gotten a job working in an accounting office in Vancouver. That was where she'd read Christian's newspaper ad and applied for the job with Hard Luck Power and Light.

"You know why she came to Hard Luck, don't you?"

"Yeah." John knew, and frankly he was surprised Duke did, too. After moving to Vancouver, Sally had become involved with a fast-talking man who'd ultimately broken her heart. He'd been married; she'd found out because his wife had shown up at her door.

According to what she'd told him, Sally had walked away from the relationship feeling both heartsick and foolish. When she read about Midnight Sons offering land, housing and jobs, she'd jumped at the opportunity to start over. This time she'd do it in a small-town environment, the kind of place she was comfortable with.

"Are you sure she's over this other guy?" Duke asked.

"I'm sure." Although he made it sound like there could be no question, John wasn't entirely convinced. He was grateful Duke didn't challenge his response.

"What about her family?" the other pilot asked instead.

"What about them?" John said defensively. He didn't much like where Duke's questions were leading.

"From what you've said, they're the old-fashioned sort. If you're serious about marrying their daughter, the thing to do is talk to her father first. Meet him face-to-face and tell him you love Sally and—"

"How am I supposed to do that?" John wanted to know. "Sal's dad lives in some dinky town on the coast. It's not like I can leave here. Especially now."

Winter had set in full force. Temperatures had dipped into the minus range every day for a solid week. Whenever it fell to minus thirty, Midnight Sons had to cancel all flights. The stress to the aircraft was too great a risk.

Snow accumulations measured forty inches or more in the past month alone. Thanksgiving was two weeks away, and there didn't seem to be any break in the weather ahead. In a word, they were snowed in. No matter how much he wanted to meet Sally's family, for the time being it was impossible.

"First," Duke said, and held up his hand. He folded down one finger. "You got a woman who's only recently turned twenty-one, so she's young. Younger than any of the others who've come to Hard Luck. Secondly—" he bent down another finger "—she moved here on the rebound, hoping to cure a broken heart."

"Third," John said, fighting back his frustration, "she comes from a family who wouldn't appreciate their daughter marrying a man they haven't personally met and approved."

"If you start out on the wrong foot with her parents, it could take years to make up for it," Duke said. "If you truly love her—"

"I do," John insisted, then added in a lower voice, "I've never felt so strongly about anyone."

His friend nodded in understanding. "Then do this right. I can't think of a single reason to rush into marriage, can you?"

John could list any number of reasons to marry Sally that very day, but said nothing.

"If she's the one for you, then everything will work out the way it's supposed to, and you've got nothing to worry about."

John shrugged. He didn't like it, but Duke had a valid point. The engagement ring could continue to wait in his pocket until he'd had a chance to square things with Sally's father. Until he could be sure she loved him for himself—and not as an instant cure for a broken heart.

"Daddy, I don't feel good." Chrissie came slowly into the kitchen, clutching her Pooh bear to her chest. The stuffed animal was a favorite from her preschool days. Now she sought it out only on rare occasions.

Worried, Mitch slid the casserole into the oven, then pressed the back of his hand against his daughter's forehead. She did feel warm. Her face was flushed and her eyes were unusually solemn.

"What's wrong, pumpkin?"

She shrugged. "I just don't feel good."

"Does your tummy hurt?" There'd been lots of flu going around.

Chrissie nodded.

"Do you have a sore throat?"

She bobbed her head and swallowed. "It hurts, too."

"You'd better let me take your temperature."

Her eyes flared wide. "No! I don't want that thing in my mouth."

"Chrissie, it isn't going to hurt."

"I don't care. I don't want you to take my temperature. I'll… I'll just go to bed."

Mitch had forgotten how unreasonable his daughter could be when she was ill. "Don't you feel like eating dinner?"

"No," she answered weakly. "I just want to go to bed. Don't worry about me. I won't die."

Mitch sighed. He didn't know if she was being dramatic or was expressing some kind of anxiety about death. She'd known about Catherine's funeral, and maybe that had made her think about Lori….

"Will you tuck me in?"

"Of course." He followed her down the narrow hallway to her bedroom. While he pulled back her covers, Chrissie knelt on the floor and said her prayers. It seemed to take her twice as long as usual, but Mitch pretended not to notice.

Once she was securely tucked beneath the blankets, Mitch sat on the edge of her bed and brushed the hair away from her forehead. Her face still seemed a little warm.

"Stay with me, okay?" she asked in a voice that suggested she was fading quickly.

Mitch reached for the Jack London story he'd been

reading to her. Chrissie placed her hand on his fore-arm to stop him. "I want you to read the story about the Princess Bride. That's my favorite."

Mitch figured he'd read the book about a thousand times. Chrissie could recite parts of it from memory, and Mitch knew he could repeat whole sections of it himself without bothering to turn the pages. Although his daughter was quite capable of reading on her own, there were certain stories she insisted he read to her.

He picked up the book and flipped it open. He made it through the first page by merely glancing at it now and then.

"Daddy."

"Yes, pumpkin?"

"Are we going to Susan's for Thanksgiving?"

Mitch closed the book. "Sawyer asked this after-noon if we'd join them for dinner." Naturally Susan would've said something to Chrissie. Sawyer had also let it drop that Bethany would be there, then waited for his reaction. So Mitch had smiled politely and said he looked forward to seeing her again. Actually it was true.

"Did you tell Sawyer we'd come?"

Mitch nodded.

Chrissie's eyes lit up, as if this confirmation had given her a reason to live. "I hope I won't be sick then." She made a show of swallowing.

"You won't be."

Mitch didn't know what was wrong with his daugh-ter, but he had a sneaking suspicion it wasn't nearly as serious as she'd like him to believe. He sat with her for a few more minutes, then moved into the kitchen to check on dinner.

"Daddy!"

He made his way back down the hallway and stuck his head in her bedroom door. "Now what?"

"I want Ms. Ross."

Mitch's heart rate accelerated. "Why?"

Chrissie nodded. "I just want to talk to her, all right?"

Mitch hesitated. Of all the things he'd expected Chrissie to ask of him, Bethany wasn't it. A game of checkers. A glass of juice. Anything but her teacher.

"Please, oh, please, Daddy. Ms. Ross will make me feel *so* much better."

If Mitch was looking for an excuse to call Bethany, then his daughter had just offered it to him. He and Bethany hadn't seen much of each other in the past few weeks, but *she* seemed to be the one avoiding him. Embarrassed by what had happened in his office during Catherine Fletcher's service, Mitch had decided to leave her alone. He'd done enough damage.

But it didn't change the way he felt about her. They couldn't be in the same vicinity without his heartbeat accelerating frantically. It had been years since he'd felt this vulnerable with a woman, and it made him nervous.

Since their meeting at Ben's place, they'd greeted each other cordially—nothing personal. Just noncommittal chitchat, of the kind he might have exchanged with a near stranger.

None of that, however, was enough for Mitch to forget the feel of Bethany in his arms, Bethany's lips on his, warm and welcoming. And so blessedly giving that he wanted to kick himself every time he thought about the way he'd treated her.

"Daddy." Chrissie gave him a long look. "Will you call Ms. Ross?"

He nodded helplessly. Walking into the kitchen, he reached for the phone. Chrissie couldn't possibly realize what she'd asked of him. Even while that thought formed in his mind, he admitted he was grateful for the excuse to call Bethany.

He punched out the phone number and waited. Bethany answered on the second ring.

"Hello."

Now that he heard her voice, he felt a moment's panic. What could he say? He didn't want to exaggerate and make it sound as if Chrissie was seriously ill, nor did he wish to make light of her request.

"It's Mitch."

No response.

"I'm sorry to trouble you."

"It's no trouble." She sounded friendly, but not overly so.

"Chrissie seems to have come down with the flu." Then, on a stroke of genius, he invented the reason for his call. "Did she mention not feeling well at school today?"

"No, she didn't say a word." Concern was more evident in her voice than irritation.

"It's probably nothing more than a twenty-four-hour virus," he said.

"Is there anything I can do?" she asked.

He'd been born under a lucky star, Mitch decided. Without his having to say a word, she'd volunteered.

"As a matter of fact, Chrissie's feeling pretty bad at the moment and she's asking for you. I don't want you to go out of your way—"

"I'll be there in ten minutes."

"No." He wouldn't hear of her walking that far in weather this cold. "I'll come for you on the snowmobile."

She hesitated. "Fine. I'll watch for you."

Mitch went back into Chrissie's bedroom. "I talked to. Ms. Ross."

"And?" Chrissie nearly fell out of the bed she was so eager to hear the outcome of the conversation.

"She'll come, but I didn't want her walking over here in the cold. I'm going to pick her up on the snowmobile. You'll be all right alone for five minutes, won't you?"

Chrissie's eyes filled with outrage. "I'm not a little kid anymore!"

"I'm glad to know that." If he'd actually been upset about asking Bethany to visit, he might have pointed out that someone who wasn't a little kid anymore wouldn't ask for her teacher.

Mitch called out to Chrissie that he was leaving. He put on his insulated, waterproof jacket and wound a thick scarf around his neck, covering his mouth, before he stepped outside. The snowmobile was the most frequently used means of transportation in the winter months, and he kept his well-maintained. The minute he pulled up outside Bethany's small house, her door opened and she appeared.

She climbed onto the back of the snowmobile and positioned herself a discreet distance behind him. Nevertheless, having her this close produced a fiery warmth he couldn't escape—didn't *want* to escape.

She didn't say anything until they'd reached his

house. He parked the snowmobile inside the garage and plugged in the heater to protect the engine.

Once in the house they removed their winter gear. Bethany was wearing leggings and an oversize San Francisco Police Department sweatshirt; her feet were covered in heavy red woollen socks. He stared at her, taking in every detail.

Mitch found he couldn't speak. It was the first time they'd been alone together since the scene in his office. This sudden intimacy caught him off guard, and he wasn't sure how to react.

Part of him yearned to take her in his arms and kiss her again. Only this time he'd be tender, drawing out the kiss with—

"Where's Chrissie?" Bethany asked, mercifully breaking into his thoughts.

"Chrissie... She's in her bedroom."

The oven timer went off, and grateful for the excuse to clear his head, Mitch walked into the kitchen. He opened the oven and pulled out the ground-turkey casserole to cool on top of the stove.

He entered his daughter's room and discovered Bethany sitting on the bed, with Chrissie cuddled close. The child's head rested against Bethany's shoulder as she read from the story he'd begun himself. When Chrissie glanced up to find Mitch watching, her eyes shone with happiness.

"Hi, Dad," she said, craning her neck to look up at Bethany. "Dad usually reads me this story, but you do it better because you love it, too. I don't think Dad likes romance stories."

"Dinner's ready," Mitch announced. "Are you sure you won't try to eat something, pumpkin?"

Chrissie's frown said that was a terribly difficult decision. "Maybe I could eat just a little, but only if Ms. Ross will stay and have dinner with us."

Before Bethany could offer a perfunctory excuse, Mitch said, "There's plenty, and we'd both enjoy having you." He wanted to be certain she understood that he wouldn't object to her company; if anything, he'd be glad of it.

He saw her gaze travel from him to Chrissie and then back. He leaned against the doorway, hands deep in his pockets, trying to give the impression that it made no difference to him if she joined them or not. But it did. He *wanted* her to stay.

"I… It's thoughtful of you to ask. I, uh, haven't eaten yet."

"Oh, goodie." Chrissie jumped up and clapped her hands, bouncing with glee. Then, as if she'd just remembered how ill she was supposed to be, she sagged her shoulders and all but crumpled onto the bed.

In an effort to hide his smile, Mitch returned to the kitchen and quickly set the table. By the time Chrissie and Bethany joined him, he'd brought the casserole to the table, as well as a loaf of bread, butter and some straight-from-the-can bean salad.

Dinner was…an odd affair. Exciting. Fun. And a little sad. It was as if he and Bethany were attempting to find new ground with each other. Only they both seemed to fear that this ground would be full of crevices and strewn with obstacles. He'd take one step forward, then freeze, afraid he'd said something that might offend her.

He noticed that Bethany didn't find this new situation any easier than he did. She'd start to laugh, then her eyes, her beautiful brown eyes, would meet his and the laugh would falter.

Following their meal, Chrissie wanted her to finish the story. Since Mitch was well aware of how the story ended, he lingered in the kitchen over a cup of coffee.

He'd just begun washing the dishes when Bethany reappeared.

"Chrissie's decided she needs her beauty sleep," she told him, standing at the far side of the room.

Mitch didn't blame her for maintaining the distance between them. Every time she'd attempted to get close, he'd shoved her away. Every time she'd opened her heart to him, he'd shunned her. Yet when he'd desperately needed her, she'd been there. And although she'd accused him of settling for any woman who happened to fall into his arms, *she* was the only one who could fill the need in him.

"I imagine you want to get back home," he said, experiencing a curious sadness. He dumped what remained of his coffee into the sink. The way her eyes flickered told him she might have enjoyed a cup had he offered one.

"Stay," he said suddenly. "Just for a few minutes."

The invitation seemed to hang in the air. It took her a long time to decide; when he was about to despair, she gave him a small smile, then nodded.

"Coffee?"

"Please."

His heart reacted with a wild burst of staccato beats. He poured her a mug, grabbing a fresh one for himself. His movements were jerky, and he realized it was because he felt afraid that if he didn't finish the task quickly enough, she might change her mind.

He carried the mugs into the living room and sat across from her. At first their conversation was awkward, but gradually the tension eased. He was astonished by how much they had to talk about. Books, movies, politics. Children. Police work. Life in Alaska. They shared myriad opinions and stories and observations.

It was as though all the difficulties between them had been wiped out and they were starting over.

Mitch laughed. He felt warm and relaxed, trusting. Alive. She seemed curious about his past, but her occasional questions were friendly, not intrusive. And she didn't probe for more information than he was willing—or able—to give her.

He brought out a large photo album and sat next to her on the sofa, with the album resting partially on his lap and partially on hers. Mitch turned the pages, explaining each picture.

He wondered what Bethany thought about the gap in his past. It was as if their lives—his and Chrissie's—had started when they came to Hard Luck. There wasn't a single photograph taken any earlier than that. Not one picture of Lori.

He turned a page and his hand inadvertently brushed hers. He hadn't meant to touch her, but when he did, it was as if something exploded inside him. For long seconds, neither moved.

Slowly Mitch's gaze went to hers. Instead of accusation, he found approval, instead of anger, acceptance. He released his breath, tired of fighting a battle he couldn't win. With deliberate movements, he closed the photo album and set it aside.

"Mitch?"

"We'll talk later," he whispered. He wrapped his hand around the back of her neck and gently pulled her forward. He needed this. Ached for this.

He kissed her slowly, sweetly, teasing her lips until her head rolled back against the cushion in abject surrender.

"Mitch…" She tried once more.

He stopped her from speaking by placing his finger against her moist lips. "We both know Chrissie manipulated this meeting."

She frowned.

"She's no sicker than you or I."

Bethany blinked.

"Let's humor her."

Her eyes darkened. "Let's," she agreed, and wound her arms around his neck.

"Thank you so much for coming," Bethany said to Ben. It had taken a lot to convince him to speak to her students.

Ben had resisted, claiming he wasn't comfortable with children, never having had any himself. But in the end Bethany's persistence had won out.

"You did a great job," she told him.

Ben blushed slightly. "I did, didn't I?" He walked around the room and patted the top of each desk as if remembering who had sat where.

"The children loved hearing about your job," she told him. "And about your life in the navy."

"They certainly had lots of questions."

Bethany didn't mention that she'd primed them beforehand. She hadn't had to encourage them much; they were familiar with Ben and fascinated by him.

Bethany wasn't especially proud of the somewhat devious method she'd used to learn what she could of Ben's past. Still, inviting him to speak to her students was certainly legitimate; he wasn't the only community member she'd asked to do so. Dotty had been in the week before, and Sawyer O'Halloran had agreed to come after Thanksgiving. She found herself studying Ben now, looking for hints of her own appearance, her own personality.

"Haven't seen much of you lately," he said, folding his arms. He half sat on one of the desks in the front row. "Used to be you'd stop in once a day, and we'd have a nice little chat."

"I've been busy lately." In the past week, she'd been seeing a lot of Mitch and Chrissie.

"I kinda miss our talks," Ben muttered.

"Me, too," Bethany admitted. It was becoming increasingly difficult, she discovered, to talk to Ben about personal things. Her fear was that she'd inadvertently reveal their relationship. The temptation to tell him grew stronger with each meeting, something she hadn't considered when she'd decided to find him.

Ben stared at her a moment as if he wasn't sure he should go on. "I thought I saw you with Mitch Harris the other day." It was more question than statement.

She nodded. "He drove me to the library." He'd said he didn't want her walking. The piercing cold continued, but temperatures weren't as low as they'd been earlier in the week. Bethany could easily have trekked the short distance; Mitch's driving her was an excuse—one she'd readily accepted.

"Are you two seeing each other now?"

Bethany hesitated.

"I don't mean to pry," Ben said, studying her. "You can tell me it's none of my damn business if you want, and I won't take offense. It's just that I get customers now and again who're curious about you."

"Like who?"

"Like Bill Landgrin."

"Oh." It embarrassed her no end that she'd had dinner with the pipeline worker. He'd phoned her several times since, and the conversations had been uncomfortable. Not because of anything Bill said or did, but because she'd gone out with him for all the wrong reasons.

Bethany walked from behind her desk and over to the blackboard. "I don't know what to tell you about Mitch and me," she said, picking up the eraser.

Ben's face softened with sympathy. "You sound confused."

"I am." It was easy to understand why people so often shared confidences with Ben; he was a good listener, never meddlesome and always encouraging.

With anyone else, Bethany would have skirted around the subject of her and Mitch, but she felt a connection with Ben—one that reached beyond the reasons she'd come to Hard Luck. It wasn't just a connection created by her secret knowledge. Since her arrival, Ben had become her friend. That surprised her; she hadn't expected to like him this much.

"I'm afraid I'm falling in love with Mitch," she said in a breathless voice.

"Afraid?"

She lowered her gaze and nodded. "I don't think he feels the same way about me."

"Why's that?" Ben leaned forward.

"He doesn't *want* to be attracted to me. Every time I feel we're getting close, he backs away. There's a huge part of himself he keeps hidden. He's never discussed Chrissie's mother. I've never really questioned him about her or about his life before he moved to Hard Luck, and he never volunteers."

Ben rubbed one side of his face. "But we all have our secrets, don't you think?"

Bethany nodded and swallowed uncomfortably. She certainly had hers.

"Mitch lost his wife, the mother of his child. I don't know the details but whatever happened, it cut deep. I can tell you because I was living here when Mitch and Chrissie first showed up. Mitch was a wounded soul. He's kept to himself. He's been here more than five years, and I've hardly ever seen him smile. Until now... You're good for him and Chrissie. Real good."

"He and Chrissie would be easy to love."

"But you're afraid."

She nodded.

"Seems to me you two've come a long way in a short time. I could be wrong, but not so long ago all you did was send these yearning looks at each other. Now you're actually talking, spending time together." He paused. "I heard he told Bill Landgrin a thing or two recently."

"Mitch did?"

Ben grinned broadly. "Not in any words I'd care to repeat in front of a lady, mind you. Seems to me he wouldn't have done that if he wasn't serious about you himself. Give him time, Bethany. Yourself, too. You've been here less than three months."

Bethany exhaled. "Thank you for listening—and for your advice."

"No problem," Ben said. "It was my pleasure."

Smiling, she closed the distance between them and kissed his rough cheek.

Ben flushed and pressed his hand to his face.

She felt so much better, and not just because Ben had given her good advice. He'd said the things her own father would've said.

The irony of that didn't escape her.

Seven

December 1995

"Hi." Bethany felt almost shy as she opened her front door to Mitch that Saturday night. Chrissie was with them so much of the time that whenever Bethany and Mitch were alone together, an immediate air of intimacy enveloped them.

"Hi, yourself." Mitch unwound his scarf and took off his protective winter gear. He, too, seemed a little ill at ease.

They looked at each other, then quickly glanced away. Anyone watching them would have guessed they were meeting for the first time. Tonight, neither seemed to know what to say, which was absurd, since they often sat and talked for hours about anything and everything.

This newfound need to know each other, as well as the more relaxed tenor of their relationship, came as a result of Thanksgiving dinner with Sawyer and Abbey. The four adults had played cards after dinner. Two couples. It had seemed natural for Bethany to be with Mitch. Natural and right. Conversation had been lively and wide-ranging, and Bethany felt at home with these people. So did Mitch, judging by the way he laughed and smiled. And somehow, whatever he'd been holding inside had begun to seem less important.

They'd all enjoyed the card-playing so much that it had become a weekly event. In the past few weeks Bethany had spent a lot of time in Mitch's company, and she believed they'd grown close and comfortable with each other. But then, they were almost always with other people. With Chrissie, of course. With Sawyer and Abbey. The other O'Halloran brothers. Ben. Margaret Simpson. Rarely were they alone. It was this situation that had prompted her to invite him for dinner.

"Dinner's almost ready," she said self-consciously, rubbing her hands on her jeans. "I hope you like Irish stew."

"I love it, but then I'm partial to anything I don't have to cook myself." He smiled and his eyes met hers. He pulled his gaze away, putting an abrupt end to the moment of intimacy.

Bethany had to fight back her disappointment.

"I see you got your Christmas tree," he said, motioning to the scrawny five-foot vinyl fir that stood in the corner of her living room. She would've preferred a live tree, but the cost was astronomical, and so she did what everyone in Hard Luck had done. She'd ordered a fake tree through the catalog.

"I was hoping you'd help me decorate it," she said. It was only fair, since she'd helped him and Chrissie decorate theirs the night before. Chrissie had chattered excitedly about Susan's slumber party, which was tonight. Bethany wondered if Abbey had arranged the party so Bethany and Mitch would have some time alone. Whether it was intentional or not, Bethany was grateful.

"Chrissie said the two of you baked cookies today."

"Susan helped, too," she said. Bethany had offered to take both girls for a few hours during the afternoon; Mitch was working, and Abbey wanted a chance to wrap Christmas gifts and address cards undisturbed.

Mitch followed her into the kitchen. They were greeted by the aroma of sage and other herbs. The oven timer went off, and she reached for a mitt to pull out a loaf of crusty French bread.

Mitch looked around. "Is there anything you need me to do?"

"No. Everything's under control." That was true of dinner, perhaps, but little else felt manageable. Mitch suddenly seemed like a stranger, when she thought they'd come so far. It was like the old days—which really weren't so old.

"I'll dish up dinner now," she said.

He didn't offer to help again; perhaps he thought he'd only be in the way. With his hands resting on a chair back, he stood by the kitchen table and waited until she could join him.

The stew was excellent, or so Mitch claimed, but for all the enjoyment she received from it, Bethany could have been eating boot leather.

"I imagine Abbey's got her hands full," she said, trying to make conversation.

"How many kids are spending the night?" Mitch asked. "Six was the last I heard."

"Seven, if you count Scott."

"My guess is Scott would rather be tarred and feathered than decorate sugar cookies and string popcorn with a bunch of girls."

"You're probably right." She passed Mitch the bread. He thanked her and took another slice.

Silence.

Bethany didn't know what had happened to the easy camaraderie they'd had over the past few weeks. Each attempt to start a discussion failed; conversation simply refused to flow. The silence grew more awkward by the minute, and finally Bethany could stand it no longer. With her mouth so dry she could barely talk, she threw down her napkin and turned to Mitch.

"What's wrong with us?" she asked.

"Wrong?"

She gulped some water. "We're so *polite* with each other."

"Yeah," Mitch agreed.

"We can hardly talk."

"I noticed." But he didn't suggest any explanations—or solutions.

Bethany met his eyes, hoping he'd do *something* to resolve this dilemma. He didn't. Instead, he set his napkin carefully aside and got to his feet. "I guess I'm not very hungry." He carried his half-full bowl to the sink.

"Oh."

"Do you want me to leave?" he asked.

No! her heart cried, but she didn't say the word. "Do...do you want to go?"

He didn't answer.

Bethany stood up, pressing the tips of her fingers to

her forehead. "Stop. Please, just stop. I want to know what's wrong. Did I do something?"

"No. Good heavens, no." He seemed astonished that she'd even asked. "It isn't anything you've done."

Mitch stood on one side of the kitchen and she on the other. "It's my fault," he said in a voice so quiet she had difficulty hearing him. "You haven't done anything, but—" He stopped abruptly.

"What?" she pleaded. "Tell me."

"Listen, Bethany, I think it would be best if I did leave." With that, he walked purposefully into the living room and retrieved his coat from the small entryway closet.

Although the room was warm and cozy, Bethany felt a sudden chill. She crossed her arms as much to ward off the sense of cold as to protect herself from Mitch's words. "It's back to that, is it?" she managed sadly. From the first day in September, Mitch had been running away from her. Every time they made any progress, something would happen to show her how far they had yet to go.

His hand on the doorknob, he abruptly turned to face her. When he spoke his voice was hoarse with anger. "I can't be alone with you without wanting to kiss you."

She stared at him in disbelief. "We've kissed before." There had been those memorable passionate kisses. And more recently, affectionate kisses of greeting and farewell. "What's so different now?"

"We're alone."

"Yes, I know." She still didn't understand.

He shook his head, as if it was difficult to continue. "Don't you see, Bethany?"

Obviously she didn't.

"With Chrissie or anyone else around, the temptation is minimized. But when it's just the two of us, I can't think about anything else!" The last sentence was ground out between clenched teeth. "Don't you realize how much I want to make love to you?"

"Is that so terrible?" she asked quietly.

"Yes." The only sound she could hear was the too-fast beating of her own heart. She could see Mitch's pulse hammering in the vein in his neck.

"I can't let it happen," he told her, his back straight, shoulders stiff.

"For your information, making love requires two people," Bethany told him simply. "I wish you'd said something earlier. We could've talked about this… arrived at some understanding. It's true," she added, "the thought of us becoming…intimate has crossed my mind—but I wouldn't have allowed it to happen. Not yet, anyway. It's too soon."

Without a word, Mitch closed the distance between them. With infinite tenderness he wove his fingers through her hair, and buried his lips against her throat. "You tempt me so much."

She sighed and wrapped her arms around him.

"Feeling this way frightens me, Bethany. Overwhelms me."

"We can't run from it, Mitch, or pretend it doesn't exist."

His hands trembled as they slid down her spine, molding her against him. His kiss was slow and melting, and so thorough she was left breathless. She rested her head against his shoulder.

"I guess this means I can put away the celery," she whispered.

"The celery?"

"When the catalog order came, I didn't receive the mistletoe. The slip said it's on back order. I talked to my mom earlier today and told her how disappointed I was—and she suggested celery as a substitute. So I nailed a piece over the doorway. Apparently you didn't notice."

Mitch chuckled hoarsely. "You know what I like best about you?"

"You mean other than my kisses?"

"Yes."

The look in his eyes was as potent as good whiskey. "You make me laugh."

She shook her head. "Don't shut me out, Mitch. I can't bear it when you shut me out of your life. There isn't anything you can't tell me."

"Don't be so sure." Mitch eased her out of his arms and stared down at her, as if testing the truth of her words.

"Mitch," she said gently, touching his face, "what is it?"

"Nothing." He turned away. "It's nothing."

Bethany didn't believe that. But she had no choice other than to end this discussion, which obviously distressed him. When he was ready he'd tell her.

"Didn't you say something about decorating your Christmas tree?" he asked with feigned enthusiasm.

"I did indeed," she said, following his lead.

"Good. We'll get to that in a moment." He took her by the hand.

"Where are we going?"

"You mean you don't know?" He grinned boyishly. "I'm taking you to the celery, er, the substitute mistletoe."

Soon she was in his arms, and all the doubts she'd entertained were obliterated the second he lowered his mouth to hers. She felt only the touch of his lips. Slow and confident. Intimate and familiar.

Christian had expected Mariah to move away from Hard Luck before December. He wasn't a betting man, but he would've wagered a year's income that his secretary would hightail it out of town right after the first snowfall. Not that he would've blamed her, living as she was in a one-room cabin. He cringed whenever he thought about her in those primitive conditions.

It wasn't the first time Mariah had shown him up. Christian was positive she stayed on out of pure spite. She wanted to prove herself, all right, but at the expense of his pride.

He walked into the office to find Mariah already at her desk, typing away at the computer. Her fingers moved so fast they were a blur.

At the sound of the door closing, she looked up—and froze.

"Morning," he said without emotion.

"Good morning," she said shyly. She glanced away, almost as if she expected a reprimand. "The coffee's ready."

"So I see." He wasn't looking forward to this, but someone had to reason with her, and Sawyer had refused to take on the task.

Christian poured himself a cup of coffee, then walked slowly to his desk. "Mariah."

She stared at him with large, frightened eyes. "Did I do something wrong again?"

"No, no," he said quickly, wanting to reassure her. "What makes you think that?" He gave her what he hoped resembled an encouraging smile.

She eyed him, apparently not convinced she could trust him. "It seems the only time you talk to me is when I've done something wrong."

"Not this time." He sat down at his desk, which wasn't all that far from her own. "It's about you living in the cabin," he said.

He watched her bristle. "I believe we've already discussed this," she answered stiffly. "Several times."

"I don't want you there."

"Then you should never have offered the cabins as accommodation."

"I'd prefer it if you moved in with the other women—in Catherine Fletcher's house," he said, ignoring her comment. Actually, having Catherine's house available to them had been a godsend. Two women—Sally and Angie—had moved in, and the arrangement was working out well.

The pilots Midnight Sons employed lived in a dorm-size room. It was stark, without much more than a big stove for heating and several bunk beds and lockers, but the men never complained. The house was far more to the women's liking. As soon as they could, he and Sawyer were bringing in two mobile homes for the women, as well.

Until then Christian wasn't comfortable thinking about Mariah—or anyone else—living in a one-room cabin. Not with winter already here.

"I'm just fine where I am," Mariah insisted.

Sawyer thought she was all right there, too, but Christian knew otherwise. At night he lay awake, thinking of Mariah out there on the edge of town in a cabin smaller than a rich man's closet. It had no electric power and no plumbing, and was a far cry from what she'd been accustomed to.

"I'm asking," he said, being careful to phrase the words in a way she wouldn't find objectionable, "if you'd move in with Sally and Angie. Just until the spring thaw."

"Why?"

Arguing with her was an exercise in frustration. And the amount of time he wasted worrying about her! That in itself made no sense to him. The fact was, he didn't even *like* Mariah. The woman drove him crazy.

"I'm asking you to move in with them for a reason other than the cabin's primitive conditions." This, of course, wasn't true, but he had to figure out *some* way of getting her to move. He said the first thing that came to mind.

"I… I think one or two of the women are considering leaving Hard Luck," he lied. "We don't want to lose them."

"Who?"

Christian shrugged. "It's just rumors at this point. But I need someone who can encourage them to stick out the winter. Someone the others like and trust."

She looked at him as if she wasn't sure she should believe him.

"The others need someone they feel comfortable with. They like you, and I think you could help."

Mariah paused. "But I don't feel it's necessary for me to move in with them."

"I do," he answered automatically. "How often do you get a chance to talk with your friends? I can't imagine it's more than once a week." He was stabbing in the dark now.

Mariah nibbled on her lower lip and seemed to be considering his words. "That's true."

"A few of them aren't having an easy time adjusting to life in the Arctic. Will you do it, Mariah?" he pleaded. Heaven knew he'd tried every other means he could think of to get her to get out of that godforsaken cabin. "Will you move in with the other women?"

She hesitated. "I'll still get the deed to the land and the cabin at the end of the year, won't I?"

"You can have both now." It wasn't the first time he'd made that offer. The sooner she accomplished her goals, the sooner she'd leave Hard Luck.

"Giving me the title now wouldn't be right. The terms of my contract state that at the end of one year I'll be entitled to the cabin and the land. I wouldn't dream of accepting the deed a moment sooner."

"Then I'll assure you in writing that the time you spend living with the other women will in no way jeopardize our agreement. You can type up the papers yourself."

He watched her and waited. Waited while the interminable minutes passed. He couldn't believe that one small decision would require such concentration.

"Will you or won't you?" he demanded when he couldn't stand the silence anymore.

"I will," she said, "but on one condition. I want to talk to the others first and make sure I won't be intruding."

Christian groaned, resisting the urge to bury his face in his hands. "Midnight Sons is paying the rent!"

"I'm well aware of that," Mariah said coolly.

"If I wanted to move the entire French Foreign Legion into that house, then I'd do it."

"No, you wouldn't," Mariah said with a know-it-all grin. "First, Sawyer wouldn't let you and—"

"It was a figure of speech." Christian now fought the urge to pull out his hair. No one on earth could anger him as quickly as Mariah Douglas. The year she was contracted to work for him couldn't end fast enough. Not until she left Hard Luck would he be able to sleep through the night again.

A wreath hung inside the door of the Hard Luck Café. Flashing miniature lights were strung around the windows. Christmas cards were pinned to one wall in a straggling triangle. Bethany guessed the shape was supposed to represent a Christmas tree.

The thank-you notes the children had written following his visit to the classroom were taped against another wall for everyone who came into the café to see. The worn look of those notes told her Ben had read them countless times himself.

"It's beginning to look downright festive around here," Bethany said as she stepped up to the counter.

"Christmas is my favorite holiday," Ben declared. "How about a piece of mincemeat pie to go with your coffee? It's on the house."

"Actually I don't have time for either," Bethany said regretfully. She was on her way to church for choir practice and only had a few minutes. "I came to invite you to my house for Christmas dinner."

Ben's mouth opened and a look of utter astonishment crossed his face. "I thought... Me? What about Mitch and Chrissie? Aren't they spending the day with you?"

"I invited them, too. I'm sure I'm not half as good in the kitchen as you are, but I should be able to manage turkey and all the trimmings. Besides, you might enjoy tasting someone else's cooking for a change."

He frowned as though this was a weighty decision. "I like my turkey with sage dressing and giblet gravy."

"You got it. My mom always stuffs the bird with sage dressing, and my dad makes giblet gravy. I wouldn't know how to do it any other way." When he seemed about to refuse, she added, "If you want to contribute something, you can bring one of those mincemeat pies you're trying to fatten me up with."

Ben turned away from her and reached for the rag. He began to wipe the already clean countertop. "I... I don't know what to say." His eyes continued to avoid hers.

"Just say yes. Dinner's at three."

He gestured weakly. "I always keep the place open."

"Close it this year." She almost suggested he should spend the holiday with family, but managed to stop herself. Still, she felt close to Ben; she *did* feel he was family. Perhaps this was emotionally dangerous, but being with him on Christmas Day might help ease the ache of missing her parents.

"Folks generally spend Christmas Day with family," he said. It was as if he'd been able to read her thoughts. "I don't have any left," he told her in a low voice. "At least, none who'd want me dropping in unannounced at Christmas."

"I'll be your family, Ben," she offered, waiting for her heart to stop its crazy beating. He had no way of knowing how much truth there was in her words. "And you can be mine. For this one day, anyhow."

"Won't I be in the way? I mean, with you and—"

Bethany reached for his hand. "I wouldn't have invited you if that was the case."

"What about you and Mitch? You two are spending a lot of time together lately—which is good," he hastened to say. "I don't think I've ever seen Mitch look happier, and what I hear is that there's a night-and-day difference with Chrissie. She used to be a shy little thing."

Bethany had the feeling he would've rambled on for an hour if she hadn't stopped him.

"Ben!" She laughed outright. "I'm asking you to Christmas dinner. Will you come or not? I need to know how much food to prepare."

She watched his throat work convulsively. "No one ever asked me to Christmas dinner," he said in a strangled voice.

"Well, someone is now."

He met her look and his eyes grew suspiciously bright. "What time do you want me there again?"

"Dinner's at three. You come as early as you like, though."

"All right," he said with some difficulty. "I'll be there, and I'll bring one of my pies."

"Good. I'll see you Christmas Day." Having settled that, Bethany left the café.

"Bethany," Ben called, "if you need any help making that gravy, you let me know."

"I will. Thanks for offering."

Not until she was outside, with the cold clawing at her face, did she realize there were tears in her eyes. She quickly brushed them away and hurried to the church.

Christmas was supposed to be a joyous time of year. It would be, Matt Caldwell thought, if Karen was with him. He glanced around the Anchorage church. The harder he tried not to think about his ex-wife, the more difficult it became to concentrate on the hymn-book in his hands.

Perhaps it was because the last time he'd been in this church was after his grandmother's death. The sadness that had taken hold of his heart then hadn't faded in the weeks since.

Matt hadn't made church a habit of late. The fact was, he and God weren't on the best of terms. He was quite comfortable ignoring the presence of an almighty being, since evidence of God had been sorely lacking in his life these past few years.

It didn't help that he was once again the only family member who was alone. His parents stood on one side of him, and Lanni and Charles on the other. Those two were so much in love it was painful just being around them.

Although Lanni enjoyed her work with the *Anchorage News,* she hated the long separations from Charles. April couldn't come soon enough as far as she was concerned.

The Christmas Eve church services continued, and the members of the congregation lifted their voices in song. Matt wasn't in any frame of mind to join in. He'd worked hard during the past few months. Damned hard. Other than his obvious purpose of getting the lodge ready, he'd driven himself in a single-minded effort, but whether it was to impress Karen or get her out of his system, he no longer knew.

He couldn't help wondering how his ex-wife was spending Christmas. He was pretty confident she wouldn't have a white Christmas in California.

Was she alone, the way he was? Did she feel empty inside? Was she thinking of him?

Somehow he doubted it, considering how impulsively she'd left Alaska. It still bothered him that she hadn't so much as told him she was moving. Instead, she'd contacted his sister, knowing Lanni would tell him.

Once the interminable singing ended, there was the predictable Christmas pageant. Despite his misery, Matt found himself smiling as the Sunday school children gave the performance they'd no doubt been rehearsing for months.

This year, instead of a doll, they had a newborn infant playing the role of the baby Jesus. This child was anything but meek and mild. In fact, he let out a scream that echoed through the church and started all the children giggling.

Well, that was what they got for using a real baby. A baby.

He froze on the thought. Babies. Children. He glanced around the congregation and noticed a number of families with small children.

Karen had wanted children. They'd had more than one heated discussion on that subject. Matt had been against it; he didn't feel ready for fatherhood. Not when his future and career remained unsettled. In retrospect, he could see he'd been right. Dragging a child through a divorce would've been criminal.

Now the likelihood of his having a family was remote at best. He discovered, somewhat to his surprise, that the realization brought with it a new pain. Great. Just what he needed. Another resentment to harbor. Another casualty of his dead marriage. Something else to flail himself with.

He was relieved when the church service ended. At least he hadn't been subjected to a lengthy sermon on top of the singing and the pageant.

Once they were home, his family gathered around the Christmas tree. Traditionally they opened their gifts on Christmas Eve. It had taken some doing for him to dredge up enough energy to spring for gifts, but he'd managed it.

"How about hot apple cider?" Lanni asked.

"Sure," he said, faking a smile. It didn't seem fair to burden everyone else with his misery.

His sister brought him a cup, then sat down next to him. Their mother was busy in the kitchen and his father was talking to Charles.

"I hoped we'd have a minute alone before opening the gifts," Lanni whispered. She searched through the mound of gaily wrapped presents; beneath one of them she found what she was looking for. An envelope. She handed it to him.

Matt looked at his name on the envelope and instantly recognized the handwriting as Karen's. His heart skipped a beat, and he raised his eyes to his sister's, not sure what to think.

"How'd you get this?"

"Karen mailed a gift to me and to Mom and Dad. It was in the same package."

"I...see." His hand closed tightly over the envelope.

"There's something else," Lanni said, her gaze avoiding his.

"Yes?" He was eager to escape to his room and read what Karen had written.

"Our wedding..."

"What about it?"

"Would you mind very much if Karen served as my maid of honor?"

Matt stared at his sister, not understanding. "You want her in your wedding party?"

"Yes," she said, then quickly added, "But only if you don't object. I wouldn't want it to be uncomfortable for you, Matt. You're my brother, after all, and she was your wife—but she's still my friend."

"Why should I care?" he mumbled. "It's your wedding." With that, he left the room.

Once he was inside his old bedroom, Matt threw himself on the bed and tore open the envelope. A single sheet of paper fell from the card. Heart pounding, he unfolded it and read:

Merry Christmas, Matt.
It didn't seem right to mail gifts to Lanni and your parents and send you nothing. But at the same time, it's a bit awkward to buy my ex-husband a Christmas gift.
I hope this card finds you well.

Sincerely,
Karen

Sincerely. She'd actually signed the note *sincerely.* As if it was some kind of business letter or he was merely a casual acquaintance. He picked up the Christmas card he'd discarded earlier and found she'd written nothing but her name.

Still, sending a Christmas card was more than he'd done for her. He supposed he'd have to add that to his long list of failures and regrets.

Eight

Mitch woke early Christmas morning.

Not wanting to wake Chrissie, he moved silently into the living room, where the miniature lights on the tree glittered like frosted stars. He smiled at their decorations—paper chains, strung popcorn and hand-made ornaments.

He rearranged the gifts under the tree. He'd placed them there the night before, after Chrissie had gone to bed. He knew she didn't believe in Santa Claus anymore, but it was fun for both of them to keep up the pretense.

The largest present wasn't from him but Bethany. A Barbie thingamajig. Town house or some such nonsense. Only it wasn't nonsense to Chrissie; the kid took her Barbie seriously. She'd be thrilled with this. He knew Chrissie would be happily absorbed with her gifts all morning, and then later, in the afternoon, they were going to Bethany's place for a turkey dinner with all the fixings.

Bethany.

He needed these quiet early-morning moments to clear his thoughts and make sense of his feelings.

It had happened.

Despite his resistance, his best efforts to prevent it, despite his vows to the contrary, despite the full force of his determination, he'd gone and fallen in love with Bethany Ross.

He didn't *want* to love Bethany, and in the same breath, he found himself humbled that this remarkable woman had entered his life. Especially after Lori. Especially now.

Mitch paced the living room, too restless to sit. Admitting that he cared deeply for Bethany required some sort of decision. A man didn't come to this kind of realization without defining a course of action.

He knew he had nothing to offer her. While it was true that he made enough money to support a family, his financial status wasn't impressive. Somehow he doubted this would matter to Bethany, but still...

He was dismally aware, too, that he came to her with deep emotional scars and a needy child in tow. The mere thought of loving again, of trusting again, terrified him. It made him break out in a cold sweat. On top of everything else was the paralyzing fear that he'd fail Bethany the way he had Lori.

Then again, he reminded himself, he had options. He could do what he'd done since September—deny his feelings. Ignore what his heart was telling him.

He might've continued that way for months, possibly years, if it wasn't for one thing.

Chrissie.

From the moment his daughter had met Bethany, she'd set her sights on turning the teacher into her mother and his wife. Watching the two of them to-gether had touched him from the very first. In ways he'd never fully understand, Bethany ministered to his daughter's need for a mother in the same way she satisfied his own long-repressed desire for a companion. *A wife...*

As the weeks progressed, Chrissie had started looking to Bethany for guidance more and more often. There wasn't *anything* Chrissie wouldn't do to be with her—including feign flu symptoms.

What confounded him was the fact that Bethany seemed to share his feelings. He felt her love as powerfully as those brief moments of sunlight every day, brightening the world in the darkness of an Arctic winter.

Admitting his love for Bethany—to her and to himself—wasn't a simple thing. Love rarely was, he suspected. If he told her how he felt about her, he'd also have to tell her about his past.

Love implied trust. And he'd need to trust her with the painful details of his marriage. With that came the tremendous risk of her rejection. He wouldn't blame her if she *did* turn away. If the situation were reversed, he didn't know how he'd react. He was laying an enormous burden on her.

Telling her all this wasn't something he could do on the spur of the moment. Timing was critical. He'd have to wait for the right day, the right mood.

Not this morning, he decided. Not on Christmas. He refused to spoil the day's celebration with the ugliness of his past. No need to darken the holiday with a litany of his failures as a husband.

"Daddy?" Chrissie stood just inside the living room

doorway yawning. She wore her pretty new flannel pajamas—the one gift he'd allowed her to open Christmas Eve.

"Merry Christmas, pumpkin," he said, opening his arms to her. "It looks like Santa made it to Hard Luck, after all."

Chrissie leapt into his embrace and he folded his arms around her, slowly closing his eyes. His daughter was the most precious gift he'd ever been given. And now, finding Bethany... His heart was full.

"I can't believe I ate the whole thing," Ben teased, placing his hands on the bulge of his stomach and sighing heavily. He eased his chair away from the kitchen table. "If anyone else finds out what a good cook you are, Bethany, I'll be out of business before I know it."

Bethany smiled, delighted with his praise. "I don't think you need to worry. Those pies of yours were fabulous, especially the mincemeat. I'd like to get your recipe."

Ben grinned. "Sure. No problem. It's one I came up with myself—I like to try new things when I cook. How about you? Have you always been this good in the kitchen?"

It was another trait she shared with her birth father, but once again this wasn't something she could mention.

She nodded. "While other little girls were playing with dolls and makeup, I was using my Betty Crocker Baking Center to concoct all kinds of cookies and cakes."

"Well, all that practice sure paid off," Mitch said.

Bethany blushed a little at the compliments. She'd

done her best to put on a spread worthy of their praise. The meal had taken weeks of careful planning; she'd had to special-order some of the ingredients, and her mother had mailed her the spices. A lot of the dishes she'd made were traditional family recipes. Mashed sweet potatoes with dried apricots and lots of butter. Sage dressing, of course, and another rice-and-raisin dressing that had been a favorite of hers, one her grandmother made every year.

"You miss your family, don't you?" Mitch asked as he helped her clear the table.

"Everyone does at Christmas, don't you think?" This first year so far away from her parents and two younger brothers had been more difficult than she'd expected; this morning had been particularly wrenching. She knew they missed her, too. Bethany had spoken to her family in California at least once a day for the past week. She didn't care how high her phone bill ran.

"I must've chatted to Mom three times this morning alone," she told Mitch. "It's funny. For years I've helped her with Thanksgiving and Christmas dinners, but when it came to doing it on my own, I had a dozen questions."

"You need me to do anything?" Ben asked, getting up from the table. He carried his plate to the sink. "I've done plenty of dishes in my time. I wouldn't mind lending a hand, especially after a meal like that. Seems to me that those who cook shouldn't have to wash dishes."

"Normally I'd agree with you, but not today. You're my guest."

"But…"

"I should think you'd know better than to argue with a woman," Mitch chided.

Laughing, Bethany shooed Ben out of the kitchen.

"We were going to continue our game of Monopoly, remember?" Chrissie reminded him eagerly. "You said you wanted a chance to win some of your money back."

"Go play," Bethany said with a laugh. "I'll rope Mitch here into helping."

"You're sure?" Ben asked.

"Very sure," she told him, glancing over at Mitch with a smile.

Mitch mumbled something she couldn't hear. She looked at him curiously as she reached for a bowl. "What did you say?"

His eyes held hers. "I said a man could get lost in one of your smiles and never find his way home."

Bethany paused, the bowl of leftover mashed potatoes in her hands. "Why, Mitch, what a romantic thing to say."

His face tightened, as though her comment had embarrassed him. "It must be the season," he said gruffly. He turned away from her and started to fill the sink with hot, sudsy water.

Bethany smiled to herself. It was rare to see Mitch Harris flustered. She fingered the polished five-dollar gold coin he'd had made into a pendant and placed on a fine gold chain. The coin had been minted the year of her birth, and he'd had it mounted in a gold bezel. The necklace was beautiful in its simplicity. The minute she fastened it around her neck, Bethany knew this was a piece of jewelry she'd wear every day for the rest of her life.

She felt that her gift for Mitch paled in comparison. Mitch was an avid Tom Clancy fan, and through a friend who managed a bookstore in San Francisco, she'd been able to get him an autographed copy of Clancy's latest hardcover.

When Mitch had opened the package and read the inscription, he'd looked up at her as though she'd handed him the stone tablets direct from Mount Sinai.

Chrissie had been excited about her Barbie town house, too.

The one who'd surprised her most, however, was Ben. He'd arrived for dinner with not one pie but four—all of them baked fresh that morning. In addition to the pies, he'd brusquely handed her an oblong box. Bethany got a kick out of the way he'd wrapped it. He'd used three times the amount of paper necessary and enough tape to supply the U.S. Army for a year.

Inside the box was a piece of scrimshaw made from a walrus tusk. The scene on the polished piece of ivory was of wild geese in flight over a marsh. Mountains rose in the distance against a sunlit sky.

Ben had dismissed his gift as nothing more than a trinket, but Bethany knew from her brief stay in Fairbanks how expensive such pieces of artwork had become. She tried to thank him, but it was clear her words only embarrassed him.

"I would've thought you'd want to fly home for Christmas," Mitch said, rolling up his sleeves before dipping his hands in the dishwater.

"I seriously considered it." Bethany wasn't going to minimize the difficulty of her decision to remain in Hard Luck. "But it's a long way to travel for so short a time. I'll probably stay in Alaska during spring break, as well. After all, my commitment here is only for the school year."

"You're going home to California in June, then?"

"Are you asking me if I plan to return to Hard Luck for another school year?"

"Yes," he said, his back to her.

Something in the carefully nonchalant way he'd asked told her that the answer was important to him.

"I don't know," she said as straightforwardly as she could. "It depends on whether I'm offered a contract."

"And if you are?"

"I...don't know yet." She loved Alaska and her students. Most of all, she loved Mitch and Chrissie. Ben, too. But there were other factors. Several of them had to do with Ben—should she tell him he was her biological father, and what would his reaction be if she did? More and more, she felt inclined to confront him with the truth.

"Well, I hope you come back" was all the response Mitch gave her. The deliberate lack of emotion in his voice was clearly meant to suggest that they'd been talking about something of little importance.

Why, for heaven's sake, couldn't the man just say what he wanted to say?

Hands on her hips, Bethany glared at him. Mitch happened to turn around for another stack of dirty dishes; he saw her and did a double take. "What?" he demanded.

"All you can say is 'Well, I hope you come back,'" she mimicked. "I'm spilling my heart out here and *that's* all the reaction I get from you?"

He gave her a blank look.

"The answer is I'm willing to consider another

year's contract, and you can bet it isn't because of the tropical climate in Hard Luck."

Mitch grinned exuberantly. "The benefits are good."

"But not great."

"The money's fabulous."

"Oh, please," she muttered, rolling her eyes. She took an exaggerated breath. "My, my, I wonder what the appeal could be."

Mitch looked at her in sudden and complete seriousness. "I was hoping you'd say it was me."

She regarded him with an equally somber look. "I do enjoy the way you kiss, Mitch Harris."

The first sign of amusement touched his lips. He lifted his soapy arms from the water and stretched them toward her. "Maybe what you need to convince you is a small demonstration of my enjoyable kisses."

A second later Bethany was in his arms. The water seeped through her blouse, but she couldn't have cared less. What *did* matter was sharing this important day with the people she loved. And those who loved her.

John Henderson wanted to do the right thing by Sally. He loved her—more than he'd thought possible. Proof of that was his willingness to delay asking her to marry him. He was determined to wait until he'd talked to her father.

He'd been carrying the engagement ring with him for weeks now. Every once in a while he'd draw it out and rub the gold band between his index finger and thumb. He figured that his patience—difficult though he found it to be patient—was a measure of his love

for Sally. Still, he cursed himself a dozen times a day
for listening to Duke.

John told himself that the other pilot didn't know
any more about love than he did. But it wasn't true;
Duke had given him good, sensible advice. John desperately wanted everything to be right between Sally
and him, especially after her recent heartbreak.

It would've been selfish to rush her into an engagement and then a wedding without first knowing that
she shared his feelings—and was sure of her own. He
had to be certain she wasn't marrying him on the rebound. Duke was right about her family, too. Her parents were traditional, old-fashioned, even, and it was
important to meet them, give them a chance to know
him. Important—but the waiting had become harder
with every week that passed.

Now he was ready to make his move. And ask his
questions...

Naturally, John would rather have delayed this initial awkwardness. No man likes to be scrutinized by
strangers, especially when he's about to ask these very
people for permission to marry the most precious,
beautiful woman God ever made. Their daughter.

If he were Sally's father, John thought, he wouldn't
blame the man for booting him out of the house. He
hoped, however, that it wouldn't come to that.

He'd bought a new suit for the occasion. It wasn't
a waste of money, he'd decided, seeing he'd probably need it for the wedding and all. *If* Sally agreed
to marry him, and he hoped and prayed she would.

Sally's true feelings for him seemed to be the only
real question. They'd been seeing each other on a regular basis, but John had noticed certain things about

her that left him wondering. Her eyes didn't light up when she saw him, the way they had in the beginning. If he didn't know better, he'd think she was avoiding him lately.

Mariah Douglas had recently moved into the house with her, and Sally seemed almost relieved to have an excuse not to invite him over so often. Of course, he'd been busy at Midnight Sons, with the holiday rush and all.

Other signs baffled him, as well. These puzzling changes in Sally's behavior had started after he'd spent the night with her. It wasn't like they'd *planned* to make love; it had just happened.

John regretted not waiting to initiate their lovemaking until after the wedding. He'd known for a long time how he felt about Sally. Immediately following their one night together, he'd gone out and bought the engagement ring, but then Duke had talked him out of proposing until he could meet her family.

It might not be such a good idea to show up unannounced on Christmas Day, but John didn't have a lot of spare time. Midnight Sons was shorthanded in the wintertime as it was. The holidays had offered him the opportunity to make the trip. That was why he was here in British Columbia, in a small town with an Indian name he couldn't pronounce, dropping in on Sally's family uninvited and clutching a somewhat travel-worn bouquet of roses.

John checked the address on the back of the Christmas card envelope and walked up to the white house with the dark green shutters and the large fir wreath on the door. He pressed the doorbell, swallowed nervously and waited.

His relief was great when Sally answered the door herself. Her eyes grew huge with surprise and, he hoped, with happiness when she saw who it was.

"John? What are you doing here?"

He thrust the flowers into her hand, grateful to be rid of them. "I've come to talk to your father," he told her.

"My dad?" she asked, clearly puzzled. "Why?"

"That's between him and me." He found it difficult not to stare at her, seeing she was as pretty as a model for one of those fashion magazines. They'd made love only that once, and although he cursed himself for his lack of self-control, he couldn't regret loving Sally. He looked forward to making love to her again. Only this time it would be when his ring was around her finger and they'd said their *I do*'s.

"John?" She closed the door and stepped onto the small porch steps, hugging herself with both arms. Her eyes questioned his. "What's this all about?"

"I need to talk to your father," he repeated.

"You already said that. Is it because I've decided not to return to Hard Luck? Who told you? Not Mariah, she wouldn't do that, I know she wouldn't."

John felt as if someone had punched him. For one shocking moment, he thought he might be sick. "You... you didn't plan on coming back after Christmas?"

"No." She lowered her gaze, avoiding his.

"But I thought... I hoped—" He snapped his mouth shut before he acted like an even bigger fool. He was about to humble himself before her father and request Sally's hand in marriage. Yet she'd walked out of his life without so much as a word of farewell.

"You mean you didn't know?"

He shook his head. "You weren't planning on telling me?"

"No." She tucked her chin against her chest. "I... I couldn't see the point. You got what you wanted, didn't you?"

"What the hell is that supposed to mean?" he shouted. Standing outside her family home yelling probably wasn't the best way to introduce himself to her father, but John couldn't help it. He was angry, and with good reason.

"You know exactly what I mean," she replied in a furious whisper.

"Are you referring to the night we made love?"

Mortified, Sally closed her eyes. "Do you have to shout it to the entire neighborhood?"

"Yes!"

Sally glared at him. "I think we've said everything there is to say."

"Not by a long shot, we haven't," John countered. "Okay, so we made love. Big deal. I'm not perfect, and neither are you. It happened, but we haven't gone to bed since then, have we?"

"John, please, not so loud." Sally glanced uneasily over her shoulder.

His next words surprised him, springing out despite himself. "I wasn't the first, so I don't understand why you're making such a big deal of it. Too late now, anyway." He would never have said this if he hadn't felt so angry, so betrayed.

Tears leapt instantly into her eyes and John would've given his right arm to take back the hurtful words. He'd rather suffer untold agonies than say anything to distress Sally, yet he'd done exactly that.

The door behind her opened and a burly lumber-jack of a man walked out onto the porch. "What's going on here?"

Sally gestured weakly toward John. "Daddy, this is John Henderson. He—he's a friend from Hard Luck."

Finding his daughter sniffling back tears wasn't much of an endorsement, John thought gloomily. He squared his shoulders and offered the other man his hand. "I'm pleased to meet you, Mr. McDonald."

"The name's Jack. I don't understand why my daughter hasn't seen fit to invite you into the house, young man." He cast an accusatory frown in Sally's direction. "Seems you've come a long way to visit her."

"It doesn't look like I was as welcome as I thought I'd be," John muttered.

"Nonsense. It's Christmas Day. Since you've traveled all this distance, the least we can do is ask you to join us and give you a warm drink."

John didn't need anything to warm him. Spending time with the McDonald family would only add to his frustration and misery, but Jack McDonald gave him no option. Sally's father quickly ushered him inside.

Swallowing his pride, John followed the brawny man up a short flight of stairs and into the living room. The festivities ceased when he appeared. Sally's father introduced him around, and her mother poured him a cup of wassail that tasted like hot apple cider.

"I don't believe Sally's mentioned you in her letters home," Mrs. McDonald said conversationally as a chair was brought out for John.

He felt his heart grow cold and heavy with pain. Forcing himself to observe basic good manners, he thanked Sally's brother for the chair. All those months while he was pining over Sally, he hadn't rated a single line in one of her letters home. Although he'd told her their making love had been no big deal, it *had* been. For him. He loved her. But apparently their relationship wasn't important enough for Sally to even mention his name.

"I told you about John," Sally said.

John wondered if that was true, or if she was attempting to cover her tracks.

"John's the bush pilot I wrote you about." Sally sat across the room from him and tucked her hands awkwardly between her knees as if she wasn't sure what to do with them.

"Oh yes, now I remember. Don't think you said his name, though." Her father nodded slowly. And her mother sent him a bright smile.

John drank the cider as fast as he could. It burned going down, but he didn't care. He drained the cup, stood and abruptly handed it to Sally's mother.

"Thank you for the drink and the hospitality, but I should be on my way."

Jack bent down to the carpet and retrieved something. "I believe you dropped this, son," he said.

To John's mortification, Sally's father held out the engagement ring.

He checked his pocket, praying all the while that there were two such rings in this world, and that the second just happened to be in Sally's home. On the floor. Naturally, the diamond Jack held was the one he'd bought for Sally. Without a word, he slipped it back inside his suit pocket.

"It was a pleasure meeting everyone," he said, anxiously eyeing the front door. He'd never been so eager to leave a place. Leave and find somewhere to be by himself.

Well, he told himself bitterly, he'd learned his lesson when it came to women. He was better off living his life alone. To think he'd been one of the men eager to have the O'Hallorans bring women north!

One thing was certain; he didn't need this kind of rejection, this kind of pain.

"John?" Sally gazed at him with those beautiful blue eyes of hers. Only this time he wasn't about to be taken in by her sweetness.

He ignored her and hurried down the stairs to the front door. He'd already grasped the door handle when he realized that Sally had followed him. "You can leave without explaining that ring, but I swear if you do I'll never speak to you again."

"I don't see that it'd matter," he told her, boldly meeting her eyes. "You weren't planning on speaking to me anyway."

He gave her ample time to answer, and when she didn't, he made a show of turning the knob.

"Don't go," Sally cried in a choked whisper. "I thought…that you'd gotten what you wanted and so you—"

"I know what you thought," he snapped.

"Maybe we could talk about this?" It sounded like she was struggling not to break into tears. He dug inside his back pocket, pulled out a fresh handkerchief and handed it to her.

"Could we talk, John?" she asked and walked down the second flight of stairs to the lower portion of the house. "Please?"

John guessed he was supposed to accompany her.

He looked up to find her mother, father, brother and a few cousins whose names he'd forgotten leaning over the railing staring at him.

"You'd better go with her," Sally's younger brother advised. "It's best to do what she wants when she's in one of these moods."

"Do you love her, son?" Jack McDonald demanded.

John looked at Sally, thinking a response now would be premature, but he couldn't very well deny it, carrying an engagement ring in his pocket. "Yes, sir. I meant to ask Sally to marry me, but I wanted everything to be right with us. So I thought I'd introduce myself and ask your permission first."

"It's a good man who speaks to the father first," Sally's mother said, nodding tearfully.

"Marry her with my blessing, son."

John relaxed and grinned. "Thank you, sir." Then he figured he should give himself some room in case things didn't go the way he hoped. "In light of what's happened, I'm not sure Sally will say yes. She wasn't planning on returning to Hard Luck—I'm not sure why, but she hadn't said a word about it to me."

"I believe my daughter's about to clear away any doubts you have, young man. She'll give you plenty of reasons not to change your mind."

"Daddy!" This drifted up from the bottom of the stairwell.

John winked at his future in-laws. "That's what I was hoping she'd do," he said and hurried down the stairs, his steps jubilant. "Oh, and Merry Christmas, everyone!"

Nine

It shouldn't upset her. If anything, Bethany thought, she should be pleased that Randy Kincade was getting married. The invitation for the March wedding arrived the second week of January, when winter howled outside her window and the promise of spring was buried beneath the frozen ground.

Bethany wasn't generally prone to bouts of the blues. But the darkness and the constant cold nibbled away at her optimism. Cabin fever—she'd never experienced it before, but she recognized the symptoms.

Her hair needed a trim, and she longed to see a movie in a real theater that sold hot, buttered popcorn. It was the middle of January, and she'd have killed for a thick-crust pizza smothered in melted cheese and spicy Italian sausage.

The craving for a pizza brought on a deluge of other sudden, unanticipated wants. She yearned for the opportunity to shop in a mall, in stores with fitting rooms, and to stroll past kiosks that sold delights like dangling earrings and glittery T-shirts. Not that she'd buy a lot of those things. She just wanted to *see* them.

To make everything even worse, her relationship with Mitch had apparently come to a standstill. As each week passed, it became more and more obvious that her feelings for him were far stronger than his were for her.

Whimsically she wondered if this was because God wanted her to know how Randy must've felt all those years ago when she didn't return the fervor of his love.

So now she knew, and it *hurt*.

Not that Mitch had said anything. Not directly at least. It was his manner, his new reserve, the way he kissed her—as if even then he felt the need to protect himself.

That reserve of his frustrated Bethany. It angered her, but mostly it hurt. In some ways, she felt their relationship had become more honest and open, yet in others—the important ones—he still seemed to be holding back. He seemed to fear that loving her would mean surrendering a piece of his soul, and she'd begun to wonder if he'd always keep his past hidden from her.

On another front, she increasingly felt the urge to let Ben know she was his biological daughter. Perhaps this was because she missed her family so much. Or maybe it was because she'd come to terms with Ben's place in her life. Then again, maybe it was because she felt frustrated in her relationship with Mitch. She didn't know.

This wasn't to say the soulful kisses they shared weren't wonderful. They were. Yet they often left her hungering, not for a deeper physical relationship, but for a more profound emotional one. She longed for

Mitch to trust her with his past, and clearly he wasn't willing to do that.

Their times alone, she noted, seemed to dwindle instead of increase. It almost seemed as though Mitch encouraged Chrissie's presence to avoid being alone with Bethany. It almost seemed as though dating Bethany satisfied his daughter's needs, but not his own.

On this January Saturday evening, when Bethany joined Mitch and Chrissie for their weekly video night, she couldn't disguise her melancholy. She tried, she honestly tried, to be upbeat, but it had been a long, drawn-out week. And now Randy was engaged, while her own love life had stalled.

Mitch must have noticed she hadn't touched the popcorn he'd supplied. "Is something wrong?" he asked, shifting beside her on the couch.

"No," she whispered, fighting to hold back the emotion that bubbled up inside her, seeking escape. Tears burned for release. She was about to weep and could think of no explanation that would appease him. No explanation, in fact, that would even make sense.

Mitch and Chrissie glanced at each other, then at her. Mitch stopped the movie. "You look like you're going to cry. I understand this movie's a tearjerker, but I didn't expect you to start crying during the previews."

She smiled shakily at his joke. "I'm sorry," she said. Her throat closed up, and when she tried to speak again, her voice came out in a high-pitched squeak. "I—"

"Bethany, what's wrong?"

She got to her feet, then didn't know why she had. She certainly didn't have anything to say.

"I—I need a haircut," she croaked.

Mitch looked at Chrissie, as if his daughter should be able to translate that. Chrissie regarded Bethany seriously, then shrugged.

"And a pizza—not the frozen kind, but one that's delivered, and the delivery boy should stand around until he gets a tip and act insulted by how little it is." She attempted a laugh that failed miserably.

"Pizza? Insulted?" Her explanation, such as it was, seemed to confuse Mitch even more.

"I'm sorry," she said again, gesturing forlornly with her hands. "I really am." She tucked her fingers against her palms and studied her hands. "Look at my nails. Just look. They used to be long and pretty—now they're broken and chipped."

"Bethany—"

"I'm not finished," she said, brushing the tears from her face. Now that they'd started, she couldn't seem to stop them. "I feel claustrophobic. I need more than a couple of hours' light a day. I'm sick and tired of watching the sun set two hours after dawn. I need more *light* than this." Even though she knew she wasn't being logical, Bethany couldn't stop the words any more than she could the tears. "I want to buy a new bra without ordering it out of a catalog."

"What you're feeling is cabin fever," Mitch explained calmly.

"I *know* that, but…"

"We all experience it in one way or another. It's not uncommon in winter. Even those of us who've lived here for years go through this," he said. "What you need is a weekend jaunt to Fairbanks. Two days away will make you feel like a new woman."

Men always seemed to have a simple solution to everything. For no reason she could explain—after all, she *wanted* to visit a big city—Mitch's answer only irritated her.

"Is a weekend trip going to change the fact that Randy's getting married?" she muttered. Her hands were clenched and her arms hung stiffly at her sides.

It took Mitch a moment or so to ask, "Who's Randy?"

"Bethany was engaged to him a long time ago," Chrissie said in a whisper.

"Do you love him?" Mitch asked in a gentle tone.

His tenderness, his complete lack of jealousy, infuriated her beyond reason. "No," she cried, "I love *you,* you idiot! Not that you care or notice or anything." Bethany went to retrieve her coat and hat.

"Bethany—"

"You don't understand *any* of what I'm feeling, do you? Please, just leave me alone."

To add insult to injury, Mitch stepped back and did precisely as she asked.

By the time Bethany had walked home—having refused Mitch's offer of a ride—she was sobbing openly. Tears had frozen to her face. The worst part was that she *knew* how ridiculous she was being. Unfortunately, it didn't seem to matter.

She was weeping uncontrollably—because she couldn't have a pizza delivered. Mitch seemed to think all she needed was a weekend in Fairbanks. Except that he didn't suggest the two of them fly in together.

"Fairbanks," she said under her breath. "How's *that* going to help?"

Restless and discontented, Bethany found she

couldn't bear to sit around the house and do nothing. She was lonely and heartbroken. This type of misery preyed on itself; what she needed was some kind of distraction. And some sympathy...

On impulse, she phoned Mariah Douglas, who was living in Catherine Fletcher's house now. She hoped she could talk Mariah into inviting her over. Mariah sounded pleased to hear from her and even said she had a bottle of wine in the fridge.

Before long, the two of them sat in the living room, clutching large glasses of zinfandel and bemoaning their sorry fate. It seemed that Mariah shared Bethany's melancholy mood. Not long afterward, Sally McDonald and Angie Hughes, Mariah's housemates, showed up and willingly raided their own stashes of wine and potato chips.

Bethany acknowledged that it felt good to talk with female friends, to divulge her woes to others who appreciated their seriousness. Soon it wasn't the lack of a decent pizza they were complaining about, but a bigger problem: the men in their lives.

"He wants me gone, you know," Mariah said, staring into her wineglass with a woebegone look. "He takes every opportunity to urge me to leave Hard Luck. I don't think August will come soon enough for him. I've...tried to be a good secretary, but he always flusters me."

Bethany knew Mariah was referring to Christian O'Halloran and wondered what prompted the secretary to stay when her employer had made his views so plain.

Then Bethany understood. Mariah was staying for the same reasons she was.

Bethany swirled the wine in her goblet. Her head swam, and she realized she was already half-drunk. A single glass of wine and she was tipsy. That said a lot about her social life.

"Let's go to Fairbanks!" she said excitedly. Although she'd rejected Mitch's suggestion out of hand, it held some appeal now. Escape by any means available was tempting, especially after a sufficient amount of wine.

"You want to leave for Fairbanks now?" Mariah asked incredulously.

"Why not?" Sally McDonald asked. Of them all, Sally was the one with the least to complain about—at least when it came to men. She and John Henderson had become engaged over the Christmas holidays.

"I don't fly. Do you?" Mariah asked. They looked at each other, then broke into giggles.

"I don't fly, either," Bethany admitted. "But we aren't going to let a little thing like the lack of a pilot stop us, are we? Not when we live in a town chock-full of them."

"You're absolutely right." Mariah's eyes lit up and she wagged her index finger. "Duke'll do it. He's scheduled for the mail run first thing in the morning and we'll tag along. Now, which of you girls is coming? No, *are* coming. No…"

There weren't any other volunteers. "Then it's just Beth and me. No, Beth and *I*…"

It was at this point that Bethany realized her friend was as tipsy as she was. "How will we get back?"

"I don't know," Mariah said, enunciating very carefully. "But where there's a way there's a will."

Bethany shut her eyes. That didn't sound exactly

right, but it was close enough to satisfy her. Especially when she was half-drunk and her heart dangled precariously from her sleeve.

"He doesn't love me, you know," she said, making her own confession.

"Mitch?"

It was time to own up to the truth, however painful.

"He cares for you, though." This came from Sally.

Bethany fingered the gold coin that hung from the delicate chain around her neck. The gift Mitch had given her for Christmas. Touching it now, she experienced a deep sense of loss.

"Mitch does care," she agreed in a broken voice, "but not enough."

Mariah looked at her with sympathy and asked with forced cheer, "Who wants to go to Ben's? A few laughs, a dance or two…"

Mitch lost count of the number of times he'd tried to reach Bethany by phone. He'd left Chrissie with a high school girl who lived next door and then walked over to Bethany's house. He stood on the tiny porch and pounded on the door until his fist hurt, despite the padding provided by his thick gloves.

Clearly she wasn't home. He frowned, wondering where she could possibly have gone.

Even as he asked the question, he knew. She'd gone to Ben's. Folks tended to let their hair down a bit on Friday and Saturday nights.

It wasn't uncommon to find Duke and John lingering over a cribbage board, while the other pilots shot the breeze, talking about nothing in particular. Every now and then, some of the pipeline workers would wander in on their way to Fairbanks for a few days of R and R. Things occasionally got a bit rowdy; Mitch had broken up more than one fight in his time. He didn't like the idea of Bethany getting caught in the middle of anything like that.

When he stepped into the Hard Luck Café, he found the noise level almost painful. He couldn't recall the last time he'd seen the place so busy.

He caught sight of Bethany dancing with Duke Porter. Mariah Douglas was dancing with Keith Campbell, a pipeline employee and friend of Bill Landgrin's. Mitch didn't trust either man.

Christian O'Halloran sat brooding in the corner, nursing a drink. Mitch noted that he was keeping a close eye on Mariah. Mitch suspected she wouldn't tolerate or appreciate Christian's interference and that Keith knew it and used it to his advantage.

Frowning, Mitch made his way into the room. He wanted to talk to Bethany, reason with her if he could. He understood her complaints far better than she knew. Her accusations had hit him like a…like a fist flying straight through time. Those were the words Lori had said to him day after day, week after week, month after month….

Before he'd really grasped that it was Bethany talking to him and not his dead wife, Bethany had left. He needed to explain to her that he *did* know what she was experiencing. He'd been through it himself.

In January, when daylight was counted in minutes instead of hours, people did feel trapped in their homes.

He wanted to sit down and tell her what had been burdening his heart for weeks now. Since Christmas.

He loved her. So much it terrified him. He wanted to tell her about Lori; he hadn't, simply because he was afraid of her response. Most of all, he wanted to tell her he loved her.

Bill Landgrin saw him, and they eyed each other malevolently. From the look of it, Bill was more than a little put out over their last meeting. Judging by the gleam in his eyes, he'd welcome a confrontation with Mitch.

Mitch wasn't eager for a fight, but he wouldn't back down from one, either.

Bill glanced from Mitch to Bethany and then back again. He set his mug on the counter and stomped over to the other side of the café, where Bethany was sitting, now that her dance with Duke was finished. Mitch started in her direction himself, scooting around tables.

Bill got there first.

"Beth, sweetie." Mitch heard the other man greet her. "How's about a dance?"

It seemed to Mitch that she was about to refuse, but he made the mistake—a mistake he recognized almost immediately—of answering for her.

"Bethany's with me," he said, his words as cold as the Arctic ice.

"I am?" she asked.

"She is?" Bill echoed. He rubbed his forehead as though to suggest he found it hard to believe Bethany would attach herself to the likes of Mitch. "Seems to me the lady can make her own decisions."

It took Bethany an eternity to decide. "I don't think one dance would hurt," she finally said to Bill.

Mitch's jaw hardened. He didn't blame her for defying him; he'd brought it on himself. But the fact that she'd dance with another man, for whatever reason, didn't seem right. Not when she'd said she loved *him!*

He sat down in the chair she'd vacated, and as he watched Bill draw Bethany into his arms, his temperature rose. He wasn't much of a drinker, but he sure could have used a shot of something just about then.

The song seemed to drone on for a lifetime. When he couldn't bear to sit any longer, Mitch got to his feet and restlessly prowled the edges of the dance area. Not once did he let his eyes waver from Bethany and Bill.

Something that gave him cause to rejoice was the fact that she didn't seem to be enjoying herself. Her gaze met his over Landgrin's shoulder, and she bit her lip in a way that told him she was sorry she'd ever agreed to this.

He resisted the urge to cut in.

Although Bethany was in another man's arms, Mitch found himself close to laughter. She'd said she loved him and in the same breath had called him an idiot. He was beginning to suspect she was right. He *was* an idiot. Love seemed to reduce him to that.

The song was finally over, and as Landgrin escorted Bethany to her table and reluctantly left her there, the tension eased from Mitch's body.

He made a beeline for her, regretting now that he hadn't been waiting for her when she returned. But he didn't want to give her reason to think he didn't trust her.

Unfortunately Keith Campbell reached her before he did. "A dance, fair lady?" Keith asked, bowing from the waist.

Mitch ended up cooling his heels again while Bethany frolicked across the dance floor in the arms of yet another man. While he waited, he ordered a soda and checked his watch.

He'd told Diane Hestead, the high school girl staying with Chrissie, that he wouldn't be more than an hour. He'd already been gone that long, and it didn't look like he'd be getting home any time soon.

With the music blaring, he used Ben's phone and made a quick call to tell Diane he'd be longer than expected.

"Bethany certainly seems to have captured a few hearts, hasn't she?" Ben commented, slapping Mitch good-naturedly on the back.

"I don't know why she needs to do that," he grumbled. "She's had mine for weeks."

"Does she know that?" Ben asked.

"No," Mitch blurted.

"What do you expect her to do, then?"

Ben was right, of course. Mitch returned to the table to wait for her. When the dance finished, he made sure he was there. "My turn," he announced flatly the minute the two of them were alone.

Bethany's eyes narrowed; she promptly ignored him and sat down. She finished her soda and set the glass aside.

"Let's dance," he said and held out his hand to her.

"Is that a request or a command?" she asked, staring up at him.

Mitch swallowed. This was going from bad to worse. "Do you want me to put on a little performance for you the way Keith did?"

"No," she answered simply.

It was now or never. "Bethany," he said, dragging

air into his lungs, "I love you. I have for weeks. I should've told you before."

She stared at him, her eyes huge. Then, as though she doubted his words, she hastily looked away. "Why now, Mitch?"

He could hardly hear her over the music. "Why now what?"

"Why are you telling me now?" she asked, clarifying her question. "Is it because you're overwhelmed by the depth of your feelings?" She sounded just a little sarcastic, he thought. "Or could the truth be that you can't bear to see me with another man?"

He frowned, not because he didn't understand her question, but because he wasn't sure how to answer. She had a point. He might well have been content to leave things as they were if he hadn't found her dancing with Landgrin.

"Your hesitation tells me everything I need to know," she whispered brokenly. She stood then, in such a rush that she nearly toppled the chair. "Duke," she called, hurrying toward the pilot. "Didn't I promise you another dance?"

Mitch ground his teeth in frustration.

He'd started toward the door when Bill Landgrin stopped him. "Looks like you're batting zero, my friend. Seems to me the lady knows what she wants, and it isn't you."

"I blew it," Bethany muttered miserably. She'd stayed behind and was helping Ben clear the remaining tables. Mariah had disappeared hours earlier after a confrontation with Christian, and she hadn't seen her since.

"What do you mean?"

"Mitch and me."

"What's with you two, anyway?" Ben asked as he set a tray of dirty glasses on the counter.

"I don't know anymore. I thought… I'd hoped…" She felt tongue-tied, unable to explain. Slipping onto the stool opposite Ben, she let her shoulders sag in abject misery. She was still feeling a little drunk—and a lot discouraged—not to mention suffering from a near-fatal bout of cabin fever.

"Here," Ben said, reaching behind the counter and bringing out a bottle of brandy. "I save this for special occasions."

"What's so special about this evening?" she asked.

"A number of things," he said, but didn't elaborate. He brought out a couple of snifters and poured a liberal amount into each. "This will cure what ails you. Guaranteed."

"Maybe you're right." At this point she figured a glass of brandy couldn't hurt.

"Cheers," Ben said and touched the rim of his glass to hers.

"To a special…friend," she said and took her first tentative sip. The liquid fire glided over her tongue and down her throat. When it came to drinking alcohol, Bethany generally stuck to wine and an occasional beer, rarely anything stronger.

Her eyes watered, and this time it had nothing to do with her emotions.

"You all right?" Ben asked, slapping her on the back.

She pressed her hand over her heart and nodded breathlessly. Her second and third sips went down far more easily than the first. Gradually a warmth spread out from the pit of her stomach, and a lethargic feeling settled over her.

"Have you ever been in love?" she asked, surprising herself by asking such a personal question. Perhaps the liquor had loosened her tongue; more likely it was the need to hear this man's version of his affair with her mother. This man who'd fathered her...

"In love? Me?"

"What's so strange about that?" she asked lightly, careful not to let on how serious the question really was. "Surely you've been in love at least once in your life. A woman in your deep, dark past maybe—one you've never been able to forget?"

Ben chuckled. "I was in the navy, you know."

Bethany nodded. "Don't tell me you were the kind of sailor who had a woman in every port?"

He grinned almost boyishly and cocked his head to one side. "That was me, all right."

Although she'd solicited it, this information disturbed Bethany. It somehow cheapened her mother and the love Marilyn had once felt for Ben. "But there must've been one woman you remember more than any of the others," she pressed.

Ben scratched his head as though to give her question heavy-duty consideration. "Nope, can't say there was. I liked to play the field."

Bethany took another sip of the brandy. "What about Marilyn?" she asked brazenly, throwing caution to the winds. "You do remember *her,* don't you?"

"Marilyn?" Ben repeated, a look of surprise on his face. "No... I don't recall any Marilyn." He sounded as though he'd never heard the name before.

Ben might as well have reached across the counter and slapped her face. Hard. She hurt for her mother, and for herself. Before she met him, she'd let herself imagine that her mother's affair with Ben had been a romantic relationship gone tragically awry.

In the past few weeks, she'd begun to think she shared a genuine friendship with Ben. A real bond. Because of that, she'd lowered her guard and come close to revealing her secret.

Bethany clamped her mouth shut. She wanted to blame the wine. The brandy. Both had loosened her tongue, she realized, but she'd been on the verge of telling him, anyway. She shook the hair out of her face and stared past him.

"Three years ago," she began resolutely, struggling to find the right words, knowing she couldn't stop now, "the doctors found a lump in my mother's breast."

"Cancer?"

Bethany nodded.

Ben glanced at his watch. "It's getting kind of late, don't you think?"

"This story will only take a couple more minutes," she promised, and to fortify her courage, she drank the rest of the brandy in a single gulp. It raged a fiery path down her throat.

"You were talking about your mother," Ben prodded, and it seemed he wanted her to hurry. Bethany didn't know if she could. Those weeks when her mother had been so sick from the chemotherapy had been the most traumatic of her life.

"It turned out that the cancer had spread," Bethany continued. "For a while we didn't know if my mother was going to survive. I was convinced that if the cancer didn't kill her, the chemo would. I was still in college at the time. My classes usually let out around two, and I got into the habit of stopping at the hospital on my way home from school."

Ben nursed his drink, his eyes avoiding hers.

"One day, after a particularly violent reaction to the treatment, Mom thought she was going to die. I tried to tell her she had to fight the cancer."

"Did she die?" Ben asked. For the first time since starting her story she had his full attention. Either she was a better storyteller than she realized, or Ben did remember her mother.

"No. She's a survivor. But that day Mom asked me to sit down because she had something important to tell me." At this point, Bethany paused long enough to steady herself. After all this time, the unexpectedness of her mother's announcement still shocked her.

"And?"

"My mother told me about a young sailor she'd loved many years ago. They'd met the summer before he shipped out to Vietnam. By the end of their time together, they'd become lovers. Their political differences separated them as much as the war had. He left because he felt it was his duty to fight, and she stayed behind and joined the peace movement, protesting the war every chance she had. She wrote him a letter and told him about it. He didn't answer. She knew he didn't approve of what she was doing."

"Whoever this person was, he probably didn't want to read about how she was trying to undermine his efforts in Southeast Asia," Ben said stiffly.

"I'm sure that's true." Bethany's voice quavered

slightly. "The problem was that when he refused to open her next letter, he failed to learn something vitally important. My mother was pregnant with his child."

The snifter in Ben's hand dropped to the floor and shattered. His eyes remained frozen on Bethany's face.

"I was that child."

The silence stretched to the breaking point. "Who took care of her?" he asked in a choked whisper.

"Her family. When she was about four months pregnant, she met Peter Ross, another student, and confided in him. They fell in love and were married shortly before I was born. Peter raised me as his own and has loved and nurtured me ever since. I never would've guessed.... It was the biggest shock of my life to learn he wasn't my biological father."

"Your mother's name is Marilyn?"

"Yes, and she named you as my birth father."

"Me," Ben said with a weak-sounding laugh. "Sorry, kid, but you've got the wrong guy." He continued to shake his head incredulously. "What'd your mother do—send you out to find me?"

"No. Neither of my parents know why I accepted the teaching contract in Hard Luck. I gave your name to the Red Cross, and they traced you here. I came to meet you, to find out what I could about you."

"Then it's unfortunate you came all this way for nothing," he said gruffly.

"It's funny, really, because we *are* alike. You know the way you get three lines between your eyes when you're troubled or confused? I get those, too. In fact, you're the one who mentioned it, remember? And we both like to cook. And we—"

"That's enough," he snapped. "Listen, Bethany, this is all well and good, but like I already said, you've got the wrong guy."

"But—"

"I told you before and I'll tell you again. I never knew any woman called Marilyn. You'd think if I'd slept with her, I'd remember her, wouldn't you?"

His words were like stones hurled at her heart. "I don't want anything from you, Ben."

"Well, don't count on a mention in my will, either, understand?"

She nearly fell off the stool in her effort to escape. She retreated a step backward. "I… I should never have told you."

"I don't know why you did. And listen, I'd appreciate it if you didn't go spreading this lie around town. I've got a reputation to uphold, and I don't want your lies—and your mother's—

besmirching my character."

Bethany thought she was going to be sick.

"It's a damn lie, you hear? A lie!"

"I'm sorry. I—I shouldn't have said anything," she stammered.

He didn't answer her right away. "I don't know anything about any Marilyn."

"I made a mistake," Bethany whispered. "A terrible mistake." She turned and ran from the café.

Ten

In all the years Mitch had lived in Hard Luck, he'd seen very few mornings when Ben wasn't open for business.

Mitch wasn't the only disgruntled one. Christian met him outside the café. "Do you think Ben might have overslept?"

Mitch doubted it. "Ben?" he asked. "Ben Hamilton, who says he never sleeps past six no matter what time he goes to bed?"

"Maybe he decided to take the day off. He's entitled, don't you think?" Christian asked.

Mitch had thought of that, too. "But wouldn't he put up a sign or something?"

Christian considered this, then said, "Probably." He frowned at his watch. "Listen, I'm supposed to meet Sawyer over at his place."

"Go ahead." It was clear Christian had the same fears as Mitch. Something was wrong. "I'll check things out and connect with you later," he promised.

Ben's apartment was situated above the café. Mitch had never been inside, and he didn't know anyone who had. Ben's real home was the café itself. He kept it open seven days a week and most holidays. Occasionally he'd post a Closed sign when he felt like taking off for a few days' fishing, but that was about it.

The Hard Luck Café was the social center of town, the place where people routinely gathered. Ben was part psychologist, part judge, part confidant and all friend. Mitch didn't know a man, woman or child in town who didn't like him.

Growing increasingly worried, Mitch went around to the back door that led to the kitchen. After a couple of tentative knocks, he walked into the dark, silent café. Flicking on the light switch, the first thing he noticed was shattered glass on the floor.

"Ben!" Mitch called out, walking all the way inside. Nothing.

The door to the stairs leading to Ben's apartment was open, and Mitch started up, his heart pounding in his ears. He paused halfway, afraid of what he might find. If Ben was dead, it wouldn't be the first time he'd come upon a body. The last had been when he'd found Lori.

He broke out in a cold sweat, and his breathing grew shallow. "Ben," he said again, not as loudly. It was another moment before he could continue upward.

The apartment itself was ordinary. A couch and television constituted the living room furniture. Small bath. Bedroom. Both doors had been left ajar.

"Ben?" he tried once more.

A moan came from the bedroom.

More relieved than words could express, Mitch hurried into the room. Ben was sprawled across the bedspread. It took him a full minute to sit up. He blinked as if the act of opening his eyes was painful.

"Are you all right?" Mitch asked.

Ben rubbed a hand down his face and seemed to give the question some consideration. "No," he finally said.

"Do you need me to call Dotty? Or take you to the clinic?"

"Hell, no. She can't do anything about a hangover."

"You're hung over?" To the best of his knowledge, Ben rarely drank.

Ben pressed both hands to his head. "Do you have to talk so blasted loud?" He grimaced at the sound of his own voice.

"Sorry," Mitch said in an amused whisper.

"Make yourself useful, would you?" Ben growled. "I need coffee. Make it strong, too. I'll be downstairs in a few minutes."

Mitch had the coffee brewing and had swept up the broken glass by the time Ben appeared, his eyes red-rimmed and clouded. His gaze shifted toward Mitch before he took a stool at the counter.

Mitch brought him a cup of coffee the minute it was ready.

"Thanks," Ben mumbled.

"I've never known you to get drunk," Mitch said conversationally, curious as to what had prompted Ben's apparent binge.

"First time in ten years or more," he muttered. "It was either that or... I don't know what. There didn't seem to be a whole lot of options. Fight, I guess, but there wasn't anyone around to punch. Not that it would've done any good, since I had no one to blame but myself. Damn, but I messed up."

"Can I help?" Mitch asked. He'd often gone to Ben for advice about something or other, including his feelings for Bethany. Most of his visits had been on the pretext of wanting a cup of coffee. It appeared that the tables were turned now—so to speak—and if he could assist Ben in some way, then all the better.

"Help me? No." Ben shook his head and instantly seemed to regret the movement. He closed his eyes and waited a moment before opening them again.

"You want me to make you breakfast?" Mitch asked. "I'm not a bad cook."

He couldn't tell whether Ben was taking his offer into consideration. Lowering his head, Ben muttered something Mitch couldn't hear.

Mitch leaned closer. "What did you say?"

"Have, ah…have you seen Bethany this morning?"

"No." He'd actually come to tell his friend what had happened between them last night and—once again— seek his advice.

"Have you tried calling?"

"No."

Ben gave a slight nod in the direction of the phone. "Call her, okay?"

Mitch looked at his watch. "It's a little early, isn't it?"

"Maybe, but try, anyway."

Mitch wasn't keen on the idea. "Is there anything in particular you'd like me to ask her?"

Ben propped his elbows on the counter and covered his face with both hands. He rubbed his eyes, and when he glanced at Mitch they seemed to glis-

ten. "I didn't know," he said in a frayed whisper. "I...
never knew."

"What didn't you know?" Mitch asked.

"Marilyn was pregnant."

Ben might as well have been speaking in a foreign
language for all the sense he made. "Who's Marilyn?"
Mitch asked in calm tones.

Ben dropped his hands. "Bethany's mother." He
paused. "Bethany's my daughter. I'm the reason she
came to Hard Luck, and when she told me... I pretended I never knew any Marilyn."

"You mean—"

"Yes!" Ben shouted, pounding his fist on the counter. "I'm Bethany's father."

Mitch swore under his breath.

"It was the shock. I... I never guessed. Maybe I
should have... I don't know."

Mitch sat on the stool next to Ben, feeling the
weight of his friend's burden as if it were his own.

"When she told me, I denied ever knowing her
mother and then—" his face contorted with guilt "—I
said some things I regret and sent Bethany away." Ben
wiped impatiently at his eyes. "She ran out of here,
and now I'm afraid she won't be back."

"I'll talk to her if you like." Although Mitch was
happy to make the offer, he didn't know if he'd be a
help or a hindrance. His own track record with Bethany wasn't exactly impressive.

"Would you?" Ben clung to Mitch's words like a
lifeline in a storm-tossed sea.

"Sure." Mitch needed to see her for his own reasons, anyway. "I'll do it right away," he said, eager
now to find her. They'd parted on such cool terms

Bethany might not be as eager for his company. But Mitch was willing to risk her displeasure. She needed him. When he'd been in pain and grief, she'd been there to comfort him. Ben's rejection must have left her reeling. Mitch suddenly understood how important it was to be the one to console her.

"Tell her..." Ben hesitated, apparently not knowing how to convey his message. "Tell her..." he began again, his voice weak. His eyes brightened and he drew in a deep, shuddering breath. "That I'm proud to have her as my daughter."

In Mitch's opinion, Bethany should hear those words from Ben himself.

Mitch left the café, and Ben was alone once more to deal with the pain and the guilt that had accompanied him most of the night. Even the brandy hadn't dulled the shock.

He had a daughter.

The words still felt awkward on his tongue. Getting used to the idea was going to require some doing. What bothered him most was the thought of Marilyn struggling alone, without him. It stung a little to know she'd married someone else so soon after his departure. But he couldn't blame her. What was she to do, pregnant with his child and unable to let him know?

Even if he'd learned the truth, he didn't think he could've helped her the way she needed. He might've been able to marry her. Maybe that could've been arranged. But he was at war, and it wasn't like he could call time-out while he dealt with his personal problems. The navy wouldn't have released him from his obligations because he got a college girl pregnant.

If there was any one thing Ben regretted most about the past, it was returning Marilyn's letter unopened. It hurt him almost to the point of being physically ill to think about her alone and pregnant, believing he didn't care. The truth of the matter was that he'd loved her deeply. It had taken him years to put his love for her behind him.

She'd done the right thing in marrying this other man, he decided suddenly. Ben wouldn't have been a good husband for her, or for any woman. He was too stubborn, too set in his own ways. It was easier to comfort himself with those reassurances, he realized, than deal with all the might-have-beens.

The fact was, he'd fathered this child. Except that Bethany wasn't a child. She was an adult, and a mighty fine one at that. Any man would be proud to call her daughter.

Bethany. Ben would give anything to take back the things he'd said to her. It was the shock. The fear, too, of her wanting something from him when he had nothing to give—emotionally or financially. He couldn't change the past or make up to Marilyn and Bethany for what he'd done—and hadn't done.

Ben poured a second cup of coffee in an attempt to clear his head. His temples still throbbed—enough to convince him not to seek solutions in a bottle again.

There was a knock at the front door. He'd forgotten that he'd left it locked. With a definite lack of enthusiasm, he shuffled across the café and unlatched the bolt. To his surprise, he saw it was Mitch.

"She's gone," Mitch announced, sounding like a man in a trance.

"Bethany gone? What do you mean, gone?"

"I just saw Christian. Duke flew her out this morning."

Pain shot through Ben's chest and he felt the sudden need to sit down. He'd only just found her and now—now he'd lost her.

The pizza had helped, Bethany decided, but not nearly enough. Sorry that Mariah had decided not to join her, after all, she sat on the big hotel bed in front of the television. She was halfheartedly watching a movie she'd seen before she'd left for Alaska and paying the same price as she had in a California theater.

Earlier in the day, she'd had her hair trimmed, and while she was at it, she'd sprung for a manicure.

Following that, she'd found a shopping mall and lingered for hours, just poking around the shops and watching the people. It didn't take long, however, for the doubts and regrets to crowd back into her mind.

She'd ruined everything. With Ben feeling the way he did, she wasn't comfortable returning to Hard Luck, and at the same time she couldn't leave. Not with everything between her and Mitch still unresolved. If the situation had been different, she could've phoned her parents, but of course neither of them knew the real reason she'd accepted the teaching assignment in Alaska. She hadn't wanted them to know.

What about Chrissie? And Susan and Scott and Ronny… She couldn't leave her students or break the terms of her contract. She had a moral and legal obligation to the people who'd hired her. The state and the town had entrusted her with these young lives. She couldn't just walk out.

On the other hand, how could she go back? It was

all she could do not to hide her face in her hands and weep. She had no idea what had possessed her to confront Ben with the truth last night. Her timing couldn't have been worse. The information had come at him with the stealth and suddenness of a bomb, exploding in his life. She hadn't prepared him in any way to learn she was his daughter.

No wonder he— Her thoughts came to a crashing halt at the loud knock on her door.

"Bethany."

"Mitch?"

"Please open up."

She didn't know how he'd learned where she was staying. She scrambled off the bed and ran to open the door.

He stood on the other side, feet braced, as though he was surprised he hadn't been forced to kick the door in. He blinked, then blurted, "Don't leave."

"Leave?" She followed his gaze to her small suitcase.

"You've packed your things."

True, but only for a short stay in Fairbanks. She wondered where Mitch thought she was going. Then she understood—he assumed she was returning to California.

"Give me one good reason to stay," she invited.

He walked past her and into the room. As he moved, he shoved his fingers through his hair. Unable to stand still, he paced the area like a man possessed.

"I love you, and I'm not saying that because there's another man wanting to dance with you. I'm saying it because I can't imagine living without you." He stopped, his eyes imploring. "I need you, Bethany. I didn't know how much until I discovered you were gone."

"You love me?"

"I haven't given you much reason to believe that, have I? There are reasons... I know you don't want to listen to excuses, and I don't blame you. Bethany, I'm not saying any of this for Chrissie. I need you for *me*. I love you for *me*." He paused and dragged in an uneven breath.

All at once it didn't seem fair to mislead him any further. "I'm not going anywhere," she confessed. "I was coming back, and when I did, I planned to work all of this out with you."

He closed his eyes as if a great weight had been lifted from him.

"I need to settle things with someone else, too," she said.

"Ben." His eyes held hers. "He wants to talk to you."

Bethany struggled to control her emotions before she asked, "He told you?"

Mitch nodded. "You're his daughter."

"He admitted that?" Her eyes welled with tears.

Again he nodded.

"Is he all right? I shouldn't have said anything—you don't know how much I regret it." She found it difficult to maintain her composure. "I shouldn't have confronted him the way I did. I can only guess what he must think. Please," she begged, "tell him I don't expect anything of him. I realize he lied, but I understand. I don't blame him. Who knows what any of us would have done in similar circumstances."

"He wants to talk to you himself."

"He doesn't need to say a word. I understand. Please assure him for me that I don't want anything from him," she said again.

"You can tell him yourself. He's here."

"Here?"

"Actually he's downstairs in the bar waiting. We tossed a coin to see which of us got to speak to you first. I won."

He gestured to the bed. "Please sit," he said. "This seems to be a time for confessions." Bethany obediently perched on the edge of the bed and looked up at him expectantly.

"There's something important you need to know about me," he said. "I should've told you sooner—I'm sorry I didn't. After I've told you, you can decide what you want to do. If you'd rather not see me again…well, you can decide that later."

"Mitch, what is it?"

He couldn't seem to stay in one place. "I love you, Bethany," he said urgently. "I'm not a man who loves easily. There's only been one other woman I've felt this strongly about."

"Your wife," she guessed.

"I—I don't know where to start." Mitch threw her a look of anguish.

"Start at the beginning," she coaxed gently, patiently. She'd waited a long time for Mitch to trust her enough to tell her about his past.

He resumed his pacing. "I met Lori while we were in college. I suppose our history was fairly typical. We fell in love and got married. I joined the Chicago Police Department, and our lives settled down to that of any typical young couple. Or so I thought."

He paused, and it seemed to Bethany that the light went out of his eyes.

"I see," she said quietly. "Go on."

Moving to stand in front of her, he said, "Chrissie was born, and I was crazy about her from the first. Lori wanted to be a good mother. I believe that, and I believe she tried. She honestly tried. But she was accustomed to being in the workforce and mingling with other people, and staying home with the baby didn't suit her. About this time, I was assigned to Narcotics. From that point, my schedule became erratic. I rarely knew from one week to the next what my hours would be."

He stared somewhere above her head, as if the telling of these details was too painful to do face-to-face.

"Lori became depressed. She saw her physician about it, and he explained that post-partum depression is fairly common. He prescribed something to help her feel better. He also gave her tranquilizers. A light dose to take when she had trouble sleeping."

"Did the medication help?"

"For a while, but then Lori found she couldn't sleep nights at all. Chrissie suffered from repeated ear infections, and Lori often had to stay awake with her, which added to the problem."

He frowned. "I don't know when she started doubling up on the tranquilizers, or even how she was able to get so many of them. I suspect she went to a number of different doctors."

Bethany held out her hand to him and Mitch gripped it hard between his own. Then he sat on the bed beside her, turning his body toward her. "What's so tragic about all of this is that over and over again

Lori told me how unhappy she was, how miserable. She didn't like being home. She didn't like staying with the baby all the time. She wanted me home more often. She clung to me until I felt she was strangling me, and all along she was so terribly sick, so terribly depressed."

"Did you know she was hooked on the tranquilizers?"

"I suppose I guessed. But I figured she was under a doctor's care—and I didn't want to deal with it just then. I couldn't. I was working day and night on an important case," he said, his eyes bleak with sorrow. "If she wanted to dope herself up at night with tranquilizers, what could I do? I'd cope with it when I could, but not then." He closed his eyes and shook his head. "You see, I might've saved her life had I dealt with the problem immediately, instead of ignoring it and praying she'd snap out of it herself."

"What happened?" Bethany asked. She intuitively realized there was more to the story, and that it would only grow worse.

"If the signs had been any plainer, they would've hit me over the head."

"It happens every day."

"I worked with addicts. I should've known."

It was clear that this was one thing Mitch would never forgive himself for.

"She killed herself," he said in a stark whisper. "Her family thought it was an accident, but I know better. She needed me, but I was too involved in chasing down drug dealers to help my own wife. She was depressed, unhappy and addicted to tranquilizers. I turned my back on her. I might as well have poured the pills down her throat."

"Oh, Mitch, you were under so much stress. You can't blame yourself."

"Yes, I can," he said, "and I have. I should've been able to tell what was happening to her. She paid the penalty for my neglect—with her life. I can understand if you don't want to marry me..."

"Is that what you're asking me, Mitch? To be your wife?"

"Yes." His gaze held hers. "I realize how much Chrissie loves you, but like I told you, it isn't for my daughter I'm asking. It's for me."

The lump in Bethany's throat refused to dissolve. She nodded and swallowed her tears.

"Is that a yes?" he asked, as if he was afraid of the answer.

She nodded again, more vigorously.

Mitch briefly closed his eyes. "I live a simple life, Bethany. I don't want to leave Hard Luck."

"I don't want to leave, either. My home is wherever you are."

"You're sure? Because I don't think I could let you go. Not now." He reached for her and kissed her with a hunger and a longing that left her breathless. A long time passed before he released her.

"We'd better stop while I still can," he told her. "Besides, Ben's waiting."

"Ben." She'd almost forgotten.

"He's downstairs bragging to the bartender about his daughter," Mitch said. "Would you like to join him there? I know he wants to talk to you."

"In a little while," she whispered and leaned her

head against his shoulder. They'd both come to Hard Luck for a purpose. His had been to hide; hers had been to find her biological father. Together they'd discovered something far more precious than the gold that had drawn generations of prospectors to Alaska.

They'd found each other. And together they'd found love.

Epilogue

Half an hour later, Bethany made her way into the dimly lit cocktail lounge and came upon Ben sitting alone at a table, nursing a bottle of beer. His shoulders slumped forward and his head was bowed. It looked, she thought sadly, as if the weight of nearly thirty years of regret rested solidly on his back.

He raised his eyes to meet hers when she walked over to his table. "Do you mind if I sit down?" she asked, feeling tentative herself. She understood that the way she'd confronted Ben had been a mistake; she wished more than anything that they could start over.

He nodded, his expression concerned as she slid out the chair and sat across from him.

"Do you want a drink?" he asked.

"No, thanks." The wine and brandy last night had loosened her tongue. She didn't want to repeat *that* mistake. "I'm so sorry…"

"I'm the one who's sorry," Ben cut in. "I'm not proud of the way I reacted yesterday—my only excuse is shock."

"I couldn't have done a worse job of it," she said.

His face tightened, and his eyes grew suspiciously bright. "It's so hard to believe I could have a daughter as beautiful as you, Bethany. My heart feels like it's going to bust wide open just looking at you."

Bethany smiled tremulously, close to tears herself.

"Your mother...the resemblance between you is striking. I didn't see it at first, but now I do." He took a swallow of his beer and Bethany suspected he did it to hide his emotion. He set the bottle back on the table. "How's Marilyn? The cancer?"

"She's better than ever, and there's no sign of the cancer recurring."

"She's...she's had a good life? She's happy?"

Bethany nodded. "Very happy. Mom and Dad have a good marriage. Like any relationship, it's had its ups and downs over the years, but they're still in love, and they're truly committed to each other." She paused and drew in a deep breath. "They don't know that I've— that I found you."

He lowered his head. "Do you plan on telling them?"

"Yes, and you can be assured I'll handle it a lot more diplomatically than I did with you. I accepted the teaching contract in Hard Luck because I knew you were here, but originally I'd never intended to tell you."

"Not tell me?"

"All I wanted was to get to know you, but once I'd done that, it didn't seem to be enough. We're very alike, Ben, in many important ways. But before I knew that, I was afraid of the kind of man you'd be."

He sipped from the beer bottle. "I'm probably a disappointment...."

"No," she rushed to tell him. "No! I'm *proud* to be your daughter. You're a warm, generous, caring person. Hard Luck Café is the heart of the community, and that's because of you."

"I can't be your father," Ben murmured. "Your mother's husband—Peter—he'll always be that."

"That's true. But you could be my friend."

His face brightened. "Yes. A special friend."

Bethany stretched her hand across the table and Ben squeezed her fingers. "Where's Mitch?"

"He's in the lobby waiting for us." Bethany smiled, and the happiness bloomed within her. "This seems to be a day for clearing the air."

Ben placed some money on the table and they walked out of the lounge. "Are you going to marry him?" he asked. "Put him out of his misery?"

"Oh, yes. I came to Hard Luck wanting to meet you, and instead I found *two* men I'll love for the rest of my life."

Mitch hurried toward them, and they met him halfway. Grinning widely, Ben slung an arm around their shoulders, drawing them close. "Well, my friends. This seems to be an evening to celebrate. Dinner's on me!"

* * * * *

BECAUSE OF THE BABY

Prologue

February 1996

She would always be his valentine, according to the card.

The man was a low-down, dirty rat! Furiously Karen Caldwell tossed the card into the garbage. She stood there in the middle of her kitchen, with the California sun pouring through her windows, and battled down tears.

Leave it to her ex-husband to do something like this. In the four years of their marriage Matt hadn't once bought her a valentine card. *Or* an anniversary card. Oh, no, he waited until they were divorced to do that. Waited until she was convinced he was finally out of her life—and her heart. Only then had he bothered to send her a card. A sweet, funny card celebrating a day meant for lovers. He'd purposely postponed contacting her until she'd managed to persuade herself she was almost happy.

Karen drew a deep, shaky breath, determined to put the man and his valentine out of her mind.

Her ex-husband infuriated her. This was just another example. Put a hundred, a thousand, of these examples together, and it explained why she'd divorced him. Matthew Caldwell was irresponsible. Thoughtless. Unreliable. In the four years of their marriage he'd changed careers four times. Four times!

Without fail, whenever she'd begun to think he'd finally found his niche, Matt would casually announce that he'd quit his job. Not once had he discussed his plans with her. He seemed to believe his decision was none of her concern.

Over and over he'd tell her he didn't know how unhappy he was until the moment he quit, as if that should be all the explanation she needed.

Giving his notice at Curtis Accounting had been the final straw. When that happened Karen had done the only sensible thing a woman could do in the circumstances. She left him.

No one blamed her, least of all Matt's family. His parents and sister were as exasperated with his penchant for shifting careers as she was herself.

Right after the divorce Karen had been offered the transfer to California. Leaving Alaska had sounded like a perfect solution, and it didn't hurt that a promotion went along with the relocation. The move would help her put the unpleasantness of her failed marriage behind her. Sunny California was just the distraction she needed.

Or so Karen had thought.

Now she wasn't so sure. She missed Alaska. Missed her friends. And…she missed Matt.

Karen avoided looking at the garbage can. Every time she thought of the valentine card, it made her mad. What irritated her most was that she knew he'd had to go out of his way to buy it.

Karen had been to Hard Luck, where Matt was living now. In a town that small, there wouldn't be anyplace that sold greeting cards. Matt would've had to order it by mail, or fly into Fairbanks.

He'd moved to Hard Luck because of the lodge—his latest folly.

Karen rolled her eyes. Her ex-husband had used the trust fund his grandmother had left him to purchase the burnedout lodge from the O'Halloran brothers. What Karen had gathered from a conversation with his sister, Lanni, was that Matt had begun to renovate it and hoped to attract tourists. Tourists north of the Arctic Circle!

But then, it made as much sense as anything else Matt had done in the past few years. If he wanted to waste his inheritance on another one of his grand schemes, *she* wouldn't try to stop him. Besides, it was none of her business.

When she couldn't stand it anymore Karen pulled the valentine out of the garbage. Below the printed message, he'd written "love" and his name.

Tears blurred her eyes. If this was how she reacted to a simple card, what would happen at the wedding? Lanni had asked Karen to serve as her maid of honor, and Karen had said yes.

True, it might be a bit uncomfortable, since Matt would be at the wedding, too, but Lanni had assured her that she'd discussed the situation with him. Matt hadn't objected. They might be divorced, but they were both adults.

It had been eighteen months since she'd last seen

her ex-husband. The wedding wouldn't be so bad, Karen decided. She'd smile a lot and let him know how happy she was. How much she liked California. How well she was doing at her job.

She'd make sure she looked her best, too. Lose five pounds, get her hair trimmed, buy some new clothes. After one glance, he'd be ready to hand her his heart on a silver platter.

And Karen? She'd hand it right back.

One

"She's just beautiful," Pearl Inman whispered to Matt as his sister walked down the center aisle, escorted by their proud father. "A perfect spring bride."

"Yes, she is," Matt agreed, but his eyes weren't on Lanni. He hadn't been able to stop watching Karen from the moment she'd entered the church.

Matt had been too busy getting the lodge ready for his first guests to pay much attention to his sister's wedding. He knew Lanni had asked his ex-wife to be her maid of honor. He'd gone so far as to assure her it didn't matter to him. He'd managed to sound downright nonchalant about it, too.

It wasn't any big deal, he'd told Lanni. Their marriage was over. Finished. Kaput. Nope, it wouldn't bother him if Karen came to Hard Luck. He didn't plan to give it another thought.

All right, if he was being honest—and he should be, since he was in a church—he *had* thought about Karen coming to Hard Luck. Okay, so he'd counted the days. The hours. The minutes. But he wasn't going to beat himself up because of it. They'd been married for four years and divorced nearly two. It was only natural he'd be anxious about seeing her.

To his dismay, Matt soon discovered he was completely unprepared for the emotional impact of being with Karen again.

Especially at a wedding.

She was so beautiful. His heart ached just from looking at her. She wore an elegant rose-colored dress that was perfect for her tall, lithe frame. A halo of flowers circled her glossy brown hair and Matt was convinced he'd never seen a more beautiful maid of honor.

A more beautiful woman.

The church was packed. It surprised and pleased Matt that Lanni and Charles had decided to be married in Hard Luck. He'd assumed his sister would choose Anchorage, where the majority of their friends and family lived. When he'd asked her, Lanni said she'd chosen Hard Luck since this was where she and Charles would make their home. She'd met and fallen in love with Charles O'Halloran here, so it seemed fitting to have the wedding here, as well. In time, Lanni hoped to start a community newspaper, but until Hard Luck was large enough to support a weekly, she'd be content to write freelance articles.

Matt was happy for his sister. He didn't doubt that Charles and Lanni were deeply in love. But watching them together had been almost painful. Their closeness, their delight in each other—he remembered what those feelings were like. Before his marriage fell apart...

With an effort Matt pulled his gaze away from Karen.

This winter had been long and bleak, with only his hopes for the lodge to sustain him.

At least the wedding was a bright spot, midway between the Christmas holidays and Alaska's summer months. It would be another six weeks before the snow melted. Another month before he got any response to the advertising he'd sent to travel agencies around the country.

Matt had risked a whole lot more than his inheritance in buying the lodge. He closed his eyes, refusing to allow any worries to crowd his mind. On the positive side, every room had been booked for tonight. Never mind that his guests were family and friends and that he wasn't getting a dime for his hospitality. Never mind that his ex-wife was one of those guests.

The wedding was a sort of dry run for the lodge. Unfortunately the kitchen wasn't in working order yet, but he'd have everything up and running by mid-June. Just in time to welcome his first real customers.

Love. Honor. As Charles O'Halloran repeated his vows, Matt felt a wrenching ache in his chest. He'd purposely let his thoughts wander in the attempt to avoid just this.

The marriage vows were a painful reminder of how he'd failed Karen. Difficult as it was to admit, he'd never been the right husband for her. She wanted a man who was content to hold down a nine-to-five job. A husband who'd work forty years for the same company and retire with a decent pension.

Matt had tried to give her the stability she craved. But it hadn't worked. Within months of taking on a job, he'd grow restless and bored. He'd always brought hard work and creativity to every new position; if he put that kind of effort into something, Matt wanted to be the one who profited from the outcome. Karen had never understood or appreciated that.

Lanni's sweet voice echoed Reverend Wilson's words. His sister's eyes lovingly held her husband's. It was a poignant moment, and more than one person was fighting back tears. Charles and Lanni had bridged the pain and anger of two families to find happiness. The O'Hallorans and Catherine Fletcher— his and Lanni's grandmother—had become bitter and enduring enemies when Charles's father married another woman. But the enmity was over now. And it was largely due to Lanni, Matt reflected, looking at her with pride.

Despite all his resolve, his eyes wandered back to Karen. Her head was bowed as if she, too, had a hard time listening to the exchange of vows.

They hadn't spoken since her arrival in Hard Luck. He didn't think she was deliberately staying out of his way, but he couldn't be sure. Her flight had landed in Fairbanks early that morning; Sawyer O'Halloran had picked her up, along with the other two bridesmaids, who'd flown in from Anchorage. The three women had been closeted with Lanni ever since, getting ready for the wedding.

He knew Karen was scheduled to fly out first thing the next morning. But for this one night she'd be sleeping in the lodge. *His* lodge.

Matt had made sure when he assigned the rooms that Karen got the most elaborate one. The one with the big brass bed and feather mattress. He'd polished the hardwood floor himself until it shone like new. Matt wondered if she'd guess all the trouble he'd gone to—then decided he didn't want her to know.

The ceremony was soon over, and Matt heaved a sigh of relief. Nothing like a wedding to remind him of his own shortcomings in the husband department. In failing Karen, he'd failed himself.

He and Karen had once been as much in love as Lanni and Charles. In fact, he'd still loved her when she left him and filed for divorce. And despite everything, he loved her now.

His jaw tightened as he remembered the night he'd come home to find she'd packed her bags and moved out—and then had him served with divorce papers. It rankled to this day that she hadn't so much as talked to him first.

He'd asked her about that once, and she'd shrugged as if it was of little concern. She had warned him, she'd said. Besides, he'd never talked to *her* about quitting his jobs. Now it was his turn to see how it felt.

In all these months his bitterness hadn't faded. It would be best if they didn't talk to each other, Matt decided. Nothing would be served by dredging up the past, especially when that was all they had to discuss.

Music crescendoed, filling the church as Lanni and Charles turned to greet their guests. His sister's face radiated happiness. Arm in arm, the couple strolled down the aisle.

Karen followed with Sawyer O'Halloran, one of Charles's younger brothers. It didn't escape Matt's notice that his ex-wife did everything humanly possible *not* to look in his direction.

So she didn't want any eye contact? Well, he wasn't

too keen on it himself. This whole affair was difficult
enough without their having to confront each other.
He'd managed to get through the wedding; now all he
needed to do was survive the reception. That shouldn't
be so difficult.

It took Matt all of ten minutes to retract those
words.

He delayed going to the school gymnasium, where
the reception was being held, as long as he could. By
the time he arrived, the music had started and a half-
dozen couples were already in the area cleared for
dancing.

The first person Matt saw was Karen—dancing with Duke Porter, one of the pilots for Midnight
Sons, the Arctic flight service owned and run by the
O'Hallorans. The sight of another man with his arms
around Karen made Matt so damn mad he walked
directly over to the bar and downed a glass of champagne. He knew that getting drunk wouldn't serve any
useful purpose, but it might help cut the pain—or so
he told himself. This probably wasn't the first time a
man had held her since their divorce, but it was the
only time he'd been around to witness. He didn't like
the experience one bit.

"Where were you?" The question came from his
mother, Kate. "I was beginning to get worried."

"I'm fine." It was another moment or two before
he could force himself to stop looking at Karen and
Duke. "I, uh, was making sure everything was ready
at the lodge."

"Your aunt Louise is looking for you."

Matt didn't bother to disguise a groan. "Mother,
please, anyone but Aunt Louise." The first thing his

meddling aunt would do was quiz him about his divorce. Matt figured he'd need more than one glass of champagne if he was going to be trapped in a conversation with his father's oldest sister. He doubted an entire bottle would fortify him for Aunt Louise and her shamelessly prying questions.

His rescue came from the most unlikely source. Chrissie Harris, eight-year-old daughter of Mitch, the town's public safety officer.

"Will you dance with me?" the child pleaded, widening her dark, seal-pup eyes.

"Sure thing, kiddo." He grinned. The kid's timing couldn't have been better.

"Dad's dancing with Bethany," Chrissie explained, sounding a little disappointed. "Dad and Bethany are getting married this summer."

Great, another wedding. "I know."

"I think Scott would like to ask me, but he's afraid." Scott was Sawyer O'Halloran's adopted ten-year-old son—one of his wife's two children by a previous marriage.

Matt held out his arms. "Well, we can't let the prettiest girl here be a wallflower," he said. Mitch's daughter slipped off her patent-leather Mary Janes and stepped onto the tops of his shoes. He waltzed her from one end of the dance floor to the other. For a whole minute, perhaps longer, he was able to enjoy the dance without thinking of Karen.

However, his pleasure was short-lived. The next time he happened to catch sight of her, Karen was with Christian O'Halloran, Charles and Sawyer's younger brother. At the end of the dance, Matt thanked Chrissie and refilled his glass.

The second glass of champagne gave him enough courage to approach his ex-wife. It was ridiculous to pretend they weren't aware of each other.

Karen was sitting, no doubt for the first time since the music had started. He picked up two full champagne glasses and walked over to her. Although she wasn't looking in his direction, she knew he was coming. Matt could tell by the way her body stiffened.

"Hello, Karen," he said evenly.

"Matt."

He handed her one of the glasses and took the empty seat beside her. "You look like you could use a drink."

"Thanks."

Neither seemed to have anything more to say. Matt struggled to find some safe, neutral topic.

"How's California?" he finally asked.

She stared into the champagne as if she expected to see her response written in the bottom of the glass. "Wonderful."

"You look good." It was best to begin with a compliment, he figured; besides, it was the truth. She looked fantastic.

"You, too."

It was nice of her to lie. He'd lost fifteen pounds because he'd been working his butt off for months. He rarely got enough sleep and wasn't eating properly.

She took a sip of champagne, then asked, "Why'd you mail me a valentine card?" He thought her voice shook ever so slightly.

He'd regretted sending that stupid thing the moment he slipped it in the mailbox. If there'd been a way to retrieve it, he would have.

"We were married for four years," she said, "and not once in all that time did you buy me a card."

He didn't have an argument, so he said nothing.

"You claimed cards were silly commercial sentiments, remember?"

He wasn't likely to forget.

"Why this year?" she demanded, and the tremble in her voice was more apparent than ever.

"Maybe I was trying to make up for the years I didn't give you one." It wasn't much of an explanation, but the only one he had to offer. When he hadn't heard back from her—not that he'd expected to—Matt knew she hadn't appreciated the gesture.

"Don't mail me any more...sentiments, Matt. It's too little and it's much too late."

He frowned. "Fine, I won't."

They both stood up, eager to escape each other. Unfortunately they came face to face with his aunt Louise. Karen looked to Matt to rescue her, but he was fresh out of ideas.

"Dance, you two."

Aunt Louise issued the order like a drill sergeant. The woman always did enjoy meddling in other people's affairs. It was either obey her dictates or be trapped in a thirty-minute question-and-answer ordeal.

Karen glanced at Matt; he shrugged. "Shall we?" he asked, motioning toward the dance floor. Judging by the look she gave him, Karen had weighed her choices and decided that dancing with him was the lesser of two evils.

Matt had often observed that when one thing went wrong, others were sure to follow. The music, which to this point had been fast and lively, abruptly changed to something slow and soft. Matt couldn't avoid touching Karen, nor could he avoid holding her close.

He slipped his arm around her waist and she held herself stiffly in his embrace. Matt did his utmost to concentrate on the music and not on the woman in his arms.

He could feel her reluctance with every step.

"Don't worry," he whispered, "I promise not to bite."

"Your bites don't worry me."

"What does?" he asked.

"Everything else."

He smiled to himself and unconsciously moved his head closer to hers until his jaw pressed against her temple. Matt never had been light on his feet, but when he danced with Karen he somehow managed to look as though he knew what he was doing. It was as though they were born partners.

Neither spoke for the rest of the dance. The second the music stopped he released her and stepped back. The ache in his chest intensified, and he wondered how much longer he'd have to stay at the reception. He didn't want to slight his sister and brother-in-law, but being with Karen was pure agony. Pretending he didn't still love her was becoming impossible.

"Lanni and Charles are getting ready to leave," Karen said quickly. He sensed that she felt as awkward as he did. "I'd better see if she needs my help."

"Thanks for the dance."

Her eyes briefly met his and filled with an unmistakable sadness. "It was good to see you again, Matt," she mumbled, then hurried away.

Much as he longed to escape, Matt observed the

proprieties—he kissed his sister and shook hands with Charles. They were honeymooning in the Virgin Islands for two weeks. He wished them a great trip, made the rounds to say his farewells and returned to the lodge.

Because he felt about as low as he ever had since his divorce, he brought out a dusty bottle of whiskey and poured himself a stiff drink. He didn't drink a lot, but there were times when little else would do.

This was one of those times.

He sat on the leather sofa in front of the massive stone fireplace, his feet propped up on the raised hearth. He held the glass in one hand and the bottle in the other.

Soon his guests began to arrive. His parents came in first. It had been a long, exhausting day, and after a few words of greeting, they wandered up the stairs. The two bridesmaids followed and then another couple, married friends of Lanni's.

Karen was the last to show up. Matt didn't ask who'd escorted her to the lodge. Probably Duke, but he didn't want to hear that.

She paused in the large hall and looked around. Plenty of work remained to be done, but it was a pleasant, inviting room. Besides the sofa, Matt had set a couple of big overstuffed chairs close to the fireplace. The other half of the room was set up with hardwood tables and chairs.

"This is very nice," Karen said, sounding surprised.

"Thanks." He'd worked hard, getting this place in presentable shape. For just a moment he wondered what she'd thought when she heard he'd purchased the lodge. Years before, a fire had destroyed much of the kitchen, plus a number of rooms upstairs.

After the fire, the O'Hallorans had boarded up the place, unable to decide what to do with it. So the lodge had sat vacant and deteriorating for years. None of the brothers was interested in running a tourist business, and repairs would've been costly and time-consuming.

"Your room's at the top of the stairs. The farthest one down on the left-hand side." He gestured with the shot glass, afraid that if he stood, he might fall over.

"You've been drinking." Karen moved closer to the fireplace.

"Nothing gets past you, does it?" he muttered sarcastically.

"You hardly ever drink." The problem was, she knew him too well.

"That's true, but sometimes the occasion calls for it." He raised his glass to her with a sardonic smile and gulped down the last of the whiskey. It burned its way down his throat. He squeezed his eyes shut, clenched his teeth and shook his head like a wet dog.

When he opened his eyes Karen sat on the other end of the sofa. "What's wrong?" she asked—as if she didn't know.

"Nothing," he answered cheerfully. "What could possibly be wrong?"

She didn't make the obvious reply. "I think I must've had a little more to drink than usual myself." Her eyes seemed unnaturally bright.

She got up and headed toward the stairs, and Matt realized he didn't want her to leave. "Do you want to see what I've spent the last few months doing?" he asked.

"Sure." Her eager response surprised him.

He gave her a quick tour of the downstairs area, pointing out the renovations as he did. He was pleased with them and didn't conceal his pride. "The kitchen should be ready soon," he explained when he'd finished showing her around. "The stove's what's holding me up, but I expect delivery in the next month or so."

"Who's going to do the cooking?" she asked.

"Right now, me." Matt shrugged. "I don't have the budget to hire anyone else. At least not yet. I need to bring in paying guests first."

"Well, you're certainly qualified to cook."

She was referring to his stint as a chef. He'd enjoyed cooking school well enough, but had lost interest during his first restaurant job. He'd gone on to commercial fishing shortly after that, abandoning his sketchy plans to open a restaurant of his own.

"I wish you the very best with this venture, Matt."

"Thanks." He knew he sounded flippant.

"I mean that," she insisted.

He'd probably offended her, and he hadn't meant to. "But you don't believe it'll last, do you?"

"No." She didn't so much as hesitate. "You'll get bored with the lodge just like you did with everything else."

"Maybe." He wasn't going to argue with her. Time would prove her wrong. He'd worked harder on this than anything he'd done in his life. Now, finally, he had something that was entirely his. The business would sink or succeed by his own efforts, no one else's.

"I'll show you to your room," he said without emotion, then led her to the staircase.

He hadn't gone more than a few steps when she stopped him. "Matt." His arm tingled where her fingers touched him. "I apologize—I didn't mean to discourage you. I can tell you've put a lot of thought and effort into this lodge. I hope it succeeds. I really do."

He turned to face her. "Do you, Karen?"

Her eyes had never been more intent. In them he found a reflection of the loneliness he'd felt these past eighteen months. He hadn't wanted to admit, even to himself, how much he'd missed her. For months he'd worked himself into a state of exhaustion, rather than face a night without her.

This evening, for the first time since their divorce, he was forced to admit how good it was to hold her. He couldn't deny how empty his arms felt without her. How empty his *life* felt.

Her face was slightly flushed. She still wore the rose-colored dress.

"I've missed you, Karen." She must know what it had cost him to admit that.

Her eyes drifted shut, and when she spoke her voice was so low the words were hardly discernible. "I've missed you, too."

His breath caught in his throat, and Matt figured if he didn't touch her soon he'd die. He raised his hand and cradled her cheek with his callused palm. She was so smooth, so soft.

Karen moistened her lips.

It was the invitation Matt had been waiting for. He drew her toward him, and to his surprise, to his delight, she came without resistance.

He was almost afraid to kiss her, fearing she'd pull away from him, fearing she'd throw the past in his face. Karen did neither. When she brought her arms up to circle his neck, Matt nearly shouted for joy.

He didn't give her time to object. His kiss was raw with need. He'd intended to be gentle, to coax her, but it wasn't what either of them wanted. He possessed her mouth. No other word described their kiss. His lips slanted over hers, twisting, seeking, *urgent*.

Controlling the kiss was beyond him. Matt didn't know how long it went on. Too long. *Much* too long. When he did find the strength to ease his mouth from hers, they were both breathless.

He held her and waited for her to say something. Like telling him he shouldn't have done that. Perhaps she expected an apology. If so, she wouldn't be getting one.

He felt her shift, and afraid that she was about to move out of his arms, he tightened his grip. She snuggled close to him, creating a new kind of torture. They'd been intimate too many years for him not to be affected by the sensation of her body against his.

When she ran her tongue along the underside of his jaw Matt finally stepped back. They stared at each other. Neither spoke, and he suspected it was because they each feared what the other would say. Her lips were moist and slightly swollen; her breath came in soft, disjointed gasps, as if she was struggling not to weep. His own was ragged and made a light hissing sound through his clenched teeth.

He kissed her again and this time forced himself to keep it slow and gentle. But when he ended the kiss the sensual impact had stripped him of all his painfully gathered control. He pulled her close against him.

"I never was much good at these games," he said, his eyes holding hers.

"Games?"

"You know what I mean."

She lowered her lashes and her face filled with color.

"Don't expect me to silently lead you into my bedroom," he said. "If we're going to make love, I need to know you want me as much as I want you."

Still she said nothing.

"What's it going to be, Karen? You can share my bed or go upstairs alone." The temptation to kiss her again was strong, but he resisted.

Tears brightened her eyes, and she bit her lower lip. "I don't want to be alone," she whispered.

He shook his head. "That's not good enough. Tell me you want me."

"Yes," she said stiffly, "I want you, Matt. I've missed you."

Two

Karen awoke with Matt's arm securely tucked around her waist. In the carefree state between sleep and complete wakefulness, she reveled in the comfort of being held in her husband's arms.

Husband.

It took her far longer than it should have to remember that he *wasn't* her husband. Not anymore. Her eyes flew open as her brain started putting together the events of the night before.

The wedding.

She was in Hard Luck for Lanni and Charles's wedding. She should never have agreed to serve as Lanni's maid of honor. That had been her first mistake. The divorce had been final for more than eighteen months. Karen had thought, no, hoped that any lingering emotion she carried for Matt was long dead. Her reaction to the valentine card should have told her otherwise. If she'd had any common sense at all, she would've phoned Lanni and begged off. Instead, she'd set out to prove she was over Matt.

She'd proved that, all right—by spending the night

with him. Mortified, Karen closed her eyes and forced back a sob. She'd had more to drink than usual, but she hadn't been even close to drunk.

She wanted to blame Matt for this. In fact, she'd feel a whole lot better if she could accuse him of seducing her, of luring her into his bedroom. But bless his black heart, he'd made sure she knew exactly what she was doing before they'd gone to bed.

The lovemaking had been incredible. It had always been good between them, but she'd forgotten just *how* good. They'd been so hungry for each other, so needy.

Afterward, Matt had held her in his arms and she'd wept. Not because she felt any regrets—she hadn't, not then. But because she had to admit how miserable she'd been without him. It wasn't fair; she loved him so much, yet she realized how wrong they were for each other. Just as her own mother must have realized at some point how wrong her own marriage had gone, how mismatched she and Karen's father were. Yet she'd steadfastly hung on for reasons Karen had never understood.

She and Matt had such contradictory expectations and needs. She had to have some predictability in her life, some certainty. He preferred just to drift along, following his whims. Of course, she hadn't known, when she first met him, that he'd have trouble staying in a job. It wasn't until after they were married that he'd started his pattern of changing from one occupation to the next. Karen had felt blindsided.

Every time Matt quit a job, Karen faced an unhappy memory from her childhood. Her father had shared the same lack of ambition. Her mother's meager paycheck had supported the family. It wasn't that Eric

Rocklin was lazy; far from it. His garden had been the neighborhood showpiece, and his model airplanes won contests. He was a good father, an attentive husband, a decent person.

His one failing was his inability to keep a job.

Her family had declared bankruptcy when Karen and her brother were in high school. One of her most humiliating memories was of the time her friends were visiting and two men came to repossess the family car. Later they were turned out of their rental house.

From the moment she introduced them, Matt and her father had gotten along famously. Now Karen knew why. As the saying goes, they were two peas in a pod.

Wearily she closed her eyes. She refused to make the same mistakes her mother had, refused to allow her husband's weakness to destroy her future. Painful though it was, she'd taken the necessary steps to correct the problem and get on with her life.

One small lapse wasn't the end of the world. It was only natural, she decided, to still have feelings for Matt. He was a gracious, compassionate person. And she was undeniably attracted to him. But he wasn't right for her. She resolved to put their night together behind her and go back to California, her lesson learned. The farther away she was from Matt, the safer she'd be.

As carefully as she could, Karen folded back the covers and slipped one leg over the edge of the mattress. She eased herself out from under Matt's arm and glanced around for something to cover herself. She caught sight of her dress, carelessly discarded in last night's haste; it lay crumpled on the floor across the room. She blushed, remembering how eager they'd been for each other. They hadn't been able to remove their clothes fast enough.

"Mornin'," Matt rolled onto his back, stretched his arms high above his head and yawned.

Karen rolled back into bed, covered herself with the sheet and ground her teeth in frustration. She'd hoped to be gone by the time Matt awoke.

Her ex-husband slid over to her side and propped up his head with one hand. "Did I ever tell you how beautiful you look in the morning?"

"No." She wanted to groan aloud. It would have saved them both a lot of embarrassment if she could've silently slunk away.

"Then let me correct that error." Brushing the hair from her face, he bent forward to kiss her. "You're beautiful in the morning. You brighten my life, Karen. Without you—"

"Don't say it. Please don't say it."

"Don't say it?"

"Last night was a mistake," she said coldly.

Matt looked stunned. "That's not what you said when—"

"I was drunk," she interrupted him, offering the first excuse that came to mind, although she'd already rejected it earlier.

He laughed harshly. "And pigs fly. Neither of us had *that* much to drink."

"But enough—"

"Yes," he said, "enough to loosen our inhibitions. It was a good thing, too, because we belong together, Karen. I never did understand why you left me."

His words reminded her of the decision she'd already made—the decision to leave again. And why. "That says it all, don't you think?"

He ignored her question, something he'd done often. "Sure, you were upset about me quitting my job, but I hated it. Would you really want me to continue working someplace that made me miserable?"

"Yes!" she cried. It was too late for this, but he'd provoked her the way he always had. "If it was the first time I wouldn't have cared, although you might've talked it over with me, but it *wasn't* the first time. It was the fourth time in as many years, and now you're running a lodge. You'll never find the perfect job. Twenty years from now you'll still be searching for a career that suits you. Nothing's going to change."

"Come off it, Karen. I'm only thirty-one."

"I don't have the time or energy to argue with you." There was no other option, so she tossed the sheets aside and hurried across the room to retrieve her dress. With the zipper in the back, she had two choices— to either ask him to close it for her, or scurry to her room with the dress gaping open. She chose the latter.

"All right, all right," he muttered, lying on his back and staring up at the ceiling. "I don't want to argue with you, either."

As fast as she could, Karen collected the rest of her things, stuffing them in her arms.

"You aren't leaving, are you?" He sounded shocked.

"Yes." The sooner she retreated to her room, the better. Then she'd change clothes and get out of here.

"What about last night?"

Karen didn't know what to tell him. "Let's say it was for old times' sake."

He frowned. "Do you do this sort of thing often?"

It would have hurt less if he'd punched her in the stomach. "That was a cheap shot, Matt, and unworthy of you. You've been my only lover and you know it." Then, with as much dignity as she could marshal, she marched barefoot out of his bedroom. Halfway up the stairs she met Matt's parents. They stared at her, mouths open.

"Good morning." She greeted them as if she were dressed for a church meeting, ignoring the panty hose and underthings bunched in her arms.

"Karen." Matt's father nodded; his mother managed a belated "Good morning."

As she continued up the stairs, Karen heard Kate call out to her son. "Matt, is everything all right with you and Karen?"

Matt didn't respond right away. "Nothing's changed."

His father's warm chuckle followed Karen into her room. "You could've fooled me."

Two hours later, Karen was sitting in the Midnight Sons mobile office, waiting for a pilot to fly her out of Hard Luck. She studied the worn floor, impatient to be gone and fully aware of why.

Matt made her weak when she believed she was strong.

Pressing her hands to her face, Karen closed her eyes and drew several deep breaths. It was better for them both that she lived in California now. The temptation to be with him would be too great if she stayed in Alaska. Even Anchorage, hundreds of miles from Hard Luck, was too close.

Sick at heart, Karen willed herself to forget the night with Matt. Before she knew it, she'd be back in Oakland where she belonged.

Paragon, Inc., the engineering company she worked for, had been more than generous in giving her time off to attend Lanni's wedding, but now she had to prove to her boss, Mr. Sullivan, that he'd invested the company's money wisely when he promoted her. She'd throw herself into the job, and she'd forget Matt once and for all.

Her heart ached at the thought of him. She did wish him well. Contrary to what he might believe, she wanted him to succeed. She just didn't think he would. If Matt was anything like her father, and he was, he'd find some way to sabotage himself. Only she refused to be like her mother, refused to stick around and pick up the pieces. She'd gotten out while she could and was determined to make a better life for herself.

To be on the safe side, Karen decided to curtail any contact with his family. It would be difficult, though. Karen loved Matt's parents as much as she did her own. They were wonderful, caring, loving people, and Lanni was like the sister she'd never had.

If this wedding had taught Karen anything, it was that she'd never get Matt out of her life if she clung to his family.

That decision made, she swallowed her disappointment and resolved to make more of an effort to meet new people once she got back to California.

Matthew Caldwell wasn't the only attractive man in the world.

* * *

"You're looking a little down in the dumps," Ben Hamilton, owner of the Hard Luck Café, said as he automatically filled Matt's coffee mug.

"What do you expect the day after a wedding?" Matt returned, fending off Ben's inquisitiveness. Matt hadn't come to socialize, but to escape.

His parents had been full of questions after seeing Karen parade barefoot up the stairs in the dress she'd worn to the wedding. Where she'd spent the night was all too obvious.

"I must say your sister made a mighty pretty bride," Ben said casually.

Matt cupped the thick ceramic mug with both hands. "Thanks."

"Two weddings in Hard Luck within a year. Now that's something."

Matt merely grunted in reply.

"Mitch and Bethany set their wedding date for this summer," Ben added conversationally.

Mitch Harris, the public safety officer—usually described as "the law around here"—and teacher Bethany Ross had announced their engagement earlier in the winter. Leave it to Matt to settle in a community where Cupid had run amuck. While he was divorced and miserable, everyone around him was stumbling all over themselves, falling in love. Not Matt. Once was enough for him, and the worst of it was, he still loved Karen.

"Bethany and Mitch's wedding's going to be in San Francisco, but we're throwing a big reception for them when they come back from their honeymoon."

San Francisco was across the bay from Oakland. Karen lived in Oakland.

Karen. Karen. Karen.

No matter what he said or did, everything seemed to point back to Karen. At this rate he'd never be free of her.

Was that what he wanted, though?

Ben wiped the perfectly clean counter with slow, methodical strokes, patiently waiting for Matt to confide in him. Matt was well aware that a lot of the men in Hard Luck used Ben Hamilton as a sounding board. He was the kind of guy who made it easy to talk about one's troubles, but Matt wasn't interested. He wasn't in the mood to talk to anyone. About anything.

He was half tempted to take his coffee and move to one of the tables. He might have, if Duke Porter hadn't chosen that moment to walk into the café. The bush pilot sidled up to the stool next to his and sat down.

Matt glared at the other man.

Duke glared back. "What's your problem?"

It was unreasonable and irrational to take his frustration out on Duke just because he'd had the gall to dance with Karen. "I've got woman troubles."

Duke snorted. "Me, too."

"You?" Ben poured a cup of coffee for the pilot and set it on the counter. "What're you talking about?"

"Well, not me personally. It's that attorney again. Tracy Santiago." His eyes narrowed as he mentioned the lawyer Mariah Douglas's family had hired to investigate Hard Luck after the town started advertising for women. Their daughter, Mariah, was the Midnight Sons secretary. "She's trying to stir up trouble. Mariah got a phone call from her on Friday. Christian told me the Santiago woman's threatening to fly up here again in a couple of months to check things out."

"That's Christian and Sawyer's problem, isn't it?"

"Yes," Duke agreed, "but it makes me mad, you know? The way that woman keeps butting into everyone's business. Here the O'Halloran brothers've done everything on the up and up—giving women jobs and housing—and what do those poor guys get in return? Hassles from some troublemaker who's accusing them of exploiting women and…and…"

"She's not your worry," Ben reminded him.

Duke didn't respond. "What's eating you?" he asked Matt, instead.

Matt didn't feel like discussing his ex-wife, especially with Duke.

Duke didn't wait for Matt to answer him. "I'll bet it's got something to do with Karen. What's with you two, anyway? The whole time she was dancing with me, she was asking about you."

"Me?" From the way she'd behaved, Matt had assumed he was the farthest thing from her mind.

"Oh, she tried to be subtle about it, but I could see through her questions. She wanted to know about the lodge and what I thought of your plan. I told her it was a damn good one."

Matt was grateful. "I appreciate that."

"So, what's going on with you and your ex?" Duke asked again.

Matt frowned. He wasn't accustomed to discussing his personal business with anyone, not even his family. He certainly had no intention of confiding in a casual acquaintance. "We're divorced. What else do you need to know?"

"It's pretty obvious that you're still in love. I don't know what it is with couples these days," Duke complained to Ben. "Can anyone tell me why people who care about each other decide to call it quits? It just doesn't make sense."

Matt would've liked to argue the point, but he couldn't come up with a single, solitary thing to say. There was only one thought in his mind—what happened last night had proved beyond a doubt that he wasn't over Karen and never would be.

He leapt off the stool. Duke was right; instead of sitting here bemoaning his fate, he should confront Karen. She loved him. She must. Otherwise she'd never have gone to bed with him.

All she needed was a little reassurance. Okay, he'd made a few errors in judgment, but that was behind them now. The lodge was their future, and if she'd give him another chance he'd prove he could make a success of it.

Matt was going after her. When he found her, he'd convince her they'd both be fools to throw away the love they shared.

He was tired of pretending he didn't care, tired of pretending he didn't miss her. His life was on course now, and once she was back everything would be perfect.

All he had to do now was explain that to Karen.

"Has she left yet?" he demanded of Duke.

"Karen?"

"Who else do you think I'm asking about?"

Duke checked his watch. "My guess is John's about to take off. You'd better hurry if you want to catch her."

Matt didn't need any further incentive. He slapped some money on the counter, grabbed his coat and ran out the door. The mobile unit that housed the Midnight Sons office was close by, and he sprinted the distance.

He saw John Henderson heading in the same direction and noticed the Baron 55 sitting on the gravel runway, ready to depart for the flight to Fairbanks.

Both men reached the door to the office at the same time. "I need a few minutes alone with Karen," Matt said. He blocked John's way.

The pilot began to complain bitterly that this was messing up his schedule, but Matt didn't care. "Listen." Matt pulled a five-dollar bill out of his pocket. "Go have a cup of Ben's coffee and give me ten minutes with Karen. That's all I'm asking."

John stared at the money, then scratched his head. "All right, all right, but make it fast, will you? I'm on a schedule." He turned away mumbling, waving away Matt's profuse thanks. "Ten minutes," he called over his shoulder. "Not a second more."

Matt waited until he'd composed his thoughts before walking inside to confront his ex-wife. Karen sat on a worn vinyl couch, staring at the floor. She glanced up when he stepped into the waiting area, and her eyes widened when she saw who it was.

"What are you doing here?" she asked, jerking herself upright. She shrank back from him, almost as if she was afraid.

"We need to talk," he said gently.

"No, we don't. Everything's already been said. It's over. It was over a long time ago."

"Last night says otherwise."

She shook her head. "Last night was a big mistake.

Please, Matt, just let me go. I don't want to talk about what happened. It didn't change anything."

"I think it did." He eased his way toward her. Grabbing a chair, he turned it around and straddled it. "I'd been thinking about buying the lodge for a while. I saw it shortly after the fire, and I'd forgotten about it till Lanni came up here. I finally made a deal with the O'Halloran brothers. I've spent nine months now, working fifteen-hour days, doing everything I can to get it ready for the summer tourist trade."

"Matt, listen—"

"Let me finish," he pleaded. "I'm telling you about the lodge because I consider it our future."

Karen squeezed her eyes shut.

"I realize you've heard those words before, but this time it's true. This isn't just another one of my ideas. I sank the entire trust fund my grandmother left me into this venture. I'm so far out on a limb I could pick fruit. I'm giving this my best shot, Karen. I'm risking everything for us."

"There is no us," she reminded him in a whisper.

"But there *should* be! If last night proved anything, it's that we belong together. We always have. Come back to me, Karen. You want promises? I'll give you promises. You want reassurances? Fine, you've got them. Everything will be different. We'll start over again—"

Tears rolled down her face as Karen leaned forward and brought her fingers to his mouth, silencing him. "Don't. Please, don't." She pressed her lips tightly together and swiped at the tears, then continued. "You want me to quit my job and come back here, right?"

He nodded. Of course he wanted her back here—as his wife. He wanted them to work together to build their marriage and their business. He needed her, wanted her, loved her. That had never changed.

"I've heard all this before. My mother heard it from my father, too. She loved him. She believed him every time, and he led her down one garden path after another."

"Karen, I'm not your father."

She looked away. "I'm not my mother, either. I can't—I *won't* do what you're asking. My future is with Paragon. My home isn't in Alaska anymore, it's in Oakland. Don't you realize how many times you've said almost those identical words to me? Six months from now, you'll be bored again and you'll have some other wonderful dream to follow. I can't live that way. I tried. I honestly tried."

"But—"

"Matt, stop, please. The bottom line is that I'm not willing to throw my career down the drain for another one of your reckless schemes, no matter how promising it sounds."

Matt stood, his mind racing frantically as he tried to find a reason that would convince her to stay.

"I have my own life now," she said. "I won't give up everything I've worked to achieve. Not for *your* dreams. Because for the first time in years, Matt, I have dreams of my own."

He was fighting a losing battle and he knew it.

"I'm going to find a man with a steady job and a savings account. I'm going to settle down in a house with a white picket fence and raise a bunch of children." A sob shook her shoulders. "And I'm going to do everything I can to put our marriage behind me." Having said that, she reached for her suitcase and rushed out the door.

"Mom!" Ten-year-old Scott O'Halloran burst in the front door with Eagle Catcher, his husky, trotting behind him.

Abbey looked up from the magazine she was reading.

"Sawyer—I mean Dad—let me fly his plane this afternoon," her son announced proudly.

Abbey's gaze instantly connected with that of her husband as he followed her son into the house.

"I didn't actually fly the plane," Scott quickly amended, "but Sawyer let me hold the control stick, and he told me all about the different instruments on the panel."

"It's time, honey," Sawyer said, kissing her on the cheek.

Abbey wasn't so sure of that. "But, Sawyer, he's only ten."

"Aw, Mom, you gotta stop treating me like a little kid."

Abbey swallowed a laugh. She recalled the day she'd arrived in Hard Luck with her two children in tow. She'd been one of the first women lured to town with the promise of a job, a house and land. She'd come hoping to make a new life for herself and her children.

Neither she nor Sawyer had been looking for love. But they'd found it, with each other. They must've had the fastest courtship in Hard Luck's history, Abbey mused. In retrospect, she wouldn't change a thing.

Not only was she deeply in love with her husband, but Sawyer had legally adopted Scott and Susan, and he worked hard at being a good father.

"My dad was teaching me the basic elements of flying when I was ten," he assured her. "Trust me, I'm not going to do anything to put either of us in danger."

Abbey knew that went without saying; nevertheless, she couldn't help worrying.

"I'm gonna find Ronny Gold," Scott told them. "I'll be back before dinner." He was out the door with another burst of speed. The silver-eyed husky raced along at his side.

"I wonder what Charles and Lanni are up to about now," Sawyer said with a grin.

"They're probably lying on a sandy beach soaking up the sunshine."

Sawyer sat next to her on the sofa. "Remember our honeymoon?"

Abbey smiled. They hadn't seen too much of Hawaii.

"If you recall, we didn't spend a lot of time on any of those beaches. As far as I was concerned, all we needed was a bed and a little privacy."

"Sawyer!"

"I'm crazy about you, Abbey."

"Good thing, because I'm crazy about you, too." She turned, sliding her arms around his waist. The happiness she'd found with him continued to astound her. When she'd least expected it, Sawyer had given her back her heart, given her a second chance at love.

"Don't worry about cooking tonight," he said. "I thought I'd treat us all to dinner."

"On a Monday night?"

"Sure." He grinned. "Ben's started a frequent-eater plan, and—"

"A *what?*"

"You know, like the airlines' frequent-flyer programs."

"Oh. Of course."

"He's trying to drum up a little business, and I figured we should support his creativity."

Abbey gave Sawyer a quick kiss. "And have some of Ben's apple pie into the bargain."

"Then, later," Sawyer said, cozying up to her, "I thought you and I could relive some of those wonderful moments from our own honeymoon."

Abbey suspected he wasn't talking about lazing around on a beach, either.

May 1996

Karen had never felt worse, emotionally or physically. Bad enough to make a doctor's appointment.

Spring was one of her favorite times of year. The changes in the California weather weren't as dramatic as those in Alaska, but the heavy Oakland air seemed to hold less smog.

Even though she'd been living in California for a while now, she wondered if she'd ever grow accustomed to seeing nothing but a brownish haze on the horizon.

She'd hoped to adjust more quickly to life here, but so far she hadn't. True, there were compensations—a staggering variety of stores and restaurants, lots of TV channels, consistently moderate weather. But daylight in the winter months had taken some getting used to.

Freeways continued to unnerve her. Traffic intimidated her. And so many people! The contrast between California and Alaska was never more striking than on the freeways.

Karen had made friends. All female. It might've helped if she'd been able to get involved in another relationship. But she wasn't ready, and she didn't know how long it would be before she was.

Still, no matter how many months or years it took, she was determined to forget Matt.

First, though, she had to get over this strange malady of hers. A friend in her office had recommended Dr. Perry, and if the patients filling his waiting room were any indication, he must be good.

She flipped through a women's magazine as she waited for the nurse to call her name. Glancing at her watch, she saw that it was already twenty minutes past her appointment time. Actually Karen didn't mind the wait because she didn't know what she'd say once she saw him. She didn't have any real symptoms. She just felt…bad. She slept more than she should. Her appetite was nonexistent. And she cried at the drop of a hat. The other night she'd found herself weeping over a television advertisement for a camera. A camera, for heaven's sake!

Her real fear was that Dr. Perry would say she had all the symptoms of someone who was chronically depressed and tell her she should make an appointment with a mental-health professional. She was prepared to do that if he suggested it.

When her name was finally called, she followed the nurse to the cubicle and sat on a molded plastic chair.

Considering what this appointment cost, she'd think Dr. Perry could at least afford a decent chair.

The nurse, Mrs. Webster, according to her name-plate, read over the questionnaire Karen had completed earlier. "It says here you haven't been feeling well."

"Yes," Karen responded crisply. "I think it might be the smog."

"The smog." Mrs. Webster made a notation on the chart.

"You see, I'm from Alaska. I've never been exposed to smog before. My lungs don't like it."

"I don't imagine they do."

"I believe it's affecting my general health. I just feel crummy." Although she felt fine at the moment, Karen found herself battling back tears. "And I—I seem to have developed the ability to weep at nothing."

Mrs. Webster's eyes searched out hers. "Oh?"

Karen fumbled in her purse for a tissue and blew her nose. "I tear up at the most ludicrous things. I can't tell you how embarrassing it is."

"You miss Alaska?"

"Yes…no. I don't want to go back… I mean I do, I really do, but I can't. You see, I accepted this promotion, and Paragon, the company I work for, moved me here." She stopped and blew her nose a second time. "Sorry."

"Let's go back to the part about not feeling well. Do you have any other symptoms the doctor should know about?"

She shrugged. "Not really."

Mrs. Webster walked over to the drawer and took

out some medical instruments. "I'm sure Dr. Perry's going to want a blood sample."

"Fine." She held out her arm for the nurse. "I feel sluggish. That's one of my symptoms," she clarified. "I wake up in the morning and I don't want to get out of bed."

"I'll mention that to the doctor."

"Do you think it might be the smog?" she asked hopefully, watching the older woman.

"I don't know. I'll let the doctor decide. But we've recently seen several people with low-grade flu symptoms."

That was reassuring. Maybe all she had was a simple case of the flu.

Ten minutes later, after the nurse had taken some blood and Karen had changed out of her clothes and into a flimsy paper gown, she met Dr. Perry. He was much younger than she'd expected. Early thirties, if that.

"Hello, Karen," he said. His voice was kindly.

"Hi." She felt more than a little ridiculous in her blue paper outfit.

While she tucked the gown more securely under her thighs, Dr. Perry read her chart. "I understand you haven't been feeling like your usual self lately."

"No. As I told your nurse, I think it must be the smog."

"Tired. Sluggish. Weepy."

"Yes, all those things."

He glanced up from the chart and held her gaze.

"Mrs. Webster said there's a low-grade flu going around," she suggested.

"Yes," Dr. Perry agreed, "but this sounds like something else. Tell me, Karen, is there any possibility you could be pregnant?"

Three

June 1996

Matt stood in the main room of the lodge and handed Lanni the glossy brochure he'd produced. He studied her closely, eager for his sister's response. Since Lanni was a writer, he'd gone to her for advice about the text and even the design. Now the brochure was ready to mail out.

"Matt, this is really great!"

"Yeah, it looks good, but does it make you want to spend several thousand dollars to fly to northern Alaska?"

"Sure," she said.

Matt remained unconvinced. "What about the section on dogsledding?"

"I think it's a good idea." But her enthusiasm sounded forced, and when she hesitated, Matt wondered if she was going to be honest or just tell him what she thought he wanted to hear.

"Do you really believe people want to learn how to run a dog team?" she asked after an awkward moment.

"Positive. It's becoming very popular. Men, and plenty of women, too, are looking for more than relaxation when they take their vacations." He strived to keep his voice calm and matter-of-fact. "They want adventure. Sure, lounging on a beach might sound good, but after two or three days most folks with A-type personalities are bored to tears. The people who can afford this kind of vacation are generally professional people who're driven to succeed. Always looking for new challenges. I'm offering them something unique."

Lanni grinned. "I'll say. But city folks aren't going to know how to harness dogs or hitch them to a sled."

"That's where the mushers come in, and I've got the real McCoy." Matt was thrilled with the response he'd gotten from the professional mushers. "Anyone who signs on is going to learn it all. That's part of the thrill."

"I hope this works." But it was plain Lanni remained skeptical.

"My gut instinct tells me this is going to catch on big."

Matt sincerely hoped he was right. The survival of the business depended on his ability to convince travel agents across North America—and beyond—to book their clients into Hard Luck Lodge. His vacation packages included guided fishing tours during the summer months and dogsledding in the winter.

"Imagine taking a hundred-mile trek above the Arctic Circle, driving your own team of dogs," Matt said excitedly. He figured if he could convince his sister, then he could sell this package to just about anyone. "I've got everything spelled out right here."

He pointed to the listing of six-and eight-day trips between February and April.

"Several of my guides have run the Iditarod themselves. They know all there is to know about dogs and sledding. This venture helps them, too. The mushers can use the money, and I've been more than fair in giving them a cut."

Lanni's attention returned to the brochure. "I like the way you talk about the history of the Iditarod. 'In January 1925, Leonhard Seppala, a Norwegian musher,'" she read aloud, "'rushed diphtheria serum 675 miles from the end of the Alaska Railroad to Nome. The trip took just over five days.'"

"The Iditarod's still called the most rugged race on earth." Matt wasn't telling Lanni anything she didn't know. "People dream about this kind of adventure."

"Then it's the thrill-seeking vacationer you're hoping to attract?"

"Exactly." Matt wanted this venture to succeed for more reasons than he cared to contemplate. He had something to prove to himself—and to Karen. "But it'll appeal to lots of other people, too.

"I'm listed with the Airline Report Corporation now," he said, although he suspected his sister didn't fully understand the significance of this. It meant that Hard Luck Lodge was formally listed with professional travel agents around the country. If a client came in looking for a place to fish, he or she would learn about the lodge.

"Good."

"I'm mailing out thousands of the brochures and offering incentives to agents to book their clients."

"Incentives? Like what?"

"Well, for one thing," he said, "the first ten agents who call me with reservations will receive a two-night fishing package."

"That's a great idea!"

"I thought so." He leaned against the registration counter, crossing his arms, and surveyed the room. A fire flickered in the massive stone fireplace. What the room really needed was those little touches a woman gave a home. He'd wanted to ask Lanni, but she'd already helped with the brochure; besides, she and Charles were newlyweds and he didn't want to intrude on their lives.

Karen had always been great at that sort of thing. He'd always been impressed with the way she could turn a dinky apartment into a real home, with the colors she used and plants and the placement of a few carefully chosen things. She had a gift for making a room look inviting.

"Now tell me about this trip you're taking," Lanni said, breaking into his thoughts. Actually he was grateful. He didn't want to think about Karen. She'd made her position clear—she didn't want him in her life—and he was determined to accept that.

"It's a ten-city West Coast tour to meet personally with travel agents," he explained. "I'll be giving a presentation in each city, along with other lodge owners. That way, the agents can ask me any questions they have."

Lanni nudged him playfully. "One thing's for sure—not too many of the others are going to offer dogsledding."

"Probably not," Matt agreed.

Lanni glanced over his travel itinerary and slowly raised her eyes to meet his. "You'll be in Oakland."

"Yeah." He didn't pretend not to know what that meant. Karen lived in Oakland. Well, he'd made up his mind that he wasn't going to see her.

A man had his pride, and she'd trampled his for the last time. Despite their night together, she wasn't interested in a reconciliation; okay, fine, then that was the way things would be.

"I mailed Karen one of your brochures."

Matt stifled a groan. This was the problem with Lanni and Karen being such good friends. A part of him wanted Karen to see the brochure because he was proud of it. Proud of everything he'd accomplished in less than a year. But at the same time, he didn't want to hear her tell him that this venture was another— what had she called it?—reckless scheme. Contrary to what his ex-wife might believe, buying the lodge wasn't a passing fancy.

"Don't you want to know what Karen said?" Lanni asked.

"No," he lied. "She's out of my life now."

"But you still care about her."

Matt wasn't about to let his sister meddle in his life. "Stay out of it, Lanni. What's happened between Karen and me is none of your business."

"Don't be so quick to shut me out, big brother," his sister said, making her eyes wide and innocent. "As I recall, *you* tried to interfere in my relationship with Charles. You manipulated us into meeting so we'd settle our differences."

"As I recall," he echoed, "you didn't appreciate my

interference. Karen and I won't, either. I love you, Lanni, but I want you to stay out of this."

Lanni suddenly looked uncomfortable.

"What did you do?" Matt demanded.

"I... I wrote and told her you were going to be in Oakland."

That wouldn't make any difference, Matt figured. "She won't look me up, and I'm certainly not going out of my way to see her, if that's what you're thinking." And he wouldn't. Karen wanted nothing more to do with him.

Too bad, but he'd adjust. It wasn't like this was earth-shattering news. He'd been a little slow to get the message; he should have taken the hint when she filed for divorce.

"Whether or not you see her is up to you," Lanni told him softly, almost as if she was aware that she'd risked offending him, "but I gave Karen the name of your hotel."

Anger caused him to clench his fists. He didn't want *anyone* interfering in his life, least of all his kid sister. Irritated though he was, he understood that her intentions were good. Lanni and Charles were so much in love themselves, it influenced the way they looked at everyone else's life.

"Don't be angry with me," she pleaded.

Matt said nothing.

"Remember, I'm the one who volunteered to take reservations when you're down in the lower forty-eight rounding up business."

It could be wishful thinking on his part, but Matt hoped his tour would generate enough interest in Hard Luck Lodge that bookings would immediately start pouring in. Lanni had offered to run the office while he was away. Actually the arrangement suited them both, since she needed a quiet place to write.

His sister left soon afterward, and Matt wandered into the kitchen with its gleaming new appliances. He was eager for paying guests. Eager to host tourists from all over the world.

So far, he'd managed to acquire only a handful of reservations. His listing in the ARC had been entered late—too late to attract much of the lucrative fishing business. He had a lot to learn about attracting tourists, but he was willing and able. And determined. He would make a go of this lodge or die trying.

"Matt has a right to know about the baby." Lanni's voice sounded tinny on Karen's telephone line. "You don't know how close I came to telling him myself last week."

"But you didn't, did you?" Karen cried in alarm. If anyone told her ex-husband she was two months pregnant, it should be her. Except that was turning out to be even harder than she'd expected.

"No, I didn't," Lanni assured her. "Listen, Karen, if you don't want to tell him face-to-face, why don't you write him a letter?"

"I can't." After the things she'd said to him, she wouldn't blame him if he returned her letter unopened. Besides, this was the kind of news that was better given in person.

"You should've called him right away." The censure in Lanni's voice was strong. It might've been a mistake to confide in her ex-sister-in-law, but she'd had to tell *someone*.

"You've already waited a month longer than you should have," Lanni reminded her.

Karen had no defense. "I know."

"But you have a chance to rectify it all now. He's going to be in Oakland on Friday."

Karen bit her lower lip. "So you said."

The pause lasted long enough for Karen to wonder if Lanni was still on the line. When she spoke again, her voice was gentle. "How are you feeling?"

Karen rested her hand on her abdomen. "Better," she said, although that wasn't entirely true. No one had warned her how dreadful morning sickness could be. During her first few weeks of pregnancy she'd suffered few such symptoms, but now...

At the time of her original doctor's appointment she'd felt tired and restless and depressed. But that had changed dramatically after the first month. She wasn't depressed anymore—but not a day passed when she didn't view parts of a toilet that were never meant to be seen at such close range.

Despite the past month's discomforts, Karen was thrilled to be pregnant. She'd always wanted children but hadn't started a family with Matt because she'd wanted him to settle into a permanent job first— which, of course, had never happened. Furthermore, he'd seemed reluctant to have a child, which was one reason she'd delayed telling her ex-husband he was about to become a father.

To some women a pregnancy at a time like this would have been a disaster. However, Karen couldn't help being excited. She *wanted* this child. Despite everything, she loved Matt. But as far as their relationship was concerned, the baby would be an additional complication in an already complicated situation.

"I hope you'll reconsider," Lanni said, and Karen realized she hadn't been listening.

"Reconsider?"

"Going to see Matt. You should, if for no other reason than to watch his presentation. He had Charles and me sit through it before he left, and I have to tell you, Karen, I was impressed."

"He's talking to travel agents?"

"That's right. He's put together this wonderful slide show. I was so busy this winter finishing up my commitments to the newspaper in Anchorage that I didn't pay a lot of attention to what Matt was doing. Did you know he spent ten days on the tundra with a musher and a team of sled dogs?"

"Matt?"

"He told me he couldn't very well sell the adventure if he hadn't experienced it himself. And his pictures—they're fabulous."

Karen could easily imagine Matt standing in front of an audience. He was good with people, outgoing, friendly. And a persuasive kind of guy.

"When he talked about the dogs," Lanni went on, "his eyes just sparkled with excitement. If the number of phone calls I'm getting here is any indication, he's doing a good job of selling the winter packages."

"You mean to say he's actually convinced people to visit the Arctic in winter?" Karen had trouble believing it, but then, what did she know about vacations? In the four years of their married life, they hadn't been able to afford even one.

"I've taken at least ten reservations, and Matt's only

been gone a week," Lanni said proudly. "More are coming in every day."

"Oh…" Karen couldn't quite hide her surprise.

"Are you going to see him or not?" Lanni prodded.

"I…don't know yet."

"Well, you'd better decide soon because he'll only be in Oakland one night. He's scheduled to go to—" Karen heard a rustle of papers "—Portland, Seattle and then home."

"I'm not making any promises," Karen said, but she knew Lanni was right. Matt deserved to learn that he'd be a father in seven months. She just didn't know how he'd react to the news.

Matt saw Karen the moment she slipped into the back row of the meeting room. Even from this distance, the first thing he noticed was how pale she looked. He sat on the stage with a number of other lodge operators, all working hard to sell their tour packages. Luckily he'd already given his presentation, so the pressure was off and he could study his ex-wife.

She'd lost weight, and he wondered if that was intentional. If so, she was too thin, but she wouldn't appreciate hearing that, especially from him.

The temptation to walk off the stage and confront her then and there was almost overwhelming. He might have done it if not for their last conversation.

Well, this time, she could come to him. He was tired of having his teeth shoved down his throat whenever he attempted to reason with her.

Then again, maybe she didn't intend to seek him out. Maybe she was only here to satisfy her curiosity. Or because she'd promised Lanni. Fine, so be it, he decided. With effort he managed to keep his eyes resolutely trained on the current speaker. But again and again, his gaze drifted back to her....

The moderator walked to the microphone. "Are there any questions?"

A hand went up in the middle of the room. "I have one for Mr. Caldwell."

Matt stood.

"Do you have any response to the animal-rights people who question using dogs to pull sleds?"

Matt had gotten the same question in almost every city. "First, I want to assure you that the dogs are loved and cared for the way most people look after their own children. As for the rigors of life on the trail, the huskies are thoroughly happy. Running was what they were born to do, and they love it. Their comfort range is amazing. Until the weather drops to around thirty below, many sled dogs prefer to sleep outside rather than in a kennel."

"Are the dogs dangerous?" someone called out.

"No," Matt said, smiling. "Mostly they're playful and fun. At rest stops along the winter trails, they cool down by rolling in the snow. For the first mile of a run, they're excited and excitable, but even an inexperienced musher can learn to manage them. After the first day or so, everyone will come to know the dogs by name and personality."

Since he offered something new and interesting, Matt fielded the majority of the questions. As with his audiences in other cities, he felt he'd accomplished his purpose. The travel agents certainly seemed enthusiastic. But even as he was speaking, his gaze was drawn back to Karen. Pride be damned. He wasn't letting her off the hook so easily. If she wanted to walk out, fine, but he made sure she knew he'd seen her.

Following the question-and-answer session, the applause was vigorous. Matt gathered his notes, glancing up only once to see if he could find Karen. His heart fell when he realized she was nowhere in sight.

Then, when he was convinced she'd run away like a frightened rabbit, he turned around and found her standing no more than a foot away.

At close range, she looked paler than she had from the other end of the room. His concern was immediate.

"Karen, have you been ill?"

"No. Well, you wouldn't call it ill."

The woman spoke in riddles.

"Matt, do you have time for a drink?"

She was actually inviting him. That was progress. He frowned at his watch, wanting her to sweat it out. "I suppose." He tried to make it sound as if he was squeezing her in between appointments.

Carrying his briefcase, he led the way to the hotel's cocktail lounge and ordered two glasses of white wine.

"No, just one glass," Karen said to the waitress. "I'll have an herbal tea. Any kind."

Matt looked at her in astonishment. "Tea? I thought you liked wine."

"I'm avoiding alcohol," she explained, her eyes averted.

He wondered why, but he wasn't going to ask. She was the one with the agenda here, and frankly he was more than a little curious about what she wanted to say.

"I was impressed with your answers to the questions," she began. "I'd hoped to be here for your presentation, but… I wasn't feeling well earlier," she said, sounding shaky and uncertain. She rallied and continued. "Lanni mailed me one of your brochures. They look terrific."

"Thanks." He wasn't going to make this easy for her. Not after the grief she'd given him, the pain she'd caused.

"She told me you've been getting reservations ever since you went on tour."

"So I understand."

Their drinks arrived and Matt signed the bill with his room number. He noticed that when Karen sipped her tea, her hand trembled. Now he was beginning to get worried.

"Karen, what did you mean earlier about being sick?"

"I'm not sick."

"Oh, yeah, I can tell. How much weight have you lost?" He hadn't intended to be sarcastic, but he hated cat-and-mouse games. If she had something to say, he wished she'd just spit it out.

He waited for her answer, determined not to speak again until she'd said something relevant; she remained silent. His resolve lasted all of one minute.

"How's the career coming?" he asked, hoping she noticed his choice of words. She'd worked for the engineering firm for three years. She was an employer's dream—conscientious, organized, efficient. He hadn't been surprised that when her boss was promoted he'd made her his executive assistant and moved her to California with him.

"Great."

Somehow Matt didn't believe her.

"Mr. Sullivan giving you problems?" he asked. In some ways, the older man was more like a father to Karen. Matt couldn't imagine Sullivan creating difficulties for her.

"Actually he's been very understanding about the time I've missed from work."

"Missed work?" That didn't sound like Karen, either. In the four years of their marriage, he couldn't recall her taking a single day of sick leave.

"I've been having some trouble…mostly in the mornings." She leveled her gaze at him, as though she expected him to make some logical deduction from that bit of information.

"Ah, you've got PMS," he said, attempting a small joke.

From the disapproving scowl she sent him, he gathered she didn't find it humorous. "Matt, you can really be obtuse."

"Me? Listen, Karen, you're the one who wouldn't allow me to finish our last conversation. As far as I'm concerned, if you've got something to say, just say it, because I have a flight to catch in the morning."

Lifting her chin to a dignified angle, she reached for her purse and stood. "You're absolutely right," she said in a clear voice. "I've been beating around the bush." Her purse strap slipped off her shoulder and she quickly secured it. "I don't have a perpetual case of PMS, Matt, as amusing as you appear to find that. The reason I've lost weight can be attributed to something else. I have what's known as morning sickness. Now, if you'll excuse me, I'll leave you to mull that one over." She turned abruptly and walked out of the lounge.

"Morning sickness," Matt repeated, and downed the last of his wine in one swallow. The words echoed in his brain and his gaze flew to her retreating figure. He bolted upright. "You're pregnant?"

Karen turned the corner and was gone.

"She's pregnant," Matt shouted to the cocktail waitress. Then, before he completely lost Karen, he raced to the lobby in time to see her walking out the front doors.

"Karen, wait!"

Either she didn't hear him or she was determined to ignore him. It was just like her to drop that kind of news and then leave him to deal with the repercussions on his own.

He didn't catch up with her until she'd reached her car.

"What do you mean you're pregnant?" he demanded. "How did that happen?"

She whirled around and glared at him.

"Weren't you on the pill?"

"Why should I be?" she asked. "We were divorced, remember?"

As if he'd forgotten!

"Don't you *dare* suggest birth control is entirely up to the woman," she said from between gritted teeth.

Matt was having trouble taking all this in. "But... how?"

"Well," she muttered sarcastically, "here's what I remember from biology class. The woman provides the egg and the man supplies the sperm."

"I know all that!" he snapped. "What I'm talking about is us. We're both responsible adults. I can't believe we didn't consider the possibility of your getting pregnant." He leaned against the side of her car, his legs like gelatin.

"It might've helped if you'd broken the news a bit more gently," he said.

"It would help if you weren't looking for someone to blame."

"That's not true," he flared. He rubbed the back of his neck. "You're going to need financial assistance." Since his budget was tight, money was the first thing that came to mind.

Karen made a growling sound, and he looked up to find her glaring at him again, her eyes bright with unshed tears. "You're impossible!" she shouted.

"What did I say now?"

"Nothing." She shook her head. "I've fulfilled my obligation. I told you about the baby. I do apologize for any inconvenience this might cause you." Sarcasm dripped from every word. "Perhaps the best alternative is to have my attorney talk to your attorney. Goodbye, Matt."

With that, she unlocked her car door and climbed in.

"You can't leave!" he shouted as she started the car. "We have to talk." But she ignored him as if he hadn't even spoken. "Karen, would you listen to me?"

She twisted around to look over her shoulder before shoving the car into Reverse. Then she backed out of the space and drove off, leaving him standing in the middle of the parking lot, seething with frustration.

Karen barely slept that night. She wasn't sure what she'd expected from Matt, but not the sarcastic arrogance he'd dished up and served her while they were in the cocktail lounge. He'd seemed to…to enjoy her discomfort.

When she'd finally garnered enough courage to tell him about the pregnancy, he'd reacted as if she'd plotted against him. As if it was important to somehow assign blame for the unexpected pregnancy.

What bothered her most, Karen decided sometime in the wee hours of the morning, was the fact that his reaction was completely contrary to the romantic picture she'd painted in her mind. For weeks she'd envisioned telling Matt about their baby and watching his eyes go soft as he regarded her with tenderness and love.

After being married to Matt for four years, she should've known better. The man didn't possess a romantic bone in his body. Furthermore, why should he be excited and pleased because she was pregnant? *He'd* never wanted a baby.

He didn't want a child now, any more than he had when they were married. A baby was an inconvenience. A baby got in the way of his plans.

She'd listened to his arguments about financial security often enough to know exactly what he'd been thinking. If Matthew Caldwell lived to be a hundred, he'd never be financially secure—simply because he'd never hold a job long enough to make it possible.

She was better off without him. On a conscious level she knew that, but on an emotional one, it hurt. It *really* hurt. If there was ever a time in her life she needed coddling and comfort, it was now.

Although the doctor assured her the morning sickness would lessen, she hadn't seen any evidence of it. The next morning, like every other morning for weeks, she rose, managed to down a breakfast of tea and soda crackers, then promptly lost it. Spending most of the night agonizing about Matt hadn't helped her physical condition.

By nine she was stretched out on the sofa with a blanket. She'd placed a bucket on the floor beside her because of the queasiness in her stomach.

The doorbell chimed, but she was in no mood for company and ignored it.

"Damn it, Karen! Open the door."

Matt.

"Leave me alone," she shouted, draining what little energy she had left.

Disregarding her demand, Matt opened the door himself and stepped into her small apartment. She never had learned to keep her door locked. Unfortunately the habit had followed her to California.

Matt looked as pale as she had the night before. He wore the same clothes he'd had on then. If she was guessing, she'd say he hadn't been to bed.

He lowered himself into the chair across from her, and glanced at the bucket.

"No one told me getting pregnant was like suffering the worst case of flu known to womankind," she muttered. She sipped flat soda pop through a straw.

"Is it always like this?"

"Every morning for the past four weeks. And the occasional evening."

He frowned, and although he didn't say anything, his expression was apologetic. "That's the reason you've missed so much work?"

She nodded. "Listen," she said, "I'm sorry for hit-ting you with the news. Lanni's been telling me for weeks that you had a right to know. I—"

"Lanni knows?"

Karen nodded again.

He expelled his breath loudly. "Anyone else?"

"No. I wouldn't have told her, but—"

"Never mind," he said, cutting her off. "It's not important." He leaned forward and rubbed his palms together. "I've been giving this a lot of thought. For the past twelve hours, as a matter of fact."

She stared at him, waiting.

"I want you to move up to Hard Luck with me. The sooner we can remarry—"

"No," she returned adamantly. "The baby is the last reason on earth for us to remarry."

Four

"You won't remarry me?" Matt had the audacity to look shocked. "What about the baby?"

Karen closed her eyes. She wasn't feeling well enough to argue with her ex-husband. The nausea seemed to be worse than usual this morning and it was difficult enough to think clearly without Matt's questions.

"Karen—"

"I'm fine." She wasn't, but explaining how awful she felt required more strength than she could muster.

His brow creased with concern. "Will you be this sick throughout the pregnancy?"

"I don't know." Good heavens, she prayed that wouldn't be the case. Her doctor seemed to think the bouts of vomiting would pass after the first three months. So far, eight weeks into the pregnancy, Karen had experienced no lessening of symptoms.

"Are you able to work?"

"Yes…no. I've used up all my sick leave." It upset her to admit that. Her boss had been wonderfully understanding, but she knew being away from her desk for days on end was a terrible inconvenience to Mr. Sullivan.

In the past four weeks, Karen had spent an average of two to three hours a day at the office. Even when she did manage to show up, she couldn't give one hundred percent.

Matt got abruptly to his feet and started pacing. "Who's your doctor? Maybe I should talk to him myself. You shouldn't be this ill. Is there something you're not telling me?"

"Like what?"

"There's no possibility this will be a multiple birth, is there?"

Twins? Triplets? The doctor hadn't mentioned it, and Karen hadn't given the matter a thought. "Of course not," she assured him, but it made her wonder. How could she ever cope with twins? Then, because he'd raised the question, she asked, "What makes you think I could be having twins?"

"I read about something like this once where the wife—the woman suffered acute bouts of morning sickness and it ended up she had quints."

"Quintuplets!" Matt's words horrified Karen, but when she glanced up at him, he was grinning from ear to ear as though the idea brought him considerable enjoyment. "Just imagine all the publicity that would bring the lodge."

Naturally he'd think of his precious lodge and not her. "Wipe that smile off your face, Matthew Caldwell."

Matt sat back down and leaned forward. "This is pretty incredible, you know."

That wasn't the impression he'd given her the night

before. Okay, the news had come as a shock, but he had a long way to go to play his part in her fantasy. She'd pictured him bringing her a huge bouquet of flowers and a large teddy bear. So far, all he'd brought her was a bunch of silly questions and an outrageous demand. He assumed that because she was pregnant they should remarry as soon as possible. Sweep their difficulties under the rug and pretend they didn't exist—that was Matt's way of dealing with most things, including her pregnancy.

"Think about it, Karen," he went on, cocky grin firmly back in place. "In all the years we've known each other, the night of Lanni's wedding was probably the only time we ever made love without protection."

That was the last thing she wanted to be reminded of, especially when she felt so wretched. She stayed on the sofa with her head hanging over the edge to be sure her aim for the bucket was on target.

"The odds of your getting pregnant from our one and only…lapse must be astronomical."

Leave it to Matt to get egotistical over something like this. The man was marinating in his own testosterone. Men and their pride! Karen would never understand it.

"Trust me, Matt, this is not the time to gloat." The nausea worsened and she closed her eyes, fearing she was about to lose whatever was left in her stomach.

He chuckled, then seemed to realize she wasn't joking. She must have gone even paler, because he reached over and smoothed the hair from her brow.

"What can I do?" he asked gently.

It was his tenderness that nearly did her in. Karen had to fight back tears. "Nothing," she whispered, taking a deep breath. "It'll pass in a minute." Sometimes it did, and other times it didn't. "It might be best if you left—I don't feel up to company."

"Oh, no, you don't," Matt warned. "I'm not walking out of this apartment until you and I have made some decisions."

"We have nothing to decide."

"What about the doctor and hospital bills?"

Karen hated to admit her pocketbook was hurting. The medical bills were beginning to mount. The health insurance provided through Paragon, Inc., paid eighty percent, but the twenty percent she had to pay herself grew with each doctor's visit. She didn't need a calculator to realize that with the difficulties she'd already experienced, she would soon run into the thousands.

"Are you offering to help?" she asked stiffly. Matt had never been good with money. It used to drive her crazy the way he'd write checks without keeping a balance in their checkbook. He'd often stack up two or three months' worth of bank statements before he'd reconcile their account. He claimed he wasn't irresponsible or reckless; he just wanted to make the effort worth his while.

The moment he'd mentioned his plans to be an accountant Karen should've realized that effort was doomed. He'd never been interested enough in numbers.

"The baby's my responsibility, too," he told her.

But it went without saying that Matt was in no position to be giving her money. Not with launching Hard Luck Lodge. He'd sunk every penny he could scrounge plus his entire inheritance into this venture.

Knowing Matt the way she did, Karen doubted there was anything left.

"I know, but—"

"Karen." He clasped her hand between his and got down on his knees beside her. "It makes sense to put this nonsense aside once and for all. We belong together. We always have—now more than ever."

"Nonsense?" Did he honestly believe that the agony of their divorce had been a trivial decision on her part? Leaving Matt and filing for divorce had been the most difficult, painful thing she'd ever done. For him to make light of what it had cost her emotionally proved he'd never understand her.

"Okay, so you don't want to move to Hard Luck," he said as if living in the Arctic was all that held her back.

She closed her eyes, stunned that he knew so little about her.

"Do you?" he asked hopefully.

She opened her eyes, confused by his question.

"Would you agree to marry me and move to Hard Luck?"

"Oh, Matt, please don't ask that of me. Not now when I feel so sick."

"I want to take care of you."

He was going to have his hands full running the lodge. As for taking care of her, well, she'd been doing a fair job of that herself.

"No," she said. She needed him, perhaps for the first time, yet as hard as she tried, Karen couldn't put the past behind her. Matt had fallen short of her expectations so often. He'd made promises in the past and let her down. There was so much more at stake now.

"No," Matt echoed, his face tense. He stood and

moved to the living room window, staring quietly out for several minutes. When he turned around, anger and frustration seemed to radiate from him. The tightness around his mouth and eyes made his expression piercing and grim.

"I've never understood what I did that was so terrible," he said, his voice low. "Okay, I agree I fumbled around for a while looking for the right career. I knew that bothered you but, Karen, I'm not your father. You complained about my tendency to bounce from job to job, but was that really so bad? We never went hungry, the rent was paid and we had a decent life."

Karen wanted to argue that it was pure luck he found work so easily and you couldn't always count on luck. It was the uncertainty of the situation that drove her crazy. She'd worry about the rent, although somehow, they'd always managed, just as he'd said.

"I'm faithful and loyal. I never drank or abused you in any way."

"Matt, please—"

"I've always loved you. The day we stood before the judge and he pounded his gavel and proclaimed that we were no longer married, I still loved you. You're carrying my child, and I love you more than ever—but I can't force you to care for me."

Karen covered her face in an effort to hold back the words that would tell him how much she cared.

"You want to shut me out of your life," he said starkly. "You want to ignore the fact that the child you're carrying is mine, too. I never thought I'd say it, but maybe you were right—having my attorney talk to yours might be the best way to handle this." Without another word, he walked to the door and left.

The sharp and sudden pain in Karen's abdomen took her by surprise. The unexpectedness of it was one thing, but the intensity of the attack took her breath away. She gasped and doubled up.

Something was very wrong.

Darkness crowded her vision, and she was afraid she might faint. With what little strength she had, Karen heaved herself from the sofa and stumbled to the door.

"Matt." She screamed his name, frantic now with fear.

He was halfway to the parking lot when he heard her.

"Help me..." she pleaded, sobbing uncontrollably. She stretched one arm toward him and clutched her stomach with the other. "I think I'm losing the baby."

Matt sat in the waiting area outside the emergency room at Oakland Hospital. He'd tried a dozen times in the past two hours to see Karen but had been told the doctor was still with her. Two hours!

The waiting room was packed. There were several crying, sick children, a man with a bloody towel wrapped around his hand and a young mother singing a lullaby to her fussing two-year-old. A couple of girls were staring at the fish in an aquarium, while two or three men seemed glued to the TV, which was tuned to CNN.

Matt hadn't glanced at the television or the aquarium once. He was too worried about Karen and the baby. He was afraid the length of time she'd been with the doctor didn't bode well for the pregnancy.

He closed his eyes and forced himself to concentrate on breathing. A crushing sadness lodged in his chest. He'd known about the baby less than twenty-four hours, yet he deeply grieved the loss of his son or daughter. He would never hold this baby in his arms, never change a diaper or hear his child's first word.

Glancing toward the swinging doors, Matt willed someone—anyone—to come and tell him what was happening with Karen.

What he'd said earlier about loving her had never seemed truer than at this moment. He hurt more now than he had when she'd served him with the divorce papers. She'd made it clear that she wanted nothing to do with him, and heaven help him, he'd abide by her wishes. But no matter what the outcome of this day, it would be hard.

He leaned forward and clasped his hands, bracing himself against a fresh wave of pain. It was so sharp, so constricting, that he had difficulty breathing.

Distracted by his thoughts, Matt wasn't immediately aware of the doctor who'd entered the room and called his name.

"Matthew Caldwell."

Matt leapt to his feet and nearly tripped over a toddler sitting on the floor, stacking wooden blocks.

"I'm Matt Caldwell," he told the lanky older man in the white coat. "What's going on with Karen? What about the baby?" He prepared himself to receive the news that they hadn't been able to save the pregnancy.

"Your wife is resting comfortably."

Matt didn't bother to explain that Karen was his ex-wife.

"We've run a number of tests, and as far as we can tell the pregnancy is progressing just fine."

Matthew was too stunned to respond. "The baby's fine? What happened? Karen thought she was having a miscarriage."

The other man patted him on the back. "Your wife has a severe bladder infection."

"But...she was in such terrible pain."

"I suspect the infection was complicated by stress and fatigue. We're giving her an antibiotic that's completely safe for the baby, and as a further precaution, we've decided to admit her for the night. Her obstetrician will call on her later."

"She's been very ill with morning sickness. Is that normal?"

"Sometimes. You might talk with Dr. Baker when he's in. Would you like to see your wife now?"

"Please."

Matt followed the ER physician down a corridor crowded with gurneys and IV stands to a semidarkened room. He pulled aside the thin curtain around the bed. Karen lay there, her hands resting protectively over her abdomen.

Matt barely noticed the doctor's leaving. He gazed down at Karen; their eyes met. She looked deathly pale against the white sheets. Matt figured he probably didn't look much better. He'd never spent a more harrowing two hours in his life.

"How're you feeling?" he asked gently. Needing to touch her, Matt reached for her hand and brought it to his lips. It wasn't until her fingers closed around his that he remembered their disagreement.

"Oh, Matt," she whispered, "I'm so sorry for causing you all this trouble."

"I'd never consider helping you trouble." He kissed the back of her hand.

Tears filled her eyes and she turned her face away from him.

"The doctor said you should sleep," he urged her softly. "Don't worry about a thing."

"What about your plane? You were supposed to have left Oakland long before now." She shifted her position to look at him again.

"I canceled my reservation. Now stop worrying about it."

Ever so lightly, he touched her tear-stained face.

"But the tour—what about your presentations in Portland and Seattle?"

That she knew so much about his schedule surprised him. "There'll be other tours."

"I feel bad about messing up your plans..." Her voice faded. Whatever drug the hospital had given her seemed to kick in just then, because she closed her eyes and was asleep within seconds.

Matt sat next to her bed until the orderly arrived. Then he followed Karen to the room she'd been assigned. He stayed until she started to stir, at which point he quietly slipped out, assuming he was the last person she'd want to see.

Later that afternoon, Karen woke up, feeling more rested than she had in weeks. She pressed her hand to her stomach, forever grateful that the pregnancy remained intact. She'd been so afraid.

A brief smile touched her lips. Generally she was the calm, cool one in a crisis, not Matt. The reverse had happened that morning. Consumed as she was with the pain, weeping and nearly hysterical, Karen had felt sure she was suffering a miscarriage.

Although he hadn't known where to even find a hospital, Matt had been clearheaded and efficient, calling 911 for instructions and accompanying her in the ambulance. Not until they arrived at the emergency room had he displayed any emotion. And then only because the medical staff insisted he wait in the outer room.

She caught a movement out of the corner of her eye and turned her head to see her boss, Doug Sullivan, entering the room.

"Karen, how are you feeling?" He'd brought a large bouquet of arranged flowers and set the vase down on the nightstand.

Karen was so surprised to see him she didn't answer. "How did you know I was here?"

"Matt called me."

"Matt?" At the sound of her husband's name she swallowed hard. Apparently he'd left Oakland, because she hadn't seen him again. She'd asked the nurses about him, but no one seemed to know where he'd gone or when.

"Matt thought he should tell me you'd been hospitalized, and he was right." Doug moved to the foot of her bed. "What happened?" he asked gently.

"All at once I had these excruciating pains. The doctors seem to think they're related to a bladder infection. That, plus stress and fatigue."

"So Matt said."

"Was there anything else he told you?" she asked, resenting the way her ex-husband had taken it upon himself to interfere in her life. It wouldn't bother her nearly as much if he hadn't disappeared without a word—which just went to prove what she'd been saying all along. The man wasn't reliable.

"Matt did mention that he wanted you to return to Alaska and move to— What's the name of that town again?"

"Hard Luck," Karen supplied.

"Right, Hard Luck. How could I forget that?" Doug Sullivan smiled, then said in a kind voice, "It might not be such a bad idea, Karen."

"But—"

He raised his hand, stopping her. "Just until the baby's born. Matt has every right to be concerned about you...and his baby."

The last person Karen had thought would side with her ex-husband was her boss. Typical of Matt to have someone else do his arguing for him! "Do you realize how far Hard Luck is from Fairbanks or a town of any real size?" she asked. "There isn't a doctor within a five-hundred-mile radius."

"True, but Matt says the public-health nurse is a fully qualified midwife. I believe he said her name's Dotty something. She's one of the women who went up there last year—she married the shopkeeper, I think."

Karen looked away, annoyed that Matt had brought Doug in to make a case on his behalf. He was obviously very serious about getting her to move to Hard Luck.

Doug's blue eyes twinkled as he spoke. "We got quite a chuckle out of that story, remember?"

Karen wasn't likely to forget. The news article about a group of lonely bush pilots advertising for women had attracted national attention. Her own connection with Alaska had made the topic especially fascinating for everyone at the Paragon office. Karen had laughed and joked with her friends—until she'd learned that Matt had moved to Hard Luck. Then the whole story had ceased to amuse her. With women said to be arriving every week—a gross exaggeration, according to Lanni—Matt could easily fall in love with one of the newcomers. Why that should concern her, Karen didn't care to question.

"So this Dotty was recruited by the O'Hallorans?" Karen asked, reining in her memories.

"Yes, and then she married a guy named, let me see, Pete. Unusual last name. Lively or Liver or something."

"Livengood," Karen remembered. A man with a thick gray beard came to mind. She'd briefly danced with him at Charles and Lanni's wedding reception.

"In addition, a doctor flies in once a month."

"You sound like you want to be rid of me," Karen complained.

"Not at all," the older man reassured her, patting her hand. "You know as well as I do that I'm a mess without you. Why else do you think I personally requested you for my executive assistant when I was promoted? You deserved it as much as I did—heaven knows I wouldn't have gotten my promotion without you."

"Nonsense." But hearing him say so helped smooth her ruffled ego.

"Come back to work next spring after the baby's born," Doug suggested. "You've been very ill these past few weeks."

Karen bit down on her lip, upset at the way everyone was making decisions for her. She felt trapped and helpless. And angry.

"Nancy's doing a reasonable job filling in for you. She's not you, but she'll do until you're back on your feet."

Karen said nothing, unwilling to agree.

"Your job will be waiting for you," Doug promised. "But right now, you need to take care of yourself and the little one."

"Did Matt put you up to this?" she asked.

"No." Once again her boss was quick to set her straight. "He came to me with a number of questions, told me what had happened and left it at that. He's worried about you, like any husband would be."

"Matt is no longer my husband."

"I'm well aware of that, my dear, but did anyone tell him? He's fiercely protective of you, Karen. I know that bothers you, but in this instance I agree with the young man. Your health and that of the baby is what's most important."

"Yes, but—"

"Now, because I want you back, I've talked with the good people in the employment office, and if you agree, I'll arrange to have your furniture and other personal belongings placed in storage. Then later, when you're ready to return to California, everything will be here waiting for you."

The resentment she'd experienced earlier flared back to life. She didn't want anyone making that kind of decision for her. But her anger died a quick death as Karen acknowledged that Doug was acting out of genuine concern and affection. Besides, she would've come to the same conclusion herself. Her health and that of her baby had to take priority over her distrust of her ex-husband.

Moving to Hard Luck with Matt wasn't the ideal situation, but it made more sense than any of her other options.

"What do you say, Karen?" Doug prompted.

"All right, but just until the baby's born."

"Take as long as you like," he told her, patting her hand again. "When you're ready to move back to Oakland, your job will still be here."

Doug Sullivan left after their discussion, and Karen must have fallen asleep, because the next thing she knew a small noise jarred her awake. It took her a moment to realize she wasn't alone in the room.

"Sorry." Matt stood at the foot of her bed, looking sheepish. "I guess this wasn't meant to be used as a flower vase, huh?" He'd thrust a bouquet of roses into the water pitcher.

Karen couldn't keep from smiling. "You brought me flowers?"

He seemed almost embarrassed that he'd been caught. He shrugged and mopped up the spilled water with some tissues.

"Doug Sullivan was in to see me," she said.

Matt's hand stilled as he raised his eyes to meet hers. "I suppose you're angry because I talked to him. You might as well know I phoned Dr. Baker while I was at it. You've made it plain that you don't want me meddling in your life, but there's more to consider here than—"

"I'm not angry."

His head came up as if he wasn't sure he'd heard her correctly. "You're not?"

"No. I've decided the best thing for me and the baby is to do as you suggested and move to Hard Luck with you. But I want it understood right here and now that I'm returning to California as soon as the baby's born."

Matt's expression was astonished, then ecstatic. "Whatever you say."

"Don't think you're going to change my mind, Matthew Caldwell, because it isn't going to happen."

"Whatever you say, sweetheart."

Karen groaned. "I'm not your sweetheart or anything else."

"Maybe not, but you're the mother of my baby, and for now that's all that matters."

Matt felt lighthearted. If he'd ever needed to prove that sometimes the quickest route to what you want is an indirect one, he'd done it with Karen. He was convinced he could have argued with her until the twelfth of never and gotten nowhere. Only when he'd received Doug Sullivan's support did he get the results he wanted.

He stared out the window of the small aircraft as it passed over the rugged Arctic terrain, heading due north toward Hard Luck. The Midnight Sons plane, piloted by Ted Richards, had picked them up in Fairbanks.

Karen slept peacefully at his side. He restrained himself from placing an arm around her, although he'd been dying to do that from the moment they'd left Oakland a day earlier.

She wasn't happy about all this, but she'd finally listened to reason. The way he figured it, once she was in his home, he'd have her back in his bed in no time, and the rest would fall naturally into place.

To begin with, he'd make sure she understood that he wasn't going to ask anything from her physically. They'd need to sleep in the same room, though, so he'd be able to look after her properly when she was ill. That made perfect sense. Still, it might take some talking to persuade her to share a room—and a bed—with him, but he'd talk as long as he had to. Wear her down, he thought wryly.

Getting Karen back in his bed had haunted Matt from the night of his sister's wedding. Nothing had ever felt so right to him. That Karen should get pregnant from their one night together struck him as a kind of poetic justice.

Their lovemaking had always been incredible. That night was no exception. But it *was* an exception in another way—they'd made love without arguing first. During the last two years of their marriage, that had become a pattern, a negative one. They'd had a lot of fights—and always ended up in bed afterward.

No one would guess that his sweet-natured wife had such a temper. Their fights used to escalate quickly to comedy, with Karen throwing anything she could lay her hands on. Over the years he'd dodged books, cups, pillows. A turkey drumstick, once. And the madder she got, the more passionate she became. The hotter her temper, the hotter her desire. The fact that, with them, passion was usually tied to anger disturbed him.

And he knew it was something Karen hated about herself, this tendency to flail at her husband in anger, then reconcile in bed.

They'd broken the pattern the night of Lanni's

wedding. The reality that they'd created a baby still hadn't fully sunk in. Every time he thought about it he grinned.

In the airport that very day he'd found himself watching mothers with children. It was all he could do to keep from approaching total strangers and declaring that he and Karen were having a baby.

"We're almost there," he whispered. He slid his arm carefully around her; if she was going to be angry with him, then so be it.

Her beautiful long lashes fluttered open and she glanced out the small window on the opposite side of the plane. "How long have I been asleep?"

He was tempted to tell her that the length of time she'd been awake would have been easier to calculate. "Not long," he assured her with a straight face.

She raised her eyebrows. "I'll bet. Well," she said, stretching, "I hope I can sleep tonight."

She would—he'd make sure of that. Once upon a time they'd slept spoon fashion, cuddled up against each other, perfectly content. Now they would again. Every night if he had anything to say about it.

The plane descended slowly, aligning itself with Hard Luck's narrow gravel runway. A number of planes lined the field, and several more were parked alongside nearby homes, like cars in a carport.

Matt resisted the urge to point out that the wildflowers were in bloom, to exclaim how beautiful the countryside looked with the snow all gone. June was probably his favorite month here in the high Arctic. The days lasted well into the evening, and nights were only long enough for the stars to blink a couple of times, then disappear over the horizon, blinded by the light of approaching day.

"Lanni should be there to greet us," Matt told her. When he'd called his sister to tell her that Karen was returning with him, Lanni had shrieked with delight. She'd advised him to go slow with Karen, but he didn't need anyone to tell him that.

The Baron came down gently on the runway and coasted to a stop.

Sawyer O'Halloran opened the side door and lowered the steps. He offered Karen his hand as she climbed out of the aircraft, then greeted her with a warm hug.

"It's *great* to see you again."

"Thanks, Sawyer," she said a bit shyly.

It gave Matt a small degree of pleasure that she didn't just blurt out that she wasn't staying once the baby was born.

Sawyer loaded the luggage into his trunk, and ten minutes later they were at the lodge. Matt was eager to see the place after his two-week absence—and eager to learn how many new reservations Lanni had taken. Thanking Sawyer, he lugged in their suitcases and set them in the lobby, then called, "Lanni!"

"She's not here," Karen informed him with perfect logic after he'd called for his sister two more times. Then he saw a note propped up on the registration desk.

"So I see," Matt said, not entirely concealing his frustration. "Well, make yourself comfortable while I put our suitcases in the bedroom." He lifted the heavy bags and headed toward the master bedroom in his private quarters—a small apartment on the main floor.

"Matt."

He set the cases back down. "Yes?"

"Where are you taking my things?"

He'd just explained that, but he was a patient man. "To the bedroom."

"You appear to be carrying them into *your* bedroom."

"Mine? It's ours now, darlin'."

Her mouth thinned in a way that told him she wasn't pleased. "I believe *my* room is upstairs—*darlin'.*"

Matt's gaze followed the staircase that led to the second level and the rooms beyond. "But I thought—"

"I know exactly what you thought, Matthew Caldwell, and it's not going to happen."

Five

Abbey hummed softly to herself as she arranged the new books on the front display table. The town council had allotted her a small budget, and she'd quickly purchased the latest hardcover releases. She didn't expect them to remain on display for very long. Now that the Hard Luck Library was in full operation, almost everyone in town took advantage of it. Abbey had been hired to organize the library, but it was thanks to the generosity of Sawyer's mother, Ellen O'Halloran—now Ellen Greenleaf—who had donated a vast majority of the books, that the place even existed. It had been Ellen's dream. And now the people of Hard Luck had access to fiction of all kinds and for all ages, as well as a variety of resource materials.

Abbey bent down to replace one of the children's books and experienced a dizzy sensation. The room started to spin. She lost her balance and flopped onto the floor.

"Honey, I've been thinking…" Sawyer walked into

the library, halting abruptly when he found his wife sitting, dazed, on the floor. "Abbey? Are you okay?"

She gave him a wan smile. "My goodness, that was a shock."

"What happened?" Sawyer asked, helping her to her feet. He framed her face between his large hands and studied her intently. His frown deepened. "You're pale."

"I'm a little light-headed, that's all," she said, dismissing his anxiety.

"Light-headed?" His voice turned gravelly with concern. "I think you'd better talk to Doc Gleason the next time he flies in."

"Sawyer," she said, smiling softly, "I already know why this happened."

"You do?"

"I'm about ninety-nine percent sure I'm pregnant."

"Pregnant?" Her husband's mouth fell open. "You think we're going to have a baby?" He pulled out a chair, one she thought was meant for her, then promptly sat in it himself.

Abbey laughed out loud when Sawyer placed his hand over his heart and croaked, "You might have prepared me."

"Sawyer, we've talked about having a baby."

"I know, but this is different… You're pregnant!"

Abbey poured him a glass of water, which he swallowed in giant gulps. "We're going to have a baby." His eyes were loving as he gazed up at her. "Oh, Abbey, I can't begin to tell you how—"

"Stunned," she said.

"No, pleased. Happy. *Thrilled.*" His lips curved in a slow smile.

She smiled back. "I know." She'd never seen her husband react quite this way before.

"Have you told anyone else?"

"No. Sawyer, I'd tell you first. Anyway, it's still early...." But despite that, she was sure. The joy and excitement that welled up inside her were as unmistakable as the physical symptoms of pregnancy.

"Can I tell someone? This is too good to keep to myself. We should let Charles and Lanni know, don't you think? My mother!" he cried. "Mom will go nuts. She's dying for a granddaughter. Just look at the way she's taken to Scott and Susan, and after three sons who can blame her for wanting a girl? We should tell Christian." He was talking so fast the words nearly ran together. "I remember the morning he started talking about bringing women to Hard Luck. I kept thinking this was the craziest idea I'd ever heard. Then I met you, and now I'm so grateful for my brother's loony ideas. Charles is grateful too—he'd never have met Lanni if we hadn't needed more housing for the—"

"Sawyer," she said, interrupting gently. She touched his arm. "Don't you think we should let Scott and Susan know before we tell anyone else?"

"Scott and Susan...of course. You mean they don't already know?"

"No, sweetheart. Of course not." He made such a comical sight it was all Abbey could do to keep from laughing.

Sawyer stood up, then immediately sat back down. "Scott can help me build a cradle. But I don't want to ignore Susan, so maybe we should—"

She placed her arms around his neck and did the

only thing she could think of to silence him. She kissed him.

Slowly Sawyer eased his mouth from hers. "Abbey, we've got to—"

Determinedly she brought his mouth back to hers and kissed him again, revealing without words how much she loved him and how joyful she was to be carrying his child. This time she met with far less resistance.

Sawyer groaned and his arms circled her waist as he pulled her onto his lap. "Abbey..."

"Hmm?"

"I love you."

"I've never doubted that. We can tell the kids about the baby this evening, and then we'll phone your mother and let the rest of the family know."

Her kisses had mellowed him considerably. "All right, but I think you should come home and rest first."

Abbey sighed and pressed her forehead against his. "Someone needs to be at the library. Besides, we both know that if I went home neither one of us would rest."

"This is the trouble with having a wife," Sawyer muttered, grinning broadly. "You know me too well. You're right—resting *wasn't* what I had in mind."

As soon as she heard that Abbey O'Halloran was pregnant, Karen stopped by the library. She knew the building had originally been the home of Adam O'Halloran, Hard Luck's founder, and she gazed around with interest.

"Karen, it's good to see you." Abbey was sitting at the large desk in the main room, working on the card catalog. "You look great."

"Thanks. You, too." To Karen's mixed relief and chagrin, her bouts of morning sickness had all but disappeared in the two weeks since her arrival in Hard Luck. Matt gloated, certain that her return to health could be attributed to him. Karen preferred to believe it was the fresh Alaska air.

"I understand congratulations are in order," she said to Abbey, pleased that another woman in town was pregnant, too.

"So you heard about the baby," Abbey responded with a smile. "But then, I can't see how you *wouldn't* know. I swear, Sawyer's personally announced our news to everyone in Alaska. You'd think I was the only woman in the world who ever got pregnant."

"And I thought Matt was the one who believed that."

The two women chuckled. "I'm happy for you," Karen said, "and on a purely selfish note, I'm glad there's someone I can talk to about all this."

"The morning sickness is better?"

"Oh, yes." Karen sighed gratefully. "I can't understand it. When I was in California I considered it an accomplishment if I managed to get out of bed and dress. I arrive here, and it's like a miracle cure. Oh, I still have an occasional bout of nausea, but it's nothing like before." She didn't mention how much Matt wanted to take credit for that.

"It happens that way sometimes," Abbey told her with the wisdom of two pregnancies behind her. "Can I help you find something?" she asked. "I can recommend a couple of good books on pregnancy and infant care."

Karen grinned. "Matt bought about a dozen books

in California," she said. "Actually I came to volunteer my services."

"At the library?"

"If I could." She was eager to find something to occupy her time. Matt was busy with the lodge, and she rarely saw him more than twenty minutes a day. Although she was living with her ex-husband, Karen was lonelier than before. The first set of guests had arrived, and Matt had left for a two-day fishing expedition; he wouldn't return until later that afternoon. But before leaving he'd hired Diane Hestead, a local high school girl, as a part-time maid. Matt's sister, Lanni, was still handling reservations, but Karen hesitated to interrupt her. She knew Lanni was working on some travel pieces, articles she hoped to sell as a freelance writer.

"I'd like to volunteer my services for the wedding reception for Mitch and Bethany Harris, too." Lanni had told Karen that the couple had been married ten days earlier in San Francisco. A huge welcome party was planned for when they returned from their honeymoon.

"We'd love to have you if you're sure you feel up to it," Abbey said excitedly.

Karen was tired of sitting around the lodge with nothing to do—no defined tasks. No responsibilities. Twiddling her thumbs. She'd even organized Matt's office, although she wasn't sure how he'd feel about it. He might have studied accounting, but the man didn't know the meaning of the words *filing system*. Earlier that morning, Karen had gone into his office to set the mail on his desk and couldn't find a space.

How he could manage anything in such clutter was

beyond her. She'd left the mail, determined to remind her ex-husband that this was no way to run a business. Ten minutes later she'd gone back into the office and tackled the mess herself. Before she realized it, the morning was gone and she'd set up a filing system for him.

Although she told herself she'd done it out of her own need for organization, she knew that wasn't entirely true. She wanted to help Matt. Contribute.

He hadn't asked one thing of her. He treated her like a guest, and that wasn't what she wanted. If she was going to make the lodge her home for the next five or six months, it was important to do something in return. She wanted to be part of the community, too, and helping with this reception was a good start.

Abbey beamed. "Ben insisted on doing all the cooking. Mariah Douglas—she's the Midnight Sons secretary, in case you haven't met her—is working on the decorations. Dotty Livengood's helping, too."

Karen was eager to make friends with the other women in Hard Luck. She hadn't ventured far from the lodge and was still finding her way around the small community. Everyone seemed to know her, though, thanks to Matt.

"The reception's on Saturday," Abbey continued, "and Mariah and Dotty are hoping to get everyone together Friday evening around seven to decorate. We'd love it if you'd come."

"I'll be there," Karen promised.

The July sun shone brightly as she wandered slowly back to the lodge, enjoying the day's warmth and the friendly greetings. Matt hadn't given her a specific time to expect him home, but she hoped it would be soon.

The first thing Karen noticed when she stepped into the lodge was the inviting smells coming from the kitchen. Savory spices mingled with the scent of simmering beef and vegetables.

"Matt?" She found her ex-husband in the kitchen, wearing a starched white apron. He stood in front of the stove and grinned wryly when he saw her.

"Hi, honey, I'm home."

Karen begrudged the way her heart leapt with excitement at seeing him again. She was lonely, she told herself, that was all. What did she expect when her family and friends were in Anchorage, hundreds of miles away?

"How'd everything go?" she asked in an effort to take her mind off her pleasure at having him home.

"Great. The guys are showering now. We had a fabulous time."

"Did you catch any fish?" Matt wasn't likely to get much repeat business unless he supplied the fishing experience of a lifetime. Karen had read in one of those glossy travel publications that it was cheaper to go on a safari in Africa than an expedition in Alaska.

"Both guys said this was the best fishing of their lives. They've already given me a deposit for next year."

Karen couldn't help sharing in his pride. "That's wonderful!"

Matt added chopped potato to the stew. "Did you miss me?"

She had, but she wasn't about to admit it. "You were only gone two days."

"That doesn't answer my question."

She knew what he was hoping to hear, but she didn't think it was a good idea to reveal how lonely she'd been. "It was…quiet around here," she said unwillingly.

He couldn't seem to take his eyes off her. "You know, you're looking more beautiful every day. Pregnancy obviously agrees with you."

Compliments made Karen uncomfortable. "I can't button my jeans. And I'm only three months along," she complained. "At this rate, I'll end up resembling a battleship."

He stepped away from the stove and made a show of studying her. He twisted his head one way and then the other. When he'd finished, he said in a thoughtful tone, "Maybe, but you'll be the prettiest battleship around."

Matt always knew how to cheer her up. But she didn't *want* to laugh and joke with him; that kind of camaraderie was dangerous. She had to remind herself repeatedly that after the baby was born, she was returning to California. It was becoming more and more difficult to think about her life away from Matt.

"Let me help you with dinner," she insisted.

"No way." He was prepared to chase her out of the kitchen, but she stood her ground.

"Matt, I *want* to help. If you don't let me, I'll go crazy with nothing to do."

He gave in. "Fine. You can set the table for our guests."

Then, because she was pleased to see him, and because she forgot for a moment that they were divorced and sleeping in separate rooms, she stood on tiptoe and briefly brushed his mouth with hers.

Matt stared at her as though she'd suddenly sprouted wings. Or antennae. His expression said he didn't understand why she'd done this. She wasn't sure herself. But it felt right. It felt more than right—it felt *good*.

The folks in Hard Luck were getting to be experts at celebrating weddings, Ben Hamilton mused contentedly. He worked in the kitchen beside the school gymnasium, assembling hors d'oeuvres for Bethany and Mitch. First there'd been a wedding and reception for Sawyer and Abbey, and almost directly afterward another one for Pete and Dotty. Come spring, there was Charles and Lanni's, and now a reception for Bethany and Mitch.

His gaze followed the couple as they circulated among their guests. Pride filled him as he regarded Bethany—his daughter. The realization still took some getting used to. He actually had a daughter. One he'd never known about until she'd arrived in Hard Luck last year.

It saddened Ben to acknowledge that he hadn't been there for either Bethany or her mother, Marilyn. Instead, he'd spent twenty-odd years in the United States Navy, first in Vietnam and later on in various ports around the world. When he'd retired ten years ago, only in his forties, he'd come here to Alaska and opened his café. He hadn't married; his affair with Marilyn was a brief episode he'd never forgotten. One that, it turned out, had left him with a daughter.

And my, oh my, Bethany was pretty. Looking at her now with her husband and stepdaughter, Chrissie, Ben wondered how he could have produced such a charming, caring, lovely young woman.

With more than a touch of regret, he realized he hadn't. Her mother and Peter Ross, the man who'd loved Marilyn, had raised Bethany; *they* were the ones responsible for the woman she'd become. His contribution to the effort had been strictly genetic. Still, he took a good deal of pleasure in his daughter—in the kind of person she was. It thrilled him no end that Bethany and Mitch had decided to continue living in Hard Luck. He hadn't figured out what role he'd play in her life—that was up to Bethany—but he was grateful for the opportunity to know her.

"What are you doing in the kitchen?" Christian O'Halloran demanded. "You should be out there with everyone else, enjoying the party."

Ben wasn't comfortable outside a kitchen. He found he related to folks far more easily when he had something to occupy his hands, when he had coffee to pour and food to serve. He'd never been one to mingle and mix at parties.

"I've got plenty to do right here," he said. He had the hors d'oeuvre platters ready, plus the fruit and vegetable trays. Fine-looking trays, too, even if he did say so himself.

He'd spent a lot of time making sure everything was as appealing to the eye as it was to the palate. The fact that he'd borrowed a cookbook by Martha Stewart from the library was his and Abbey's secret.

"But this is Bethany and Mitch's reception," Christian told him, as if he didn't already know.

"Ben, what can I do to help?" Mariah Douglas stepped into the kitchen and stopped abruptly when she saw Christian O'Halloran. The two regarded each other like wary dogs.

Ben had never considered himself much of an expert when it came to dealing with women. He was a crusty old bachelor, set in his ways. Nevertheless, he liked to think he was a good judge of people. It seemed to him that Mariah Douglas was sweet on Christian—which was unfortunate, because the youngest O'Halloran brother avoided Mariah like a communicable disease.

"Hello, Christian," she greeted him stiffly.

Considering that they worked together every day, it astonished Ben that Mariah was actually blushing.

"Mariah." Christian nodded once, formally, and Ben noticed that he backed up several steps.

Mariah returned her attention to Ben. "Can I help?"

"I've already offered," Christian said.

If Christian hoped those curt words would dismiss her, his plan failed. Ben decided it was time to intervene. "These trays could do with replacing, and that punch bowl needs to be refilled and set out on the table," he said briskly. Someone had brought the almost empty bowl into the kitchen. "Must be plenty of thirsty folks."

Ignoring Christian, Mariah headed for the punch bowl.

Christian started to lift a tray, then hesitated when he saw Mariah. "Don't do it like that."

"Like what?" she snapped.

Ben didn't blame her for using that tone. He wasn't privy to what was going on between them, but he'd listened to Christian's complaints about his inept secretary often enough to feel some sympathy for her.

"Don't fill the punch bowl here," Christian muttered as if that should have been obvious. "Did you stop to think how much easier it would be to carry the bowl to the table first and *then* mix the punch?" He gestured to the wine, soda water and fruit juice lined up on the counter.

"Yes, but—"

"Here, I'll do that and you carry the trays out."

"No," Mariah insisted. "I said I'd take care of this. Stop worrying about me."

Christian and Mariah reached for the punch bowl at the same time. Ben could see it coming even before it happened. As they tugged at opposite sides of the bowl, the bright red remains of the punch swirled around the bottom and upward in a wave—which slapped Christian's white dress shirt and ran down the front of his pants. He gasped and leapt back.

"Christian!" Mariah cried with alarm. "Oh, no."

"Now look what you've done!" Christian shouted.

"Me? You brought this on yourself!"

Ben was proud to see that Mariah had learned to hold her own against her employer. She didn't even blink as he glared at her.

Christian's eyes narrowed and he whirled around to leave the kitchen. "Tell Mitch and Bethany I'll be back as soon as I've changed clothes," he said to Ben.

The instant Christian was out the door, Mariah sagged against the counter.

"You all right?" Ben asked.

"I'm fine," she muttered. "It's just that Christian and I... Oh, never mind. I'm sorry, Ben."

"No need to apologize to me." He picked up the food tray himself and carried it out to the table, then stepped back to admire his work. He grinned, inordinately pleased with his efforts. It was a small thing, but he felt pride in being able to contribute to his daughter's reception.

"Ben." Bethany joined him. "I don't know how Mitch and I can possibly thank you. Everything looks so beautiful."

Ben decided he could live on those words and the happiness gleaming in her eyes for at least a week. "It's nothing," he said with a nonchalant shrug, as if he'd whipped up the entire display that morning. In actuality, he'd been planning and working on it for weeks.

"The food's fabulous," Bethany told him. "And I know what those grapes and watermelons cost. You've done such a beautiful job." She stood on tiptoe to kiss his cheek.

"I wanted your party to be special," he said, uneasy with emotion, even positive emotion. Damn, but he was proud of Bethany.

She'd chosen a good man in Mitch, too. Ben grinned. He was pretty gauche about this romance business, but he was well aware that Mitch's daughter was responsible for bringing her father and Bethany— her teacher—together. Who knew an eight-year-old could be so smart? Ben was convinced he couldn't have picked a better man for Bethany had he sought out a husband for her himself.

"Dad told me what you did," Bethany said, slipping her arm around Ben's waist. "Writing Mom and Dad that letter was really thoughtful."

He shrugged again, making light of the single most difficult letter he'd ever written. "It was nothing."

"Dad told me you thanked him for raising me so well. It wasn't easy telling my folks I'd found you, and I think Dad might've been afraid that you'd replace him in my life."

Ben had given that some consideration, too. Peter Ross deserved a lot of credit for marrying a young woman pregnant with another man's child, and raising that baby to become such a beautiful, generous woman. Ben wanted to thank this man he'd never met, and at the same time reassure him that he had no intention of stealing his daughter away. Peter was her real father; he respected that. Ben felt it was time to clear the slate with Marilyn, too. He'd written his regrets to Bethany's mother and asked her to forgive him for having left her to deal with the pregnancy alone.

"Dad said he'd be pleased to count you as a friend," Bethany told him, eyes glistening with tears.

Ben already knew that. Peter's letter had arrived two days before Bethany's wedding, and Marilyn had also written him. He'd loved her, Ben realized; perhaps he still did. But he was content. She was happy and he'd discovered a woman who was not only his daughter but his comfort, his friend. Everything had worked out for the best.

"Are you going to dance with me?" Bethany asked, hugging him.

"Dance? Me?" Ben experienced a fleeting moment of panic. "Not on your life. That's what you've got a husband for. Now let me go back to the kitchen before your guests get hungry." He hurried back to where he felt most at home but turned to study his daughter one last time. His heart seemed to expand a bit as Bethany stepped onto the dance floor with Mitch.

* * *

Matt knew Karen was having a good time. He'd been relying on this wedding reception; the last time the people of Hard Luck had gathered to celebrate a wedding was the night Karen had spent with him. Matt sincerely hoped that history was about to repeat itself.

He'd certainly been restraining himself with his ex-wife—he'd been as good as a choirboy. In three weeks he hadn't even *tried* to kiss her, which was a real feat, considering how he felt about her.

Matt feared she was looking for an excuse to leave, something that would prove she'd be better off living elsewhere. True, her options were limited right now; nevertheless she did have some. For instance, he knew that her parents had invited her to move home if things became too uncomfortable. But Matt had decided he wasn't giving Karen any reason to leave Hard Luck. He had five and a half months to prove himself. Five and a half very short months.

His hands-off policy was working, too; Matt could tell. She was much more relaxed with him. And almost against her will, she was beginning to appreciate life in Hard Luck. She'd become part of the community, made new friends. And having his sister in town had been more of an advantage than he'd anticipated. The two women got together at least twice a week. Karen had started helping with the reservations, gradually taking over from Lanni when Matt was away, and responding to queries left on the answering machine.

Because she wanted to keep busy, Karen was also volunteering two afternoons a week at the library. In a matter of days she was more familiar with the townsfolk than he was after living in Hard Luck for nearly a year.

Another thing that boded well was the interest she'd taken in the lodge itself. Without his saying a word, Karen had started adding those small feminine touches he'd hoped for.

Before he knew it, she'd draped a patchwork quilt over the back of the sofa. A vase of wildflowers magically appeared at the registration desk. She'd even brought in some pieces of scrimshaw and jade figurines. One day, out of the blue, a hand-carved totem pole appeared over the fireplace; it looked perfect, as though it had always stood there. She never said where she'd got it or how much she'd paid. Now and again, he found her looking at it and smiling happily to herself.

Over dinner a couple of nights before, she'd offered him a suggestion—a good one too. She'd pointed out that the lodge was attracting tourists from all over North America, and in order to reach Hard Luck they had to fly over the Arctic Circle. Karen came up with the idea of having certificates printed for everyone who stayed at the lodge, making them official members of the Arctic Circle Club. Soon she was flipping through catalogs and making more suggestions. Like selling coffee mugs with the lodge's name and logo. That was a good idea, he agreed, especially if people took them home and used them at the office. Nothing like free advertising.

He was encouraged by all these indications of her growing attachment to Hard Luck and the lodge. But the most promising sign so far was the difference in her attitude toward him. Even if their relationship was more comradely than romantic. Or perhaps because of that.

Okay, so he'd been out of line thinking they should sleep together right away. It was an innocent mistake. They weren't exactly strangers; besides, she was pregnant with his child. He'd assumed...and he shouldn't have. It was taking far longer than he'd expected for her sensibilities to right themselves.

Damn it all, Matt wanted her with him. His bed had never seemed so big...and so empty. Every night he lay on his back and stared at the ceiling, knowing the woman he loved, the woman pregnant with his child, slept in the room directly above him. If ever there was a guarantee of insomnia, Karen had provided it.

On a more positive note, everything else in his life seemed to be falling satisfactorily into place. With reservations coming in for the dogsledding tours, plus the business he'd managed to pick up this summer, there was a good possibility he'd break even. Well, perhaps not this year, but next year for sure. At the moment he was content just to meet his expenses. The lodge was an investment, and for the first time since he'd told Karen about it, she was beginning to see the promise.

He watched her now, laughing with her friends, hugging Bethany, wishing the young couple well, and Matt grew impatient. Dancing had started an hour ago, and he wanted her in his arms.

Joining Karen, he slipped an arm around her waist. If he hadn't known she was pregnant, it would've been hard to tell. But he did know, and he found himself conscious of her thickening middle. Matt believed this baby was giving him a second chance with Karen.

"How about a dance?" he asked. He'd had a couple

of beers with the guys and was feeling mellow. Mellow enough to put aside his inhibitions.

"A dance?" She gazed up at him, frowning slightly as if she wasn't sure they should.

"One dance," he pleaded softly. They were halfway onto the dance floor already; she could hardly refuse.

"One dance," she echoed.

God was on his side, Matt decided, because the song was a lovely old ballad from the sixties, the music slow and sultry. Matt drew Karen into his arms, maintaining a respectable distance between them. Just enough to reassure her.

To his delight she leaned closer and pressed her head against his shoulder. "I love weddings," she murmured.

She hummed along with the music, and Matt closed his eyes, remembering the days when she came to him without restraint, without reserve. Remembering the times she'd freely shared her love.

One dance quickly became two, and then three. It felt so familiar—as if she'd never left him, never stopped loving him, never gone through with the divorce.

When Matt looked up, he noticed that a number of people had already left. By tacit agreement, he led Karen outside; together they strolled back to the lodge.

Once home it seemed only natural to kiss her. It was what he'd longed to do for weeks, what had been on his mind for days, ever since he'd learned they'd be attending the reception.

Karen sighed when his lips met hers. Knowing this was what they both wanted, Matt deepened the kiss. His heart nearly flew out of his chest at the way her arms tightened around him. He caressed her back, savoring her softness. He investigated the slender curve of her spine and sought the fullness of her hips. He pulled her closer, needing her, wanting her to know exactly how much.

"Karen, I love you. I'm crazy about you," he whispered between kisses.

"Oh, Matt…"

He kissed her again with sweet desperation. "You know what I want," he said huskily when the kiss ended.

Karen braced her forehead against his shoulder and drew in several deep breaths. "I… I think it's time I went upstairs."

"Upstairs? You mean you aren't—you won't—" He stopped abruptly. He opened his mouth to argue with her, then closed it, knowing there wasn't any point.

"Good night, Matt," she said, and kissed his cheek. "Thank you for a lovely, romantic evening." With that, she turned and walked up the stairs. Alone.

Six

Karen had been more tempted to sleep with Matt than she ever wanted him to know. It shocked her how susceptible she was. She'd been in Hard Luck less than a month, and already he'd half persuaded her to accept his dream, the same way he had so many times before.

Already he had her believing in the lodge, in the feasibility of its success. Only, Karen should have known better—*did* know better. She'd walked that path too often not to recognize what awaited her at the end.

This latest scheme would be like all the others. Matt would completely win her over and then, when she least expected it, he'd abandon the entire venture for some ridiculous reason. Their past was riddled with such incidents. Her father had repeatedly done the same thing to her mother. It still astonished Karen that out of all the men in the universe, she had to marry one just like him. Yet, Karen reminded herself, she dearly loved her father. He had his faults, true, and they were glaring, but like Matt, he was a good man.

She could feel herself weakening. She loved living in Hard Luck and had quickly formed friendships. The sense of community and family was strong, and that appealed to her, especially now. People cared about each other. And like all of Alaska, the scenery here was spectacular.

From her bedroom window she had a stunning view of the Brooks Mountains. She could see blooming tundra, awash with colorful wildflowers. The beauty of the landscape was almost more than she could absorb.

It went without saying that in January, when the baby was due, the world outside her window would be a very different one. In the dead of winter, daylight would be minimal. Temperatures would dip to thirty and forty below. She'd lived in Alaska a long time, though, and that didn't really alarm her.

Karen stood gazing out her window at the morning and mulled over the situation with Matt. What was it about weddings and slow dancing that weakened her resolve every time?

A bright red warning light had started flashing in her mind the moment Matt led her onto the dance floor. She'd known even before he kissed her what was likely to happen. Yet, wanting him the way she did, she'd been powerless to stop.

If she didn't develop some control over her sexual attraction to him, it could definitely become a problem....

The obvious solution was to accept her parents' offer to move to Anchorage and stay with them until the baby was born. The thought depressed her so much she immediately dismissed it. She closed her eyes, remembering all the places she'd lived as a child.

They'd moved so often, never set down roots in any one town. Karen refused to live that migratory existence ever again. And she didn't want to be reminded of all those distressing emotions, all those sad childhood times—especially when she was about to have a child of her own.

It took some doing to admit the truth: she didn't want to leave Hard Luck. Nor did she want to be separated from Matt, not now, not while she was pregnant.

Later, she told herself, after the baby was born she'd visit her parents before she headed back to California.

She dressed and wandered downstairs. Yawning, she stretched her arms high above her head, surprised by how good she felt.

Matt, who stood behind the reservation desk, glanced up at her. "You look well rested," he murmured dryly.

"I am." Briefly she wondered what had happened to his usual cheerful greeting. She'd heard a joke long ago that said there were two kinds of people in the world—those who woke up and said, "Good morning, God," and those who said, "Good God, morning!" Karen had her own observation to add; she'd noticed that these two very different types of people often found one another—and married.

Matt fell into the chipper, lighthearted category and she into the other. Morning had never been her favorite time of day, although it was easier when she had a regular schedule. This basic difference between them went further than simply the way they reacted to mornings. Matt was an optimist; she, however, was a realist. Or so she'd always insisted.

This particular morning, however, she felt good—for no particular reason. She poured a glass of orange juice and carried it to the front desk. "I'm meeting Lanni today," she said, sipping the juice.

Matt gave her a perfunctory nod, then resumed his study of the ledger.

"Is something bothering you?" she asked.

"Not a damn thing," he snapped.

"My, my, we're in a grumpy mood this morning."

He glared at her.

Then it hit Karen like a ton of glacial ice. Her ex-husband was actually sulking because she'd refused to go to bed with him. This wasn't like Matt, either. As long as she'd known him, he'd never been subject to mood swings. Rarely, if ever, was Matt in a bad mood.

Some of the difficulties in their marriage had resulted from his almost childish insistence that everything would work out. Everything would be fine. He refused to look at any problem seriously, or even acknowledge there *was* a problem. This moody self-absorption was a side of him she hadn't seen, and frankly it amused her. She smiled.

"What's so funny?" he demanded.

"You. Matthew Caldwell, you're pouting."

"I most certainly am not." He slammed the ledger closed. "If there's anything wrong with me—and rest assured there isn't—it's that I didn't sleep well last night."

Karen didn't ask why; she knew. Their pattern had been broken. The fighting, followed by the intense lovemaking. They'd made progress, whether Matt recognized it or not.

He released a long sigh and shook his head. With a quick wave Karen started out the door, eager to see Lanni.

"Karen." Matt stopped her. "You said something last night that intrigued me."

"I did?"

"Before you went upstairs, you thanked me for the romantic evening."

"Yes?" she asked, not understanding his question.

"What made last night romantic?"

She shrugged. "I don't know. The way we danced, I guess. The way you held me, the way we kissed…"

"But you didn't spend the night with me."

This was another area of dissension that had often annoyed Karen. "Don't confuse sex with romance. A woman likes to be…wooed." She raised her eyebrows. "It's an old-fashioned word, I know, but it's exactly what I mean."

"Wooed." Matt repeated the word as if it contained magic. His eyes brightened.

"I suspect it's not a good idea to tell you this, but you tempted me last night," Karen said. "It was all I could do to refuse you."

A cocky grin spread across his face. "Really." A second later, he started to frown. "If that's the case, why *did* you refuse me? You've got to know how much I love you, how much I want us to get back together again."

She stared down at the floor, not ready to admit that she wanted it, too. "I need more time," she said, knowing that sounded lame. But it was the truth.

"What if I wooed you like you said?" he suggested. "Would that help?"

She looked at Matt and trembled with dread. Because, without a doubt, it was already too late. She loved him, loved the lodge, loved living in Hard Luck.

"Karen?" he asked again.

"I think it might be a good thing for us both," she answered. And then, afraid of what the future held, she hurried out the door.

Matt gleefully tossed his ballpoint pen in the air and caught it. He didn't know why he hadn't thought of this sooner. The solution was so simple! All this time, and he'd overlooked it.

He needed to prove to Karen that he loved her and—perhaps just as important—appreciated her. And he needed to do it clearly and conclusively. He had to give her a reason to marry him again—other than the obvious one that she was pregnant with his child. He'd assumed that should be enough, but if he'd learned anything in his four-year marriage it was that women were rarely practical when it came to matters of the heart.

With the same determination he'd brought to rebuilding the lodge, he decided to take on the project of wooing back his ex-wife.

Soon, however, his grin faded. He set the pen down on the registration desk and wiped a hand across his suddenly damp brow.

Karen wanted to be wooed. How was he supposed to do that?

"What do you think?" Lanni asked, studying Karen as her friend turned to the last page. This was agony, and Lanni chewed her lower lip, anticipating Karen's reaction to her latest article.

Charles had read the piece and raved about it, but Charles was her husband and, crazy as she was about him, she doubted he was a good judge of her work. According to him, she was brilliant. Although she loved him for believing that, she needed a less biased opinion.

Karen, on the other hand, could have been an editor.

Her former sister-in-law sighed and straightened the stack of pages.

"Well?" Lanni asked, barely giving Karen time to breathe. She yanked out the chair and sat across the table from her. "Tell me what you think. You don't need to worry about upsetting me. I just want the truth."

"The truth," Karen repeated. "Lanni, this is a beautifully written piece."

Lanni loved hearing it. "You think so? You really think so?"

"Have you decided where you want to submit it?"

Lanni named a nationwide, glossy travel periodical and waited for Karen to suggest she aim for a regional magazine, instead.

"Sounds like a good idea."

"You think so?" Her vocabulary seemed to be limited to those three words.

"Lanni, you should have more confidence in your talent. This article about Mt. McKinley is one of the best-written and best-researched I've ever read. This past year..." She hesitated. "I'm not sure how to put it, but there's a maturity to your writing that was lacking earlier. I'm sure the apprenticeship program with the

Anchorage paper helped, but you've acquired more than style or technical skill."

Lanni hung on every word.

"Your work shows a new...depth."

Loving Charles had done that for her; Lanni was convinced of it. Their love, their marriage, had changed her view of life, deepened her understanding of people, given her a greater sympathy and tolerance. Charles had also helped her develop a more profound appreciation for the land.

They'd waited eight months, until she'd finished the apprenticeship program, before they got married. If it had been her decision she would've married Charles last Christmas, but he'd been the one to insist they hold off until she'd fulfilled her obligation to the paper. He'd worried about the fact that he was ten years older, and it was almost as if he expected her to change her mind. But not once had she doubted that she was meant to be with Charles O'Halloran. Nor did she doubt his love.

For years their two families had hated each other. Catherine Fletcher, Lanni's grandmother, had brought nothing but pain into the O'Hallorans' lives. David O'Halloran, Charles's father, was the only man her grandmother had ever loved. Yet Catherine had done all she could to hurt him, because he'd hurt her. Wrongs had been committed on both sides.

David and Catherine were both dead now. Lanni was sure they'd approve of her marriage and the reconciliation it had brought. Despite the animosity between their families, she and Charles had fallen in love. In some ways, she believed they were soul mates. Meant for each other. It sounded fanciful, but she'd come to think they'd been given this one opportunity to make up for the wrongs of the past.

"There're a couple of typos," Karen murmured, flipping through the pages. She pointed them out, then swallowed the last of her cold drink. "I wish I could put my finger on what's changed in your writing."

Lanni smiled to herself. She didn't need Karen to tell her. She already knew.

Matt slid onto a stool in the Hard Luck Café. Anyone who needed advice sought out Ben Hamilton. Although he'd never been married most people thought of him as something of an expert when it came to relationships.

"Coffee?" Ben asked, gesturing with the pot.

"No, thanks. I came in for a little advice." Matt wanted to get straight to the point.

"You're not going to order anything?"

"No, I wanted to ask—"

"Listen, advice is no longer free," Ben said. "You sit back and chow down on a piece of my homemade apple pie, and then I'll tell you whatever you want to know."

"I'm not hungry," Matt objected. He'd never known Ben to push food on anyone. "Business slow or something?"

"All these women in town aren't exactly helping, you know? Every one of them's got a kitchen, and if they don't already have a family to cook for, they're inviting the men in town to dinner. Business is down twenty percent from a year ago."

It looked like Matt was going to be the one with the sympathetic ear.

"So that's what the frequent-eater program's all about?"

"Exactly."

Matt understood Ben's concern, and he did want to support the Hard Luck Café. "All right, give me a cup of coffee." He was desperate enough to pay for coffee he didn't want if Ben could help him win over Karen.

Ben nodded, obviously pleased. He filled Matt's cup, then pressed his hands against the counter. "What can I do for you?"

"It's about Karen."

Ben's mouth quivered with the telltale signs of a smile. "Goes without saying."

Once more Matt was as direct as possible. "She wants to be, uh, *wooed*."

"Wooed," Ben repeated as though he'd never heard the word before. "What does that mean?"

Matt hadn't considered that Ben wouldn't know. It would be a shame to waste a couple of bucks on a cup of brew if Ben wasn't going to help him. "Why do you think I'm asking you?"

The door opened and Sawyer O'Halloran walked in.

"Sawyer," Ben called out, looking relieved. "You got a minute?"

"Sure." Sawyer perched on the stool next to Matt's.

"Matt, here, has a problem. Maybe you could help."

"Be glad to do anything I can," he said, righting his mug.

"Karen wants to be wooed," Matt told him.

"Any suggestions?" Ben asked the pilot.

Sawyer frowned as he took his first sip of coffee. "You're asking the wrong guy. I know what the word means, in a general way, but how to go about it is another question."

"You convinced Abbey to marry you," Ben reminded him.

"Sure, but it wasn't easy."

"How'd you do it?" Matt asked. True, he'd been married himself, married to Karen, but they were both young then. He didn't remember that he'd done anything special. She'd apparently thought marriage was a good idea, and he'd gone along with it. There hadn't been any talk of this wooing business; it sure hadn't been the problem it was now.

"First, I didn't realize I was in love with Abbey," Sawyer confessed. "All I knew was I didn't like any of the other men bugging her. When I heard Pete Livengood had proposed I went ballistic."

"Pete's married to Dotty," Matt said, confused.

"That was before Dotty arrived," Ben explained.

"Okay, so Pete proposed to Abbey."

"It made me furious," Sawyer muttered. "I told myself that Christian and I had brought these women up to Hard Luck and it had cost us a lot of money. I hadn't gone to all that trouble and expense so the local grocer, twenty years Abbey's senior, could steal her away."

"So what'd you do?" Matt asked.

"I did the only logical thing I could think of. I told her if she was that desperate to find a husband, I'd marry her myself."

Wow, maybe this'll be easier than I assumed, Matt thought. "And that worked?"

Ben chuckled. "It worked so good the next thing I heard, Abbey had packed her bags and was planning to leave on the first flight out of here."

"You're joking." Matt could see they weren't. "So what'd you do after that?"

Sawyer held his mug with both hands and frowned. "What could I do? I begged."

"Begged?" Matt figured he'd already tried that and it hadn't worked.

"I'd never felt lower in my life," Sawyer said. "One thing I knew for sure—if Abbey left I wouldn't be worth a damn. I loved her, and Scott and Susan."

"What did you say that convinced her?"

Sawyer considered that, then shook his head. "Don't know. I was just so grateful she agreed to marry me I never asked."

The door opened again, and ten-year-old Scott O'Halloran flew into the café.

"Don't be bringing that dog in here," Ben warned.

Scott said something to Eagle Catcher, who stopped abruptly, tail drooping between his legs, and turned around. With a backward glance he ambled out the door.

"I swear that dog understands English," Matt said.

"I'll only be a minute," Scott told the husky. He hurried to the counter and slapped down a dollar bill. "You got any of those ice cream bars left, Ben?"

"Sure do." Ben turned and headed for the freezer in the kitchen.

"So Karen wants to be wooed," Sawyer said to Matt. "She wants to be courted."

Wooed. Courted. Whatever you called it, Matt still didn't have any clearer idea of what she was seeking than before he'd asked his friends. He knew the results he was after, he understood the general strategy, but he didn't have any specific plans.

"That's a good idea," Scott murmured absently.

"What is?" Matt asked the boy.

"Courting Karen. I wish she'd marry you again, because then Angie or Davey would have someone to play with after they're born."

"Those are the names Abbey, the kids and I've picked out for the baby," Sawyer explained. "You might listen to Scott—he offered me some valuable advice when I needed it with Abbey."

"Really?" Matt said eagerly. He didn't believe a ten-year-old kid could supply him with the answer three adult men couldn't. "So you think it's a good idea for me to, uh, court my ex-wife?"

Ben returned with the ice cream bar. Scott regarded the others suspiciously. "Yeah," he said as if he thought this might be a trick question.

"So, how's a man supposed to go about that?" Ben asked Scott, leaning halfway over the counter.

"Well," Scott said, clearing his throat, "he could flatter her."

The three men exchanged glances. "That sounds like a plan," Ben said.

"Yeah. Tell her…tell her that her eyes are as brown as a bear's winter coat," Sawyer suggested.

"She's got blue eyes," Matt said.

"Blue…blue…" Sawyer repeated in an apparent effort to find something to compare to her eyes. He must've said the word ten times before he stopped, defeated. "Anyone else got any ideas? I'm not exactly a poet, you know."

Matt had already figured that out for himself.

"Be affectionate," Scott said next.

The three leapt on that like hungry wolves on fresh kill. Matt was the first one to realize it wouldn't work.

"But… Karen's already pregnant," he babbled. Good grief, he couldn't get any more affectionate than that.

"True," Sawyer agreed.

"What about flowers?" Ben threw out. "Women are crazy about getting flowers. Aren't they?"

Matt had thought of that, but he didn't have the money for such extravagance. And second… "Why would she want flowers when the tundra's in full bloom?"

"Maybe you should pick her some," Ben said.

Matt dismissed the idea with a shake of his head. "I've got better things to do than traipse around there looking for tulips."

"There aren't any tulips on the tundra," Sawyer told him.

"I know that!" Matt snapped, losing patience. He glanced at Scott again. "Any other ideas?"

The kid was busy eating his ice cream bar, and Matt could tell from the way Scott kept looking over his shoulder that he was eager to get back outside with his dog. "Romance her," he said tersely.

"Romance," Matt echoed. That was what he'd thought this entire conversation had been about in the first place.

"Can I go now?" Scott asked him.

"You can go." Matt removed the dollar bill from the counter and handed it back to the boy. "Put that on my tab, Ben," he instructed. "Thanks for your help, Scott."

The boy was gone in a flash.

"Just a minute!" Sawyer jumped off his stool.

"Man, why didn't I think of this sooner? I've got the perfect solution!"

Matt was paying attention now. "You do?"

"Hot damn, I can't believe I didn't think of this sooner." Sawyer paced the floor, threading his way between the tables. "One of the most romantic things Abbey and I ever did was fly out to Abbey Lake."

"Abbey Lake?"

"Yeah, I named it after her. She got a real kick out of that."

"I don't have any lakes to name after Karen." Matt was losing confidence again. Unlike him, the O'Hallorans owned a lot of land in these parts and could easily afford to name lakes after the women in their lives. Besides, land wasn't available to the everyday citizen the way it used to be, before statehood.

Sawyer gave an exasperated sigh. "I'm not saying you should name a lake after Karen. I'm saying you should take her into the wilderness with you."

"Fishing?"

"Why not?" Sawyer asked.

"Yeah," Ben echoed, "why not?"

Matt couldn't think of a reason not to do it. "You seriously think she'd like that?"

"Abbey thought it was a lot of fun. I flew her and the kids out to the lake. Must've been a little more than a year ago now," Sawyer continued. "It was one of those really hot summer days we get now and then."

"Had quite a hot spell last year about this time," Ben commented. "That was when I served sweet-and-sour meatballs with pineapple for dinner one night. Sort of my salute-to-the-tropics night. John Henderson ate two platefuls." Ben grinned proudly. "I had those little umbrellas sticking out of the meatballs. They looked real festive."

"Go on," Matt encouraged Sawyer, afraid that Ben might have distracted him.

"I remember it was one of the first times I ever kissed Abbey. The kids were playing in the water." His eyes grew warm with the memory. "That was when I realized how much I liked being with her."

"You must have if you were kissing her," Ben muttered. He reached for the coffee and topped up their mugs.

Still, Matt was skeptical. "I'm not so sure Karen's the outdoor type."

"You think Abbey is?" Sawyer asked.

Sawyer had a point. The idea started to build in Matt's mind. The two of them out in the Alaskan tundra. Alone... It led to all kinds of interesting possibilities.

"Tell her if she's answering the phone at the lodge she should have fishing and camping experience herself," Ben counseled. "That way she can answer the travel agents' questions."

Matt nibbled his bottom lip. "That sounds plausible."

"Then take her out there the same way you would any tourist."

Well, yes, except that they'd share a tent. And a couple would zip their sleeping bags together, wouldn't they? Oh, yes, the thought of them crowded together in a small tent held plenty of appeal. Karen curled up against him in a double sleeping bag would be heaven after the frustrating nights he'd spent tossing and turning in his huge bed.

"You might've hit on something here," he said slowly.

"Give it a try," Ben said, looking pleased with the outcome of their conversation. "I'd say let her do the cooking, though."

"But I generally do all that myself," Matt explained. When people paid him a thousand dollars or more for the Alaska fishing experience, they didn't expect to fry up their own dinners.

"Women are really particular when it comes to that sort of thing," Ben said. "They like to do their own cooking."

It had proved true so far, Matt thought. Karen had done all the cooking unless they had guests, in which case he took over.

"I think you might be right." Matt eased himself off the stool. "Thanks for everything."

"No problem," Ben and Sawyer said together as Matt left the café.

"Did you get everything settled with Matt?" Scott asked Sawyer over dinner that evening.

"Settled?" Abbey looked from her husband to her son.

Scott stabbed his fork into the soft, pink flesh of fresh salmon. "Dad was giving Matt Caldwell advice about how to romance Karen."

"Sawyer? Giving Matt advice? On romance?" Abbey wasn't sure what to think.

Sawyer grinned from ear to ear. "Yup. The poor

guy came into Ben's all depressed. No idea how to get his ex-wife back."

"And *you* told him?" This should be interesting.

"Yup." Sawyer made an exaggerated display of polishing his fingernails against the flannel sleeve of his shirt.

"You?" Abbey almost choked holding back a giggle.

"And Ben," Sawyer added defensively.

"They asked me a bunch of questions, too," Scott informed her.

"They asked you?" This was getting better by the minute.

Scott nodded.

"And what did you tell these three great romantics?" she asked her son. It took considerable restraint to keep the laughter out of her voice. Although she loved Sawyer, the man knew as much about romance as she did about flying a plane. To his credit he tried, but she'd had to coax him every step of the way.

"I told Matt he should be affectionate," Scott muttered.

Sawyer frowned. With an air of superiority, he said, "Well, Scott, to my way of thinking, affection is something you give a dog. Women require a whole lot more."

"Is that right?" Abbey asked, and took a bite of her dinner in an effort to hide her smile. "What else?"

Scott's eyes narrowed as he concentrated. "Um, I told Matt to flatter Karen. Tell her how pretty she is and that kind of stuff."

"That's good."

"You think so?" Sawyer looked surprised. "We had a problem with that one."

"Oh?" This didn't come as any surprise to Abbey.

"Karen's got blue eyes and we couldn't think of something poetic to compare her eyes to."

"What about the sky?" Susan suggested, joining in the conversation.

"The sky," Sawyer repeated, pointing his fork at the eight-year-old. "I'll have to tell Matt about that."

Abbey rolled her eyes. "Just what did you three masters of romance finally suggest?"

Sawyer set aside his fork and planted his elbows on the table. He leaned forward as if he was about to confide a wonderful secret.

"We're all ears," Abbey told her husband.

Sawyer spoke to the children. "Remember the time I took you and your mother to Abbey Lake?"

Both children nodded enthusiastically.

Sawyer beamed. "That's it."

"You mean you suggested Matt take Karen swimming?" Abbey remembered how cold the water had been, and the water fight that had ensued.

"Not swimming exactly," Sawyer said.

Abbey studied him expectantly.

"I thought the most romantic thing he could do was take Karen camping."

"Camping?" Abbey exploded.

"And fishing. Ben made a point of telling him he should let Karen do the cooking, too. Women feel real proprietary about those sorts of things," he added as though he was an expert on the subject.

"Oh, Sawyer," Abbey groaned, closing her eyes.

"Yup," he boasted. "That's what romance is all

about. Taking a woman into the wilds, letting her share the wilderness experience."

Abbey buried her face in her hands.

"Great idea, don't you think?"

Abbey slowly shook her head. "Where, oh, where did I go wrong?"

Seven

"You know what I was just thinking?" Karen said over dinner. She studied Matt, who sat across the round oak table from her. Without guests, it made sense for them to dine in the kitchen, something they'd done all week.

Matt's look was absent, and he seemed absorbed in his own thoughts.

"Matt?"

"Sorry," he said, glancing up.

"I went over your books this afternoon." Karen half expected him to complain that his finances were none of her affair, and he'd be right. The lodge was his business, not hers.

"Did I make a mistake, mark the debits as credits?" he joked.

Matt would never make such an error, not after the months of training he'd received while working for one of Anchorage's largest accounting firms. "No, of course not."

The fact was, Matt was far more qualified than she to handle the books.

"I'm surprised at how well you're doing financially."

"It looks promising, doesn't it?" According to his reservation list, the dogsledding tours were booked solid. He'd collected a nonrefundable advance fee from each client. Despite herself, Karen was impressed with the way he'd handled the lodge's finances.

"You might think about hiring someone to help you this winter."

"Really?" Her suggestion appeared to surprise him. "You mean other than housekeeping?"

"Eventually you'll need some help in the kitchen and a couple more maids," Karen said. "And I was thinking you might want someone to pinch-hit for you with the winter tours." Since the baby was due in January, shortly before the first tour was scheduled, Karen was beginning to worry that Matt would be too busy to spend time with her. Although he'd arranged for professional mushers to train, supply and escort the participants, he'd be on the trail himself, hauling food, tents and other essentials. He'd be the one setting up camp each evening, cooking the meals, getting everything ready for the arrival of the dog teams.

"Why would I want to hire anyone just yet?"

Karen studied her stir-fry and pushed the snow peas around her plate. How could the man not realize that the dates of his winter tours conflicted with her due date? She wanted Matt with her when the baby was born, but more than that, she wanted him to *want* to be with her. However, it wasn't something she'd ask of him.

"No reason," she murmured, doing her best to hide her disappointment. "Looking over your ledgers, I thought you'd be able to afford a couple of extra employees."

"I don't see why," he said without elaborating.

"Oh." Her appetite gone, Karen carried her plate to the sink. She stood with her back to him, collecting her composure.

Karen had done everything she could think of to push Matt out of her life. It shouldn't surprise her that he wasn't going to be available when she needed him. Maybe she should let him know how she felt, but the words stuck like a fish bone trapped in her throat.

"You sound disappointed," Matt said.

"No, no, the lodge is your business. It was a suggestion, that's all. Don't worry about it."

Later that evening, Karen was sitting on the porch knitting a blanket for the baby when Matt eased himself into the chair next to hers.

"I've been doing some thinking," he said.

"About what?" The knitting needles made soft clicking noises, and she jerked the soft pastel-green yarn.

"You've been taking a few phone reservations for the fishing tours lately."

"Yes." Karen was astonished by how many people booked their vacations a year or more in advance. If the orders coming in for the next summer were any indication of what was to follow, Matt would be sold out before the end of the current year. She'd had no idea that people would be willing to spend this kind of money to catch a few measly fish.

"I, uh, suspect there's been the occasional question you couldn't answer." He knew that to be true. More than once, she'd had to write down questions, ask Matt for the answers and then phone back.

"Yes," she said.

"It seems to me you'd be able to deal with that type of question better if you'd gone out on a fishing trip yourself."

"You want me to fly hundreds of miles from here to fish and camp so I can answer travel agents' questions?" That seemed a little extreme to her.

"Sure," Matt replied as though this made perfect sense to him. "You'll love it."

"We'll camp…in a *tent?*" Perhaps there was some other accommodation he hadn't told her about.

"It's the only way to go," Matt said, looking delighted with the idea.

"We'll cook over a camp stove?"

"You've never had better-tasting meals."

Karen didn't quite believe that.

"So, what do you say?"

She looked at him in shock. They'd been married four years and he apparently hadn't noticed she wasn't the camping type. She opened her mouth to tell him exactly what she thought, then stopped herself.

Matt was right. This was exactly the sort of thing she should do.

"If you agree, we can leave in the morning," Matt coaxed, his eyes twinkling.

"Will we be gone one night or two?"

"Whatever you want."

"One night… You're sure you want to do this?" Karen didn't want to be difficult, but she did enjoy the more basic comforts.

"Of course I'm sure," Matt said. "We'll have a wonderful time, just you wait and see."

Karen would've been more than willing to wait. But she wanted to support Matt, and if that meant traipsing around the tundra, then she'd prove what a good sport she was by doing it.

Mariah Douglas waited for the paper to come out of the printer, then reread the letter she'd composed on Sawyer's behalf.

The phone rang and she reached for the receiver. "Midnight Sons. Mariah speaking. How may I help you?" The static on the line told her it was a long-distance call.

"Mariah?"

"Tracy!"

She was thrilled to hear from Tracy Santiago. They'd become good friends and corresponded regularly. Tracy was the Seattle attorney Mariah's family had hired when they'd learned she'd accepted the position with Midnight Sons.

At the time there'd been a lot of publicity, some positive and some negative, about the O'Hallorans "luring" women north.

Although Mariah had repeatedly reassured her parents that everything was fine, they'd insisted on having the O'Hallorans investigated. They'd hired Tracy to fly up and check everything out. The attorney had asked a lot of questions, which made some people uneasy, and she'd inadvertently stirred up bad feelings. Mariah didn't blame her; Tracy was only doing her job.

Unfortunately Mariah had already started out on

the wrong foot with one of her bosses—Christian O'Halloran. When Tracy showed up, the youngest O'Halloran brother had held Mariah personally responsible and labeled her a troublemaker. From that day forward, he'd actively looked for an excuse to fire her. Mariah was certain she would've been laid off long before now if it hadn't been for Charles and Sawyer.

From that rocky beginning, things had quickly deteriorated. Lately her relationship with Christian had become worse than usual. The incident at the wedding reception—when he'd spilled punch on himself—hadn't helped. He hadn't actually said so, but she knew he blamed her.

"I'm calling in an official capacity," Tracy explained. "It's been a year now, and your commitment to Midnight Sons is over."

"Yes, I know."

"Will you be moving back to Seattle?"

Mariah's family had probably put Tracy up to this, but Mariah didn't even consider the suggestion. In the past twelve months, she'd come to love Alaska and Hard Luck. For the first time in her life, she was out from under her family's dominance. She made her own decisions—and, consequently, her own mistakes.

"I'm staying right here," Mariah said.

"You're happy, then?" Tracy asked, sounding unsurprised, perhaps even a bit wistful.

"Very happy."

"What about the other women?"

"So far, everything's worked out really well."

The door swung open, and Duke Porter walked into the mobile office. Mariah's gaze followed the bush pilot. She didn't know what it was about Tracy and Duke, but those two definitely rubbed each other the wrong way. Mariah had watched the sparks flash whenever they were together—and yet they seemed to gravitate toward each other. It was an interesting phenomenon.

Personally Mariah liked Duke. True, he was a bit of a chauvinist, but a lot of what he said was simply for show. Or provocation. He'd toss out the most ridiculous comments just to rile everyone, then sit back and look pleased with himself. Tracy's problem was that she'd taken Duke at his word.

"I don't know if you remember Matt," Mariah said conversationally. "He's the one who bought the old lodge from the O'Hallorans. It's in full operation now, and his ex-wife, Karen, is back with him. Oh, and Abbey's pregnant. Karen, too. And Mitch and Bethany are married. So how's everything with you, Tracy?" She purposely used the other woman's name, expecting a reaction from Duke.

He didn't disappoint her. No sooner had the lawyer's name left her lips than Duke wheeled around. "Is that highfalutin lawyer bugging you again?" he demanded.

"Just a minute, Tracy," Mariah said and held her hand over the mouthpiece. "Did you say something, Duke?"

"Is that Tracy Santiago?" he asked.

"Yes." Mariah nearly laughed out loud at the way fire seemed to ignite in Duke's eyes. Tracy was probably the only woman to challenge the laughable things Duke said and did. He didn't much like it.

Mariah always got a chuckle out of Duke's heated

response to Tracy. In fact, everyone laughed; never-theless, Mariah sensed that Duke and Tracy could be good friends if they'd put their differences aside.

"What's she want?" Duke asked.

"To talk to me," Mariah informed him sweetly, turning her back to him. "I'm here," she told Tracy.

Duke strolled over to Mariah's desk in a blatant effort to catch what he could of the conversation. He didn't bother to hide his eavesdropping.

"Is that Duke Porter I hear?" Tracy's usually con-trolled voice went chilly.

"If you two ever made the effort, you might be friends," Mariah said to them both.

"I'd rather be friends with a skunk," Duke said loudly enough to be heard in Fairbanks.

"You tell Mr. Chauvinist I'd rather clean fish than have anything to do with him," Tracy snapped.

"Does she have a reason for calling or is she just hoping to stir up more trouble?" Duke asked, making sure Tracy heard that, as well.

"Mariah, listen, this doesn't sound like a good time for us to talk. Why don't you give me a call if you need anything." Tracy hesitated. "You know, I've come to think of you and the other women as my friends."

"You *are* a friend," Mariah assured her.

"With a friend like that, who needs—"

"Duke, enough," Mariah said, glaring at him.

"All right, all right," he muttered as he moved away from her desk.

"You'll keep in touch?" Tracy asked.

"Of course," Mariah promised. "Thanks for call-ing, Trace. It was good to hear from you."

She was about to replace the receiver when Tracy giggled and said, "Mariah?"

"Yeah?"

"Is Duke still there?"

"Yup."

Tracy giggled again. "Do something for me, would you?"

"Sure."

"Go over to him and kiss him and tell him it's from me. Then ask if I'm still his favorite feminist."

Mariah grinned. "You're *sure* you want me to do this?"

"Positive. I just wish I could see the look on his face when you tell him that kiss is from me."

"You got it," Mariah said, and she hung up the phone.

Duke studied her quizzically. "What did she want *this* time?"

Mariah rolled back her chair. Her eyes on his, she stood and walked slowly toward him. He was obviously uncomfortable with the way she'd focused her attention on him.

"Mariah?" Duke glanced around, then started moving backward as she continued her approach. He cleared his throat and glanced in both directions. "What's the matter with you? You look like something out of *The Exorcist*."

"Tracy asked me to give you this," she said, making her voice low and sultry.

When Duke was backed right up to the wall, Mariah braced her hands on both sides of his face. Duke's eyes widened, and he opened his mouth to speak. He didn't get a chance.

Mariah planted her mouth firmly over his.

Duke squirmed.

Mariah heard the door open, but paid no heed.

"Mariah!" Christian yelped. "Duke! What the hell is going on here?"

"You didn't tell me my feet were going to get wet," Karen complained as they trudged along the marshy banks of the lake. Sawyer had delivered them by float plane to the prime fishing area where Matt brought his clients. The plane had taxied as close to shore as possible, but they'd had to walk the rest of the way in. Through the water. No one had bothered to tell her this, Karen thought with some bitterness.

Something bit her and Karen slapped her neck. The mosquitoes swarming about her face were evidently thrilled with her arrival. Already she had two huge swellings on her neck. She'd be lucky to get out of this place whole at the rate the bugs were dining.

"If your feet are wet you'd better put on a fresh pair of shoes," Matt said after he finished unloading their supplies.

"I only have the one pair. You told me to pack light, remember?" If Sawyer was late picking them up the following afternoon, Karen swore she'd kill him. Her enthusiasm for this undertaking had never been high. The little interest she did feel was vanishing rapidly.

"We'll make camp by that cluster of trees," Matt told her, pointing into the far distance. "The river's directly behind it."

Karen drew a deep breath as she remembered Lanni's adventure with the brown bear when she'd taken Abbey's children out to gather wildflowers on the tun-

dra. Scott had delighted in telling Karen how he was
sure they were about to become "dead meat" that afternoon.

Matt had tried to reassure her about bears, but she
wasn't taking any chances. She'd had Mitch Harris
teach her how to shoot off the can of pepper spray.
Karen gave a heartfelt sigh. Matt seemed to believe
this trek in the wilds would be one grand adventure.
He'd talked excitedly about the wildlife they might see,
mentioning moose, caribou, Dall sheep and wolves.
Then he'd blithely told her she didn't have a thing to
worry about.

"Why do mosquitoes love me so much?" she grumbled, although she didn't really expect an answer.
"You'd think they were holding a dinner party and I
was the main course."

"They're always more of a problem by the water,"
he reminded her.

Karen's feet made squishy sounds with every step
she took. Matt might have advised her about adding
an extra pair of shoes to her pack, she thought again—
but she didn't want to be a complainer.

He was trying to make this a positive experience for
her, and she felt guilty every time she found something
else to gripe about. Unfortunately a camping-and-fishing trip wasn't even close to anything she considered
fun. If Matt and his buddies enjoyed this kind of stuff,
fine. Just leave her out of it.

It seemed they'd been walking for miles, but in actuality, she realized, it couldn't have been more than
a few hundred yards.

Matt slid the large backpack from his shoulders and

set it on the ground. "We'll make camp here." Quickly and efficiently, he began to unpack.

He'd carried almost everything, and feeling equal parts guilt and exhaustion, Karen leaned against a large boulder and simply watched him.

"First I'll pitch the tent and then we'll do some fishing."

"What about dinner?" She was already hungry. It must have something to do with running around in the great outdoors, breathing fresh air. But then, you couldn't find air any purer than what she'd been breathing in good ol' Hard Luck. It seemed unnecessary to travel hundreds of miles north when the air at home was just as fresh and unpolluted. Besides, she could feel a cold coming on and would've preferred the comfort of her own surroundings. The truth was, she wouldn't mind crawling into bed right this minute. A *real* bed. *Her* bed.

"Dinner?" Matt said, his eyes twinkling with mischief. "That's why we're doing the fishing first."

Karen groaned. He expected her to catch her own dinner. A crucial question occurred to her. Namely, what would she do if she struck out—did no fish mean no dinner? This was the first time she'd ever gone fishing. *And probably the last,* she muttered to herself.

She felt decidedly annoyed that her very own ex-husband would assume she knew anything about this camping and fishing business when she'd never so much as baited a hook.

"It won't take me long to set up camp," he said, removing a few more things from the huge backpack.

Karen was astonished that he could carry everything they'd need for the night in that contraption.

And she was impressed at how easily he assembled the small tent. Before she knew it, Matt stood in front of her, holding two fishing poles. "Ready?"

She wasn't. "I guess so," she said, forcing some enthusiasm into her voice.

It was an effort to ease herself away from the rock. Matt offered her his hand.

"I'm not good at this kind of thing," she said, slapping at another mosquito. Then she sneezed. Twice.

Matt led her to the river, whose rushing water emptied into the lake, and in no time Karen had a fishing pole in her hand. However, she soon learned that whatever it was that attracted fish—and she refused to believe it was the offensive-smelling egg at the end of her hook—she lacked it.

Clearly Matt didn't suffer the same affliction. He cast his line into the water and almost immediately got his first bite. He'd brought in two fish, one after the other, and all Karen had caught was a cold.

She sneezed once more and rubbed her nose with her sleeve.

Matt stood in the middle of the river—or "stream," as he called it—wearing rubber hip boots. Water swirled around him as he held his fishing pole in one hand and fed the line with the other. He glanced over at her and smiled in perfect contentment.

"It doesn't get any better than this!" he shouted over the sound of the surging water.

"You mean it gets worse?" she shouted back. Matt laughed; he seemed to think she was joking, but she was serious. Dead serious.

Uneasy about walking into the middle of a river, despite the protection of the hip boots Matt had given her, Karen remained close to shore, feeding her line into the clear, tumbling water. She'd about given up hope of snagging one of the rainbow trout that seemed to migrate toward Matt's line when she felt something nibble at her bait. She actually *felt* the fish nibble. Her eyes lit up, and she gasped with excitement.

"Matt." She didn't dare shout for fear of alerting the fish that it was about to become their main course. Matt didn't respond, so she raised her arm above her head and waved.

At that precise moment, the fish decided to take the bait and the fishing pole shot out of her hand.

"Matt!" she screamed.

"Grab that pole," he yelled, wading toward her, his eyes filled with panic. His expression told her she was replaceable, but the rod and reel were not.

Karen didn't have any choice but to go splashing into the fast-rushing stream after the rod. It would've been lost if the reel hadn't caught between two rocks. She just managed to rescue it, but lost her fish.

By the time she made her way back to shore, she was drenched.

Matt reached her side and jerked the pole away from her. "I thought I explained that this is expensive equipment! I can't afford to lose a rod and reel, so hold on to it, will you?"

She looked up at him and blinked back tears. When she spoke her voice sounded muffled—probably because she was trying not to cry. Or sneeze. "I had a fish on the line. I... I wanted you to watch me bring it in."

He exhaled sharply, then placed his arm around her

shoulders. "I'm sorry, honey. I shouldn't have yelled at you."

Karen sniffled, more than ready to abandon the whole venture, but Matt wouldn't hear of it. Against her will she found herself standing on the edge of the flowing water less than five minutes later. Sneezing. It seemed to take an eternity to attract another trout.

Then, suddenly, she experienced the same sense of exhilaration as a fish nibbled at her bait. This time she was ready when the trout encountered the hook. She gripped the fishing pole with both hands, prepared to catch a trout or die trying.

"That's it, honey!" Matt hollered, his excited voice carried on the wind. "Give the line more slack," he ordered.

Karen had no idea what he was talking about, but she must have done something right, because she didn't lose the fish. Her arms ached with the strain, but she held on as the fish leapt and fought.

Matt was there to lift her prize out of the water, using the net. "He's a beauty," her ex-husband told her with a proud grin.

"He sure is." Karen gazed at the fish fondly as it flopped around in the net.

Matt deftly removed the hook from the trout's mouth and was about to place it in the basket when Karen stopped him.

"Put him back," she said.

"Back?" Matt's eyes held a look that said he must've misunderstood her.

"He's too beautiful to eat. And too brave and noble."

"Karen...you're not serious."

"I mean it, Matt!" she cried. "I don't want him

killed." Not after the way he'd struggled to live. Not after she'd looked him in the eye.

Matt did as she asked, but he wasn't pleased.

From that point forward, their afternoon went downhill. Karen thought wryly that from her vantage point there was nowhere else for it to go. By dinnertime she was tired, hungry and in no mood to commune with nature. She wanted dinner, a hot bath and her own bed, in that order. No luck on any score, however.

Her contribution to dinner was a disaster. Fortunately, Matt had caught a couple of trout, which he cleaned while Karen prepared the vegetables. She dumped a can of beans in a pot, then sliced some potatoes to fry in a pan. By accident, she charred them. Smoke got in her eyes, blinding her, and she coughed and hacked. When she could see the potatoes again, they resembled dried cow chips. And the beans had become a mass of soggy lumps. To her relief, Matt took over then, and handled the frying of the fish. The result was delicious—even though Karen's misery didn't allow her to truly enjoy it.

Matt's festive mood had dissipated by the time they crawled into the tent that night. Tired as she was, Karen had assumed she'd immediately fall asleep. That wasn't the case.

For one thing, the atmosphere in the tent was…intimate. If she'd understood that they were going to be holed up inside this tiny space together, she would've insisted they bring an additional tent.

"Something smells," she said after a few minutes. Every time she closed her eyes, her nose was assaulted by a repugnant scent. It reminded her of skunk.

"It's your mosquito lotion," Matt suggested.

"No, it isn't."

"It is, Karen. I've been smelling it on you all day."

"Fine." She rolled away from him, presenting him with her back. Just like a man to stink up a place and then claim it was the woman's fault. Anyway, if it *was* the bug repellent, which she doubted, he had it on, too. Maybe not as much as she did, but still…

Ten minutes must have passed before Matt spoke again. "I didn't mean that as an insult," he said gently.

"I know. I'm just tired and cranky." What she wouldn't give for a hot bath and clean sheets…

"You comfortable?" he asked next.

"No." She itched and her back hurt. Matt had put an air mattress under the sleeping bag, but it was a poor substitute for a real bed. The ground was still hard.

Five minutes later she announced, "I've got to go to the bathroom."

"You went half an hour ago."

"I can't help it. These things happen when a woman's pregnant. You don't need to come with me—I'm perfectly capable of marking my own territory."

Matt chuckled, but followed her out of the tent nonetheless. When they crept back inside, the smell of the bug repellent wasn't as strong as it'd been earlier. Or maybe she'd just grown used to it.

Matt sprawled out atop the sleeping bag. He lay on his back, hands tucked behind his head.

Karen glanced at him, then released a slow, pent-up sigh and lay down again. She was careful to keep a respectable distance between them.

This wasn't so bad, she decided. It wasn't nearly

as comfortable as the lodge, but she'd survive for one night. As long as they weren't attacked by any wildlife.

"Are you asleep?" Matt asked.

"No."

"Why don't you put your head on my shoulder?"

In other circumstances Karen might have worried that Matt was planning to seduce her. She doubted it now, since she wore half a bottle of bug repellent and hadn't bathed. Tentatively she rested her head on his shoulder and closed her eyes.

That felt better. A lot better.

"I'm a disappointment to you, aren't I?" she asked softly.

"No."

"I don't think I'm a good advertisement for the business. If any of the travel agents ask me about the fishing, I guess I can tell them about the one I set free."

Matt ran his hand along her hair. "You're doing okay."

"Well… I do have to confess this isn't my idea of a fun time."

"Really?" Matt seemed surprised.

"I'm sure plenty of women enjoy camping-and-fishing trips, but unfortunately I'm not one of them."

"But I thought—" He bit off the statement.

"What did you think?" she prodded.

He hesitated.

"Matt?"

"I thought…you'd consider this…romantic."

"Romantic?" The man needed therapy. Or maybe just a good dictionary.

"You said you wanted to be wooed."

"I do," she told him, "but not like this."

Matt pulled away from her, raising himself up on one arm. Karen was unprepared for the sudden movement, and her head hit the ground.

"Ouch." Her eyes smarted. She rubbed the back of her head.

"Why isn't this romantic?" Matt demanded.

"You have to ask?" She made a sweeping gesture with one hand. "My feet have developed jungle rot. I've been the main course and every other course for the entire mosquito population. Then you set me in this river, and when I nearly lose your precious rod and reel, you act like it's worth more than I am!"

"I'll have you know that reel cost five hundred dollars."

Karen gasped at the news, but it didn't slow her down. "*Then* you insist I cook dinner, probably to punish me because I had the audacity to set free a brave, beautiful trout who deserved to live."

"Oh, please."

"And you call this romantic?" she sat up, crossing her arms. "I call it torture."

The silence fell like a landslide between them.

"All right," Matt said after an awkward few minutes. "We got off to a bad start. I'll do better next time."

"Next time?" There was more?

"You wanted wooing, didn't you?" He had the nerve to sound angry. "And wooing means romance, right?"

"Right."

"Then that's what you're getting."

Eight

"Just look at me," Karen told Lanni, holding out her bare arms for inspection. A number of red, swollen mosquito bites marked her pale skin. "The bugs ate me alive."

Lanni walked over to the library table where Abbey kept the newest hardcover releases. She chose a murder mystery Duke Porter had returned earlier that afternoon. "Are you telling me you didn't have a good time?"

Karen shrugged, not sure how to answer her friend, who also happened to be Matt's sister. She realized she was placing Lanni in an uncomfortable position by asking her to side against her own brother.

"I had the experience of a lifetime—and I've never been more miserable." Karen sighed heavily and made a dismissive gesture. "I didn't mean to put you on the spot. It's just that this whole fishing business has left me flustered. And cranky." She sighed again. "Matt seemed to think he was doing me a favor."

Karen began to look through the library books, grateful for an excuse to get away from the lodge.

Matt had been sullen and uncommunicative ever since they'd returned. Granted, she hadn't exactly been cheerful herself. She didn't understand how two people who clearly loved each other could find themselves at odds over something as ridiculous as a fishing trip. Matt had been trying to share his vision of the future. And she'd…well, she'd been looking for a way to survive a night in the wilderness.

"It may not have been the vacation of your dreams," Lanni commented, "but now you'll be able to answer any questions the travel agents ask, won't you?"

"I'm convinced that was just a ploy Matt used to get me to come with him," Karen muttered. "It turns out that his sole purpose was to romance me, if you can believe it."

Abbey came in at that moment, carrying a tray filled with tea things from the library kitchen. "I'm afraid Sawyer and Ben are to blame for that," she said, setting the tray on the desk.

"What do they have to do with this?" Karen wanted to know.

As she poured them each a cup of tea, Abbey said, "Apparently Matt decided to, uh, seek their advice on how to win you back."

"Ben and Sawyer?" Lanni cried. "Why, Ben's never even been married!"

"I know," Abbey said, attempting to conceal a smile and failing. "Frankly, Sawyer isn't much better when it comes to romance. He tries, but I'm afraid he was a bachelor for too many years. I planned to warn you, but one thing led to another, and before I realized it you and Matt had already left."

"He dragged me into the wilds in the name of romance." Karen shook her head. How could Matt possibly have thought she'd consider it romantic to traipse around for two days in wet shoes, with mosquitoes, the threat of bears and no hot water?

"I'm crazy in love with Charles," Lanni said, "and I do happen to like camping. Nothing romantic about it, though. In fact, I can safely say Charles knows as much about romance as Matt. In other words, nothing."

"What man really does?" Abbey murmured as she handed around a plate of homemade cookies to accompany the tea.

Karen shook her head. "I guess I was asking the impossible when I suggested Matt woo me. Instead, he woed me." She chuckled at her own witticism.

The other women laughed, too.

"When we were first married," Abbey said, "I could see that this romance business was going to be a problem. I love Sawyer so much—he's a good man, a wonderful husband and father. I guess women are more sentimental than men. We occasionally want a symbol or an expression of love. I mean, I want him to understand there are certain dates that are important to me—dates I want him to remember. Not that I expect anything extravagant. The price of the gift isn't important."

Karen and Lanni nodded in agreement.

"It's the thought that goes into it," Karen added for good measure. "And knowing that he cares enough to make the effort. No woman likes to be taken for granted."

"Exactly," Abbey said.

"What dates did you give him?" Lanni asked. "That is, if you don't mind my prying."

"Not at all." Abbey stirred a spoonful of sugar into her tea. "I explained to Sawyer that Valentine's Day, my birthday, our anniversary and Christmas were important to me. I asked that he remember me on those days." Her eyes grew warm. "He said there wasn't a chance on this earth that he'd forget me any day of his life—which was sweet, but not the point."

"How'd you clue him in on buying you a gift?" Karen asked.

"Actually, Scott was the one who told him that when I said I wanted to be remembered I was really saying he should buy me something."

"What did Sawyer say to that?"

Abbey grinned. "He took out a pen and a piece of paper and wrote down all the dates, then tucked it in his wallet."

"So, *has* he remembered?" Lanni asked eagerly. "You know, this is good advice."

"Yeah, he has." Abbey grinned even more widely. "He's never had to buy a woman presents before—apart from his mother—so he generally seeks advice from the kids."

"Scott and Susan?" Karen couldn't suppress a laugh.

"I know. At least my husband had the sense to figure out that I wouldn't be interested in Barbie's Playhouse or a new computer game. For my birthday this year he bought me a cookbook about homemade bread."

"Not bad," Karen said, impressed. She recalled that

for her birthday the last year she and Matt were married, he'd bought her a lens for his camera.

"It *was* a thoughtful gesture," Abbey agreed, "but he had an ulterior motive. He was mostly interested in having fresh-baked bread," Abbey said. "Like his mother used to make."

"What did he give you on Valentine's Day?" Lanni asked.

Abbey sipped from her tea. "He wasn't very imaginative. He bought me a box of chocolates and then promptly picked out his favorites."

"Matt mailed me a card for Valentine's Day," Karen murmured, remembering how that card had affected her. She'd dug it out of the garbage and kept it.

"I know why he did," Lanni told her. "At least I think I do. You sent a Christmas card for Matt last year, along with your gifts to the family, remember?"

Karen wasn't likely to forget. She'd agonized over that card. She hadn't wanted to ignore him, but at the same time, she didn't feel it would be a good idea to encourage him to think there was any possibility of reconciliation. He'd never mentioned the card, or said anything about the note she'd sent with it. She wondered if he'd kept it, the way she had his valentine message.

The valentine card was meant to be a reminder that he still loved her and wanted her with him, she suspected. It had come when she was most vulnerable, when she'd been trying her hardest to put Matt and their marriage behind her. As if she could *ever* forget Matt, no matter how hard she tried.

"What's going to happen with you and my brother?"

Lanni asked, her expression serious. "Will you really go back to California after the baby's born?"

Karen didn't know how to answer that. "I'm not sure… I want us to make a new start together. Heaven knows I love him enough, but we still have things to work out."

"He's trying," Lanni said.

Karen scratched at the mosquito bites on her arms. "I'm afraid if he tries any harder it'll do me in."

Charles was reading a scientific journal when he heard someone on the porch. Setting aside the magazine, he walked into the living room, half expecting Lanni's return from the library.

To his surprise his visitor was his youngest brother. "Well, hello, Christian. Come on in."

"Thanks." Christian stepped inside and glanced around. "Where's Lanni?"

"Over at the library."

Christian seemed relieved. "I hope I'm not disturbing you," he said, with an uneasiness that wasn't like him.

"Not at all. Can I get you anything?"

"Yeah," Christian said stiffly. "A new secretary."

Charles didn't bother to conceal his impatience. "What's the matter with Mariah?"

"We don't get along," he spat out. He sank onto the sofa. "I don't know what's wrong, but I don't like the woman. Never have."

"What does Sawyer think?"

Christian shrugged. "He doesn't seem to have a problem with her, and since we went to the expense of flying her up to Alaska, he isn't that keen on firing her."

"So you've come to me, hoping I'll talk Sawyer into agreeing with you."

Christian's eyes brightened. "Yes," he blurted, and then shook his head. "No. I don't know what I want. Yes, I do. I want Mariah out of that office. If she chooses to stay in Hard Luck, fine. As far as I'm concerned, she has as much right to stay here as anyone else."

"What about employment?"

A pained expression came over Christian's face. "Ben's been talking about hiring some help."

"But Mariah's not a waitress."

Christian rubbed a hand along the back of his neck. Charles could tell he'd given the matter thought. "Matt will need to take on an employee or two at some point. Let him deal with her. Just get her out of my sight."

Charles mulled this over, unsure how to respond. "It could be a while before Matt can afford to take on an employee. And it wouldn't surprise me if Karen decides to stay after the baby's born. That'll mean extra expenses—and an extra person to help out at the lodge. Karen's already filling a lot of the gaps. Do you honestly think Mariah can afford to wait around till Matt's ready to hire her?"

"No." Christian frowned. "Darned if I know what to do with her. There's got to be somewhere she can go. I wish Sawyer and I could agree on this."

Charles sat on a chair across from his brother, gazing down at his feet. He was reluctant to involve himself in areas like hiring—and firing. Although he was a full partner with his two brothers in Midnight Sons, he was a silent one. He left these types of decisions to Sawyer and Christian.

"Has Mariah made expensive mistakes?" he asked, buying time to consider the situation. Charles couldn't remember ever seeing Christian so flustered. Just the fact that he'd come to him for advice said quite a bit.

It took Christian a long moment to answer. "Mistakes," he finally repeated. "She made plenty of those in the beginning, but she seems to manage adequately enough now."

If the increase in profits was any indication, the woman had been a godsend, Charles mused. She'd skillfully organized the office and developed a system of rotation for the pilots that they felt was fair. That was something Sawyer and Christian had never accomplished. Mariah had even started an advertising program that had attracted new business. But Charles didn't think Christian would appreciate his singing Mariah's praises.

"Her year's up," Christian pointed out. With a deepening scowl, he said, "She's fulfilled her contractual obligation. The property and the cabin are legally hers."

"But you'd prefer it if she left."

"No," Christian muttered, then almost as if he wasn't aware he was speaking out loud, he added, "She spilled punch down the front of my suit at Mitch and Bethany's reception."

"The way I heard it, you were as much to blame for that as she was."

Christian didn't respond, apparently caught up in his own thoughts. "I've reviewed the applications I took last year, and there's another woman I'd like to bring in."

"To take Mariah's job?"

"Yes," Christian admitted. "You probably don't remember, but I never intended to hire Mariah. I wanted Allison Reynolds."

"Who?"

"You never met Allison. She flew up and only stayed one night, but she was perfect, Charles. I took one look at her and…well…" He shook his head. "That doesn't matter now."

"Then how'd you happen to hire Mariah?"

Christian stood and walked around the living room, pausing in front of the fireplace. "As I said, Allison left after a…short stay. I was discouraged, so I reached for the first application on the top of the pile. In retrospect, I'm fairly sure I didn't read it."

"But you phoned and asked Mariah if she wanted the job?"

"Yeah. I didn't even remember who she was. I can't be expected to recall every person in every interview, can I?"

"No, I suppose not."

"Mariah's the one responsible for that lawyer snooping around, asking questions." Christian seemed to be looking for excuses to get rid of her.

"I know," Charles said. But in his opinion, Tracy Santiago had been a blessing in disguise. Without realizing what they were doing, his brothers had set themselves up for trouble with this scheme of theirs. Tracy Santiago had opened their eyes to the legal problems they'd invited. Luckily, as it turned out, any women who might have created serious difficulties for them had already moved on.

"You're sure firing her is what you want?" Charles asked, sympathetic to both sides. He liked and respected Mariah, but he'd known for a long time that Christian didn't get along with her. He was also aware that it could be uncomfortable to work with someone who was a constant source of irritation, whatever the reason.

The intense look in his brother's eyes revealed just how uncomfortable he was. "I don't know," he muttered. "I just don't know."

"Can you figure out what it is about Mariah that bothers you so much?" Charles asked, hoping Christian could come up with a solution of his own.

"That's the thing," Christian confessed. "When everything's said and done, Mariah's become a pretty decent secretary. The truth is, I simply don't want to be around her."

His brother was one contradiction after another.

"Never mind," Christian said with a deep sigh. "I have a feeling the problem will take care of itself, anyway."

Now Charles was confused. "What do you mean?"

"I think Duke's going to marry her."

"Duke?"

"Yeah, I found the two of them kissing the other day."

"Duke and Mariah?" Charles couldn't picture it.

"That's what I said," Christian snapped.

"You're sure?"

"I saw them myself. This isn't hearsay, Charlie. I saw them kissing with my own two eyes."

Charles struggled to visualize them as a couple. Certainly stranger things had happened. Lanni had fallen in love with him, hadn't she? Heaven knew, she could've had any man she wanted. That she fell in love with *him* struck Charles even now as nothing short of incredible—but a gift he wasn't about to question.

"Forget we had this conversation." Christian seemed eager to be on his way. "I probably just needed a sounding board and you were handy."

"Fine. I've wiped it from my memory."

"Good." Christian was at the door. "I don't begrudge them happiness, you know."

"Who?"

Christian cast a baffled glance at Charles. "Mariah and Duke. Who else?"

"Right," Charles called after him. He stood in the open doorway and watched his youngest brother head off down the dirt road. Charles recognized that woebegone look. The first time he'd seen it, Sawyer had it plastered all over his face. Abbey was about to leave Hard Luck and Sawyer was beside himself, wondering how he could persuade her and the kids to stay.

Charles knew he'd worn that look himself the afternoon he discovered Lanni was Catherine Fletcher's granddaughter. It had felt as if his entire world had come crashing down.

Now that same look was in Christian's eyes. Charles chuckled, almost pitying his brother. Christian didn't know what was about to hit him.

Matt stepped into the Hard Luck Café and let the screen door slam in his wake. He didn't walk up to the counter the way he usually did, but stared out the window at the airfield. John Henderson was picking up guests for the lodge, two retired college professors, who'd taken the afternoon flight into Fairbanks. John and company were due at Hard Luck in about ten minutes.

"You want any coffee?" Ben called from behind the counter.

"No, but I'd like a refund for the last cup."

"A refund? What for? I make the best coffee in town and you know it." Ben sounded insulted.

"The coffee was fine, but the advice stank."

Although Ben chuckled, Matt didn't find this amusing. He should've known better than to take romantic advice from a confirmed bachelor. And Sawyer hadn't been much of an improvement. Matt didn't know what he'd been thinking; he'd been desperate, he decided. Desperate enough to seek the counsel of two men who were as ignorant in the ways of women as he was himself.

With guests at the lodge, Matt was afraid his relationship with Karen would become even more strained. He'd genuinely wanted her to enjoy their camping-and-fishing adventure. What he'd hoped, he admitted now, was that she'd be so impressed with him and his operation here she'd throw her arms around his neck, declare how much she loved him and promise never to leave again.

Instead, they were barely on speaking terms.

Matt's intention had been to romance her, but he'd consider himself fortunate if she didn't pack up and return to California by the end of the week.

"I guess things didn't work out like you wanted," Ben said.

At least the old coot had the good grace to sound contrite. "You could say that. Now on top of everything else, Karen's furious with me because she got a couple of bug bites and her feet were wet for two days."

Ben chuckled again, and if the situation hadn't been so critical, Matt was sure he would've seen the humor in it himself.

"Did she catch any fish?" Ben asked.

"One." Matt still had trouble believing Karen had set the trout free. Leave it to a woman to assign human characteristics to a fish. Brave and noble. For crying out loud, she was talking about a trout. A trout! Karen looked at this fish and saw a poor, maligned creature. Matt looked at the same fish and saw dinner.

If that two-day trek in the wilds was any indication of how their relationship was going, Matt might as well give up now.

"I take it you've got guests flying in."

"A couple of college professors," Matt explained, his thoughts still on Karen. He hadn't seen her since early that morning. He'd gotten everything ready for the evening meal himself, then spent the remainder of the day gathering the necessary supplies for the next trip. He'd be away three days this time. He'd venture a guess that Karen would be pleased to have him gone. His biggest fear was that she'd leave before he returned.

He wished he could find a way to settle their differences once and for all, but every attempt he made seemed to backfire.

Early that evening, as the four of them sat down to dinner in the lodge dining room, Matt felt torn. Despite his natural sociability, he would've liked nothing better than to spend a quiet evening with his ex-wife; he wanted a chance to right any wrong he'd unintentionally committed.

Unfortunately he found himself reluctantly sitting across the table from the two white-haired professors—likable though they were—and chatting with them. Both men, Donald and Derrick, were in their early sixties and full of vigor. They'd been friends for years and often traveled together. One was married, the other divorced. They talked freely about their lives in a relaxed, companionable way.

Karen was her usual gracious self throughout the meal. She asked a question now and then and listened intently to the answer. She was a perfect hostess, making their guests feel interesting, valued, important. It was a real skill she had, one he'd noticed from the first moment they met.

"I hope Matt had you sign the guest book," Karen said as she passed around the basket of fresh-baked rolls. They were still warm from the oven.

"I had them sign it this afternoon," Matt answered on their behalf, since both were busy eating.

"I understand this is your first season operating the lodge," Donald, the more animated of the two, said a few minutes later.

"That's right."

"We're still pretty new at this," Karen added.

"So far, it's been a delightful experience," Derrick said, smiling at Karen. "I must say, Mrs. Caldwell, dinner is delicious."

"Thank you, but I can't accept the credit. Matt's the chef at the lodge."

"The grilled salmon is excellent," Donald told him.

Matt shrugged off the compliment. "Thanks," he said gruffly.

"I'd be interested in knowing your background," Derrick said conversationally. "It seems to me you must be a jack-of-all-trades."

"And a master of none." Matt wryly completed the old saying. "Actually that pretty well sums up the situation. I've dabbled in a number of careers in the past few years."

"When I first met Matt he was a psychology major," Karen explained, avoiding his eyes.

"Did you graduate?" Derrick directed the question to Matt.

"No." If he was uncomfortable with compliments, he was even more uncomfortable discussing the twists and turns his life had taken since college.

"He knows just enough about human nature to make him dangerous," Karen teased, her voice affectionate.

Matt couldn't take his eyes off his ex-wife. She looked radiant that evening. He wondered if she was ready to put their differences behind them. He knew *he* was. He hoped that if he got down on his knees and promised never to take her camping again, she'd be willing to forgive and forget. If she wanted romance he'd find some other method of providing it. He didn't know what, but he'd figure it out.

"You're an excellent cook, as well," Donald was saying.

"At one point in my illustrious past I decided I wanted to cook. That was soon after Karen and I were married." He saw no need to mention that they were currently divorced.

"Matt developed some excellent recipes and an extensive repertoire," Karen said.

It actually sounded as though Karen was boasting, but Matt was sure he was mistaken. He remembered how furious she'd been the day he'd announced he didn't want to be a chef, after all. When he'd finished his course at a culinary institute, he'd been hired as a sous-chef by a major hotel. The job had allowed for no creative freedom, and after ten months, Matt felt that his inventiveness had been stifled to the point that he could barely stand going into work.

Karen hadn't been pleased when he'd quit, but she'd supported his decision. That was when he'd decided to become a commercial fisherman and had hired on with a fishing vessel. The money was good—no, great—but the dangers were high. Fishing some of the roughest seas in the world was risky, and a number of vessels were lost every year.

"Not exactly," Matt said, and glanced at Karen. This conversation had become disquieting. The last thing Matt wanted was to have his lack of direction discussed and dissected by his guests. It had always been such a contentious issue between him and Karen. He didn't want her to recite the litany of his failings. Not now, when he was struggling to win back her approval.

"After leaving cooking school, Matt decided to become a commercial fisherman," she said.

"Where'd you fish?" Once more the question was directed to him.

"The Bering Straits," Matt answered with little enthusiasm. His eyes briefly met Karen's, and he realized she was thinking the same thing he was. Those months apart while he was at sea had been some of the most difficult in their marriage.

Sure, the money had helped them pay their bills, but it hadn't been worth the strain on their marriage.

"How long did you fish commercially?" Donald asked.

"One season." He didn't elaborate, didn't say that when he'd gone into the trade he'd dreamed of one day buying his own boat. But then, he'd also fantasized about running his own restaurant.

Although he'd bet Karen would deny it, he'd given up fishing for her. She'd worried herself sick the entire time he was at sea, and Matt knew he couldn't do that to her anymore. So he'd left at the end of the season and joined an accounting firm.

"After that Matt worked for an accountant—for a while," Karen said.

"Accounting," Derrick echoed. "You have led a varied life."

"It's interesting to note how everything's pulled together for you now," Donald said thoughtfully. He helped himself to seconds on the salmon and while he was at it reached for another roll.

Matt looked at him curiously.

"You're happy with the lodge?" Donald asked.

"Very happy." Matt said this as much for Karen's benefit as to answer the question.

"Yes, it's all pulled together for you now," Donald repeated. He had everyone's attention.

"How do you mean?" Karen made it sound as though Matt couldn't be trusted not to sell the lodge at the drop of a hat. Not that he would've blamed her. He'd certainly given her enough grief with his erratic work history during their marriage.

"You were interested in psychology first, isn't that right?" Donald asked.

"Yes," Matt murmured, wondering how their conversation could have veered so far off course.

"Then cooking school?"

"Yes." Karen was the one to reply this time.

"For which he shows remarkable talent." Another dinner roll disappeared.

"Followed by a stint as a commercial fisherman," Donald went on.

"One season was all," Matt insisted. He'd tried to make that clear in his arguments with Karen. While the fishing had been adventurous and lucrative, it hadn't been a real career.

"Followed by accounting."

"Nine months' worth." Again it was Karen who supplied the details. "And now the lodge."

"This lodge means everything to me," Matt said. He yearned to explain that he'd invested his trust fund in this venture, rebuilt the place with his own two hands and was personally involved in every phase of its operation.

The professors exchanged looks.

"If anyone were to design a course on opening a lodge, I think they'd follow this exact same pattern," Donald said. "It's as if everything you've done in the past five or six years has steered you in this direction. I predict that Hard Luck Lodge is destined to be a success."

"You have a basic understanding of human nature." Derrick smiled. "Naturally Donald and I came up for the fishing, but if you continue to feed us like this, we'll certainly be coming back—even if we don't catch a thing."

Both men chuckled. "The fact that you've fished commercially is bound to be an asset."

"True," Matt admitted.

"Plus your accounting experience."

"It's a perfect fit." Donald nodded with evident satisfaction.

"Thank you," Matt said. Funny, he'd never realized all this before. The two men were absolutely right. It was as though he'd spent the past years in training for this very thing.

"If you gentlemen would kindly excuse me?" Unexpectedly Karen stood up.

"By all means." The professors rose politely to their feet and thanked her for her hospitality.

She threw them a quick smile and rushed into the kitchen.

Matt didn't know what was wrong, but he knew he'd better find out. He decided he'd give her a couple of minutes, then excuse himself from the table, too.

Fortunately the professors made some comment about going to bed, since they'd spent most of the day traveling. Matt waited until they were on their way up the stairs, then hurried into the kitchen.

"Karen, what's wrong—" He'd no sooner walked through the door than Karen hurled a wet sponge at him. It stuck to his shirt.

"What was that for?" he asked, stunned.

Nine

"Karen," Matt whispered, approaching her slowly.

She reached for the next-closest item at hand, which happened to be half a head of lettuce. "Stay away from me, Matthew Caldwell." Tears streaked down her face.

"Why are you so upset?"

She flung the lettuce at him, but Matt ducked in the nick of time. Not that she really wanted to hit him. She wasn't sure *what* she wanted to do.

"Karen?"

She couldn't bear it when he said her name like that. As if she was the most precious, the most beautiful woman on earth. As if he'd treasure her for all eternity.

"I'm warning you—stay away from me." She backed up, edging toward the door, hoping to make a clean escape. If she got past him, she'd run up the stairs and flee to the haven of her room. Then, and only then, would she try to analyze the reason for her tears. She felt a confusing mix of emotions—anger, guilt and a sudden, overpowering sadness that she could neither define nor explain.

"Tell me what's upsetting you," he pleaded.

"I can't." She shook her head helplessly; she didn't understand it herself. She didn't know *why* she felt so furious, or where to direct her anger.

But everything was somehow linked to their dinner conversation. The two professors had taken the apparent chaos that had ruled her marriage and Matt's life and seemed to find logic in it. Karen had been blinded by her complete lack of faith in her husband. She suspected that was a result of her unsettled childhood.

"Why can't you explain?" he coaxed.

"Just leave me alone, Matt Caldwell," she wailed.

"No." His stubbornness was showing. "You know I can't stand to see you cry."

"Then I'll stop." She sniffled hard in an effort to stem the tears. Matt wasn't the only one upset with her crying; it troubled her, too. Karen *hated* to cry. It made her nose red and runny, it made her eyes puffy and, worst of all, it made her weak. Vulnerable. Whenever she wept she wanted to be held. While they were married, it was Matt who held her. His comforting often led to lovemaking, which only complicated the issues between them.

Matt stretched out his arms to her. "Honey, let's talk about this."

She wavered, the lure of his embrace strong. It took every ounce of fortitude she had to shake her head. She was at the kitchen wall now, easing her way toward the door.

"Karen, I love you so much."

She pressed her hands over her ears. "Don't tell me that," she sobbed.

"Why not?" he demanded. "Don't you know by now that I'd move heaven and earth to have you back?

I want you and our baby here, with me. I want us married."

"You only want me because of the baby."

"That's not true," he argued vehemently. "Do you know any other man who would've agreed to live the way we do? Damn it, Karen, I'm going crazy. Do you think it's been easy living with you day after day, loving you as much as I do and not touching you? We hardly even kiss."

"We can't kiss," she mumbled. Kissing was always the beginning for them; it rarely stopped there.

"If you want to be angry with me, fine, but let me at least hold you."

That was generally how their fights went. She'd be unhappy over something that Matt found trivial and unimportant, and she'd explode. She'd throw things, and in an effort to calm her, Matt would offer her comfort. The comforting led to kissing and the kissing to much more. She didn't want it to happen that way now.

"No," she said. "Not again. You seem to forget I'm not your wife anymore."

"The hell you aren't," Matt growled. "Sure, you've got some judge's decree in your hot little hands, but that doesn't change how I think of you—or how you think of me. You're my wife as much tonight as you were the day we got married. I never understood this whole divorce business. You're the one who wanted it, but are you happy?"

She couldn't answer. Besides, he already knew. She'd divorced him, moved to California—and had never been more miserable in her life.

Removing herself from the temptation of being close to Matt simply hadn't worked. Here she was, pregnant with his child, living with him. Difficult as this was to admit, she was happier than she'd been in two years. And it infuriated her.

The tears came in earnest then.

"Karen, for heaven's sake…"

She lacked the energy to run from him, and she slumped against the wall. In giant strides, Matt crossed the kitchen and gathered her in his arms. "Honey, listen, nothing can be that terrible."

"Yes, it can," she sobbed, hiding her face in her hands.

The warmth of his body seeped into her bones, chasing away the chill from her heart. Karen could feel his breath at her temple, gently mussing her hair.

She didn't know who reached out first; it didn't matter. She was as hungry for him, as needy for her husband, as he was for her. His touch no longer merely comforted but excited. His lips were warm as they covered her mouth. Soon their need for each other was consuming them.

"Matt, oh, Matt…" She breathed his name again and again as he buried his face in her neck. She slid her arms around him and pressed her body against his solid strength.

"I've been crazy for you for weeks," he muttered, whisking open the buttons of her blouse. "But I refuse to make love to you in the kitchen."

"Do you think this is a good idea?" she asked as Matt swung her into his arms. He opened the door with a push of his shoulder and carried her past the registration desk and toward his private quarters.

"It's a brilliant idea," he said, walking past the dining room table.

"Matt, the dishes," she said, pointing.

"Forget the dishes."

"You're angry." She was always the one who flew off the handle. Not Matt.

"Not angry," he corrected, "frustrated with this foolishness. I want my wife back."

She slipped her arms around his neck and kissed him hungrily. His eyes briefly met hers before his strides took them into his darkened bedroom. He placed her gently on the bed and knelt over her. "You asked for romance. I swear I'd do anything in the world to give it to you if only I could figure out what it is," he said before he kissed her again.

"You seem to be doing a pretty good job at the moment," she whispered.

"I am?" He sounded both pleased and surprised.

"But I still think we should talk first."

"Not on your life," he said, removing her shoes and carelessly tossing them aside. He kicked off his own. "Not when there's a chance you might change your mind about us making love."

"I… I promised myself we wouldn't."

"You can unpromise just as easily."

Karen held out her arms in open invitation. "I guess I'll have to."

When Karen awoke it was still dark. The space beside her on the bed was empty. "Matt?" She sat up, clutching the sheet to her chest. She saw his shadowy figure in the dim light and realized he was dressing.

"Is it morning?" she asked, yawning luxuriously.

"Unfortunately, yes." He sat on the edge of the bed.

"I've got to get the professors up and fed before Sawyer flies us out."

"You're leaving?" She'd completely forgotten about the professors and that Matt would be taking them fishing. "But we need to talk," she said urgently.

"It'll have to wait until later. I'm sorry, honey, but I don't have any choice."

"How long do we have to wait?"

"Three days," he told her. "Besides, what's there to talk about? Everything's already settled, isn't it? You're moving into this bedroom with me and we're getting married again as soon as I can arrange it."

"Aren't you taking a lot for granted?" she asked, piqued that he'd assume everything was settled simply because they'd made love. She wanted to remarry him, too. But contrary to Matt's assertion, there was still a great deal to discuss.

"You love me. I love you. What else is there to say?"

"Listen to me, Matthew, we have to clear the air. We need to—"

"I don't have time, honey," he said. "Hold that thought and I'll be home in three days."

Discouraged, Karen fell back against the pillows. *Nothing* was settled, although thanks to what the two professors had pointed out, Karen had a far better understanding of Matt, of their history and his ambitions for the lodge…and of her own reactions the night before.

The professors were right, but neither she nor Matt had seen the obvious. He'd found his calling, had unconsciously been working toward this for as long as she'd known him. The lodge wasn't another phase; it was his life's work. And it had taken two strangers to make both Matt and her aware of that.

Now Karen understood the reason for her tears the night before—they'd been prompted by anger and sadness. And, she had to admit, guilt. She hadn't trusted Matt to find his way, to find the work that suited him. She'd allowed her fears and insecurities to cloud her judgment.

Not only had she brought grief into her own life, but into Matt's, as well.

Lanni stood at the kitchen sink and stared unseeingly at the world outside the window. Her thoughts were troubled as she reviewed her conversation with Karen the day before.

Charles stepped up behind her and slid his arms around her waist. "You're pensive this morning," he said, kissing her neck. "What's up?"

"It's Matt and Karen," Lanni murmured. She set aside her cup and turned to wrap her arms around her husband, hugging him close. "Something's happened between them."

"Good or bad?"

"I don't know," Lanni confessed. She closed her eyes and savored the feel of Charles's arms. When Matt and Karen had separated she'd been careful not to take sides. Karen was one of her best friends, but Matt was the brother she idolized.

Following the divorce, she knew he was feeling lost and confused. In retrospect, Lanni wished she'd been more sympathetic. Karen's leaving him had undermined the very foundation of his life.

"I ran into Karen this morning, but where's Matt?" Charles asked, breaking into her thoughts.

"He's off doing his wilderness thing." Lanni leaned her head back far enough to look into her husband's eyes. "I couldn't bear to lose you," she said fervently, offering him a blurry smile.

Charles stroked her hair. "What brought that on?" he asked.

"I was just thinking about my brother and Karen. When Karen left him and filed for divorce, it was as if someone had pulled the rug out from under him. He was miserable.

"Yet when I saw Karen soon after they'd separated, I realized she was just as heartbroken. I couldn't take sides or interfere—at least I didn't feel I could—and now I wonder if that was a mistake."

Charles kissed the top of her head. "What I hear you asking is whether you should involve yourself now."

"Yes. That is what I'm wondering. My brother's a private person, and I doubt he'd appreciate my meddling in his affairs, but at the same time…" She hesitated.

"What makes you think you should?"

"I went over to see Karen yesterday," Lanni said, then bit her lip. "I knew Matt was gone, and I thought I'd pop in and see how she was doing. At first everything was fine. We chatted and laughed the way we normally do, and then out of the blue Karen started to cry."

"About what?"

"That's the sixty-four thousand dollar question," Lanni said. "When I asked her what was wrong, she shook her head, hugged me and told me I was the best friend she'd ever had."

"Hmm."

"What does 'hmm' mean?"

"Nothing," Charles answered. "Do you think this bout of melancholy is related to her pregnancy? I've heard that pregnant women sometimes get a little moody."

"How would I know? I've never been pregnant."

She felt Charles smile against her hair. "Not for lack of trying."

"Stop it, Charles. We're talking about Matt and Karen here, not my insatiable appetite for my husband."

"Being that husband, I should mention how grateful I am for such a loving wife."

"That's just it," Lanni said urgently. "Can you imagine how awful it would be if something ever drove us apart?"

The smile in her husband's eyes faded. "I couldn't bear it, Lanni. Loving you has changed my life for the better. It's transformed everything. For the first time I have a healthy relationship with my mother. I've got you to thank for that. Even the way I feel about my brothers is different because of you."

Charles dropped his arms, pulled out a kitchen chair and sat down heavily. "I remember when I learned that Sawyer and Christian had brought women to Hard Luck. I was furious. Then I found out my two brothers expected Abbey and her kids to live in one of those old cabins. I decided to put an immediate end to their idiotic plan."

Lanni pulled out a chair for herself and sat opposite him. "Don't forget the twenty acres."

He snickered at that, then shook his head. "I was the one who suggested Abbey leave Hard Luck. When Sawyer heard what I'd done, this look of shock came over him. It was as if I'd stabbed him in the back. Betrayed him. Then he told me something I've never forgotten."

"What did he say?" Lanni asked when he didn't continue right away.

"Sawyer told me I was tempting the fates with my arrogance. He'd never expected to fall in love, and if it happened to him, I was just as vulnerable. Someday I was going to fall in love myself, and he hoped he'd be there to see it, because then and only then would I appreciate what he was feeling." Charles laughed softly. "Not long after that I met you, and I felt like I'd been smacked upside the head with a two-by-four."

"I felt the same way after meeting you," she said.

Charles reached for her hand and kissed her fingertips.

"Remember how Matt tried to bring us back together?" Lanni asked.

Charles nodded.

"I can understand now why he did something so uncharacteristic." She blinked back tears at the memory. "He was hoping to spare us the kind of heartache he was suffering."

"And now you want to help him...."

"Yes," Lanni said fervently. "But I'm not sure how, and I'm afraid that anything I say or do might hurt more than it helps."

"I don't know what to tell you, sweetheart. Perhaps

you should talk it over with another woman, someone you trust and respect."

Lanni's eyes brightened; she leapt out of the chair and dropped a grateful kiss on his lips. "You mean someone like Abbey."

Fat raindrops plopped down on the dirt road. Karen studied the pattern they made on the hard ground as she leaned against the porch railing.

She folded her arms around her waist and gazed up at the dark, angry sky. Matt and the professors weren't due back until the following day. In her loneliness it felt like an eternity.

Scott O'Halloran came racing down the road on his bicycle, with Ronny Gold behind him. Their legs pumped the pedals furiously. Eagle Catcher easily kept pace with the two boys, staying closest to Scott's side.

Scott saw Karen and slammed on his brakes. "Hi, Mrs. Caldwell!"

"Hello, Scott."

"Do you have a name for your baby yet?" he asked.

"Not yet," she told him. "Do you have any suggestions?"

Scott pinched his lips as he mulled over the question. Then, with a look of excitement, he said, "Scott's a good name."

"So's Ronny," the other boy shouted.

"I'll keep both of those in mind," she assured them. "Don't you think you should get out of the rain?"

"Nah," Scott said, answering for them both. "I used to live in Seattle. I'm used to this. Once you've lived in the Pacific Northwest, you learn to take rain in your stride."

"I'll remember that," she said, smiling a little at his grown-up manner.

"Look," Ronny said, tugging at the sleeve of Scott's jacket. "The girls are right behind us. We gotta split."

"'Bye," Scott said, leaning over the handlebars in an effort to make a fast getaway.

Chrissie Harris and Susan O'Halloran raced after them. "Hello, Mrs. Caldwell!" Chrissie shouted.

"Hello, Chrissie. Hello, Susan."

Susan gave her a swift wave and paused only briefly, saying, "Scott let Ronny read my diary, and he's gonna pay."

"Do you really think your brother would do something like that?" Karen asked, not quite hiding a smile.

"I'm sure," Susan said with righteous indignation.

"Ronny wrote her a note in the margin of the page. Boys," Chrissie Harris said with wide-eyed wisdom, "are not to be trusted." The girls disappeared, chasing after the two boys.

Now for the first time it came to Karen that Hard Luck would be a good place to raise her child. Although the town was small, the sense of family and community was strong.

She knew there were occasional problems. Friday nights when Ben served alcohol, some of the local trappers and pipeline workers drifted into town, and now and then a fight broke out. But Mitch was routinely there to take care of things.

Karen remained on the porch, musing about life in Hard Luck, when Abbey strolled past, carrying an umbrella.

"Howdy, neighbor," her friend called.

When Karen returned her greeting, Sawyer's wife

stopped and studied her carefully. "How're you feeling?"

"Fine." She was, if a little lonely. She missed Matt and wished he was home. Her heart was full of everything she wanted to tell him.

Abbey moved onto the porch. "Do you have time to sit and chat for a while?"

"Sure." Karen was grateful for the company.

They sat side by side on the steps. "So how's life treating you these days?" Abbey asked.

Karen raised her shoulders in a shrug. "I can't complain." But she could. In truth, Karen felt wretched, although her condition wasn't physical. Her malady was one of the heart.

Her eyes brimmed with tears, and she knew Abbey saw her struggle to keep them at bay. She was thankful that her friend didn't comment or ply her with questions. Instead, Abbey gave her a moment to compose herself.

"I imagine the lodge must feel empty when Matt's away," Abbey said in a quiet, conversational tone.

"It does." Days like this made Karen wonder how she'd managed without Matt during their year and a half apart. In her first months of pregnancy, she'd felt alone and afraid, and the harder she'd tried to convince herself she didn't need Matt, the less true it became. She *did* need him. The fact that she'd been tempted to keep the baby a secret from him proved as much— she'd been fighting the very thing she wanted most.

"I've been feeling so blue lately," Karen said softly.

Abbey reached for her hand. "Sounds to me like you could use a little cheering up."

Karen managed a watery smile. "What do you have in mind?"

Abbey gave her a knowing smile in return. "What does every woman do when the going gets tough?"

"Shop," Karen answered automatically.

"Sawyer's flying into Fairbanks later today. Why don't you and I tag along and check out baby furniture? It's time the two of us indulged ourselves at a real, live shopping mall."

"That," Karen said, brightening immediately, "is an offer too good to refuse."

Matt had never been so eager to head home. Good thing he wasn't responsible for the weather, because it had rained for two solid days, and there was no letup in sight. Donald and Derrick, his clients, had called a halt to their expedition. They were wet, cold and miserable.

Luckily the fishing had been great, and the two men felt they'd gotten more than their money's worth. What they wanted now was a hot bath, a good dinner and a warm bed.

Matt was in complete agreement. He radioed in to Midnight Sons and requested that Sawyer pick them up a day early. Unfortunately Sawyer was in Fairbanks, but Christian said he'd meet them. It might've been Matt's imagination, but Christian sounded desperate to get out of the office.

Although the weather was dismal, that wasn't the only reason Matt felt so eager to get home. He missed Karen. He wanted to be with her, hold her, make plans for the future. The last thing he wanted to do was discuss the past. He'd always dreaded it when she wanted to "clear the air," because those conversations invariably led to more problems. He never understood why women found it necessary to dissect every aspect of a relationship.

As far as he was concerned, the situation was simple enough. He loved Karen. He wanted her and the baby with him. If she didn't want that, too, well...

But Matt knew Karen. A man couldn't live with a woman for more than four years and not become acquainted with her ways. She loved him so much it hurt. He knew that in the very depths of his heart. *She loved him.* What bothered Matt was her reason for holding out.

All right, he understood that his tendency to drift from one kind of job to another had troubled her. But that was tied to her childhood and her father.

Matt wasn't anything like Eric Rocklin, and if Karen hadn't figured that out by now, he thought with a spurt of anger, then she never would.

Christian arrived in the float plane late in the afternoon. It took the two of them more than an hour to load up the gear. Matt sat next to him in the copilot seat and watched as the landscape unfurled below them and the town of Hard Luck finally appeared. He experienced a swelling sense of pride as the lodge came into view.

But it wasn't only the lodge that beckoned him. His wife would be there, and for the first time in a long while he felt like a husband again.

It seemed to take forever to reach the lodge. He imagined Karen rushing out to greet him, and the anticipation set his heart racing. He could hardly wait to hold her in his arms again. They had a lot of time to make up for.

"Karen!" he shouted as he pushed open the heavy wooden door and strode through. "I'm home."

The two bedraggled professors followed close on his heels.

"Karen!" he repeated, louder this time.

No response.

"She must have gone out," he explained to the two men. The image of her rushing to greet him crumbled at his feet.

Donald and Derrick mumbled something about a bath and immediately headed up the stairs.

Matt wandered through the house, looking for his ex-wife. It wasn't as if she was expecting him; nevertheless, he felt a deep sense of disappointment that she wasn't home.

When she hadn't returned an hour later, he called the library. To his surprise Lanni answered.

"I don't suppose you've seen Karen?" he asked without preamble.

"Not today," Lanni told him. She seemed about to say more but stopped herself.

"Do you know where she might be?" he probed.

Lanni hesitated. "No, I don't. Let me check around and see what I can find out for you."

"I'd appreciate it." He hung up and started the dinner preparations.

Peeling potatoes, he thought about his short conversation with his sister. It suddenly occurred to him that something wasn't right. Wedging the receiver between his shoulder and ear, he punched out the number for the library.

"What's going on with Karen?" He wanted the truth, and he wanted it now. "What are you keeping from me?"

"I—" Lanni stopped.

"Tell me," he ordered.

"Something's happened between you two, hasn't it?" his sister asked.

"Yes," he said, but to his way of thinking, the changes were all good. She was back in his bed, and as soon as possible, they'd get remarried.

"Whatever it was must've really upset Karen," Lanni said.

"What do you mean?" he demanded. He'd thought, he'd hoped, that Karen would be excited. That she'd be happy. He realized she wanted to "clear the air"— have one of those discussions he disliked so much— but he'd assumed they'd scaled the major hurdles by admitting how much they loved each other and wanted to be together.

"When I saw Karen yesterday, she started crying for no reason."

"Crying? Just where is she?" he asked, losing his patience.

"If you'd give me a chance I'd tell you," Lanni snapped. "I talked to Scott ten minutes ago, and he told me Karen flew into Fairbanks with Abbey and Sawyer. They're due back anytime, so don't worry."

By ten that night it became clear that Karen had no intention of returning.

She'd left him again.

Well, it wasn't the first time, but it as sure as hell would be the last.

Ten

Abbey was right. A shopping spree in Fairbanks had done wonders for Karen's spirits. Sawyer had dropped the two of them off at the closest mall and arranged a time to meet them later.

Karen and Abbey had delighted in drifting from one store to another, from one baby department to the next. Karen felt like a child let loose in Toyland at Christmas.

The experience of shopping for baby clothes had produced a flood of tenderness for her unborn child. Choosing sleepers and nighties somehow made everything more immediate, made the baby seem *real*. Before she could stop herself, she bought a number of things, more than she could easily carry. She ordered a crib and changing table and selected several other items for a layette.

The most fun she had was trying on maternity clothes with Abbey. Karen hadn't laughed this much in ages. The smocks were huge on her. But although she barely showed, she could no longer button her pants. Abbey was an old pro at this pregnancy business, and she assured Karen that in another month or so, those smocks would be a perfect fit.

Sawyer met them at the scheduled time, and because of the rainstorm, suggested dinner in Fairbanks before flying back to Hard Luck. When they finally landed that evening it was after ten. The afternoon away had been exactly the remedy she needed. Karen felt happy—and exhausted.

Sawyer and Abbey drove her to the lodge. Sawyer climbed out of the truck, helped her down and sorted through the packages before handing Karen her purchases.

"Looks like someone's inside," Abbey said, gesturing toward the front window where a light shone in the growing dusk.

"Do you think Matt might be back?" Sawyer asked.

"I doubt it," Karen answered. Knowing her exhusband, he'd probably consider the rain and wind a bonus. She'd heard that rain made for good fishing, but then, what she knew about the sport was minimal. She could imagine Matt standing in the middle of a raging river that very minute, happily soaked and hoping to lure breakfast onto his hook.

"Thanks again," Karen called as her friends left. She shifted the sacks in her arms, pleased with her purchases and looking forward to showing Matt.

"One thing's for sure," she said aloud to the baby, "whether you're a boy or a girl, you're going to be one of the best-dressed kids around."

She suddenly realized that she and Matt had never talked about the baby's sex. She didn't know if he had any preference; he'd never said.

No sooner was she inside than her eyes connected

with those of her ex-husband. He was sprawled in the overstuffed chair in front of the fireplace. His feet were propped on the raised hearth and his outstretched arms dangled over the sides of the chair.

"Karen?" He stared at her as though she were an apparition.

"You're back early!" she said excitedly. "This is a surprise."

"You can say that again."

She ignored the sarcasm in his voice. "I've had the most marvelous day." Hurrying across the room, she set down her packages in the empty chair. "Just wait until you see what I bought for the baby!"

He continued to stare at her.

She chattered nervously, talking too quickly, describing the baby clothes and toys.

"Why are you buying these things now?" he asked in a snarling tone.

"Because I had the opportunity to fly into Fairbanks with Sawyer and Abbey," she explained as patiently as she could. Surely he wasn't upset because she'd bought things for the baby. Ignoring his sour mood, she pulled a yellow cotton sleeper from the sack. "Isn't this adorable? You wouldn't believe the incredible stuff they have for babies these days. I found the cutest pair of baby sunglasses. Abbey and I got a real kick out of them."

"Baby sunglasses," he muttered, but he didn't sound impressed.

It was clear that her ex-husband—soon to be husband again—was in a rare temper. Karen lowered herself onto the hearth, facing him. "What the matter?" she asked with a laborious sigh.

After the long, happy afternoon, she was tired and disappointed by his lack of welcome. The last thing she wanted now was a confrontation with Matt. "Didn't the professors have a good time? Do they want their money back?"

"No," Matt said irritably, obviously taking offense at the question. "They had the time of their lives and made a point of telling me so. They would've stuck it out if the rain hadn't started coming down in buckets."

"So that's why you came back a day early?"

His eyes narrowed. "I surprised you, didn't I?" He got to his feet, looming above her. "You planned to be out of here by then, didn't you?" he went on. "You were planning to be gone before I learned what you'd done."

"Out of here? Gone?" Karen had thought they'd be able to sit down and discuss where their lives were going, how their relationship would change. But she had no intention of leaving him. It was the furthest thing from her mind.

"Sure," he said with a hint of belligerence. "You intended to sneak out of Hard Luck without telling me."

"You assumed because I wasn't here when you returned that I'd *left* you?" This was by far the most ridiculous thing he'd ever said. She leapt to her feet and stuffed the yellow sleeper back in the bag.

"What else was I supposed to think?"

"If you'd bothered to look in your office, you'd have found a note."

"You wrote me a note when I wasn't expected home?" he challenged, his eyes glittering with disbelief.

"You or anyone else who happened to stop by and

needed to know where I was." She held the packages tightly against her stomach as if to protect herself from Matt's hostility. This wasn't like him; she didn't understand it, didn't know how to respond.

"You left me before," he reminded her. "What else am I to think when I return home and find you gone?"

"That was different," she said in her own defense.

His short laugh was devoid of amusement. "Last time, you filed for divorce so fast my head was spinning. Remember? You couldn't wait to get rid of me then. Nothing's changed. Certainly not you."

Karen almost gasped with pain at his accusation. Her knees felt weak, but she stood her ground. "I warned you, Matt, but you wouldn't listen. You hardly ever listened to me in those days." He didn't seem to have improved much now.

"You warned me?" he spat out.

Karen glanced over her shoulder and up the stairs, fearing his outburst would waken their guests. Well, so be it, if that was what Matt wanted.

"When you decided to become an accountant I told you to be very sure. You'd already gone through three other professions in short order, and I wasn't about to let you risk our financial security again."

"Telling me to be very sure is a long way from filing divorce papers," he said sullenly.

"You didn't even discuss it with me. I come home from work one night and you gleefully announce that you've quit." Tears threatened, but she held them back through sheer force of will. "Without so much as hinting you were unhappy, you quit. If you'd talked to me, explained that the job wasn't right for you… But you left me completely out of the decision."

"And so the next day you packed your bags and were gone," he said. He snapped his fingers as if to say her leaving had been a spur-of-the-moment decision.

"Can you blame me?" she cried. "Can you honestly blame me? I was tired of having you jerk our lives around. I'd had it up to here," she said, raising her hand above her head, "with your inability to stick to a job. Any job." She paused and dragged in a deep breath before she continued, "I'd grown up with a father who refused to accept responsibility. Then I made the mistake of marrying a man just like him."

"I am not your father." Matt made each word loud and distinct.

"You're *exactly* like him. You didn't even think about the bills. They were supposed to pay themselves, I guess. Your 'Don't worry, be happy' attitude drove me *crazy*."

"I was miserable working for the accounting firm!" he shouted.

"Just as you were miserable continuing with college, with the chef's job, with commercial fishing and with everything else you dabbled in over the past five years? Or was this a *different* kind of misery?"

He didn't answer.

"The time had come to grow up, Matt. You didn't want a family, you drifted from job to job, without revealing an ounce of responsibility or ambition, any plan for our future. What else was I supposed to do?"

"Answer me this, Karen. Would a responsible adult turn tail at the first sign of trouble? Would a responsible adult walk out on her husband and end her marriage on a whim?"

"Do you really think that was easy for me, Matt?"

Her voice shook as she stiffened herself against his accusations.

"Easy or not, you did it, and I don't trust you not to look for some excuse to do it again."

"All this because I went *shopping?*"

"I returned early and you were gone. When I called around, all I could find out was that you'd been feeling low. Then I discovered you'd gone into Fairbanks with Sawyer and Abbey."

"For heaven's sake, I went shopping!" she said again.

"I didn't know that. For all I knew, you could be going back to that wonderful job in California that you love so much."

She couldn't believe what she was hearing. It hurt that he was saying such things. "Why would I do that?"

He shrugged. "Why do you do anything? What happened two years ago makes as little sense to me now as it did then."

"You're being absurd."

"Am I?" he challenged. "The last thing you said to me before I left the other day was that I shouldn't take you for granted. Trust me, Karen, I don't. I never will again. You're as likely to walk out on me now as you were before, and I can't—I *won't*—forget that."

"Just because I didn't leap back into marriage when I found out I was pregnant? As far as I could see—"

Matt didn't allow her to finish. "If you're going to go, Karen, I advise you to do it now. I haven't got the stomach to drink away my sorrows. Nor do I enjoy living with uncertainty."

"You really think I'd do anything so underhanded?"

"Why shouldn't I? You did it before."

She tried to swallow the constriction blocking her throat. "Fine, then, I will." She moved toward the stairs. "You didn't need an excuse to get me to leave, Matt. All you had to do was ask."

Mariah was singing quietly to herself when Duke Porter opened the office door and walked in. She looked up, relieved to find it wasn't Christian. Her boss appeared to be doing his utmost to avoid her these days. Which was just as well.

"Hello, Duke." She greeted him with a cheerful smile.

Duke stayed close to the door, as if he was prepared to make a quick exit. "If I come in here, you aren't going to kiss me again, are you?"

Mariah laughed. "A lot of guys around here wouldn't complain if I did."

"Maybe not," Duke agreed good-naturedly, "but you said the kiss was from that attorney friend of yours. Tracy something or other."

"It was." Duke wasn't fooling her; he knew Tracy's name as well as he did his own. He should; he'd been complaining about her for months.

Duke rubbed the back of his hand across his lips as if to wipe away anything to do with Tracy. "Let me set one thing straight right now. The last woman I want kissing me is that…that she-devil."

"She's not so bad."

"She wouldn't be if she knew her place."

"Knew her place?" Mariah echoed in disbelief. "What century are you living in?"

Ignoring that, he walked over to the coffeepot, removed his mug from the peg and poured himself a cup. "She thinks just because she's an attorney, she knows better than anyone else," he muttered. "What that woman needs is a man to put her in her place."

Mariah opened her mouth in outrage, then felt a laugh gurgling up. Duke went out of his way to be provocative, and frankly she'd like to see him or any other man try to put Tracy in "her place." She didn't know what it was with those two. They hadn't gotten along from the first moment they'd encountered each other.

Suddenly dejected, Mariah realized it had been that way with her and Christian, too. The first day she arrived in Hard Luck her suitcases had fallen open and all her underwear had scattered across the runway. That beginning must have been an omen. Things had quickly gone from bad to worse between them. The man flustered her so much she'd made one mistake after another.

"Speaking of Tracy," Mariah said, taking her mind off Christian, "I got a letter from her this week."

"Oh." Duke sat on the edge of her desk. "She's not making a trip up here, I hope."

"She's got two weeks' vacation coming, and she wanted to know if I'd meet her somewhere."

"Like where?"

"I was thinking of Anchorage. I've always wanted to go on one of those glacier tour boats." She opened a bottom drawer and removed a brochure. "There's lots I'd like to see in Anchorage, especially Earthquake Park. It's supposed to be really something."

"Any chance you might invite her up here again?"

"Here?" She eyed the pilot, wondering if he was hoping to stir up a little trouble. Mariah sometimes thought Duke was attracted to Tracy, but she dismissed the idea. Not Duke and Tracy. Not two people who couldn't exchange one civil word.

"Maybe I will," she said, studying him.

Duke scowled. "In that case let me know so I can avoid her. I don't want to be within a two-hundred-mile radius."

He sipped his coffee, grimaced as if he found it not to his liking and left the office.

No more than a minute later, the office door opened again. Without raising her eyes, she chided, "Come on, Duke. Make up your mind. You—" She stopped abruptly when she did look up and saw not Duke, but Christian.

His gaze focused on her. "Was that Duke I noticed coming out of here? Or should I say *loverboy?*"

"Yes," she answered stiffly. "It was Duke." Judging by his expression, Christian seemed to be suggesting that she and Duke had been doing something unseemly. "And for your information, Duke isn't my loverboy."

"The two of you were in here alone?"

"Yes." She rolled her eyes and sat down at the computer, presenting him with a view of her back. It was pointless trying to reason with Christian. He'd already decided she and Duke were romantically involved, and he seemed unwilling to change his mind.

"Do you think that's a good idea?" he asked.

"What? Being in here alone with Duke? Really, Christian, he's a pilot. It isn't like he doesn't have business here." She was about to mention that she was the one who scheduled the flights, took orders and handled numerous other details, but she realized her arguments were useless.

"The last time I caught the two of you together, you were practically undressing each other."

"That's not true!" Mariah's cheeks reddened with embarrassment. "You make it sound like I need a...a babysitter."

"You do," Christian sneered. "It's a miracle you haven't destroyed the airfield by now. You've certainly got a habit of wreaking havoc wherever you go."

"That's the most unfair and unkind thing you've ever said to me, Christian O'Halloran." Pride demanded she hold her head high, but it was difficult.

Mariah had known for a long time that Christian regretted hiring her. She was also aware that he'd approached Sawyer soon after her arrival, wanting to replace her. If anything, his dislike had spurred her on; she'd tried harder to please him, to fit in and prove herself. She'd hoped that in the past year she'd done that.

She'd worked hard. When it came to Sawyer, she had a near-flawless record. But with Christian everything had gone wrong. Spilling punch on him was just the latest disaster—and relatively minor, at that. If she lost an important file it was inevitably one Christian needed. If she misplaced a phone message it was one Christian had been anxiously waiting to receive. It never failed; she was continually in conflict with him, when he was the very person she most wanted to please.

For nearly a year Mariah had lived with the threat of losing her job. Just when it seemed they were making progress and finding some common ground,

Christian had stumbled on her kissing Duke. Everything had gone downhill since then.

He avoided her whenever possible. When it wasn't possible and they were in the office at the same time, he rarely spoke to her, and then only about business. That made for an awkward situation, and Mariah didn't know how to change it for the better.

Karen's suitcases were packed and ready to be taken to the airfield. The two professors had left earlier that morning, and the lodge was strangely quiet.

Karen had been downstairs only once all morning; Matt wasn't there. Now she waited in her room, although she wasn't sure for what.

The tightness in her chest hadn't gone away from the moment she announced she was leaving. The phone call to her parents in Anchorage had assured her she was welcome to live with them as long as she needed.

She walked over to her window and stared out at the panoramic view of the tundra. She would miss all this. More important, she'd miss the friends she'd made here. Lanni, of course. Abbey and the children. Bethany, and although she didn't know Mitch well, she thought the world of his little girl. Then there was Ben. And the O'Halloran brothers. Duke and John and Ted, and the other pilots.

But she was fooling herself, Karen knew, if she believed it was the townsfolk she'd miss most. For the second time in her life she was about to walk away from the man she loved.

It had been difficult enough the first time. She didn't know if she could find the strength do it again.

A noise echoed up the stairs. The screen door slammed, indicating Matt was back.

Leaving her suitcases at the top of the steps, Karen slowly made her way down.

Matt stood at the foot of the staircase, watching her. Neither spoke.

His eyes seemed huge, twice their normal size. It took Karen a moment to realize that the tears brimming in her own eyes had distorted his image.

"Are you ready to leave?" he asked starkly.

"No," she answered. Her fingers tightened around the railing. All at once, in a rush of pain, Karen knew she'd never be ready. She couldn't make herself do it. She couldn't leave him. Not again.

Her gaze scanned the room. During dinner the night before in Fairbanks, Sawyer and Abbey had told her how hard Matt had worked to rebuild the lodge. How he'd taken on an impossible task and turned this half-burned, abandoned place into a promising enterprise. How pleased they were to have her and Matt as part of the community. They'd spoken of Hard Luck's future, and Karen had felt a vital part of that future. Until she'd arrived home. Until she'd faced Matt.

The moment she'd moved into the lodge with him she'd seen it all for herself. He'd found his calling. Everything he'd done in the last few years had steered him in this direction. The professors had revealed that truth to her—a truth that should've been obvious. All she'd had to do was watch her husband here in his lodge. His capability, the care he took, the responsibilities he assumed—they all should've told her that things were different for him now.

In the four years she and Matt had been married,

she'd never seen him this happy, with himself or his work.

"What do you need?" he demanded.

"Need?"

"In order to to leave."

It seemed he couldn't be rid of her fast enough. She didn't know how to answer him and glanced behind her.

"I'll get your suitcases," he said. He took the stairs two at a time, roaring past her.

"No." The word nearly strangled her.

He stopped midway up the stairs. "No?"

"I don't want to leave you, Matt," she choked out. "Not again. The baby needs you. *I* need you."

A strained silence followed.

"How long?" he asked, his voice taut. "How long are you willing to stay this time?"

"Forever."

He took a deep breath. "I don't know if forever will be long enough. Are you sure, Karen? Be very sure because I won't have the strength to let you go again."

"I *am* sure," she said, and the tears ran down her face.

All at once they were wrapped in each other's arms. Matt was kissing her and she was crying and kissing him back.

They both tried to speak a number of times, but it seemed more important to reassure each other with kisses.

"Never again," Matt whispered between kisses.

"No. I'm here for a lifetime."

"Partner. Lover. Companion," Matt said between kisses. "Wife."

"I'm moving," she whispered, and laughed at the way his eyes lit up like fire, "into your bedroom."

"*Our* bedroom. I remodeled that room for you."

"What about a family?"

"There's plenty of space," he said, smiling.

Tears of happiness sparkled on her lashes. "I have so many ideas for the lodge."

"Wonderful." He pressed his mouth hungrily to hers.

"But I have an even better idea for right now."

He lifted his head and his gaze probed hers. "You do?"

"It doesn't have a thing to do with the lodge." Clasping his hand, she led him down the stairs and toward their private quarters.

"Might I ask what you have in mind?"

She laughed joyously. "You'll find out soon enough, oh, husband of mine."

* * * * *

#1 *New York Times* bestselling author

DEBBIE MACOMBER

delivers a captivating tale of adventure and romance set on the stunning coast of Mexico.

Lorraine has just discovered that everything she believes about her father is a lie—starting with the fact that Thomas supposedly died years ago. Now she's learned that not only is he *not* dead, he's living in a small town south of the border. In the process of tracking him down, she manages to get framed for theft and pursued by the real thief, the police *and* a local crime boss. Her father's friend Jack agrees to help her escape, although Lorraine's reluctant to depend on a man like him.

Jack's every bit the renegade Lorraine thinks he is—an ex-mercenary and former Deliverance Company operative. He's also the one person who can guide her to safety. But there are stormy waters ahead, including an attraction that's as risky as it is intense. The sooner Jack can get Lorraine home, the better!

Available now, wherever books are sold!

Be sure to connect with us at:

Harlequin.com/Newsletters

Facebook.com/HarlequinBooks

Twitter.com/HarlequinBooks

MIRA®

www.MIRABooks.com

MDM1926R

New York Times **bestselling author**

DEBBIE MACOMBER

National Bestselling Author

SHEILA ROBERTS

Discover two heartwarming tales in one stunning collection!

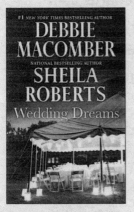

First Comes Marriage
by Debbie Macomber

Janine loves her grandfather but balks at his plan to choose her a husband. Zach, the intended groom, has recently merged his business with the family firm, and Grandfather insists it would be a perfect match. Zach and Janine agree on one thing—that Gramps is a stubborn, meddling old man. But… what if he's right?

Sweet Dreams on Center Street
by Sheila Roberts

Sweet Dreams Chocolate Company has been in the Sterling family for generations, but now it looks as if they're about to lose it to the bank. Unfortunately, the fate of Sweet Dreams is in the hands of Samantha's archenemy, Blake, the bank manager with the football-hero good looks. It's enough to drive her to chocolate.

Available now, wherever books are sold!